THE
REBEL
WITHIN

LANCE ERLICK

Finlee Augare Books (Chicago)

This is a work of fiction. All of the characters, organizations, and events portrayed herein are either products of the author's imagination or are used fictitiously, and any similarities to actual persons, organizations, or events is entirely coincidental. Also, though locations used in this work exist, for dramatic effect details have been altered. Accordingly, they should be considered fictitious.

Edited by Leah Carson

Finlee Augare Books, Chicago, IL
ISBN: 978-0-9889968-0-9 (print)
ISBN: 978-0-9889968-1-6 (e-book)
Library of Congress Control Number: 2013934668

Printed in the United States of America

To DJC, who unwittingly became my muse at a young age. May your journey be long and filled with friendships, love, and happiness. To ELA who has inspired me along this path.

To Dave and Jason, that you may follow your dreams.

To Sue, who helped bring this to life.

ONE

I'm 16. Life should be fun, right? I should be meeting guys and throwing kick-ass parties with friends. Instead, the Knoxville Public Schools, the Tenn-tucky state government, and the Federal Union plan my life down to the last nanosecond. They believe they know what's best. I disagree.

Here I am, Annabelle, late again, running down the concrete corridors I've whitewashed during detention. When I get to senior civics class just in time, someone slams the door in my face. Then a pompous voice blares over the loudspeaker, "All security-tracked students report to Auditorium B to meet Commander Samantha Hernandez."

The voice is Harmony Director Surroc. *Oh, joy.* Another "hoo-rah" for the Mechanized Female Warriors. The mechs are always on my back, trying to get me to join—but I hate them so much I want to puke.

I head for the auditorium, past girls scurrying to class. The disgust in their stares is unmistakable. Yeah, yeah, you hate me because I'm a security-tracker. Well, joke's on you. I hate *being* security-tracked even more.

I hold my head high. Out of habit, I scan my surroundings and contemplate escape. My chest fills with relief at the sight of my sister. Janine's a year younger, smarter, and drop-dead gorgeous. She catches up and squeezes my hand for reassurance.

It's bad enough that Surroc tracked me to security. It's even worse that she tracked Janine at age 12. I'm determined to look out for my sister, make sure she finishes school and doesn't turn into a rebel like me.

Eleven other girls stream into Auditorium B wearing the same "approved" outfits: bland navy skorts, bleached blouses, and flats. No makeup, jewelry or accessories, 'cause those hint at status and inequality. Hair can't reach shoulder length because long hair is pretentious and thus disharmonious. So is dyeing. When my blonde curls hold their bounce, they're off my shoulders. When they sag, because I refuse to wear my hair shorter, I get to spend quality time with Harmony Director Surroc.

Janine and I enter our small, windowless auditorium—just a classroom with a stage. I find us padded seats in the middle of the whitewashed hall. This place sure could use decorations, paintings, something. My wrist-com, standard security-track issue so cops can monitor my activities, shows I have two hours until lunch and my cop intern training.

Janine jabs her elbow into my side and whispers, "Captain Voss is here."

Yep, our intern chief. Voss the Boss with her round cow-face. She tries to look serious in her ratty brown hair and navy uniform. But those sweat stains under her arms? And the way she paces back and forth on the stage? Nervous Nellie.

Next to Voss stands Commander Hernandez, who created the Tenn-tucky mech forces during the war. It's her first time at our school. Usually she sends gung-ho warriors.

When Hernandez marches to the podium in her crisp blue military uniform with colonel emblems on her shoulder, my stomach churns. A scar runs down her right cheek. I can't help picturing horns on her tight-cropped black hair. She's the enemy telling me and other security-trackers to join the killing machine.

"Call me Sam," Commander Hernandez says in a low bass. Her voice echoes in the small room and silences murmurs behind me.

Call you vulture.

Janine must notice my fidgeting; she touches my hand to tell me to stay calm.

"I'm sure you've heard the Mechanized Female Warriors called mechs or amazons," the commander says.

And murderers.

"I assure you we're not a mythical force. We're girls like you defending Federal Union values. This is your chance to reach for

2

the sky and serve your nation in need."

How many more families will you destroy? Having Janine next to me halts my outburst and another detention.

"We have video clips to show what you can expect. Training is rugged, but don't be alarmed. We train recruits well before they get into the tournament or the arena. See how with mech gear, our warriors can outperform Olympians in running, jumping, and various sports."

A wide screen to the right of the podium shows a video of three warriors encased in black titanium-polymer shields and helmets. I hear that this gear can protect against a .45 at point blank range. The commander doesn't demo that.

"Use of advanced hydraulics gives warriors the boost."

I watch them perform onscreen against women who competed in the last Olympics in Bangalore. Compared to the robotic black-shielded mechs, the athletes look like kindergarteners. Impressive. While I'd love to have even old-model mech gear used by the cops, Captain Voss doesn't think much of me, or my adoptive mom. Feeling is mutual. Voss lurks in the shadows, smirking.

"How would you like to enhance your performance to unbelievable levels?" the commander asks. "These are not toys, not video games. They're performance aids. When you master new skills, you'll be able to compete in our prized mech tournaments."

Not prized by me.

Hernandez shows clips of the televised events. Onscreen, girls in blue spandex tights perform amazing jumps, spins and evasions as they fight–not as spectacular as with mech suits, yet still intimidating. The Union televises tournament finals every six months, which Mom makes me watch.

I'm not impressed with girls pounding on each other. It's upsetting to see how excited Janine gets over this. She even ignored my protests and followed me into cop internship three afternoons a week.

A compact woman with measured movements, Commander Hernandez resembles a proud mom showing off her girls. "Imagine holding your own with any of these opponents, and turning those skills into protecting our liberties."

While separating families, I want to add. I keep my mouth shut. Getting suspended from basketball would hurt Janine more than me. She's our star shooter.

The commander starts a new clip: the arena. I'm ready to bolt. Onscreen, a petite redhead faces a brutish man with thick muscles. He's souped-up on steroids to make these contests more challenging. It reminds me of my dad. He had to fight in the arena like a Roman gladiator. My birth mother helped him escape. Then the mechs Dad trained captured my parents, executed him, and imprisoned her.

If only I could close my eyes so I don't have to relive this. Classroom cams would pick that up, though. I'd spend more detention time with Harmony Director Surroc, or worse.

"This is the final test for a mech warrior," Hernandez says. "Stand face-to-face with any man and hold your own in hand-to-hand combat. Overcome your fears. Focus your energies to accomplish amazing things. Become a mech and be the best you can be."

You mean the best the Union will allow me. Why not let me create? Or be an architect. Let me do something other than security. Then I'll reach for the sky and be the best I can be. Oh, well. Are we done?

Onscreen, the redhead hits the huge muscleman across the head, neck, and back. He strikes back; hits air. It's like watching a bullfight. The man falls to his knees. She snaps her fist, open hand, and foot across his upper body until he falls face-first into the dirt. *No, it's an execution.*

Girls cheer the brute's demise, those around me in the auditorium as well as the audience onscreen. When Janine grips my hand, I force myself to assume the stony face I've cultivated.

Why do these videos encourage girls to sign up? And they make men look like brutes. Who knows what men are really like? Most fled to the Outlands before I was born.

The commander turns off the video and steps down from the stage. She's my height, stocky, built like a brick wall. She shakes the hands of security students and addresses us by name. She must have reviewed our files. When she reaches me, it's all I can do to keep my breakfast down. I shouldn't have had those eggs. I can't just take off without embarrassing Janine. My actions reflect on her, Mom, and the rest of my adopted family.

Hernandez nods with a look that says she has her eye on me, or sees through me. "Annabelle Scott," she says. "Such passion and drive. If only you'd let me train you to focus that energy."

"Thanks," I mumble. Feeling naked, I close my mouth, hang

4

my head, and taste bile. Strangely, her smile, distorted by the scar running down her right cheek, seems genuine. She's disarming in ways that get my guard up. *Vulture, you won't get your claws into me.* I smile and nod. *Over my dead, cold bones.*

The commander turns to my sister. "And you, Janine Scott. The sharpest mind in the security program, and a terrific basketball player. With the right training…"

I tense. *Leave her alone,* I want to scream. She's too sweet for your killing machine.

Janine's pinky locks mine behind our backs. Her gracious smile lights up her innocent face. "It's great to meet you, Commander. We all aspire to serve."

I pray she's just acting when she says this.

She digs her fingernail into my palm. "Thank you for coming today, Commander. It was an inspiring presentation."

I can practically taste honey drip off Janine, and all I want to do is hold and protect her.

* * *

After cabbage-faced Surroc dismisses us, I drag Janine down whitewashed hallways away from Auditorium B. She looks up at me with worried eyes. I say "up," though she's only an inch shorter, because she has a way of holding her head the way she did when she was little.

We burst into steamy sunlight and I'm ready to scream. Those eggs struggle to escape. They taste foul the second time around. How can I join the mechs who killed my dad for fleeing a nation that no longer wanted him? How can I forgive them for ripping my birth mother from my arms, sending her to prison, and not letting me visit, write, or even know where? I was only three, yet I remember that tear at my gut like it was this morning.

The concrete courtyard, surrounded by concrete classrooms, concentrates the morning heat. Sweat soaks my thin blouse. Or is it that this reminds me of a prison? Across the way, I spot chubby-faced Emily Battani. As the governor's daughter, she manages to dress a sliver better than the rest of us despite strict dress codes. Today it's a hint of eye shadow, makeup to cover her zit-marred face, and new clothes.

I guide Janine away. I don't need reminding how we're all equal except I'm stuck with security while Emily has options. I bump into pinched-face Daphne and her giggly friends, probably the ones

5

who slammed the door in my face. She gets to go into biology, probably medicine. She's wearing the same blah clothes as me, yet hers are spotless and fresh each morning. She probably wears each outfit only once.

"Poor little security girls get grubby in the mud?" is the best Daphne can manage. Her mousy friends giggle.

Janine nudges me: be good.

I'd rather squirm in mud than believe blah is beautiful. I'd hate for any of these worm-brains to operate on me.

Cabbage-face watches us from the steps outside the auditorium. I don't need another lecture on the importance of harmony. Mom has a phrase for people like Surroc: a True Believer. It's from a banned book by Eric Hoffer in Mom's private library.

"Tell your mom we're watching her," Daphne says.

Janine tugs me away and whispers, "Don't mind her."

I do mind. Mom, my adoptive mom, is a Tenn-tucky state senator. She's one of the few sane people opposing Governor Battani. She fights for more opportunities for girls like Janine and me, but people are afraid. Janine is, I see. "Why don't you go to class and let me walk this off."

"I know you don't like mechs, Belle. Why can't you talk to me about it? I don't like secrets between us."

"I need fresh air. Promise me you'll never join. If you want to be a cop, that's okay." I stop by her building.

"I'm not leaving you all wound up. Don't skip school today. I know you want to."

She knows me so well. "I'll be okay, Babe."

My wrist-com vibrates. Pictures flash of me caught skipping school last week. I "borrowed" an electric cycle to head up into the hills. I didn't get to use it. Next is a doctored picture of me hanging from the clock tower over the administration building, with its broken dials. Surroc leaves them as a reminder of my disharmony. I don't need reminding.

Janine views the images, turns off my wrist-com, and heads inside. "We've got a game tonight, Belle. Don't get detention. I need you. Their captain's Dara the Terror. They say she can play center, forward, and guard all at once."

"Hype," I say, though I've heard rumors the big ox punched another player.

My sister leads me up a narrow flight of stairs to the tarred roof to get my fresh air. I need to bust loose and get out of this prison. My baby sister is holding me back. Yet not a cell in my body can hate her for it. She's no goody-goody. She never rats on me when I skip school or wander into restricted areas. That counts for a lot.

Janine stops at the roof panel. "Belle, don't be mad at me for being nice to the commander."

"I'm not, Babe, but I don't want you to turn into one of those animals. You're much too sweet for that."

Grinning, Janine forces the panel. "That's because I have you to protect me."

Mom didn't ask me to take that responsibility. No, I took it upon myself the moment I moved in. To get her to sleep with lights out, I let her sleep next to me. She's followed me ever since, like my Siamese twin.

She doesn't say anything when I move to the ledge to look over the Knoxville cityscape and wonder. What would it be like to go wherever I want? Instead, I depend on crowded city-buses with restrictions based on my student and cop intern IDs. Glancing toward mountains I can't see—the Outlands—I tell myself someday, but how? Travel outside Knoxville is restricted even for cops.

With warm wind blowing through my hair, I imagine floating out there. At least the rah-rah video excused me from civics class. I couldn't handle another lecture on the history of the Second American Civil War: how the year before I was born, our nation split into the Federal Union and the Outlands. Our Union promotes harmony—blah, blah, blah. If I taught, I'd spice it up with how harmony took my birth parents. I'd follow with how Mom's husband had to flee with their son George. I've never met my adopted brother.

The only good part of security and being a cop intern is I skip school in the afternoon, though that further limits my options. Afternoons I go through cop training, which makes me wish I was in school.

Emily Battani joins us, and the world closes in around me.

TWO

"Daphne's such a bitch," chunky Emily says over my shoulder.

I hold my gaze toward distant mountains. What does the governor's lucky egg want from me now?

I shrug and glance down at the street below. A blue and gray city-bus lurches forward; bikes scramble out of its way. It reminds me of pictures I've seen in Mom's study, showing China before they opened their economy and replaced bikes with cars. This is progress?

While she says hi to Emily, Janine nudges me: be nice. I get it, though I want to be alone. I'm tempted to take my chances by jumping off the roof to escape.

Looking past the city-bus, I stare at Michael's School for Boys. It's one of a handful of boarding schools for the few boys who remain in Knoxville. The state keeps them hidden behind high walls topped with barbed wire and patrolled by mech cops.

Will I ever meet a boy?

Mom says women stopped having boys because of high rates of autism, violence, and social disruption, and they didn't read. That made it hard for them to adjust to our knowledge-based economy. After the war, most of the males fled to the Outlands. The government sent others to prisons, work camps, and institutions. Then the city zoned our neighborhood and school to exclude them. Harmony Director Surroc and Captain Voss say liberated women don't need men. Governor Battani says the only way to

8

make females safe is to eliminate the source, meaning men. Males would have all been gone long ago except for women, like my birth mother, who protested, though fewer every year.

The only other times I see the boys' school is out the window of Harmony Director Surroc's office while she lectures me. No class windows face this street. School buses bypass Michael's, as if passing near them would pollute us.

Leaning over the concrete ledge, I spot a tall, lean redheaded boy in jeans. My breath catches. He glides along the outside of the concrete wall that surrounds the boys' school. I try not to act startled as I wonder how he got past his school's electronic surveillance.

To avoid alerting Emily, I look away and watch him from the corner of my eye.

Why am I drawn toward a boy I've never met?

For months I've watched him on the roof of his school behind barbed wire. He looks out at the world like I do. He's only a few years younger than my dad was when they threw him into the arena. I hunger to meet the redhead, to be with a boy and see what happens. Maybe he won't be the brute shown in televised arena fights and news-vids.

While Mom doesn't talk about it, I've seen dogs. It doesn't seem as much fun for the bitch as for the horny bastard. Yet curiosity burns within me that I can't share with Janine or Mom. I dare not trust anyone else. No telling who might post my thoughts. Soc-net police are on the lookout for any backlash against the Federal Union.

The boy glances around as he edges his way toward the alley. Like he can fool a zillion cams! Must be desperate. *I'm with you, Red.*

"There's a boy," Janine whispers. Worry lines crease her tanned forehead. I don't think she remembers her brother George. He left for the Outland before Mom adopted me.

"A small boy," I say, aware Emily's watching. *Hurry!* I send him mind-waves to get moving, as if that ever works.

"Not a threat," I say. "See mech cops out front and…" I start to mention his green student collar, but it's masked or missing. It's horrible to have to wear a choker like a dog, which is how cops I work with track males.

Emily leans over the ledge to look and calls it in. She has to get her goody points for the day. She gives the call center the location and description of the fugitive. "If there's one, there could be more. They're like cockroaches."

Since there's no point educating the devoutly ignorant, I shake my head. The boy disappears into an alley behind the school as mech cops out front receive the call. This gives me an idea.

Sirens blare at the boy's school. Uniformed cops on electric cycles appear at nearby intersections. It pays to be the governor's offspring. I'm sure her mom will reward her tonight. Mech cops in faded black exoskeletons split up and circle the school at mech-enhanced speed. They hold up remotes that zap collars within range, intended to immobilize males until cops can round them up. This is what cop and mech training leads to, one of many security jobs I don't want.

I turn to Janine, who shows too much enthusiasm for the manhunt. *That could be your brother, Babe.* "You need to get to class. You don't want detention."

"What about you?"

"My class is nearby. Go on."

After Janine leaves, I take a deep breath and head down narrow stairs.

Emily follows. "If you cut class today, take me with you. I hate this place."

I reach the bottom of the stairs and hesitate. I'm tempted to take her. If we're caught, she could lessen my punishment. I can't trust her, though.

"Sorry, no plans today."

She withdraws into herself. At times I feel sorry for Emily. She's an early product of EggFusion Fertilization, the fertilization in the lab of one woman's egg with stem cells created from another woman's skin tissue. In other words, she has no dad but two moms. Living alone with the governor, Emily may not know who the other mom is. Maybe that's why she acts angry and depressed.

I walk with her as far as her class. After she goes inside, I turn on my heels.

No plans except escape and find that boy.

* * *

Taking whitewashed corridors down the wing where obedient freshmen are already in class, I reach our large auditorium without bumping into anyone. The broad stage is set up for another pep talk on social harmony. *Yippee.* Behind the stage, stairs rise up into rafters where stagehands handle drops and lights. I snatch a hoodie from wardrobe and cover myself despite steamy heat for early April. I relish the adrenaline rush.

I place a makeshift aluminum patch over my wrist-com. It's a trick I learned from cop intern training to mask GPS tracking. Gotta love cops and their toys. Then I wrap my student ID chip in aluminum. That's to fool the school tracking system, which logs us on and off campus like store products. I'm the toilet-bowl cleaner getting crap jobs.

I crawl through dust-covered windows onto a ledge over the stage's loading dock. It's the only gap I've found in school security. This act of disobedience brings me closer to my parents. Plus I feel electricity I've never felt in class, with my boring cop internship, or even on the basketball court.

Cycle cops swarm the boys' school while mech cops covered in dull black shields move south toward the river. It's hot and clear, too hot to be outdoors. Swooshing mosquitoes from my neck, I pull the hoodie over my face. Then I dart across the empty street and head east. That's where I'd go if I was a boy.

I want to meet him and make sure he's safe. I need to understand this obsession: to know boys despite the horror drilled into me at school and online. This one doesn't appear dangerous. No, he looks innocent, like Janine, in need of protection. I imagine catching the boy. *Would you take me with you?* Sounds stupid to trust a stranger who might be a brute.

I don't slow down.

Wishing I had my basketball shoes instead of junky flats, I jog down an alley between Union Burgers & Subs and Federal Clothiers. They carry bland, government-approved food and attire to ensure health and harmony. Someday I'll open my own shop and design variety as an alternative to becoming a security cog. *As if they'd let me.*

Seeing cops in the woods behind the boys' school, I stop, catch my breath, and savor the excitement of blood pounding in my ears. I feel alive and certain I can catch the redheaded boy. Mom says I have a nose for finding people, like when I have to hunt down one of my eight adopted sisters—a long story.

Cops and mechs fan out. Feeling the pressure of the hunted, I head toward the river where vegetation is thicker. I like to sit there and watch the world pass. The water originates in the forbidden Outland, where there are plenty of boys who escaped my world. I say a prayer this one makes it.

When I reach the broad, rippling river, I spot among tall grass and thick weeds a tuft of red hair and a boyish face. I duck behind thick brambles and struggle to breathe. My heart pounds in my throat. I've never been this close to a boy who wasn't wearing handcuffs. Close enough to count the freckles on his sweet masculine face.

I should flee. Instead, I study his eyes studying me, eyes as blue as a summer sky. My throat dries. I feel like a fawn. Yet I sense no danger except from cops. They swarm like mosquitoes from the direction of his school. Voss must have called the entire force for one boy. Cops thrash through the underbrush grid by grid, evidently without infrared. It must be too hot.

Sweat trickles down my neck. I remove the hoodie and prepare myself to approach Red. Bushes rustle nearby. I look up to see Janine's adorable face. "What are you doing here?"

She plops next to me. "I saw too many sparks flying after the mech video. Whenever you get this way, it scares me."

"I'm sorry, Babe. You can't be here." I look over at Red and no longer see his eyes. *You wouldn't hurt my sister, would you?*

Janine squeezes my shoulder to get my attention. "I knew you'd run again."

"This isn't a game. We need to get you back before they catch you." I pull Janine down behind thick bushes.

"I know you're hurting, Belle. You talk in your sleep. Don't keep things from me. I can handle it. Is this because of me?"

I study worry lines on her pretty face. "No, Babe. You've done nothing wrong, but you need to stop following me." I pull her away from the boy into tall river grasses.

Janine smiles; acts oblivious to the dangers. "I want to help, Belle. Don't shut me out. Is this about George?"

"Who?"

"You call his name in your sleep."

I tug Janine down lower behind bushes. "You're mistaken."

"Is that who you're meeting?"

"No!" I take Janine's hand, gaze into her big brown eyes, and will her to stop digging.

"Are you in love with him?"

"How? I've never met any boys." I pull Janine deeper into tall grass.

Cops move closer. My heart's ready to burst for Red and for my sister. I've been dying to tell her how she has a brother and I'm adopted: all my baggage. Yet Mom made me swear to keep this to myself. That's hard because I love Janine more than if she was my blood. My need to protect her is an open wound that can't heal. I still see her on her first day of school picked on by two older girls until I stepped in and sent the girls packing.

Janine grips my hand to say it's okay. My guilt explodes. If she knew we weren't bio-sisters, would she stop looking up to me? Will she think less of me because I lost my parents as enemies of the state? I savor the unquestioned love in her eyes. I can't let anything sour it.

I whisper, "I need time alone to think."

"Why won't you tell me what's troubling you?" Janine's most convincing pouty look tugs at me. But this isn't the time for her to get her way.

Surrounded, I see no way out unless the cops leave. They linger, scan, and tighten the circle. I push Janine down among reeds. "Stay put. No point both of us getting caught. I'll draw the cops away. You get to school before I tan your hide."

"You wouldn't."

"I'm serious. They'll hunt until they find something."

"Sisters stick together."

"Not this time," I say. "It won't help me if you get caught. Hide until the cops leave and be careful."

"Belle, I'm sorry I got you into trouble."

"You didn't, Babe. Do this for me." I steal a glance in the direction of Red. *Don't you dare hurt Janine.*

He looks more frightened than she does.

"Stay low, Babe. You don't want to bump into that boy." I see a flash of worry in her eyes and raise my voice. "If I were him, I'd slip upstream about 100 yards and find me a nice shallow cave until sundown. Then I'd make my way upstream to the Outland. So you wait here until the cops leave and head back behind Union Burgers up there."

She nods and sinks low in the weeds. Satisfied I've done what I can, I scoot out from the cover of tall grass in a crouched position. I don't see Captain Voss, though she wouldn't miss this. I spot my intern partner Lieutenant Brooks. Her coarse, wrinkled face makes her look older than her years and carries the weight of one who had to fight all her life.

After removing the aluminum shield over my wrist-com, I stand, raise my hands, and march toward Brooks. "I surrender."

"Halt!" A frightened brunette in uniform tenses her slender body and aims her zapper at me. I recognize the thin-faced recruit as new to the intern program.

I freeze. "I saw a boy on the run. I thought I could catch him."

"Nice try." It's Captain Voss, the stupid cow. Her round face twists into a scowl as she marches toward me. "Truancy is a serious crime."

"I saw a boy from Michael's School."

"You should have called it in."

"We did." I regret the "we" bit.

"Who's with you?"

"She chickened out." I should have brought Emily–not.

"Get your sorry ass to school. I'll deal with you this afternoon."

I'm sure you will. Forcing myself not to glance back and check on Janine, I hitch a ride with a cycle cop.

Back at school, I hide in the rafters over the loading dock. When I see Janine sneak in by the cafeteria, I head for class. I'm ready to slip into boring advanced algebra when cabbage-face Surroc grabs my arm.

"Annabelle, you should consider it a privilege to be in security so you can serve your community. Yet you risk it all for silly stunts."

"What have I done this time?" I inch toward Surroc's office and away from my sister's classroom.

"You know very well." Surroc follows. "I got a call from Captain Voss. You want off the intern program?"

I smile inwardly. If this visit is because of Voss, maybe Janine's safe.

"Look at me while I'm talking to you. I'd give you detention, but you seem to like that. Besides, we're out of paint." Surroc shakes her head, sending her ratty brown hair bouncing. "So, I'm suspending you from basketball for four weeks."

I don't mind until I recall promising Janine I wouldn't miss tonight's game. There's no point pleading with Surroc. That only gives her pleasure. I hold my stony-face instead.

Surroc wags her stubby finger at me. "If the governor wasn't coming to watch her daughter play, I'd suspend you tonight." She seems disappointed that my punishment hasn't upset me more. "If you keep acting disharmonious, who will take you? Not the police, not the mechs, and not security guards. Do you want environmental cleanup?"

Thinking about the nearby nuclear power plant shutdown and radioactive cleanup, I shake my head and act with such contrition I hope it releases me. I still have to face Voss and Mom.

THREE

Since I almost got Janine into trouble by skipping school, I fight the urge to blow off the cop internship. This being Monday, she joins me at the crowded bus stop across the street from school. After three city-buses and two transfers, we reach the cop station. I pat Janine's shoulder: *I promise to be good.*

"Don't forget the game," she says, before heading into the training room. She has indoctrination: tablet learning on laws, police procedures, surveillance techniques, and harmony.

I want to get out on patrol with Lieutenant Brooks. Instead, Captain Voss grins with satisfaction; she's nailed me. She pulls me up a narrow stairway, past the motherly Liz Cameron seated in a small reception area. I smile at the captain's assistant. She looks past me. It must be one of her bad days. Did Voss lecture her on too much time away from her desk?

We enter the captain's spacious office. Behind her big oak desk is a soft captain's chair, and nearby a clump of potted hibiscus plants. Standing by a round conference table is Lieutenant Brita Scarlatti. The lean, no-nonsense cop is the captain's pet. She doesn't move, forcing me into a corner when Voss closes the door.

"Don't get your hopes up about joining the mechs," Voss says in a high-pitched voice that claws at my ears. "After today's stunt, you'll be lucky to get environmental cleanup."

To stay calm, I picture a muzzle on her fat-cow face.

Voss grabs my wrist-com. "Don't ever mask the tracking chip again. You wear it for a purpose."

Voss shakes her round head in disgust. Her foul breath steams on my cheek. "You don't have the stomach for this job, let alone mechs. Did Commander Hernandez mention the final arena fight is to the death? Girls die. Let me tell you, you make it that far and wash out, you'll become a shattered person."

Do you speak from experience?

"Don't even think of stepping out of line again. Go." Voss waves her hand to dismiss me.

I hold my face blank as Scarlatti opens the door. She leads me past Liz Cameron's empty desk and downstairs into the crowded station room. Rows of metal desks have virtual computers, where I've tried to access information on Dorothy Montgomery, my birth mother. It's not that Mom hasn't been good to me; she has. I don't like the Federal Union forbidding me from finding my birth mother. The desks can't access out-of-state records without going through a department filter. That would ID my search and land me in another prison far away.

* * *

Lieutenant Scarlatti deposits me at Brooks' cluttered desk and marches off with an air of self-importance she doesn't show around Voss. Brooks is my bright spot in the intern program. Tracked to security like me, she's also on the outs. Thankfully, she helps interns whenever she can.

Brooks turns off her virtual screen and gathers her bag. "Ignore her. Let's go. I take it the captain gave you what for." Her laugh softens her coarse face.

She leads me out of the bland concrete cop station. When we reach her electric two-seat squad car, Brooks gives me a hard look. "Isn't Congresswoman Tam a friend of your mom's?"

I brace myself. I don't like people bringing up family connections, as though the sins of the mothers fall upon the daughters.

Brooks continues, "She was assassinated this morning."

"No!" My stomach knots. Like Mom, Tam is—was—in the opposition. *Another sane voice snuffed out.*

Brooks opens the tiny vehicle, which lets out a puff of steam. "Certain folk can't stand dissent."

"Who did it?"

"Lone shooter."

"Where did she get a gun?" I surprise myself at my response.

Brooks frowns. "An intern with another station."

I fold myself into the toasty passenger seat and cradle in my lap the remote that triggers electric collars. I grip a stun gun, my sole weapon as an intern, with mixed feelings. Twice I've received jolts running from cops. Brooks needs backup. I just hope I don't have to stun anybody.

The lieutenant takes the wheel and turns on the inadequate air conditioner. She zips us through the broad avenue, empty except for buses, a few electric cycles, which I crave, and dozens of sweaty bicyclists.

I don't look forward to Janine graduating from indoctrination to patrols, and putting herself at risk. She might get a partner like Scarlatti. "What's our gem assignment?" I ask.

Brooks pushes the peppy little squad car up a hill into a leafy residential neighborhood. "Enforce rezoning laws."

Oh, joy. More stupid regs. One by one, the city rezones neighborhoods to exclude males. Voss expects us to find offenders, turn them over to mech cops, and punish anyone who harbors them. I can't dodge this duty forever; the governor wants Knoxville cleared by summer.

Brooks works a grid west of town, driving the winding roads up and down hills until I'm certain we're going in circles. When she whips the two-seater around a corner into a new development, I spot a small boy, 10 or 12, wearing a green student collar. He darts into the woods. I point my remote, and hesitate. The boy reminds me of my redhead, or maybe George.

Brooks triggers her remote. The jolt sends the boy sprawling into a spread of dry leaves.

Braking hard, Brooks parks the two-seater. "Good eye." She likes to praise me, though I know she saw me hesitate.

She gets on her wrist-com and calls mech cops. I enter the woods, hold out the stun gun, and approach the little boy. He twitches on the ground. He's such a frail thing, in worn jeans and yellow tee shirt; reminds me of Janine.

Brooks holds me back. "He might be dangerous."

The boy recovers from the shock and sits up, bewildered.

His innocence tugs at me. "You got a name, boy?"

"Rod. Can I go home now?" He doesn't seem angered by the electric shock.

I'm furious, and I wasn't jolted. I can't help wondering about my redhead.

Brooks pockets her remote and holds out her service revolver. "Stay down. Don't move."

"I live over there." The small boy points to a ranch near the woods. "I want to go home." He breaks down crying.

"That's for the authorities to sort out," Brooks says.

I pull Brooks aside. "Can't we—"

"Already called it in."

Before I can protest, a mech crashes through the woods like one of those old-fashioned pickup trucks the Union banned. If I weren't already in deep trouble, maybe I'd help this kid.

The mech enters the clearing, covered head-to-toe in tarnished black shielding. Although it must weigh a ton, she sprints with ease. "Come with me, boy," the mech officer says in a silky voice. She picks him up.

Drying his eyes on his tee shirt, the boy looks at me. "Tell my mom, please."

"That won't be necessary," the mech officer says. "It's a matter for the zoning commission." The mech cop sprints down the road carrying the boy.

I want to go after him, and take him back to his mom.

Brooks grabs my arm. "Annabelle, don't even think it. Get in the car."

* * *

Sitting on the hood of Brooks' two-seater, I stare up at bushy trees. Dark storm clouds blow in from the southwest. I can't stop my eyes from fogging.

"Annabelle," Brooks says. "Let it go."

I can't.

My wrist-com vibrates. Janine texts: *Where R U? Game in 45 min.*

Brooks sees my alarm. I show her the text. "I can't miss this game. Could you drop me off?" There are no buses out here, and Brooks still has to issue the boy's mom a fine.

Smiling, she hands me her fob. "Take the car. I'll get another team out here and hitch a ride. Drop it off at the station after the game. Knock 'em dead."

I practically kiss her. She'll catch hell for giving me her car.

Taking back roads, I head toward school. I can't stop thinking about the small boy ripped from his mom like I was. I pull up along River Road behind Michael's School for Boys. Despite thunderclouds, it's still light out. Come dark, cops will use infrared to ferret out my redhead.

I ditch the car in a clearing off the road, and make my way to the cave. My heart races. Did Red hear me? Did he go to the cave? I take off my flats and wade into cool brown water, ankle deep. Squishy muck oozes between my toes.

Rain begins: sprinkles, then a torrent. Drenched, I continue, and stub my toe on a rock. *Blast.* I wince, look up and see the entrance to the cave. Water's rising. Beneath a tuft of red hair, a pair of emerald eyes looks back. I freeze. "You're not going to be a brute, are you?"

"You're a cop." He crawls out of the cave and stretches.

I look up at him, tall, slender, maybe a year older than me. He could be handsome if not covered in mud. My breath catches. I lose feeling in my feet. "An intern. Not a very good one, evidently. I'm Annabelle."

"Morgan. Why didn't you turn me in?"

"Long story. I'm late. I have a plan, sort of. Clean up and follow me."

While he rinses off in the river, I climb out. Trying not to be obvious, I watch him from the corner of my eye. Part of me is petrified of what I'm about to do. "How did you escape your school?"

"Every electronic gadget has weaknesses."

"So you're a geek?"

Morgan laughs and climbs out of the water. "Not everyone who knows electronics is a geek. Self-taught."

I'm glad to see he's fully clothed. Keeping my distance, I walk barefoot to the car. My soaked curls flop over my shoulders. "Where will you go, the Outland?" I can't believe how willing I am to join him.

"I want to help others escape, but I don't know what to do once I get them out."

I'm shaking; got to pee. What if he grabs me out here all alone? I take a deep breath and look back at him. He smiles. I'm all churned up inside.

When I reach the two-seater, I use the fob to open the trunk. How do I tuck this large boy into such a small space?

He towers over me. "You've got to be kidding."

I back away. "Climb in or don't. I've got a basketball game." *How lame.* "After dark, I'll take you across the river where it's less populated and point you toward the Outlands."

Without arguing, Morgan folds himself into the small trunk. I hand him a bag with what's left of my lunch and make sure the seatbacks allow in air. Then I rinse my feet in the rain, put on my wet flats, and climb in. Now the seat's wet.

"You okay back there?" I ask.

"I think so. It's tight and stuffy."

I speed to school. This is the stupidest thing I've ever done, yet it feels right. All I have to do is get Janine to go home with Mom and tell them I have to return Brooks' car. What could go wrong?

* * *

When I reach the assembly hall locker room, I have just enough time to change out of my wet clothes into my blue basketball uniform. While the others go out to warm up, Janine waits. "What happened to you?"

"Downpour."

"I was afraid you weren't coming."

"Almost didn't." I towel off my hair and tie it up to keep it regulation. "Come on, we have a game." *Let's get this over with.*

I race her out to where the team huddles on the sidelines, listening to instructions from Coach Winters. Rumbling conversations in the stands above drown her out. I can't focus. I have to get Morgan out of that tiny trunk. It was a mistake bringing him here.

Mom sits alone in the back of the assembly hall. Nearby, Dara the Terror stretches. She's big-boned, massive, all muscle beneath her skin-tight red uniform. Also tracked to security, she has fire in her eyes and scars across her striking Romanesque face. She looks like someone poked her and stirred an angry bear. She's intimidation on two legs—two thick, powerful legs. Her presence screams, "Submit, you've already lost," and her team's record bears that out.

My teammates look defeated, so I interrupt the coach and turn to my teammates. "If you think we'll lose, we will. We can take these guys if we don't make any mistakes. Are you with me?"

Shoulders lift, faces brighten. We clasp hands, bump fists. Janine's face lights up. That brings me back into the game.

21

When we walk onto the court, cheers resonate from the packed stands. Huge video screens above both baskets show close-ups of our team. I spot Governor Battani. *No pressure.*

This is our first game against Zola High since they acquired the amazon, Dara the Terror. She's a versatile and commanding guard, forward and sometime center. With her is slender super-shooter Margarite Olivetti, a string-bean brunette who hides in Dara's shadow. I've watched them on video. Their game consists of Dara getting the ball to Margarite or driving the basket. We can play that game.

While sluggish Emily Battani jumps against Dara, no contest, I read the situation. Dara muscles the tipoff to Margarite. I intercept and fire the ball to Janine. She doesn't disappoint. Sensors in the ball track position, speed, arc, and passage through the hoop to post her three points.

Margarite takes the inbounds from Dara and brings the ball up court. I fake right, steal, and knock the ball to Janine, who nails all net. It helps to have an intuitive connection with her.

This time Dara brings the ball down. She puffs up her chest and bears down on me. I plant my feet. *No way, bully.*

She runs over me, sends me sprawling onto the hardwood floor. Pain shoots up my back. Sensors in our uniforms register the pressure of Dara's hit and the fact that I held position. The posted result: a foul. I get to my feet, dazed.

With Dara all over Janine, I inbound the ball to Emily. She's here because Mommy Gov is in the stands. Emily gets the ball to Janine. Dara grabs my sister's wrist. Time slows as the amazon twists to throw her weight into Janine's elbow.

Get off my sister.

I hit Dara full force. She lets go of Janine and turns on me. It's like an arena fight. Dara carries at least 50 pounds of brawn and fury over me.

She swings her fist at my jaw. I flinch; fall back. She clips me, a glancing blow, an electric jolt. Dara hammers my shoulder and back. I punch at anything I can: face, stomach, neck, all wide targets. Nothing slows her. She throws me to the ground, jumps on top, and straddles me. "I'm gonna cut you up and send you back to your mama."

Good luck finding her.

Red and blue uniforms circle around. With every ounce of

strength I hit and kick. Anger, not just at Dara, but Surroc, the Union, Voss, Hernandez. Everyone tells me what to do, who to be, how to behave. The Union took my parents, grabbed that boy, hunts Morgan. Dara hurt Janine.

I can't budge the amazon.

Dara grins. I push to get her off. She hits. I block. Pain soaks me like the thunderstorm. I'm drowning in pain; can't stop her. She rolls me over and gets me into a chokehold. I can't breathe. Taste bile. I ram my elbow below Dara's diaphragm. She doesn't let go.

Someone pulls Dara off. I stare up at Captain Voss. *Not you!*

"That's enough," Voss says. "Get up."

Dara wags her finger at me. "She started it."

Before I can catch my breath, Voss cuts me off. "Not a word. You're both under arrest for breaching harmony. Think before you add to your crimes."

Fighting the pain, I struggle to my feet and glance at Janine. She's terrified. I force a smile and wink, which inflames my face. At least she's okay. No one touches Janine. And no one has until today.

Margarite pulls Dara aside and whispers. I glare at Margarite, shooting her a thought-wave: Dara can't protect you if you touch Janine.

The crowd creates its own disharmony of shouts and taunts. To make my humiliation complete, I have to stand before the grumbling crowd while Lieutenant Scarlatti cuffs my wrists behind my back. Then she slaps on a maroon criminal collar, my scarlet letter. It doesn't ease my anguish that Captain Voss does the same to Dara.

I hang my head. I've embarrassed my family. Poor Janine looks miserable. I want to hold her and tell her it'll be okay. I no longer see Mom in the stands. How will I face her?

Then I recall Morgan scrunched into the trunk of Brooks' car with no way out.

FOUR

Lieutenant Scarlatti shoves me into her black, four-seat squad car. The stuffy interior aggravates my sweaty body and nauseated stomach. Bars separate the rear seat from the front. She locks me in, as if I'm some murderous brute.

When the lieutenant pulls away from the school, giggling Daphne takes my picture to post and broadcast. At least they didn't arrest Janine.

Scarlatti drags me into the station. The buzz of chaotic activity assaults my senses. She makes me wait on a stiff bench outside her office. Cuffs chafe my wrists. I don't see Dara. Did they take her to her East Knoxville station? I expect a night in jail, no more, I pray.

Brooks gets up from her desk and examines my face. "Let's have the nurse look at you."

I shake my head; pain shoots up my neck. The nurse will only give me aspirin and cold compresses. I need to get out of here.

Cops and interns glare daggers. I've embarrassed the station. *Well, too bad. How would you react if Dara had injured Janine? She's the victim. Can't you support one of your own?*

Captain Voss grabs my arm. The pain of inflamed welts spreads like wildfire. She hauls me upstairs. We pass the empty assistant desk and enter Voss' office with Scarlatti tagging along. Voss slams the door and shoves me into a seat. I land on my hands, cuffed behind me. Pain radiates through my shoulders and down my back. I shift position to free my arms.

24

"You think you're better than us because your mom's a state senator," Voss the Boss squeaks. "That'll only cause you misery. You know better than to start a fight."

Looking down, I adopt a pathetic voice that disgusts me. "If I may speak...Dara was going to break Janine's arm."

"You don't know that."

"She was mad that Janine scored six points and was ready to nail another three. Dara—"

"I can't have my interns destroying harmony in front of the governor." Voss' fat face glares down at me. "You skip class. You interfere in police matters. Now this! I have no alternative but to send you to Hollander's Resocialization Facility in Nashville. I'm putting in for your transfer."

"No, Captain. You can't. Dara will—"

"She's not your concern." Voss pulls away as if my social disease might spread.

"But Janine—"

"Maybe they can penetrate your thick skull." Voss turns to Scarlatti. "Lock her up."

"No, Captain, please."

Scarlatti shoves me out of Voss' office and escorts me downstairs. I only wanted to protect Janine. Now she's on her own.

In the station room, sister interns and cops stare as if I'm that runaway boy abandoned in the trunk of Brooks' car. Mom? Janine? Morgan? *What have I done?*

* * *

Lieutenant Brooks intercepts us by the elevator to lockup. Her coarse face is a mask I can't read. "I'll take her from here."

Scarlatti's tight face scowls. "Captain's orders."

"I need to speak with her first." Brooks takes my sore arm and escorts me toward her desk. While Scarlatti huffs off to her office, Brooks whispers, "Don't mind her, Annabelle. I didn't see it, but I know you wouldn't start a fight unless it was important."

"I didn't start anything. I tried to get Dara off my sister."

"Come on. You're wanted in the conference room." Brooks leads me past her cluttered desk.

"Now what?"

"Don't know. It's the mech commander."

"Hernandez?"

Brooks nods and hurries me past a gauntlet of glaring faces. I enter a small interrogation room with a rectangular metal table and two wooden chairs. Brooks leaves and closes the door. For the second time today, I stand face-to-face with the stocky commander, still in uniform. She's the opposite of Dara: compact and controlled.

"Call me Sam." Her rumbling bass rattles my bones.

I gaze into the scarred leathery face of the vulture.

"You have gumption and fire in your belly when you have something to fight for," she says.

"She hurt my sister," I blurt out.

The commander motions for me to sit and takes the seat across the table from me. "She went for a compound break so Janine wouldn't play again."

"You know?"

Hernandez grins, twisting the scar on her right cheek. "You don't like authority much, do you?"

I straighten up and try to hold my practiced, stony face, like that'll keep her from looking through me. I sit with the table between us and try to get comfortable with my hands cuffed behind me. "I was protecting my sister."

"You skip school, buck intern rules, travel to unauthorized areas, sneak into parties with alcohol and other illegal substances. Shall I continue?"

"No, ma'am." I stare at the dented metal table.

"Not ma'am. Just Sam. I understand Voss plans to send you to a re-socialization facility, not that it'll do you any good."

"Ma'am...Sam." *Vulture.*

She grins. Her face relaxes. Muscles ripple beneath her uniform, a weightlifter? "I can offer you an alternative. Only you can decide if it's better. I see potential I could mold if you're willing."

I look up. "Become a mech?"

"It's not so horrible. Dangerous, yes, but better benefits than a cop. You'll get your own electric cycle, wider transit authorization, meals on base, uniforms supplied, and cool technology. Besides, you'll be doing a service to your country."

A tether tears at my gut. I can't join the service that destroyed my family. Who do I let down: my birth mother and dad, or Janine and Mom and Morgan?

"You're not convinced," the commander says. "You don't want

Voss to send you away from your family, do you? Leaving poor Janine on her own?"

My head shakes. *Leave her out of this.*

"Join the mechs and you can stay in Knoxville."

Shifting my weight, I look into the commander's dark eyes. "I'm not a fighter."

She laughs. "Don't worry about today's performance. You lacked focus. Never attack in anger."

"I had to react."

"You need training, which I can provide. I have to make this same offer to Dara, but how would you like to defeat her in the tournament?"

"She's too big."

Sam's smile comes with a twinkle. "Dara relies on bulk. It'll be her undoing."

"Fighting brutes to the death is not exactly appetizing."

"Dara scares you, doesn't she?"

I nod.

"I can improve your odds. You'll have our special training. We'll make you strong so you can be there for your family. Become a mech and you'll never fear Dara again. You won't have to fear men, either."

Like facing Morgan and nearly peeing my pants. "I need to think about it." While it's a betrayal even to consider joining mechs, I have to think of Janine and Morgan.

"I wouldn't accept an immediate yes, but don't take too long. Voss can move you within days. After that, it'll be difficult to transfer you to mechs." She unlocks my cuffs. "You won't need these."

Rubbing my wrists, I ask, "What about Voss sending me to lockup?"

"National service takes precedence. I'll clear it with her. Now go home and think this through."

The commander leaves me with thoughts of re-socialization, mechs, what they did to my family, what they'll do to me, to Janine. I brush those thoughts aside. Right now I have to save Morgan from prison and the arena.

* * *

I consider my options: being seen in public with my collar, or asking for a lift. Brooks' two-seater is at school, I hope, and no one else wants to be near me. When Voss calls Brooks to her office, I head outside into a hot thundery twilight. The bus stop is a block away.

The crimson collar chafes my swollen neck. Fear dries my throat. I don't want to take three buses with transfers to get back to school, to Morgan, to more trouble. Everyone will stare at my collar. They'll probably call to get me arrested again. I need Sam's electric cycle.

I'm about to run in the rain when something catches my eye. Janine sits curled up on the steps like a whipped puppy.

"What are you doing here?" My anger melts when she wraps her arms around me and holds tight.

"Thanks for protecting me. Sisters stick together. Don't we?"

My sister dissolves into me. I have to get her home so she isn't involved, and then deal with Morgan. I take her hand. "Let's go. We've got three buses to catch."

Janine pulls back and holds up a fob. "I couldn't let you get in trouble for not returning Brooks' car."

Looking behind her, I see the two-seater and freeze. Is Morgan still there? "Janine! You don't have a license."

"Brooks was angry at first, but she said you can drive me home and return the car in the morning." Janine rubs her forearm.

"Babe, I don't know what to say." Or do. I can't make her take the bus. And I can't drive Morgan where I planned while I'm wearing my stupid tracking collar.

I take a deep breath, hold Janine's poncho over her silky brown hair, and follow her to the two-seater. She shouldn't be here, taking risks and ruining my plans, yet her resourcefulness saved me having to take buses. I just need a different plan.

Janine climbs into the passenger seat. "You made us believe we could win. We could have. Dara knew it. That's why she got so mean."

When I get behind the wheel, I glance through the rearview mirror at the trunk. I can't risk it. I'm shaking too much to drive. Janine clutches my hand until I pull away and start the car. The electric engine purrs. I lower the window to let in fresh air that reeks of damp dog. Or is that Morgan?

I whip the two-seater through narrow empty streets, past the first bus stop where a cluster of women huddle outside a Union Burgers & Subs in the rain. They look weary. Where are all those happy harmonious people the Federal Union wants me to believe in?

We travel in silence. *Thanks, Janine. Because I'm crazy. Nuts. A lunatic.* I've put everything at risk for a boy I know nothing about. What do I say to him? How do I drop him off before taking Janine home? How do I drop her off when she won't leave my side?

We pass a second crowded bus stop that would have meant a 20-minute wait in the rain. Any deviation from a path straight home and Voss will send mech cops to pick me up. Farther on, flashes of lightning illuminate a clump of woods I visit when I want to be alone. It's a possible place to drop Morgan off. Across the street is one corner of our gated community with its crowded bus stop and night-shifters heading to work. *This is insane.*

I slow down, trying to think.

There's a small strip mall with groceries and other necessities by the bus stop, and another Union Burgers & Subs. I pull in and park. "Janine, I need you to get me something to drink. I'm dehydrated and—"

"Just pull into the drive-up."

"Please."

With a worried look, Janine gets out of the car. Approaching the shop, she looks back like I might leave her. Once Janine's away, I call out, "Morgan, are you back there?"

A grunt, then, "Annabelle?"

"I'm so sorry. I've made a complete mess of things." I look around and spot a cluster of bicyclists huddled under the canopy. They look my way. Janine's coming back. "I've gotten myself arrested. I'll think of something. Brooks keeps bottles of water back there for emergencies. Help yourself. No more talking. My sister's back."

After Janine gets into the car, I guzzle the cup of water she hands me and head toward home. I turn into the subdivision. If I didn't have this tracking collar I'd take Morgan across the river.

After the entrance gate to our community accepts my ID, I drive past cams that take my picture and Janine's. *Damn, what about infrared?*

Inside the gate is a clubhouse and commons for community activities with child care, though most families care for their own. I pass our community church, a branch of the Universal American Church of Christ. The church split from the Catholics over sex and financial scandals and liberation from Rome's patriarchy. They merged with Lutherans, Anglicans and others into a single church that supports the Federal Union's ideals. Mom takes us once a week, though I don't think she believes. There wouldn't be sanctuary in our church for Morgan, not when they preach a male-free world.

Ten-foot walls topped with barbed wire enclose our community. Battani says it's to protect us against predators, meaning males like Morgan. With my crimson collar, it feels like a prison, which we'll both get if I don't think of something soon.

Ten years ago, the city built this planned community of 400 identical duplex townhomes and had it zoned all-female. We're supposed to be a village, one of many that make up Knoxville and other cities across the nation. Living in small districts, we're expected to become harmonious and maintain equality, unless you're a lucky egg like Emily.

I suspect Mom didn't move to the tight-knit community of Battani Estates with the other state senators because of my rebelliousness. But it's probably because she's in the opposition. She won't say.

Even though it's raining, we pass neighbors cleaning common areas. They also do evening maintenance on our solar panels and wind turbines. The neighborhood association assigns work crews to schedules. Janine and I get two evenings a quarter to keep the property up to zoning standards. It's an opportunity for busybodies to pump children for family infractions, like bringing home a boy, and to spy on moms and sisters. I have to be careful. Too many secrets. To which I add Morgan.

How do I free him while I'm wearing this stupid tracking collar?

FIVE

I park Brooks' two-seater in the garage next to Mom's electric, a political perk. Janine's acting clingy, with tonight's scare etched into her soft, innocent face.

I pocket the fob and turn to Janine. "Time to face Mom."

"I'll tell–"

"Tell her nothing, Janine. Just sit tight while I sort this out." That last bit was for Morgan. To make sure Mom doesn't ambush us, I close the garage door and approach the front entrance. Lightning flashes along the ridge behind our townhome.

This is just the first step. Later I'll need an excuse to come back out, and a way to mask my wretched collar. *Damn, Brooks' car has GPS tracking, too.*

Steeling my nerve, I stand at the front door of our gray townhome. A four-bedroom place sounds spacious until it's filled with three moms and nine girls. Like other women in our community, Mom took two wives, each with two girls of their own. On top of that, each of our moms adopted a girl my age. That makes twelve people under one roof. One step inside and already I feel claustrophobic. Eyes bore into me. I've let all these people down, including Janine's bio-sister, Sarah.

Mom faces the door to the garage, ready to pounce. She's still wearing the dressy senate pantsuit she wore to the game. She hears me close the front door and turns my way.

Our warm, safe and too-cozy house becomes a hostile arena. Mama Grace, who stays home to manage the house and family,

31

drops dishes in the kitchen and ambles toward me, looking dismayed. Mama Helen pushes her reading glasses up over her short-cropped brown hair and smoothes the lines in her forehead to no avail. Mom rushes the front door with a commanding air.

Our roommate Sarah reaches me first and gives me a tearful hug. Her embrace inflames a knot of pain in my shoulder. At 12, she's sweet and homely. It breaks my heart to think that they'll track her to security this year. I hold her as a buffer against the lecture I deserve from Mom.

Mama Helen's eldest, beautiful Therese, gathers her two younger sisters to protect them from me. "Now you've gone and done it."

Though she lost her parents the same time I did, I don't think she knows. At least she doesn't talk about it. Then neither do I. Therese scowls at me. I've shown again that I'm not up to her standards of harmony and perfection. Thanks for the support, sis. I think of all the daughters as my sisters. It's so confusing.

June, Mama Grace's eldest, mumbles about how I've made it harder for her to form a family. While the state tracked Therese to medicine, like her mom, June only qualifies for service jobs like waitress or shopkeeper, which she blames on me. I doubt I'm the cause.

June's two younger sisters fade into our harmony-approved pastel wallpaper. Now that everyone else has chastised me, I'm ready for Mom.

I figure she'll drag me to her first-floor office, carved out of the great room for times when she works at home. Instead, she pulls me upstairs. Maybe it's because of the paper-thin walls and all the listening ears downstairs.

To the left are three sister bedrooms with in-suite bathrooms, designed for two girls each. We're three to a room because of us three adoptees. My room is down the hall. I wish I could be there now, thinking up a plan for Morgan.

Mom pulls me into the large master suite she shares with Mama Helen and Mama Grace. Three queen-sized beds are separated by nightstands.

I hold my face bland as granite, though it's ready to shatter.

Mom's face creases as she takes a long moment to compose herself. "Belle, what's gotten into you?" Her whisper is harsh. She closes the door. "I got a call that you skipped school again. And now there's this fight. We've talked about this. You can't..." She holds up her hands in a futile gesture. Mom's rarely at a loss for words. My guilt piles higher.

Mom turns to me and sighs. "Why can't you be like Janine?"

The door swings open and Janine's voice startles me: "I can explain, Mom."

"Janine, you're sweet to stick up for me," I say, "but Mom's right. I have to own up to what I did. I wish I could be more like you."

"But—"

I grab Janine's hand and give her a look: *Back off. We'll talk later.* I push her out and close the door.

Mom sighs. "You want to tell me what's really going on?"

Not really.

Knowing that Janine will wait outside, I turn on the music feed, a boring melody intended to promote harmony. It's our cone of silence. I stare at the wood floor. "I deserve whatever punishment you have for me and more." *Lots more.*

"I'm not here to punish you, Belle. God knows you've suffered enough."

At times like this, I wish she'd come down harder on me and purge my guilt. "I know I've brought shame on the family."

"I shouldn't have told you about being adopted. It wasn't fair to dump my confidences on a young girl."

The worst part isn't that she shared so much. It's that I can't tell Janine, when Mom and Janine are all I have. I take a deep breath and look up into Mom's worried face. Her dark penetrating eyes soften, despite deep sadness within.

"How many girls have vivid memories from when they were three, Mom? How many have burned into their souls bawling their eyes out while mechs tore their mothers away? They gutted me like a fish. I feel like it just happened. This isn't normal. And no, I'm not going to some harmony shrink to tell me it's okay. It's not."

"Belle..."

"Maybe I didn't watch them kill my dad, but those same murdering vultures came into our school today. They forced us to watch another horrid recruiting video with girls beating on each other and fighting brutes. They made Janine watch. I won't let them get their claws into her. For God's sake, they destroyed my family. No offense, you're the most amazing mom I can imagine, but nothing erases those memories. I've tried. I know I'm a disappointment. You don't deserve this." *And I need to get out of here.*

Mom takes my face in her hands. "You haven't disappointed me, Belle, but I worry about you. I've done everything I know to make it up to you. Dorothy was in the opposition with me. To hurt her, they went after your dad. They put him in the arena. We got him out, and then I suspect they let him go so they could kill him and arrest your mom. I'm so sorry."

I wrap my arms around Mom. She remains rigid. "It's not your fault," I say. "I had to bust loose today because of the mech video. I'm sorry. I'm trying to be careful. I chew my tongue raw to keep from saying things. I don't want them to take you. I don't.'"

"I know, Belle. It's just that they killed Congresswoman Tam today."

"She didn't deserve that."

Mom holds back tears. Her eyes look hollow. "We have to be very careful."

"You think they'll come after you?" *Why haven't they already?*

"Tam is a message that no one is off-limits. Secret police could make our entire family disappear."

"Can't we go after whoever did this?"

Mom pulls away. "Not when the shooter was killed with no witnesses. Curb your rebelliousness, Belle. I hate to ask after what you've been through, but do this for your family."

I study gouges in the wood floor. "Thanks for making me part of your family, Mom. I promise not to skip school again. Less than three months. I can manage that." *If they don't send me away.*

"That's a start."

"I hold my tongue at work. I can't enforce their crazy laws, though. They hauled off a boy today. His only crime was living with his mom in a neighborhood they rezoned."

Mom nods. "Not a day goes by that I don't think about George, praying he's alive, hoping he remembers he has a mom who loves him. I can't contact him or his dad without putting us in danger. I have to control my anger for the family. That's all I ask of you."

When I smile, Mom brushes dyed blonde hair from her face. Her husband Bret fled with George before she adopted me. That drew us close, because she confides in me too much. I wish I could confide in her without making things worse.

"I want to meet George and get to know him," I say. "I think of him every night. Janine says I say his name in my sleep."

Mom's face wrinkles with distress. "I can't talk about certain things like George and the Outland to anyone else, not even Helen or Grace. I know this isn't fair to you. Honey, you can't tell Janine. Don't put her in the position I've put you in."

I take a deep breath. "I'm glad to be here for you, Mom." *Here goes.* "I want to know boys. Is that so wrong?"

"Oh, God, Belle. I've so wanted to give you a normal life. It's a terrible burden to have to hold so much inside. It wasn't always like this. We were happy before I asked Bret to take George to the Outland. When they left, I felt the same ache you do."

"I know. Funny, with all your stories, it's like I know them, too."

She smiles, which softens her face. "I got a message today. George is doing fine, helping Bret with the farm and making gadgets. Bret was an engineer before the war. Now George is catching on. He reads everything he can about history, not the sanitized junk put out by our government and theirs, but histories of the Romans and early America."

"Wow. A boy who can read!"

"Boys read fine if you give them something interesting."

"I know. Don't believe everything I hear in school. If it were true, they wouldn't have to keep convincing themselves."

Mom laughs. "They say George runs like the wind."

I smile. Mom raised me on legends: Bret as a frontiersman in the wilds of Appalachia, and George as a larger-than-life Daniel Boone. She says he killed a bear when he was 12. Fought off three escaped prisoners who attacked him on the road. Harvests a field in a day. None of this can be true, yet I hunger to meet the boy behind the legend, the most exciting person I can imagine. Part of me is jealous that Mom has more love for the one who isn't here, though I'm beginning to understand.

I pace the hardwood floor. *Got to leave.* "I won't forget George, but he has Bret. My birth mother has no one. We need to find her. She needs our help."

Mom's eyes agree with me, although she shakes her head. "The more we dig, the worse things get for Dorothy. I just heard that they transferred her to another prison out west."

"Where?"

"They won't tell me. Please, promise you'll leave this alone. I'll inquire when I can. We will find her. Just don't step on the wrong toes." Mom hesitates and clears her throat. "Did Sam talk to you? I know you hate the mechs, but you should consider her offer. I can't bear them sending you away."

"Did you have something to do with that?" I ask.

"I knew Sam before the war. She's tough but fair. She didn't kill your dad. She was upset at how her troops handled him. It was a political move that bypassed her. Almost cost her control of her mech units. She's offering you a lifeline you need right now."

I can't leave until I've gotten past the worst of this mess. I take a deep breath and blurt out: "I've done something so incredibly stupid you should shoot me for it."

Mom sets her hands on her hips. "What now?"

"I watched a boy escape from Michael's School. That's why I skipped."

She grabs my arms. "What have you done?"

"I saw an opportunity and helped him." I look down, trembling so hard it's all I can do to keep from collapsing. "At least, I thought I was helping. He's in the trunk of Brooks' car in our garage."

"Belle! Don't we have enough problems?"

"I was going to…take him…across the river after the game. If you can keep Janine from following, I'll do it now."

"Not with that collar." Mom grabs a change of clothes I've seen her wear at night, dark and plain. "Are you in love with him?"

"No! I only just met him."

"You're acting like it's more."

My stomach knots. "I've watched him across the street for months." I look at Mom. "Is this what it feels like? My insides twist and turn as if a parasite's trying to get out."

"It's only an infatuation for what you can't have." She changes into her night outfit. "Leave this to me. Not a word to anyone."

"I want to see him."

"No!" Mom glares at me.

"But, Mom…" I feel desperate. Control of this thing is dripping through my fingers. "What are you going to do?"

"Best you don't know. You're not to bring this up again. Is that understood?"

"I'm sorry. I thought I was doing the right thing."

"Next time, think of consequences first. You've put the entire family at risk. Cover for me. I'm going out. Does he have a name?"

"Morgan," I say. "Keep him safe."

* * *

While Mom goes out to clean up my mess, I remain upstairs. I can't face the family. I only want to be with Morgan. *Will I ever see you again?*

I retire to the bedroom I share with Janine and Sarah, with its three double beds pushed together.

Morgan, where are you from? What happened to your family? What music do you like? Well, the Federal Union only allows harmony junk. I haven't seen a movie in ages. They all come with harmony lessons. I don't understand how, after just meeting him, I feel the same insane connection I do with Janine. It makes no sense, and now he's gone.

I lie on my bed. Sobs work their way up from deep within my chest. It's childish to feel so sorry for myself, yet if I keep this bottled up, I'll do something even more stupid.

The door creaks open. I turn to see Janine's bob of brown hair around her sweet face.

"You need to eat with the family," I tell her.

Janine enters our room. She closes and locks the door, which Mom forbids. "I'm sorry I got you into trouble this morning, and I'm the reason you fought at the game."

"You aren't, Babe. Please go. I need to be alone."

She plants her first aid kit on the bed. "Let me tend your injuries, since you wouldn't let the station nurse look at you."

"I'm okay." I feel every punch Dara threw. Confronted by Janine's pouty face, I remove my basketball uniform. It hurts lifting my arms over my head.

"Goodness gracious." Janine takes my uniform and lays it out on her bed. Then she examines me closer.

"I'll be fine. Don't fuss." Still, I don't stop her putting ointment on my cuts or applying a penetrating cream over my inflamed shoulders.

"Sometimes you don't know what's good for you. Just lie still."

She's gentle, better than any station nurse. I drift off to thoughts of the river and Morgan as the combination of eucalyptus, ointment, and cream relaxes the pain.

"Why won't you let me tell Mom I was with you?" Janine asks.

"She thinks you're the perfect angel. Let's not ruin that for her. She has enough on her mind."

"I'm not a goody-goody. I want to be like you, if only you'll trust me."

"I do, Babe." *Though I've promised Mom not to tell you certain things.* I don't want Janine to turn out like me, frustrated all the time.

"Then tell me why you're acting like a chained beast today."

"I don't like being told I have to do security. I don't like the mechs, even though they're the best I can hope for. It frustrates me. Okay, I've confessed."

"But, Belle, isn't it nice to know you'll have a job?"

I sigh. How can I convey my deep distrust of the system? It tells me how to live, what jobs I can aspire to, and who I can be with. It's like a prison sentence, and I'm wearing the maroon collar to prove it.

"At least you won't have to worry about your job, right?" Janine persists.

I smile. "If that makes you happy." I'll fight to keep her out of the mechs another day. I sit up. "How did you know about the station nurse?"

Janine pushes me back down and applies cream to my arms. "To most people I'm part of the background, like wallpaper. When I slipped in and spoke to Lieutenant Brooks about the car, she told me."

"She's a good partner," I say. "I hope you get her."

"Then you might get Scarlatti. Yuck. Are you taking the mech offer?"

"Does everyone know about that?"

Janine grins. "It would be cool to be mechs together."

I sit bolt upright. "Promise me that no matter what, you won't do that. I can't bear to think of you fighting brutes in the arena. Promise me."

"Okay. Don't be so cross. Now lie down. Your back's a mess."

I savor the soothing effects as my back absorbs the cream.

"Now will you tell me about George, or do I have to listen to you breathless tonight as if—well?"

Feeling the heat in my face, I turn away. I hate lying to her. "I can't stand them telling us we can only be security. It feels like a big bear chasing me, a bear named George."

"Okay, keep secrets from me." Janine lies down.

While I like her next to me, I get up. I can't have Sarah coming in and getting the wrong idea. I ease into a clean blouse and skorts. There's a playful look in Janine's eyes. I don't deserve her and yet I need that unquestioned love. "Where would I meet boys, Janine?"

"You were looking at the one from Michael's School. Then you skipped. Is that his name?"

"Enough, Babe." I sit next to her. "He intrigues me because I don't like being told I can't. That's all. Now let's go eat."

Listening to Mom drive away, I hope Morgan didn't give her any trouble. I pray she can get him to safety. My mind wanders to the car. I can't see him. Instead, I see George from the picture Mom hides in her study.

SIX

My maroon collar's giving me a rash. It reminds me that Voss the Boss, that fat cow, can track my movements. I can't take a walk to clear my head because I know I'll end up hunting for Morgan until Voss picks us up. And Janine will follow.

Inside our home, ten pairs of eyes follow me. No privacy even when I tuck myself into bed. Sarah snores like a freight train. I leave the lights off, which spooks Janine, so she crawls in next to me. Even though she's too old for this, I don't push her away.

I can't stop thinking of Morgan out there all alone. Is he heading for the Outland, where I can't go? I'm not sure it isn't George I really want. Then what? Could I really survive in the wilds of Appalachia? No, I've got to make my peace here.

Curled up under my cotton sheet, I face the dark closet. Though I know what I must do, my mind hunts for ways out. It's only a few months until I graduate, early, since I'm security-tracked. I can't graduate if they send me away.

I've toyed with the idea of starting my own restaurant. I'd offer more variety than Union-approved chains. Trouble is, it's hard to stand out, what with all the restrictions on food, drink, and decor. Going to Nashville will destroy any chance to get permits or money. I'd be branded an outcast.

I consider throwing myself at Voss' mercy. I'll plead for another chance. She'd relish me groveling, and I'd be sincere.

It's not that simple, though. Talk of Hollander's Resocialization Facility in Nashville means the governor's office is involved.

Mom's opposition might be a factor, but my actions have brought this on all of us.

My only option is to grab the commander's lifeline, even though I know it's a trap. I try to talk myself into accepting the inevitable.

A mech warrior is the highest aspiration within the security track. If I have to be security, why not the best? It gets me out from under school rules, Surroc, and Voss. I get to stay with Mom and Janine. I won't have to worry about jobs. Mechs will provide for my family.

I hunger to meet George and visit the Outlands. As a mech, I'd have permission, tools, and protection. I'd get to satisfy my curiosity about guys. Why are they almost irresistible to me? Is it the attraction of the forbidden? Mom's talks about George? Or am I meant to be around guys? Our Harmony world feels so unnatural.

Adventure calls. I want to escape the cocoon of our protected Union. The Outland offers the experience of another world, untamed and free. Maybe I'll feel thankful for what I have: public transport, national healthcare, instant communication, support groups, safe diet, and all the things absent in the Outland. Yet the wilds beckon. I can't tell a soul, one of my few private thoughts kept from the Soc-net police.

Then there's the national service aspect. Warriors hunt bad guys and rescue girls from the Outlands. They protect our borders from kidnappers and drug dealers. They protect girls like Janine, who warms my back while my mind drifts into one of the commander's tournament videos.

Hernandez matches me against Dara the Terror. Big as an elephant, she tears into me, yanking my limbs from their sockets. I feel no pain, just humiliation and defeat. I'm a blob on the tournament floor, a mass of torn and bruised flesh. She pounds me like Mama Grace beats bread dough. The stands overflow with girls cheering for Dara. They become her and jump into the ring, taking turns beating me until I'm nothing but a stain on the mat.

Then I find myself in the arena before a brute twice Dara's size. His biceps are thicker than my waist. Yet, I'm smitten instead of scared, and confused. He rips into me. Pain triggers neurons up my spine and throughout my brain. He takes his time, tears my flesh. What am I thinking, signing up to fight a brute to the death? I lose consciousness.

Next, I'm running in the Outland mountains. Wearing heavy black mech gear, I chase suspects, and catch a boy. My black-shielded partner blasts him to dust. It's my dad. I've killed him by becoming a mech. All he wanted was to be left alone. I turn to see my birth mother in chains. I did this. If not for me, my dad would have left sooner. My birth mother wouldn't have returned for me and gotten arrested. Instead, she pleads for me not to send her away. The tether between us stretches and snaps. The rebound doubles me over in pain.

"Don't leave me. Don't leave."

Arms wrap around me. *Mommy?*

"It's okay, Belle. I'm here," Janine whispers, her warm breath on my ear.

I hear the freight train across the room. At least I haven't woken Sarah.

"I'm not going anywhere, Belle. I promise."

But I am. Covered in sweat, I hold Janine. She doesn't seem to mind the dampness. Her breath warms my chin. I gaze into her sweet face, though it's too dark to see, and imagine every freckle, the curve of her big brown eyes, the contours of her sculpted cheeks, her delicate ears. I need her. She replaced another bond severed long ago. I have no choice. No matter what, I'll take the mechs.

"I'm okay, Babe. Get some sleep."

Taking comfort from my calm voice, she rolls over.

* * *

After I drop Janine off at school, and before I deliver Brooks' car, I check the trunk. It's still damp. I can't believe Morgan fit in that tiny space, or that he's gone. Now that I've met him, I wish I'd driven him across the river and spent time to get to know him instead of going to that stupid basketball game. Then Dara wouldn't have attacked my sister. I wouldn't have gotten myself arrested with this stupid maroon tracking collar, putting Mom at risk, and having to join the mechs.

After Brooks drops me off at school, old cabbage-face Surroc pulls me from Civics class and hauls me down whitewashed corridors to her office overlooking Michael's School. I'm too familiar with Surroc's cozy office, with its soft pastel colors and padded chairs designed to get my guard down. She sits next to me rather than across the desk like Captain Voss.

42

I keep my face blank, which is easy since I didn't sleep, and wait for Surroc to speak. She grins like she's won something, or "passed gas" as she would say. I'm more familiar with her scowls, hand-wringing, and squeezing her tiny brain cells to decide what to do with me.

"I'm not surprised." Surroc sits like some prim, uptight, frustrated old woman. "You aren't suited for school, are you?"

You got that right. I hold my stony face and count bicycles outside.

"You won't be our problem much longer."

Too bad, being a thorn in your side gives me pleasure.

"Not laughing? I thought you'd be celebrating. You're done with school. You're also off the basketball team. We can't have violence here."

Oh? What about Dara attacking Janine? Is that okay because Mom's in the opposition? I hold my face still, hoping my eyes don't betray me. I've had years of practice.

"No surprise or shock?" Surroc seems ecstatic that I'm to be re-socialized.

Do you also know about the commander's offer?

"You'd best return to class before they send you to my office for being tardy." She grins.

Wanting to smack her, I hold my composure until I'm out in the hallway. Some people enjoy the unhappiness of others. As a mech, I might have something to say about that.

On the way to class, I use my wrist-com to call Commander Hernandez. *Please go to voicemail.*

She picks up. "Annabelle, have you considered all the implications of your decision?"

You answer your own phone? You know it's me? And you know my answer?

"Hello, Annabelle. It's customary for calls to be dialogue."

"I'm sorry, Commander." I take a deep breath and search for other options. "I want to join your mechs." I can almost see her smile with that scar tugging at her cheek.

"Very well. Be here tomorrow morning at eight sharp. I'll arrange with your school and Captain Voss, and have transit permits delivered to your house. Welcome on board. You won't regret it."

Already do. "Thanks, Commander." *You may get your grubby paws on the body of Annabelle Scott, but you'll never have the soul of Annabelle Montgomery.*

The rest of the morning crawls in a blur as I reconsider my decision. I unearth nothing new.

I watch Janine between classes, surrounded by friends. She's a better student than me, more obedient. She doesn't have my baggage. I feel like Eve eating from the Tree of Knowledge, from the banned *King James Bible* I've read in Mom's private library. Enlightenment brings burdens. Yet Mom had to tell me something to help me cope with this ache in my gut. It didn't make the pain go away, though our bond helps fill the void.

I leave my last class and savor a moment's freedom before I grab the first of three buses to the cop station and Voss the Boss. When I step off the curb to run to the bus stop, a little gray bug of a car screeches to a halt before me. I curse until the passenger door opens.

Lieutenant Brooks waves. "Get in."

I smile. *Are you dragging my ass in for another humiliation?*

I climb in anyhow. This could be my last day with Brooks. I study the coarse texture of her face for what to expect. The moment I close my door she has the peppy two-seater buzzing a cluster of bicyclists, who are either on shift change or lunch break.

"The captain called all units. You get to see action today."

I grin. *No lecture from Voss.* "What's going on?"

"Protest at the state capitol. Voss didn't want me to bring you, but I told her you're trained and I need backup."

"Thanks." *I think.*

We bounce along Kingston Pike, past crowded bus stops. It must be noon shift changes. I'll miss working with Brooks. She cares and tries to do the right thing, which is rare. I want to be more like her, though not the outcast part.

"What can you tell me about the protest?" I ask as we pass several city-buses and approach downtown.

"Every spring these women protest a war that's been over for 17 years."

"Come on, Becky. You don't expect me to believe that." I use her first name because we've gotten close, and I hope Voss hasn't poisoned our relationship.

Brooks laughs. "That's what I like about you. No BS. Okay, these same women brought the war to an end when they protested the slaughter of Outlanders by our mech forces."

I cringe. My dad was a fatality, though three years later. "Why now?"

"Annual reminder that husbands, brothers and sons disappeared. They demand an accounting."

I'm surprised to hear Brooks talk this way. "Do you support them?"

Brooks looks offended. "I toe the party line. Have to as a Knoxville cop."

"But you don't agree?"

"My dear protégé. You know I can't answer that. I will miss you. Yeah, Voss told me you're leaving. Did Sam offer you a slot with the mechs?"

I nod.

"I'd be proud to recommend you. Just don't lose your sense of self. We have to enforce the laws. We don't have to agree with them."

When we approach the cluster of government buildings and rows of parked cop cars, I turn to Brooks. "Becky, I'm glad I got to work with you. I hate that this is coming to an end. Please take Janine under your wing. She has a good heart and follows the rules, but she's fragile. I worry about her."

"I'll see what I can do. Voss may have other ideas."

On foot, we join other cops who converge on the government complex. Women hold placards: "Stop running our sons out of town. Where are our husbands, brothers, and sons?"

Mechs enter the plaza and turn fire hoses on the women. Glass shatters in a Federal Clothiers storefront. Soaked women sprawl across the sidewalk like so much debris.

While protesters scatter, cops cuff two gray-haired women and a young roly-poly girl. Several pairs of cuffs clang against Lieutenant Scarlatti's utility belt as she motions for more arrests.

I follow Brooks to a spot where a dozen cops surround two frail women, jostling over who gets to cuff them. About 50 cops surround 12 protesters. Voss the Boss is taking no chances.

With the protest over, Brooks grabs my arm and pulls me away. Scarlatti looks around for something to do, and I'm wearing the bright maroon collar. *Don't you dare electrocute me, you witch. I don't need my battered brain cells further scrambled.*

Brooks has me around the corner and out of sight before

Scarlatti can trigger my collar. "Your excitement for the day. What do you think?"

"Those women deserve answers, not what they got."

"Street protesting by a few accomplishes nothing. That's why I brought you."

"And here I thought I was your backup." I watch two protesters flee.

Brooks takes no action against them. "I know you're angry and confused. I wanted you to see that it's self-destructive unless you find the right focus. Don't waste your talents or passion on lost causes."

I shrug. "I'm a lost cause, and you waste time on me."

Brooks laughs as she squeezes into her little car. "If you were a lost cause, I wouldn't waste time on you. Now don't disappoint me."

More pressure. I scrunch in. "Now what?"

"The usual: arrest people outside approved zones, catch boys, and enforce food codes. I like the latter because we get to snack."

I laugh. "Why haven't we talked like this before?"

"This may be our last day together. You need to know you're not alone, and I don't mean family. Not everyone is out to make your life miserable."

That gets me longing to find Dorothy Montgomery, my birth mother. The only access point I haven't tried is in Voss' office. I have to do something, without getting Brooks into trouble.

Brooks touches her ear and speeds up. "Got an assignment. Abandoned store with activity."

The piercing siren announces something more intimidating than the pathetic bug bouncing along empty streets.

When the Federal Union banned most cars and expanded bus use, restaurants and stores clustered around bus stops. Those between stops shut down. Now, abandoned buildings dot Kingston Pike.

Brooks pulls up behind a two-story brick building that once housed a specialty grocery. The parking lot sprouts grass. A four-door black cop car pulls up alongside with two cops I don't recognize. They must be from another precinct.

Using her wrist-com, Brooks coordinates with the other team and hands me a stun-gun. "Watch my back."

Then she leads us to a side door along a brick and concrete wall. She breaks glass, unlocks the door, and enters. I don't see anyone outside, though I spot city-cams across the street. I aim my stun-gun behind in case anyone jumps out. I follow Brooks into a store cluttered with debris on the floor and empty shelves. Only a few dusty cans remain, cat food by the look of it.

Brooks finds creaky wooden stairs and climbs to the second story as the other team clears the downstairs. I look behind, watching her back. At the top of the stairs, we turn down a battered plaster hallway past storage rooms to an apartment; probably the store owner's when the store was open.

Brooks contacts the other team. I hear one of the cops run up the stairs. I check to make sure. A dark-haired Hispanic lieutenant glares at me. I'm not in uniform. She holds out her remote when she notices my maroon collar. I show my badge dangling from my neck and point to Brooks.

My partner knocks at the door. "Police. Open up."

There's movement behind the door. The dark-haired cop kicks the door and goes in, followed by Brooks. I scan the dust-filled hallway.

The stench of human filth gags me. I choke it back and enter the room. Six mattresses line one wall. On them lie three boys, couldn't be more than nine or ten, in dirty rags. Each boy has a collar wrapped in aluminum to mask GPS tracking and prevent us from activating the electric shock.

I touch my collar. *I'm like you.*

The Hispanic cop grabs an older boy by the window and cuffs him. I strain to see if it's Morgan. I breathe a sigh. It isn't. After the dark-haired cop pulls the boy from the window, I look down. The fourth cop cuffs two young boys in the parking lot below.

Not my redhead. Good.

My heart aches that these boys have no other home. If they were girls, we'd send them to foster homes where someone might adopt them as I was. Few neighborhoods accept boys; we'll send them to boarding schools like Michael's or worse. I've read *The Diary of Anne Frank* and imagine these boys hiding from a society that doesn't want them.

Brooks takes my arm and leads me out of the room. She covers my mouth with her hand. "Not a word. Go wait in the car."

47

My mind spins. I want to save these boys. I have no business being a cop or a mech. I should have fled with Morgan. Can I still find him?

SEVEN

Brooks returns me to the station, thankfully in silence. I feel the weight of her disappointment. I don't know what to say. I never wanted security. I stink at it. What was I thinking, signing up for mechs?

Brooks records my time from when she picked me up and disappears upstairs to talk to Voss. I'm glad she doesn't drag me along. I couldn't bear Brooks reprimanding me in front of the captain. I'd kill myself.

It's almost time to go, so I hide in the little gym behind the break room. I do warm-up exercises for basketball games I'll never play again. My mind drifts. *Mom, did you get Morgan to safety?* I think of a hundred things I'd like to explore with him if we could have escaped to the mountainous Outland.

Janine pops in wearing her intern outfit of navy slacks and pastel blue blouse. "Don't you dare do anything wild tonight." She straddles a leg-stretcher next to me. "You're wearing a collar, for God's sake."

"What are you doing here? You should be at basketball practice."

"I joined the team to be with you, Belle. Since you're off, so am I."

I stop exercising. "Janine? You're our star player. You can't quit."

"I'm only a star because of you, Belle. Besides, after yesterday I can't put my heart into it. Don't make me."

49

"I'm thinking of your future."

"Then get your stuff. I'm taking you home."

I've never seen Janine act so bossy. My actions must have really upset her. I grab my school bag and follow her to the lockers. "Are you my jailer?"

She smiles. "If need be."

We burst into the moist Knoxville air. Dara, wearing her own maroon collar, stands on the sidewalk with thin-faced Margarite. I push Janine behind me and face Dara, cringing at the thought of another beating.

Dara puts up her hands. "Hold on. Maybe I went a little crazy last night. Truce? I mean, we're both out of basketball and joining mechs."

When I step back, Janine places her hand on my hip so I'll know where she is.

Margarite steps forward. "I quit the team, too, so I could join the mechs. Look, we want to make it up to you. We were a shoe-in for the championship. You embarrassed us. I guess we deserved it, but–"

Dara brushes her friend aside and holds out her hand. "Truce. We're on the same side now. I know where we can blow off steam."

I look for a trick, don't see one, and shake her hand. It's a firm, bone-crushing grip. Dara's big as a brute, but she's all girl, just lots of her.

"What about our collars?" Mine screams criminal. It's indistinguishable from murderer and rapist, no shades of gray. I feel rebellious over yesterday, Morgan, joining mechs, what we did to those boys today, and now Dara.

Dara grabs my arm. "Let's go. I've got a plan."

Pulling away, I spot Brooks by the exit and wave her off. Don't need her involved. Janine sidles next to me with a frown. Oh yeah, she came to take me home.

I shrug. Dara's right. If I have to work with her in mechs, I should make an effort. I don't think she'll hurt Janine now.

Janine tugs my hand toward the bus stop, giving me every silent clue she can that she wants to go home. I reassure her with touch and hand gestures that I want to do this. It's like having a twin, with our own language.

I follow Dara down the street, around a corner to an electric green-cab, charged off solar and wind. It's a tight fit. Dara gets in front, while the three of us crowd into the back, me between Margarite and Janine. Margarite isn't so threatening away from Dara, though I sense she'd do whatever Dara says.

Dara passes back a small bag. "Put it on. It neutralizes the collar."

Inside the bag, I find a tan collar that opens into a hollow aluminum donut. Dara demonstrates by sliding the two pieces over her own collar. She clamps them together. This looks classier than what Morgan used. I snap the enclosure over my collar. "You've done this before."

Dara grins. It must be Margarite's shield. *I want one*. It stirs the rebel inside me.

After Dara stuffs the empty bags into her waist-pack, she directs the driver to take us into the country southwest of town. At twilight we near a checkpoint. The official word says checkpoints are there to catch brutes on the run, though I suspect Governor Battani doesn't want us talking to citizens outside our districts. We might get ideas.

Dara has the driver turn down a muddy road through trees so thick they mask the cloudy sky. We pull into a clearing and up to a grand old plantation house with pillars lining a long porch. While windows are boarded up on the first floor, second and third floor windows appear intact.

When the cab stops, Dara authorizes payment and gets out. I have a good idea of where we are if we have to walk home. Though it's a long walk.

Margarite leans over and whispers, "Don't mind Dara. She's a great friend when you get to know her."

I doubt that.

"She had it rough growing up. Her pop went nuts and attacked her. Then they took him away. She vowed never to be weak again."

Margarite climbs out of the cab before I can ask the obvious question: *Has Dara ever gone off on you?*

Janine squeezes my hand. "Let's go home."

She's right. We should go, but I need to challenge my stupid collar. "You can go. I need to work with Dara in the mechs."

Resistance narrows Janine's eyes. "I'm staying with you."

51

If I make her take the cab home, she'll force the cabbie to stop and return. I ask the driver to come back in an hour. I don't want Janine out late on a school night.

I climb onto the wide wood porch and enter through an ornately decorated doorway, unsure of what to expect. It could be an ambush, or just another bland party with Union-approved music, food, and drink, monitored so it's impossible to have fun. We follow Margarite into a marble foyer and encounter subdued lighting and energetic music. Two dozen girls lounge around ancient sofas covered in dust.

Along one side of the huge hall is an island-bar where we join Dara. She's with a tough-looking black girl, Rox, from another basketball team. I recognize other players we've faced, too.

Dara eyes me. "Basketball buddies. Relax. It's not a trap. Basketball's over. Let's be friends."

I'm not so sure. Janine pulls away and joins two guards from another team. Margarite follows, leaving me alone with the amazon.

"Lighten up," Dara says. She places an unlabeled bottle of clear liquid between us, pours two glasses and pushes one toward me. "Let's drink to kicking ass in the mechs." She downs her drink and motions for me to follow.

I hesitate. Mom lets me taste beer and wine around holidays when Mama Grace isn't looking, while she warns me about alcohol poisoning and addiction. I don't like the taste or the buzz. Still, if Dara can do this, so can I. I pick up the glass and down the clear liquid.

My throat burns. I hunt for water to put out the fire. Dara howls like a hyena. Other girls gather around as I croak, "Water."

Janine brings me a glassful, which I chug down.

"Outland moonshine," Dara says. "That'll loosen you up. Let's dance."

She grabs my arm and pulls me across the hardwood floor to the center of the hall. The music grows louder, or maybe it's the drink stirring my brain. Dara twirls me. The room spins. I reach for the bar, toward Janine. Her forehead creases with worry lines. Margarite takes her hand. They dance nearby.

I lose focus. My head fills with fluffy feathers. Dara grins. I laugh, releasing tension from deep in my gut. I scream. Other girls echo as if psyching ourselves for a game.

52

All the girls dance to the heavy beat of pulsing music, some spicy number I haven't heard before. My body responds as if it knows the beat. Something primal, denied by the Union, leaks out like a wild beast.

The harder I dance, the more tension escapes and the lighter I feel. Dara's big and muscular. I imagine being with Morgan. He shows me a world where I'm not security-tracked. Where I don't have to become a mech to stay with family. Where boys aren't scarce and feared.

* * *

I wake from dreamless sleep to an arm draped over my waist. It's not Janine. My head aches. My mind is groggy and overcast. I remove the arm and crawl out of a strange bed. My bare feet touch the cold wood floor. I'm dazed, and naked except for panties. By streaks of morning light through moth-eaten drapes, I see the amazon next to me.

What have I done? What have you done to me? Where's Janine?

I grab my clothes. Dara stirs, checks her watch. "Great night, Hon, but we've got to hustle. Two hours to get to base."

I loused that up, too? I'm off to Nashville for sure. "How do we get to base? Where's Janine?"

"Margarite took her home."

I'm stunned. Janine wouldn't leave without me, unless she drank and–

I pull on my beige blouse and navy skorts, touch my collar, and feel the shield. Dara stands. She's naked and well-proportioned, though with guy muscles. *Yuck.* I'm disgusted that I spent the night with her. "Why get me drunk?"

"Chill. Didn't you have a good time?"

I can't remember a thing. I check my wrist-com and find it turned off.

"Don't activate unless you want Sam to know where we are." Dara tugs on her clothes. Then she combs her short brown hair with her fingers, checking in a tarnished dresser mirror.

I view myself in my hand mirror. I need a comb, a shower, a toothbrush, and a way to scrub away guilt. More than that, I can't be late. "How do we get to mech base without calling a cab?"

"Not by alerting cops. I thought you were smarter than that, Hon. If you and I are gonna rule the mechs, you'll have to do better."

"Stop calling me Hon." I run my fingers through my hair, flattening my slept-in curls.

"You're touchy in the morning."

"What about last night's cab?"

"She's a friend who won't rat us out. Let's go. I've got an electric cycle around back with two helmets."

I don't want to hold onto Dara on her cycle, but there's no other way. It would take four buses from home, and I'd have to walk the last half-mile because buses don't reach the base for security reasons. Besides, I'd have to get home to begin that journey.

Dara drives the electric cycle along bumpy back roads. When we approach the concrete mech structure, which I've seen in promotional videos, Dara ditches the cycle behind bushes and removes her collar shield. "Let's rock their socks off." She sounds grumpy.

Unlike the cop station, this military base used to house a Special Forces unit. It has concrete walls topped with barbed wire and a gate we have to pass through.

Dara grabs for my collar shield. I pull away. "I don't need your help."

"Don't be such a grouch. I had a great time last night."

"I don't know what happened last night, and I don't need a girlfriend." I release my shield and toss it to her. "You want to be friends? Fine." *Or not.*

She stuffs the shield into her leather case with hers and stomps off. Dara's a tough girl to like.

When we reach the bunker-like guardhouse and gate, I realize my transit papers and anything else the commander sent me are at home. There's no time to get them. I expect the tall, uniformed guard to let Dara through and send me away. Instead, the brunette directs us both into a gated area beside the guardhouse. I'm a prisoner on a military base with my maroon criminal collar. *Now what?*

"Morning, grunts." The commander, compact and self-confident, steps out of the shadows. "We don't take criminals." She reaches up with a key and releases my maroon collar.

I rub my neck and feel the prickly heat of a rash from the chafing collar-shield.

The commander releases Dara's collar and throws it toward the guard. "You won't need those. We have our own ways of tracking you, and if you shield our units, you'll end up in the brig or worse. Do I make myself clear?"

I nod. How did she know? Was last night a test? If so, did we fail?

"Now go, before your instructor penalizes you for tardiness. I hear she's a ruthless bitch." The commander opens the inner gate.

Dara goes first. We both run across the concrete courtyard into a concrete building that looks like a huge bunker. From the inside, it looks like we entered a prison. *What am I doing here?*

EIGHT

Getting excused from school and cop internship for mech training feels like skipping class, until I enter a small classroom with 50 other girls. Walls are khaki concrete that scream military. Dara pulls two girls from their seats up front and takes them for herself and Margarite. I sit toward the back on an uncomfortable wooden seat.

Dara glares at me as if the hard seats are my fault. I can't shift from her hurting Janine to "let's be girlfriends" to hating me when she doesn't get her way. I steady my breathing.

Commander Hernandez barges into the room. *You're our instructor?*

She stands before the class and waits until everyone's quiet. "This room is intentionally uncomfortable to motivate you to master what you need and move on. No one gets comfy in the mechs. If we do, people die. You're here by invitation, which means I can invite you to leave, to wash out. You may excuse yourself from the program at any time until I accept you as a mech. At that point I'll ask you to sign on for six years."

That's a life sentence. Wouldn't Nashville be better?

"Become acquainted with each other. While you come as rivals and enemies, within this program, we work together. Is that clear?"

When all she gets in reply are groans, she scowls, highlighting that grisly scar down the right side of her face. "The proper response from a warrior is *Hoo-rah* or *We stand ready to deliver,* depending on whether you're acknowledging that you understand or committing to perform. I repeat, which I rarely do: as mechs, we operate as a single unit. We don't tolerate animosity toward sister warriors or interns. Is that clear?"

A weak *Hoo-rah* comes in response.

"You want to wash out of the program, keep slacking. You want me to treat you like mech potential, then sharpen up. Our next order of business is the release."

Above my desk appears an image that reads "Mech Trainee Release." I push my hand through the hologram.

"Those who don't think you're old enough to sign, raise your hands and leave. The state recognizes your authority to commit to this release without parental consent."

I'm not sure Mom would refuse, given the alternative.

"Read the release. It covers your commitment to the program, what I expect from you, and physical requirements and risks." The commander slows for the next part: "Risks include death, permanent injury, mental and physical duress. We tear you down and build you up to be the best. This is before you qualify as a mech warrior. If you can't agree, don't sign. Begin reading. At the end, either sign or excuse yourself."

She stops to let that sink in, and then continues, "So there's no misunderstanding, pay attention to the section on fertility. You agree to aggressive contraceptive implants in case of attack on or off assignment. Given the rigors of your work, we can't have pregnant warriors. Implants work six months on with no period and a hell-week off to purge your system. These plus the rigors of training, action, and potential injuries will likely render you infertile. It's a cost of becoming a mech. If this is unacceptable, drop out and save yourselves heartache. I'll return in half an hour. No one is to leave their seat." She marches out of the room.

I skim the lengthy document for all the reasons I don't want to become a mech. My eyes glaze over to the point that I must force myself to concentrate.

Dara grunts and tries to throw the screen off her desk. It's a hologram that merely shimmers with her efforts. "This is bullshit. No one said anything about signing an encyclopedia. Is there anything we're not releasing?"

"Then wash out." It's what I want to do.

"You calling me a chicken-shit?" Dara stands and receives a jolt from her armrest. "Shit." She collapses toward the floor and receives a second jolt before she scrambles her large frame into her seat. "What the hell kind of prison they running here?"

Everyone stares at the amazon, the biggest girl in the room. Margarite looks anxious. Dara squirms in her seat, her body tensing, her face turning red. She rips the metallic armrest off the frame and tries to throw it toward the front of the room. The thin surface clings to her arm and delivers a steady current until she slumps into her seat.

I study my armrest: a mesh with electrical circuits for holographic images. They must enable the jolt that has the amazon twitching in her seat. I don't want to see how she reacts when released.

I read the release more carefully. It lists physical risks: broken bones, diseases, organ damage, everything except pregnancy. Someday I might marry a woman or two like Mom did and consider EggFusion Fertilization to have kids. I might decide to hook up with Morgan or George, if I could find them. I haven't given it much thought until now, but it's another thing the Union denies me. What's odd is how this conflicts with their need for warriors. To the extent genes matter, they're selecting them out of the warrior gene pool. Is that the real intent?

The irony is that for years, scientists worked to perfect ways to take male skin tissue, coerce it into stem cells, and use those to fertilize eggs. It had been a boon to infertile men. Then the Federal Union turned this technique into EggFusion Fertilization with no need for men.

I sign. What choice do I have? I'll bide my time.

* * *

When the commander returns, she dismisses a mousy girl who refuses to sign and closes the door. "First phase of mech training will be history, procedures, rules, and regulations, all the fun book learning." *More brainwashing.*

Dara stews, waiting for a chance to assert herself. It's hard to keep my eyelids open after whatever happened last night. *Curse my rashness.*

"Before we begin, roll up your sleeves for your first injection."

"For what?" Dara asks.

"Number One Grunt, didn't you read the release?" The commander moves to the right front corner of the room and produces what looks like a gun. She stops at each girl's left arm, fires whatever she's injecting, and moves on. "As mechs, we use what works. This heightens your ability to absorb and retain instructions. What ordinarily would take a week of putting you to sleep with lectures will take four hours of concentrated learning, after which I'll test you. Don't fail me."

I raise my hand.

Without slowing her injection routine or looking around, the commander says, "Number Two Grunt, you have a question. You want to know what constitutes a pass on my test and what happens if you fail."

"Actually, ma'am–"

"I'm not a ma'am. You'll address me as Sam or Commander. Is that clear?"

"Yes. Hoo-rah."

"You might survive the day. As for the test, I don't teach nonsense. I provide what you need to stay in the program, what it takes to survive, and what you need to succeed as a mech warrior. If you're under fire and the enemy shoots 100 rounds at you, what percentage do you need to avoid?"

The deafening silence, punctuated by the whoosh of the injection gun, unnerves me. "A hundred percent," I say.

"That's what I expect from you. Nothing less is worthy of a mech warrior. When I was in the marines, they talked of giving 110 percent. That's bull. You can't give more than you have. But be forewarned, my standard of what you can do is much higher than yours. Don't settle, or you'll fail. I don't need slackers."

When the commander stands next to me, I brace myself. I hate injections. Along with the whoosh comes a knuckle punch to the arm, and I know I can expect more bruises. I put on my blank face.

When she finishes the injections, she stands by the door. "You grunts have four hours. The tutorial paces itself and requires your complete attention. You can't leave your seats, as Number One Grunt demonstrated, except to use the bathroom on the tutorial's schedule. When it announces your break, two at a time, I suggest you take advantage of the facilities in back of the room. Don't make us clean up after you. You have five minutes before you're penalized. After four hours, there's a brief break before the test. The test is not multiple guess. In the field, you won't get a list of options to choose from. Learn to deal with this."

When the commander closes the door, the tutorial begins. Words stream across the holographic page at such speed I have to give it my full attention. The tutorial washes away concern over what I got myself into, anger at Dara, and curiosity over where Morgan is and how Janine's doing.

The first part, history, I learned in school: how in the early decades of the 21st century, right-wing extremists tried to turn back the clock. When they failed, they seceded, bringing the Second American Civil War.

I concentrate, not because I'm interested or learning anything new, but because the commander worries me with her 100 percent. I'm amazed at how my mind absorbs like recycled paper towel. These meds could turn me into an "A" student, but I doubt it meets healthy all-natural standards of the FDA.

I read how the great Progressive CEO, Adrianne Picard, supplied mech gear and other tools that allowed Federal Union mech warriors to turn the tide in the war. It also enabled them to police 17 years of shaky peace, which the Outlanders often violate. The tutorial moves into mech history. During the brief Civil War, Commander Hernandez formed the Tenn-tucky mech corps in a matter of weeks. She brought together former marines, Special Forces, and street toughs, putting them through a grueling training program that continues through today.

Yippee. Can't wait.

Next come mech rules and procedures, just like cop internship and school harmony. One difference: the commander emphasizes excellence over harmony, although mechs have to work together.

Excellence sounds good after wallowing in the bland, average, harmonious garbage of school, Union rules, clothes and food. Being expected to be my best could work, though they used "excellence" to dispatch my parents. I push those thoughts aside before I miss vital information for the test. I stink at tests.

When it's Dara's turn to take a break, the amazon goes with Capra, a tough sandy-blonde from the plantation party. Dara stops beside me and punches my injection arm. I force myself not to react.

I hear scuffling beside me and then, "I'm gonna turn this shock treatment on Sam."

I check Dara from the corner of my eye as I focus on the virtual screen. She looks dazed. I don't even see her leave. I can't afford to miss anything before the test.

When it's my turn, the tutorial screen goes blank except for a flashing red "BREAK-TIME" and the countdown from five minutes. I launch myself out of the wooden seat. *Thanks for not electrocuting me.*

I don't wait to see who comes with me. The two-stall bathroom I enter is knee high in crumpled toilet paper.

I grab what I need, finish up, and shake my head at Jane, a small brunette with a pretty face. I rush to my seat with a minute to spare, close my eyes and take a deep breath. It's been two hours and seems like 15 minutes. My mind drowns in facts, figures, rules, procedures, and the penalties for failure: washout, the brig, and death. My brain turns to mush. I open my eyes in time to see the tutorial continue: Welcome back, Number Two Grunt. *How personal. Thanks, Commander.*

Two hours later, the tutorial screen goes blank. The commander barges into the room. "Pencils down."

Everyone stares.

"That's a joke. The best you'll get. In a moment I'll release you to go across the hall for refreshments and a potty break, which I suggest you use. Except Number One Grunt, who will clean the toilets in the back of this room." The commander stares at Dara. "The rest of you are dismissed."

Dara stands and receives a jolt that sends her big arms into spastic contractions. She slumps into her seat. "This is bullshit."

"No, Number One Grunt. This is respect. You want out of the program, keep pushing me. After everyone else leaves, you'll have 20 minutes to clean the bathroom to my satisfaction."

I take the long way around Dara, who glares back. "You'll get yours." Dara can't strike the commander, so she has her eye on me instead.

Thin-faced Margarite waits for me in a large dining hall. Sandwiches, fresh vegetables, deserts, and drinks are arranged on tables along one wall. "Don't mind Dara. She likes to boss."

Famished, I grab a wheat-bread sandwich, expecting cardboard turkey with tasteless mayo. "How long have you known her?"

"Three years. She had a tough childhood with lots of foster homes."

Haven't we all—the tough childhood bit. I head for a seat in the corner. I need to chill and let my brain relax.

Margarite grabs a sandwich and follows. "If you let her think she's in charge, things go better. Just don't challenge her."

Do you consider Dara your girlfriend? If so, why don't you seem angry over last night? I lose my appetite. "Look, Margarite. I hope we can be friends, but I don't take orders from Dara. You work it out." I sit on a thin-cushioned seat and bite into my sandwich, trying to save my strength for the test.

Margarite hesitates, as if deciding whether it's okay to eat without Dara. She sits across from me. "I'd like to be friends. You and Janine are great players. I'm glad she's not hurt." Her eyes have that withdrawn, tortured look. I bet she had a rougher childhood than Dara.

"Does Dara beat on you?" I ask.

"Heavens no. She's not like that." Margarite hangs her head. "I let her lead."

Bet you do. I finish my turkey sandwich, which has a honey taste to it, and pocket a packet of oatmeal cookies. Then I head into the bathroom before we take the dreaded test. Margarite follows. *Guess that's why you get along with Dara.*

* * *

After lunch, the commander hustles us into the small classroom where Dara sits. A dark gloom clouds her tough face, fighting mad with no way to express it. Did Hernandez talk to her while we were on break?

"You'll have one hour to complete the test." The commander moves to the door. "Don't dwell on one question too long. Make me proud."

When we stare quietly, the commander says, "The appropriate response for a warrior is *I or we stand ready to deliver.*"

She waits until she hears our chorus. "Much better." Then she leaves.

The test involves open-ended questions that require thought. I freeze, close my eyes, and take a deep breath. *I'm doing this for you, Janine, and for Mom, and so they won't send me to Nashville.*

What's the capital of South Appalachia? Biltmoor.

What's the population of South Appalachia? Two million. *So, how have they held out against superior Union mechs for 17 years? Never mind. No time to digress.*

What's the mech corps mission? To rescue females, capture or terminate male escapees, enforce borders and patrol national parks on the Outlander side. *How insane. If they're on the other side, why is that our responsibility? Never mind. Stay focused.*

When the hour ends, the commander returns to the room and studies her wrist-com.

I'm certain I've washed out. It was the hardest test I've ever taken, worse than advanced algebra. I tremble, thinking of Nashville. Then I see onscreen:

Congratulation, Number Two Grunt.

Did I get 100 percent? Can't be. I answered every question, but I didn't know the answers, unless whatever she injected created a new databank I can access.

I passed. Now what?

NINE

Exhausted from five hours of tutorial and test, I'm ready to be let go for the day. Instead, as we leave the classroom, Commander Hernandez hands us navy blue body-hugging uniforms from a battered folding table. Then she leads us down a long khaki concrete corridor to a large gymnasium with equipment lining the walls. I smile and inhale the aroma of athletic sweat.

Dara grimaces, a volcano ready to explode in my direction. Am I being paranoid? I don't think so.

Margarite stands between Dara and me to keep the peace. *Good luck.* Only one girl washed out over the test, a serious brunette I expected to do well. Did she have second thoughts?

The commander gathers us along one wall near groups of weights. "As you saw in the recruiting video, the tournament and arena require intense physical conditioning and stamina. Because you have pent-up energy after sitting, we'll commence your training. Spread out and give me full-body pushups, not the sissy kind. Twenty. Now."

I move away from the others and drop to the concrete floor. Dara arranges recruits around herself, her posse, no doubt.

A stocky girl with a round, pleasant face drops next to me. "I'm Brandy."

"No talking," the commander says. "You move like a bunch of old ladies. Maybe we should do this with sniper fire. When I give orders, you move. In the field, sluggishness kills."

The remaining girls drop where they are and start pushups.

Several struggle to do one. Full-length pushups aren't required in gym class.

"Roll over, knees bent, hands behind neck. Give me 20 full-extension sit-ups."

My arms burn from the pushups, but sit-ups loosen tension in my gut.

"On your feet, grunts. Stretch like this." The commander demonstrates leg stretches. When she finishes, she points in my direction. "Three laps around the gym. No physical contact."

When I begin jogging, Brandy joins me. "I hear Sam's tough. Some say she's the best. I want to be with the best."

I remind myself I need friends to survive here. "I'm Annabelle."

"I know. You're mom's a state senator."

"I'm not my mom, and I don't like being reminded."

"Sorry," Brandy says. "I'm just trying to make a friendly connection."

Dara joins us, moving like a nasty old truck. "Let's pick up the pace."

I respond to the challenge.

"Love to see Sam fight a professional wrestler in the arena without weapons," Dara says.

"I hear she's got the brute's balls in a jar in her office," Brandy says.

"Right."

"You don't think she's tough?" I ask.

"Question is, are you?" Dara bumps me and receives a jolt that must come from the blue workout uniforms.

I guess Sam's serious about no contact, though I can't see any circuitry in my outfit that could cause the shock. I couldn't see the circuitry in our basketball uniforms, either.

"We'll have to do something about that." Dara catches up. "Look, if you and I work together, we could rule this place."

"I don't want to rule anything."

"Yes you do. You just don't realize it. You and I could whip this crew into shape in a day."

"Enough talk." The commander opens a wide door in the back of the gym and lets in the brilliant western sun along with a blast of hot air. "You need to learn how to focus and control your energy instead of wasting it. Let's change the stakes. Two miles. Anyone who can't beat me washes out. Everyone outside."

There's a mad dash for the door. I squeeze through with Brandy right after Dara and Margarite. I squint in the blinding sun. Sweat trickles down my neck. I look around at athletic girls, many bigger and stronger than me, and at Sam. This whole mech thing won't be easy.

"We can't control the weather," the commander says. "Imagine you have two miles to find cover and the enemy is shooting. This is not a jog. It's a sprint for your life. Go!"

The commander starts running in the middle of the pack. I ease ahead, breathing harder than I want to, with sweat streaming down my back. Dara charges past along the gravel path. String-bean Margarite pumps to keep up.

Little Brandy joins me. "What's she trying to prove?"

"That she's better than us. I'm guessing the commander is. Let's pick this up." I speed up, although not a sprint, not yet.

The pack clusters behind me. While recruits jockey for position, the commander moves up. She's tough, the best. A former marine, she looks to be in superb shape. I pick up my pace. She's suckering us. Stocky and compact, she's solid muscle.

Take nothing for granted, I recall from the mech tutorial. Assume your opponent has abilities you don't know about. Anticipate them coming at you in unusual ways. I pass Dara, who can't hold her sprint.

"Showoff," she says, out of breath.

Margarite falls back with Dara. I keep distance between myself and the pack, which the commander now leads. She's gaining on me.

"I can't keep this up," Brandy pants.

"You can. You have to." I kick into a sprint. Keep my eye on the gravel path ahead and the pack behind. I sweat, breathing heavily.

Brandy struggles, lags behind. The commander picks up speed with each pace. I push myself into a hard sprint, eyeing the finish line near the gym. The commander passes Dara and Margarite. Brandy struggles to stay with the commander.

Hot, moist air burns my lungs, which crave oxygen. Nausea washes over me. Lactic acid builds up in my blood. *I can't wash out.*

I hear the commander on my heels, gaining. I imagine her as the mech warrior after my dad and me. We're running for our lives. A boost of adrenalin spikes my system. I kick as hard as I can to reach freedom, to do what my dad failed to do. I cross the finish line and collapse.

The commander catches me. "You have willpower, Number Two Grunt. I'll grant you that." She takes my arm and helps me walk off cramps that attack my right leg.

I'm panting too hard to say anything, not that I can think of anything to say.

Dara hunches over at the finish line. "Damn, you're good. You really washing us all out?"

After the other girls finish, the commander releases me and gathers everyone around. "I have a reputation for being unpredictable. Get used to it. Don't mistake my message or orders. Today was a test of what you bring me to work with. None of you will wash out over this run. But take me seriously when I say to push yourselves. When we complete your training, you need to be able to outrun an old woman like me. You're dismissed. Get changed, go home and be here Friday at eight."

She returns to me. "I have something to loosen the leg cramps. Don't think this buys you anything, Number Two Grunt. You're no better than the others. Maybe you're even more trouble because you have a chip on your shoulder. If you learn to harness it, you could amount to something. If not, I don't want you. Is that clear?"

"Hoo-rah," I whimper.

* * *

I lie on a thin mattress in a room off the nurse's station. I'm looking up at the commander with an IV in my arm. "What's in this stuff, Commander?" A middle-aged nurse with dark complexion and auburn hair watches me.

"Call me Sam." The commander continues to apply ointment to my right calf muscle. "Proprietary secret."

My leg cramps fade almost immediately. I exhale a gutful of tension and imagine myself floating. My arm no longer hurts where she injected the memory enhancer and who knows what else. Am I giving up something that will matter to me later? "What about the injection you gave us?"

Sam chuckles. "Like this ointment, it's not approved for general use, but it works. We're done here."

She removes the IV and walks out. I feel the stretch of a tether I don't want. I shake off my weariness and this feeling of connection with the vulture commander.

I roll off the narrow bed and pull on my beige blouse and blue skorts. Wish I had something more practical and exciting to wear. I long for jeans that won't tear and look blah all the time. At least I no longer wear the maroon collar; that is if she doesn't make me put it on when I leave the base.

I pass the nurse's station. There's no nurse. In the deserted front lobby, I wonder how I'll get home. The others have left. Are there still buses to the nearest stop a half-mile away? I step outside into blistering heat reflected off the concrete courtyard and take in a warm breath of fresh air, not quite mountain, though it'll do.

Sam stands at the guardhouse with a short blonde in uniform. "Come on. I don't have all day."

Yet she seems to have nothing else to do. I run over, no leg cramps. In fact I could do another two miles, just not like before.

Sam shoves a plastic card into my hand. "Since you didn't go home to get your transit papers, take this. I won't have my recruits arrested for traveling without permits. Don't you dare pull another stunt like last night or this morning. I'll not only kick you out, I'll strangle you for stupidity."

I stand at attention. "I...Hoo-rah...stand—"

"That's enough, Number Two Grunt. I know why you joined the program. I threw you a lifeline. Don't think I won't kick you out."

"Aye, aye—"

"If you say sir or ma'am, I swear I'll belt you."

"I don't know what to say."

"Then don't shatter my illusion that you have a brain by opening your mouth."

I nod.

"I accept no excuse for failing to be on time except death, yours, and I won't readily accept that. To remove all other excuses, I'm providing you an electric cycle. Make sure to charge it every night. It's not for pleasure trips. You may use it going to school, your cop station, and here. Is that clear?"

I nod.

"You're learning." Sam hands me a fob for the cycle. "No training tomorrow. I have other business to tend to. Be here Friday at eight."

"Thanks, Sam."

I hurry through the gate before she gives me another reason to feel inadequate. I've always known Janine was smarter than me, but she never rubs my nose in it. Basketball gave me confidence I could do something. Now I'm in over my head, floundering.

I turn on my wrist-com to text and call Janine. I worried all day about whether she got home safe. It's the first time I got her into trouble and couldn't cover for her. I hope Mom isn't too disappointed.

I can't reach Janine, which worries me more.

The silver electric cycle isn't new. I don't deserve that. I'm just so pleased to have it I don't mind. I start it and listen to the electric motor purr like a kitten. I fall off when it shoots forward and lands in the bushes. I drag it back to the road, mount and ease it forward. It takes until the end of the mech road to get the hang of riding.

When I turn and look back, Sam is watching. I'm puzzled; she's a pain, yet she seems to care. She won't go easy on me, and I wouldn't expect her to. I figure all the trainees got cycles, since Sam doesn't want us hung up with bus transfers during rush hour.

No traffic this far east: no buses, cars, or bikes. We're too close to the Outland border.

I check messages from Janine, addressed to "rat-fink." *Thanks and no thanks. Glad you had fun. Traitor. Rat-fink cubed. Did you drop into a sinkhole? Rat-fink to the tenth power. Where are you? Miss you. Rat-fink to the googol power. No, really, where are you? Sorry I called you rat-fink. Don't be mad at me. I quit the team and volunteered five days for the cop intern program. Lieutenant Brooks is great. Where are you?*

On my way, I text her, and I kick the cycle into high gear. I thrill at a cooling breeze through my sagging curls. If nothing else, the mechs gave me this cool toy. On the empty road, I kick it up to 70. It's like traveling supersonic. Seeing lights ahead, I slow. I don't need a ticket, or worse, cops taking my cycle away.

I set the speed governor at the speed limit and nearly fly over the handlebars when the cycle breaks to bring me down to 40.

I keep my eye out for Morgan. *Did you make it this far? Stay clear of the mech base.*

TEN

I feel like a high school senior, basketball superstar, and Olympic legend wrapped up together. Here I am on an electric cycle, free to go where I want instead of having to follow bus routes and schedules. I'm on top of the world until I walk into the station with its beehive of activity surrounding Lieutenant Scarlatti and Voss the Boss.

I scurry like a mouse down the side corridor into the break room. It's empty except for Liz Cameron refilling her thermos. She doesn't look up when she hurries out, hustling to get back to her desk before Voss notices her absence.

Surprised that the electronic scanner takes my ID, I clock in for what limited pay internship brings. I check the roster. Janine's on the clock. Brooks is out on a call. I hope she took my sister.

With all the commotion downstairs, I sneak up to Voss' reception area. Dwarfed by her desk, the plump, motherly Liz guards the captain's office while she drinks decaffeinated coffee by the quart. I swear she's addicted to caffeine and believes that if she drinks enough decaf she'll get her buzz.

"Captain's downstairs," Liz says with an exhausted smile. "I suppose you already know that."

"What's all the fuss?"

"Since you're leaving the force, I shouldn't tell you."

"Fine," I say. "I'll ask downstairs. I'm sure they're closer to what's happening."

"Not so fast, young lady. They'll tell you there was a breakout from Michael's School last night. Boys had help on the outside, Underground Railroad, I'd say. A hundred boys. Think of that, 100 ruffians stirring trouble."

I slump against her desk to steady myself. *Morgan?* I can't breathe.

Liz is too involved in talking to notice. "We can't have that, so Voss is calling all officers to hunt them down before they reach the Outlands. For transport they stole buses and cabs. For food they broke into Union Burgers & Subs."

Mom? Are you helping them? Tell me you're not. I can't lose you, too. Not again. Think of poor Janine.

"They must have bypassed checkpoints, or else they're still hiding here in Knoxville." Liz shudders. "How do you hide 100 boys? They'd stand out like ants at a picnic."

That's what I want to know. *Mom?*

"This all happened last night after you left. We simply have to find those boys and send them to a more secure facility far, far away."

I hurry downstairs, stealing a glance up at Voss' office. She has the best access to government files that might tell me where my birth mother is. How many more chances will I get before I'm off the force? Tonight doesn't look promising, but I get another idea.

Two dozen cops crowd around Voss and Scarlatti. I slip around the outside of the large room to avoid them. Voss is red-faced, embarrassed. I don't want to run into her and absorb her wrath. I don't see Brooks or Janine, so I check the electronic roster. Brooks is still out. Janine doesn't qualify to be on the posting roster.

I sneak into Scarlatti's office and root around her desk. For a bright, tough cookie, she has no memory for passwords. She recorded them on her wrist-pad, which she left in her desk next to her confirming electronic fob. How sloppy. No wonder the boys escaped.

After memorizing passwords, I pass the fob over the verifying node on Scarlatti's desk to access her files on the holographic monitor. I push through to the police database and discover that access is limited. I'm surprised Scarlatti, as Voss' favorite, can't see more. No wonder she isn't worried about her passwords.

I pull up my file. On top are transfer papers sending me to Hollander's Resocialization Facility in Nashville this Friday. There's a notation: Suspended by assignment to mech training. I don't see a termination date. I guess that means I'm still a cop intern. Am I also in school when I'm not with Sam or the cops? How confusing.

Janine's file has a bold reference to me and Mom—sins of the mothers and sisters. It pisses me off. It's criminal to hassle Janine just because Mom opposes Governor Battani, and I've transgressed.

Files dating to the Second Civil War are archived and unavailable. Prison files only show jails and prisons in the Knoxville area. A notation comes up that Scarlatti can't access what I'm looking for. So that's why she spends so much time in Voss' office.

Several notations point to local prison breaks and round-ups. Voss' name shows up next to many of the round-ups, along with Scarlatti. Many escapees died rather than return to prison. Voss' teams captured the rest. None of the prisoners made it to the Outland over the three years covered in the files.

Pulling up records on Michael's School for Boys brings a listing of students, including a Morgan McDermott, 17. His picture shows a doe-eyed redhead. He's handsome when not covered in mud. They list him as a good student, and athletic. His curriculum shows that he's years behind me, and I'm security-tracked. I wipe a tear from my cheek. *They're not educating boys for careers, are they?*

Morgan made three attempts to break out of school, the last on Monday, which I watched. There's a notation that they're transferring him to a work-farm in western Nebraska. Despite wanting to know more, I realize Scarlatti will return to her office before going on patrol. I shut down my searches and then, to cover my tracks, do mundane look-ups into food and clothing I know she likes.

I sneak out of the office. When I slip around the corner toward the break room, the crowd still gathers around Voss, who is giving painstaking directions. I hurry into the break room with its refrigerator, microwave, vending machines full of bland offerings, and Liz's decaf machine.

Someone hits my left shoulder and body-blocks me against the wall. "Damn you."

For a nanosecond I think *Dara*. Then I see Janine. She buries her face in my shoulder and sobs, holding me like a desperate child. "I thought you were dead."

I can't hold back my tears. "I'm so sorry about last night. I passed out. I feel wretched that I got you into so much trouble."

Janine pulls away. "Trouble? I've been worried sick about you all night and today. That's trouble."

"Mom wasn't angry?"

Janine whispers, "She didn't come home last night. I begged Margarite to go back for you. She refused. I would have gone myself, but I couldn't remember how."

Mom out, Underground Railroad, escaped boys. Oh, shit. Why couldn't you take me with you? Because I was stupid and got that maroon collar. Is Morgan still with you? Where are you? I can't let Janine know. *What to do?* I can't sit around. I can't let Janine follow me.

I brush tear-streaked hair from the side of her soft face. "I'm so sorry I got us into a fix last night."

"I can't believe how cozy you got with Dara."

Chills worm their way up my spine. "I don't remember what happened, Babe."

"She fancies you, doesn't she?"

"I don't fancy her. She got me drunk."

Janine pulls away.

"I'm sorry, Babe. I have to work with Dara. That's why I went. I just need to be more careful. I promise I won't let it happen again."

Her eyes soften. "Where's Mom?"

"I don't know." *And I don't.* "Why don't you finish your shift? I'll make sure she's okay."

"I'll come with you. Then you won't have to do all those bus transfers alone." Janine touches my neck. "Glad they removed that horrid collar."

"I got an electric cycle for being in the mechs. I'll find Mom and come back for you so you don't have to catch the bus."

"Don't get into any more trouble. Please. I'm sorry I got mad at you."

"I deserved it." I hug Janine and savor how she melts into my arms. "Is Brooks taking you on?"

"I guess. She took me out. I really like her."

"Do what she says and I'll come back for you. Let her know…tell her…don't tell her about Mom."

Janine nods.

* * *

Relishing the freedom the electric cycle offers, I pray that storm clouds blowing in from the southwest hold off. I hurry home, thrilled to cover 45 minutes of bus transit in 10. I text Mom, no reply. I call and get voicemail.

I park my cycle in the empty garage. No Mom, though it's early. I hurry inside. Mama Grace stands in the kitchen with the aroma of baked gingerbread cookies. My sisters don't get home from school until five. Surroc says extending our school days provide all girls the same educational opportunities. Mom says it's so schools can socialize and watch us and so women can work, most women, anyway. Mama Grace stays home.

I hug her. The sight and smell of gingerbread tempts me. Though I know the sugar-free taste will disappoint.

Mama Grace moves her treasures. "Hands off. You have explaining to do, young lady. You didn't come home last night and kept Janine out late."

"I was socializing with other mech trainees." I hope she'll see that as a good thing.

"I don't like you girls out late, particularly when we have city-wide curfew on account of that Michael's School."

Despite wanting to ask about Mom, I don't want Mama Grace to connect the dots. "Tell Mom I'll be late. I've got to work and then bring Janine home."

"Be careful. Too many hooligans out there."

Without commenting, I return to my cycle. I feel important, having my own transportation. I call and text Mom again, no response. Is the senate in session? If so, she'll have her wrist-com off. I decide to check it out, since I don't need two bus transfers to get there.

The state government building takes up a full city block, which was torn down and rebuilt with Roman columns. It's hard to reach. Nearby streets are blocked to all but authorized traffic. I reach a checkpoint set up after yesterday's "riot" and breakout from Michael's School. A pimply blonde in a cop's uniform grips her stun-gun. *Trigger happy, are we?*

"Is the senate in session?" I ask.

Pimply Blonde glares at me as if divulging such secrets could lead to revolution, successful, as opposed to civil war, failed. That gets me to wondering why we call the separation of the Outlands a civil war. The war's been over for 17 years and we're still separated.

I sigh. "My mom's in the senate. I've been trying to reach her. If they're in session, fine. If not, I need to find her." I hold up my cop intern ID.

The pimply blonde grabs my card, scans it and relaxes. "The senate's not in session. Have you tried her office?"

I want to slap my blonde head and say, duh, wish I were smart like you. Instead, I smile and nod. I ride out toward the mech base to enjoy speed on the lonely road and to satisfy myself that Mom didn't head that way. I don't see anything that looks like 100 boys. Can't imagine concealing that many. I'm proud that Mom can, and that she got George to safety.

There's nothing along the tree-lined road to the mech base to indicate boys went this way. I wouldn't. I'm certain Mom wouldn't. How would I do it? I'd flee Knoxville–too many eyes. I'd cross the river and find the most sheltered path, under cover of woods. Head toward no-man's-land and then the barrier. But the closer you get to the border the more cams, listening devices, and satellite tracking. It sounds impossible. *Way to go, Mom. Just don't get caught.*

I don't know where to look and don't want to expose Mom by tipping off Sam or the cops, so I return to Knoxville, and keep going. Janine doesn't get off for another two hours. I don't want to run into Scarlatti or Voss. I can't go to work, since I'm too worried about Mom. And I need to find alternatives to the mechs.

At each passing bus stop I study restaurant choices: Union Burgers & Subs, Tenn-tucky Bistro, American Fine Dining, our good, better, best. It's the same boring stuff in different settings. I want to believe there are others like me who relish variety. Now and then, I see a Barry's or such that adds spice within Union restrictions.

I hunger to give it a shot. I'd bring Janine in so she didn't have to do security. Might even sneak Morgan in to help, let him live in the attic or basement. A restaurant would be a perfect place to hide boys and feed them. I like this more with each mile.

As much as I hated waking up next to Dara this morning, and the way she takes charge and got me drunk, she'd know how to get a club or restaurant working. Before I know it, I'm in front of the old plantation house. Two dozen cycles nestle up to the porch like horses tied to a hitching post. It's Dara's posse from mech training.

When I turn to make my escape, Dara pops out in jeans and yellow pullover. "I wondered if you remembered how to get here."

"I'm not interested in a repeat of last night," I tell her.

75

"Don't be so thin-skinned. You've got to toughen up for the mechs. Come on in and let's party."

"I have to go. I was just trying our new toy."

"Heather's cooking up something illegal."

The thought of new tastes grabs me and won't let go. A restaurant is my ticket out. I hold up my hand. "Okay, but I can't stay long. I'm not drinking. And I'm not getting cozy." I feel ill imagining what happened after I passed out.

"Loosen up. We only go around once. Make it count."

Not your way. I park my cycle next to the others and tuck the starter fob into an inner pocket I sewed into my skorts. I follow Dara through the huge marble façade of the plantation's foyer. The dusty, expansive interior returns the nightmare of last night. I keep my distance so Dara can't put her arm around me and be buddies again. The light beat of catchy music fills my ears, something I could dance to or at least move to, since I haven't danced to anything other than Union melodies with Janine.

In the long, high-ceiling room, beanpole Margarite sits with a few of her basketball friends. Dara stands along the side with mech recruits, including the boisterous sandy-blonde Capra and Rox with her shiny cornrows. Several recruits stand at the bar drinking shots. Who will wake up next to Dara tomorrow? Will they wash out of the program when they don't make it to training? *That's right. It's not until Friday.*

Dara tugs my arm. "Come on. Just a quick drink."

I yank free and step back. "I don't like being touched. I don't want a drink, and I don't want to sleep with you."

"You find me ugly?" Dara moves closer, softens her look, and poses her elegant profile.

"You have a striking face. You're passionate about what you want. But I'm not interested in getting involved with anyone."

"You're sleeping with Janine, aren't you?"

I glare up at her. "You're joking, right? We sleep three to a room. That's all. I love my sister and won't let anyone hurt her."

"Is that a threat?"

"A promise."

Dara laughs. "You've got spunk. I like that."

The subtle implications have me on edge. I move to the counter next to the bar and find sandwiches. Starved, I grab what looks like another bland turkey-soy-on-wheat.

"Careful," Dara says. "It has kick. You might want a drink with it."

I fill a glass with tap water and taste the sandwich. I don't smell anything unusual, but the sandwich bites back, something tangy I can't place. I swig water. After the burn dies down, the taste compels me to try again. This time I get a broader taste with the kick. I savor the experience with my eyes closed. It piques long-dormant taste buds that scramble to describe the yummy taste.

When I finish the sandwich, my chest rumbles. Acid rebels against the prickly taste. "What was that?"

"Sharp mustard with jalapenos," Dara says. "From the Outlands. Here, try these." She holds out a tray of illegal chocolates.

Popping one into my mouth, I get a minty flavor, then cherry. The silky blend slides down my throat and quiets the acid burn. I'm in heaven, seduced by the dark side in rebellion against the Union.

Music grows louder with a peppy beat. Dara takes my hand, drags me to the middle of the floor and begins to dance. Not wanting a repeat of last night, I break free and head for the door. I don't need whatever she's pushing.

"Don't go." Dara taps my arm. "We caught two of the Michael's School boys. We're gonna have some fun with them."

ELEVEN

I release Dara's grip and back up toward the exit. "I said no. I can't be late."

"Your loss."

When I reach my electric cycle, I spin dirt to flee the plantation house and Dara. I feel contaminated, as if worms have taken over my body.

I call Mom, no answer. Worried, I call her office downtown.

"Haven't seen her all day," her aide says in a perky voice. "Isn't she working at home?"

"Could be. I'll meet her there." I hang up.

While I want to head home to find Mom, something tells me she's still not there. Then it hits me. Dara might have Morgan. I brake and nearly fly over the handlebars. Doubling back, I take a trail through the woods and get my legs scratched by brambles. I can't leave my redhead at Dara's mercy. She has none that I can see.

I park the cycle away from the plantation, facing the road, and continue on foot. It begins to drizzle. I have to hurry. When I reach the clearing around the great mansion, I hunker down behind bushes. *Think about consequences, Annabelle. You can't march in there and grab Morgan. Not with Dara surrounded by friends.*

I scoot around the plantation house. When I reach the back, a shed obstructs my view. A tool shed on the plantation? Not seeing anyone, I approach. There's no lock on the door, but it's bolted shut.

While keeping my eye on the mansion, I scoot behind the shed. "Anyone in there?" I whisper. "Morgan?"

"He got away."

I take a deep breath and let it out. "Who else is with you?"

"The big girl took Drake. Just him and me."

"Are you going to hurt me if I let you go?" There's a dumb-blonde question. Of course he'll say no.

"I just want to get my friend and leave."

"You got a name?"

"Brad."

"Well, Brad, you can't help him. If you try, you'll get caught and put me at risk. Do you understand?"

"Yes."

"If I let you out, will you do as I say?"

"Okay."

I push aside the bolt and open the door. Though he's in shadows, I see a boy with hands and feet bound by rope. He looks to be 16, strong, athletic. Heart racing, I approach. This isn't any easier the second time, my second boy in three days. I must be nuts. I take a brief glance back at the mansion, gray under storm clouds, and begin to untie his hands. "You won't hurt me, will you?"

Brad bows his head. His cheeks are moist. "I have to help my friend."

I stop. "Then I can't help you. If you get caught they'll make you talk. You'll tell them about me. Come with me or stay here."

He nods.

My hands tremble as I undo the rope binding his wrists. I stand back, take a quick look at the house and move toward the door. I should get away while I can. "Do you know where Morgan went?"

Brad removes the rope from his legs and gets up. "No. He was with some woman in a black disguise. She was showing us the way."

Mom? "What does she look like?"

"I couldn't see. Shouldn't we get going?"

I take a final look at the mansion before I lead Brad outside and close the shed door. Then I take him around behind the shed and back toward my cycle. Lightning strikes come from the west as we reach the cycle. The rain picks up.

"Where can I take you?" I ask as I mount the cycle. It dawns on me that he could immobilize me and take the cycle.

"I have to help Drake. He needs me."

"Listen to me, Brad. There are over 20 warriors at the house." I don't add that they're only trainees, first day even.

"You're one of them, aren't you?"

"Yes and no. I'm not into capturing boys."

Brad moves backward toward the plantation. "Thanks for letting me go. Will you help me?"

"Don't do this, Brad. I can't. I have other problems." *Namely Mom.*

"Morgan told us about you. Thanks from all of us."

My breath catches. "Thank me if you make it to the Outlands."

Brad turns and runs back toward the plantation house in the rain. Part of me wants to follow him, but I have to make sure Mom is safe. I have just enough time to check, change out of my wet clothes, and return to the station before Janine gets off.

* * *

When I reach our communal home, the garage is empty. Inside the townhouse a gaggle of girls mill about, filling the space with chatter that most times gives me comfort of the familiar, but not now, with Mom gone, and not when Therese pulls her younger sisters upstairs, away from the social misfit.

I don't ask about Mom. It might frighten the family. Mama Grace is the most likely to know, and she doesn't look worried. I hate all these secrets.

A steamy shower fails to purge the filth from Dara's touch or the guilt that I didn't help Brad rescue his friend. I can't believe I helped him only to let him go back. I can't believe I did it again, helped a boy I won't get to know.

I change into fresh blouse and skorts that match what I removed, except they're clean and dry. I exchange my muddy flats for clean ones and rush off to look for Janine. I need to keep her from showing her worry-face and stirring up trouble at home on top of everything else. I'm dying to tell her about Morgan and Brad. *Where are you, Mom? Where's Morgan?*

At the station, I find my sister at Brooks' desk. Janine listens to the lieutenant better than I do, which is why she's a better student. Bless her.

I sneak along the outside of the big room to avoid Scarlatti, who acts like an orchestra conductor in Voss' absence. She's directing teams to chase lost boys. The captain must be upstairs. I land in a seat next to Janine and grab her hand. She squeezes back: no animosity. Good.

"Told you I'd be back in time," I say.

Janine beams. "Did you—"

"Later." I turn to Brooks. "How's my sister doing?"

"Better attention to detail and procedures than some." *Meaning me.*

"Good. I'll check out. J, meet you in the break-room."

"Whoa," Brooks says. "Where have you been all afternoon?"

"Hunting escaped boys." It's the truth. After all, I did find Brad.

"Likely story. We're finished if you want to take your sister home. I hear you have one of those," Brooks lowers her voice, "personal transports."

"It's so I can get to mech base quicker."

Brooks pats me on the shoulder and winks.

I hush Janine until we're on the cycle. Then I can't shut her up. "Did you find Mom? I've tried all afternoon."

I start the cycle. It's too quiet to muffle voices. "I'm sure she's okay. She's been gone before."

"Never when so many boys got loose. Hurry. I don't feel safe, and thanks for coming back."

"Sisters stick together."

"Not last night," Janine reminds me.

"I said I was sorry. Will you ever forgive me?"

"I'll think of ways you can make it up to me."

I'm not worried. Usually she just wants me to take her somewhere.

I speed down secondary streets to avoid city-buses. When we reach home, I park in the garage next to Mom's car. I'm relieved, excited, and curious. Janine's worry-face melts into a smile as she scrambles inside. I follow.

Dinner's ready. Mama Helen sits at one end of the long table. To my relief, Mom sits at the other end. Janine gives her a hug, longer than usual. I know Mom noticed. I hope the others don't.

Not wanting to put Mom on the spot, I agonize through a vegetable stew that could use some mustard-jalapeno sauce.

When dinner is over and Mom gets up, I give Janine a look not to follow and pull Mom upstairs into the master suite. As soon as I close the door and turn on harmony music, she starts in on me.

"You didn't come home last night, and you had Janine out late."

"You weren't here, either." I lower my voice. "Mom, I know what you were doing. I'm not a child anymore."

"You're only 16, Belle. You shouldn't worry about such things, and we're not going to talk about it. Where were you?"

I stare at the worn wood floor. "At a party I shouldn't have gone to, where I got stupidly drunk. I'm sorry, Mom. I made a fool of myself and thankfully, Janine got home safe. It wasn't her fault. She's a good girl."

Mom sighs. "I know you cover for her, Belle. Problem is she copies you, and you're not setting a good example. You're taking too many risks."

"Where's Morgan?"

"I told you to forget about him. I took care of it."

"But, Mom—"

"Enough!"

"You helped those boys last night, didn't you?" I noticed mud on Mom's shoes downstairs.

"The less you know, the better."

"I see that school every day, Mom, and some of the boys. What's happening to them is criminal. I'm proud of you. It's time you let me help."

"Goodness, child, you have your whole life ahead of you."

"Every boy I see reminds me of George. I want to help them all for his sake."

Mom collapses onto her bed. "Me, too, Belle. I miss him so much." She looks up at me. "Don't think I love you or Janine or Sarah any less. You have experienced my love. He hasn't."

I sit next to her. "I know, Mom. I used to get jealous, but not anymore. Now I'm angry I can't get to know him."

She smiles. "I need you to be more careful, Belle. There are many who want to destroy us. If they learn what you know, we're finished."

"I know, Mom." I stand and pace. I want to tell her about Brad and Drake, but I can't burden her with more. Then she'll go out to clean up another of my messes.

"What is it, Belle?"

I sigh; have to give her something. "Last night I was with that bully who tried to hurt Janine. I have to learn to deal with her in mech training and, if I make it, on the force. I tried to impress her and the other girls. It was one drink. Must have been pure alcohol. I won't do it again. I promise. I'm only 16. I'm still learning."

Mom laughs.

"Mom? Why can't you get mad at me like other moms when their daughters get out of line?"

"You get mad enough at yourself. I trust you, Belle. More than you know. If anything happens to me, I know you'll protect Janine and Sarah."

"Don't talk that way."

"We almost got caught. All I thought of was losing you three."

When she hugs me, I feel that tug, heaped with guilt for being weak around Dara. I took too many risks with Morgan and Brad. I wish Mom would come down harder on me. I deserve it. I can tell her most anything. *Have I pushed you to the breaking point to test your unconditional love?* More guilt. I hold her tight. I know we came close to losing each other. Still might.

* * *

Thursday is school and cop internship, which float by in a fog. My mind is on Morgan and Brad. Friday is mech training. I don't look forward to what craziness Dara will bring. I want to help those boys like Mom does, but all I've done so far is create problems.

I park my cycle outside the base and pass the tall guard with minutes to spare. Hopefully, I won't run into Dara. I know that's coming. I don't know which is worse: that she's a bully or that she fancies me. This gets me thinking. Everyone expects I'll marry a girl and settle down, when actually I ache to find a boy and figure out what that's all about. How many other girls have my confusion? Yet if I tell anyone, somebody will plaster it on social networks and alert the Soc-net police.

Little Brandy waits for me in the courtyard outside the huge mech bunker. "Glad you're back. Hope you rested up on your day off."

Like a baby, up every two hours, wailing. I hope she doesn't expect the one who got her brains beat in on a basketball court to protect her from the amazon. I hurry down khaki corridors.

Sam greets us outside the little classroom where we did the tutorial. "It's eight. Take your same seat."

She closes the door behind us. Dara grumbles; looks like she didn't get much sleep. I drop into my wood seat and feel static electricity on my arm from the tabletop.

"We have a short time to mold you into effective warriors," Sam says. "Let's get to it. Today we'll do intense physical conditioning. We'll demonstrate mech suits and what they can do. Then you'll start sparring. First, roll up your sleeves. Signing the release and returning was your consent to contraceptive implants."

So soon?

"It's also your consent to tracking implants. Think of yourselves as products. This is your personal chip. You'll be tracked 24/7. If you're in trouble, you can activate an alarm and sister mechs will come to your aid. Do not activate as a prank or you will wash out. This contains travel permissions, which are limited until you become a warrior."

I hate putting foreign substances into my body. What about side effects? Loss of freedom? I didn't expect to cross this bridge so soon. Dara rolls up her sleeve. A dozen girls from her party follow. I guess that's leadership. Protesting will get me kicked out. I can't accept the consequences, so I roll up my sleeve and brace myself.

Sam moves around the room with the injection gun. "Aside from sit-ups and pushups, of which I expect you to master 100 each, you're to do 10-mile cross country runs at least three times a week, which we will track."

I ache already. I raise my hand to ask how we do that with travel restrictions.

Sam doesn't call on me, while she continues injecting. When she reaches me, Sam grabs my raised arm, lowers it and injects. It feels like she slugged me. I hope it's both implants at once.

"As mech trainees, you'll have limited travel access, which allows you to return to base at any time to further your training. Your permit allows access to three fields around Knoxville. I tolerate no excuses."

Sam finishes injections, returns to the front of the room, and opens the door. "I want hustle today, grunts. I want each of you to outperform this decrepit old woman. Is that clear?"

A cacophony of shouts fill the room, a disharmony of "Hoo-rah" and "We stand ready to deliver." Then a second as recruits choose the opposite and finally a third chorus of "Hoo-rah" as we figure that's the appropriate response.

I'm not a rah-rah person, even in basketball, but the crowd drags me along.

"Double-time." Sam leads the way down narrow corridors at a sprint to the gymnasium with its embedded scent of sweat. Before we can line up, she drops into pushups. "With me."

I drop to the ground and try to keep up. I can't. She's in superb shape for an old woman, probably only Mom's age. Other recruits drop and struggle to do a few. Dara keeps up, muscles rippling. Despite mine rebelling, I refuse to cave in.

Without taking a break, Sam rolls into sit-ups. We copy. Then Sam takes us to the weights, where seasoned warriors join us. They look crisp in blue form-fitted exercise pants and long-sleeve tops. I'd prefer short sleeves and shorts as I add my sweat to the gym's aroma.

While warriors demonstrate various weight programs, Dara sidles next to me. "Not so tough today, are you? Bet you can't press 50."

Dara flexes her muscles to intimidate me. It works. *Just stop telling me what I can't do.* I can't stand this competitive, buddy-buddy, Dr. Jekyll and Ms. Hyde bit, either.

She volunteers for the bench to show us lesser grunts she's boss. She has no difficulty at 50 pounds and calls for 75. At 100, she struggles to press once. "More."

Sam shakes her head. "Next. Hustle."

The muscular, black-haired spotter locks the weights, and Dara gets up. Disappointment spreads across her large face.

I step forward. I struggle to lift the fifty-pounder once, but I do it. I get my arms to full extension, feel like I'm carrying the weight of a car, and ease it down before it drops. I try a second time and lose it. The dark-haired spotter catches before the weight bar slices me in two.

"I'll try the next one," I say.

Sam shakes her head, and the spotter locks the weights.

Let me try. I hold my blank face; no point aggravating Sam.

Next come free weights, leg weights, and equipment that pulls, pushes and stretches every muscle I'm surprised I have. Dara outmatches me each time with a solid gloat of superiority on her Romanesque face.

"Maybe you aren't cut out for mechs," Dara says.

"Shut up."

"You want to make me?" She shoves me.

No! I push back and brace myself. I knew this was coming, yet

85

I'm trembling. What's more, I'm pissed that I woke up next to her with memory block after she tried to hurt Janine.

Sam grabs us by our arms and leads us toward a mat. "I thought I made myself clear. Mechs work together." She pulls us onto the mat. "Sort this out now."

Sam calls out to the group: "Everyone stand back while our wildcats give us a demo."

Not again. I've let Dara sucker me. She plunges in. I scoot backward, trying to decide what to do. She looks bigger face-to-face.

Dara reaches with long arms. I slap her hand away. She punches my arm. I punch. She keeps coming. "Pathetic. You fight like a little girl."

How original.

"You want to win in the arena, you'd better learn to fight like a man. That's the point, isn't it?"

Dara rushes in. I scoot aside, a moment too slow. Dara grabs my waist and tosses me onto the mat.

She jumps on top and straddles me. "Not so tough, are you?"

Her eyes bear down on me, a cross between victory and what: seduction? I'm a fly in a spider's web.

She has limited vocabulary. Maybe that translates into limited moves. I try to rock Dara off. The amazon weighs too much. I punch. Dara grabs my hands. "You give up?"

"I'm resting," I say. Rage builds. I let it explode in arm and leg movements that come out spastic. I can't budge the beast.

"You're pathetic. You really think you can beat me?"

I thrust forward to butt heads. Dara leans back and adjusts her weight. When she does, I swing my legs up and grab hold of Dara's head. I throw her back, which frees my arms. When I try to break loose, she gets my head into a scissor lock. I can't pry her legs loose; lose my grip on her head. I have nothing to fight back with. I refuse to yield. *Think, Belle.* My mind fades. My lungs crave oxygen.

My birth mother appears to me. I can't make out her face, never can, though I know in my heart it's her in handcuffs. They cart her away. Someone holds me. Mommy, mommy, don't leave.

She vanishes.

TWELVE

When I come to, I'm lying on a bed surrounded by khaki walls and bright LED overhead lights. It must be the base infirmary. An IV clings to my left arm, which is starting to bruise. The middle-aged nurse with auburn hair mops my brow and smiles down at me. Her nametag reads: Nurse Kristina Wells. Sam stands over me, dismisses the nurse, and closes the door.

"What am I to do with you, Number Two Grunt? You have more heart and guts than most warriors do, but you aren't using your head. You'll kill yourself if you keep playing Dara's game. She has bulk and strength and she's smarter than she acts, but she's lazy."

"Could have fooled me." My voice sounds raspy.

"If she works harder, she'll become quite a force." Sam adjusts the IV. "What about you? What's driving you? Where's your strength come from besides sheer will, which won't count for much on its own?"

"I don't know, Commander. Can you teach me to beat her?" I'm tired of being afraid.

Sam grins. "Competition? Very well. I'll teach you how to be your best. I'll offer the same to Dara, no favorites."

A moment of hope turns to despair. I don't want preferential treatment, but I can't imagine how to hold my own against Dara if Sam helps her get better.

"Enough slacking." Sam reaches over and removes my IV. "It's time to demonstrate mech suits. You can't afford to miss training. Just don't pick any more fights."

Before I can protest that I didn't pick that one, Sam pulls me to my feet. I'm dizzy, weak, in no condition for more training.

Nurse Wells looks upset as Sam drags me down the corridor.

"I'll take full responsibility," Sam says and keeps moving.

Every muscle in my body protests. My neck's swollen from Dara's scissor-lock. I feel welts on my arms, but that's nothing compared to the pain of letting myself get suckered into a humiliating fight.

I hold my head high as I march into a larger gymnasium with its high beamed ceiling. Mech suits line one wall. Standing at attention by the suits, six warriors look sharp in blue exercise uniforms. Recruits stand at attention on the concrete floor. Sam takes me to the back where I stand up straight like the others, though on wobbly legs.

Two black robot-hulks appear, warriors encased in black shielding made of a polymer of titanium and carbon-fiber-reinforced plastics. *I got that from the tutorial.* They step into the middle of the echoing hall and exercise: one-handed pushups standing on their heads, and jumps into back-flips. Then they run at each other. Colliding, one throws the other up toward steel ceiling beams. The airborne mech grabs the beam with one hand, pulls herself up, and jumps onto the other mech. They wrestle like nothing I've seen before, moves I can't describe for their speed, agility, and brutality. Then the two mechs face each other and bow.

"This is some of what the suits can do." Sam's bass voice resonates in my ears. "Each of you will examine your gear. When I give the word, break formation. In orderly fashion, sprint to your suit as designated by your number. The suits are sized for you as small, medium, and Dara." Sam glares at her.

The amazon seethes, saying nothing. *Yeah, you're saving it for me.*

"Go!" Sam says.

Have I missed something? I approach Sam. "I—"

"Number Two Grunt, are you paralyzed?"

"No, Commander."

"Then why aren't you moving?"

Since I'm Number Two Grunt, I run toward rack two, which is not next to rack one. My leg muscles cramp. I push through the tightness and reach my suit as others remove theirs from their racks.

"For the duration of training, you'll work with these suits," Sam says. "Familiarize yourself with how they work, how to put them on, what they can do. They'll become your advantage in battle and your lifeline to sister warriors."

I pull heavy black parts off the rack. Each leg comes separate with locking mechanisms that attach to each other and to the front and back torso shields. I watch Brandy assemble hers. It looks like a quick assembly and release system.

"Hydraulic components enhance muscle movements. They compensate for the weight and increase your strength, agility, and speed. It's like learning to ride a bike. You'll be clumsy at first. Your instincts will be to overreact.

"These suits offer great advantages. We introduce them now because they enhance physical conditioning by showing what you're capable of. Word of warning: don't become dependent on the suit. Your greatest danger will be when your suit is vulnerable or when you're not wearing it."

I reach into the right arm shield, heft the weight, and hope the rest of the gear will support this. My muscles resist. The fist tightens as I move my fingers. I flex my bicep. The fist flies up past my face. Yeah, I could use this fighting Dara, but then she'll have one, too.

I connect the legs with the groin plate, an awkward narrow shield. At first, I'm clumsy, like moving in molasses. When I lift my leg, the suit responds and over-reaches. I fall backward. Others tumble around me.

"You'll get used to that. For now, familiarize yourselves with each piece of the suit. The most important will be the biochip. When you put on the helmet, it begins to adapt to you. From that point on, you'll need to remove the chip and carry it with you when you're not using your suit. It's your key and includes your personal adaptations. You'll understand better as you teach the suit to work to your specifications."

While I long to wait until my muscles loosen up, Sam's on a fast schedule. I'm surprised she takes time away from running the mech corps to handle training. I guess she wants all recruits trained the same.

After getting to my feet, I attach the chest and back plates, like medieval armor, only thinner. They're glove-tight, though not to the point I can't breathe. They fasten easily to the leg and groin plates as we've seen in the tutorial. This makes movement easier, though I'm bulky with all this gear. Other recruits finish adding body armor and examine the helmet. When Dara puts hers on, she looks like a robot, tall and menacing. Despite what Sam says, size matters.

The neck plate is pliable enough so I can turn my head. I look at the helmet and the chip upfront.

Sam walks among us, examining our preparations. "Put the helmets on. We've turned off the com-links except mine so you can hear me."

The helmet is heavier than I expected. Before putting it on, I flex my mech gloves. I don't want to drop the helmet and embarrass myself. The gloves have more mobility than you'd guess with that amount of armor.

I lift the bulky helmet over my head and lock it into the neck-plate with four clasps. I'm in a fully encased coffin, and it's hot. I steady my breathing and open my eyes. I see through the visor, some clear shield, and a cam feed behind. That would be useful in a fight or in basketball.

My eyes dart about, taking in what limited view I have through the visor, while other cams give me a broader perspective. It's confusing, like looking at three movies overlaid. I turn to take in my surroundings and the other black-shielded recruits.

"One of the innovations is the visual array," Sam says. "You have a view through a bullet-proof clear polymer. It's stronger than steel. You also have other views triggered by eye movements. This is part of training the suits. You'll want to keep the rear view open at all times to alert you to threats.

"You have infrared views most helpful at night. When we get to weapons, you'll find views that allow you to aim in one direction while moving in another. The most important thing is not to get confused by all the potential views."

I sort out the cam views. Dara is to my left, the biggest, Number One Grunt. Brandy's to my right in regular light and hazy infrared. I flick my eyes one way and another. I shift views until I have only the visor, the rear shot and two views offset to the sides like a panorama. This is solidly cool.

Moving forward, I test how the suit responds to my muscles. I flex my arms, squat down, and jump. I could get used to this.

"Enough play," Sam says. "Form up."

While other recruits bump into each other and tumble like bowling pins, I navigate toward Sam. I fall, jump, and land 10 feet away on my back. Ordinarily that would knock the wind out of me. Instead, I jump to my feet and run. The sense of freedom and release from muscle strain is exhilarating. I slam into the wall before I can stop.

"I said form up!"

I bounce back, turn and run toward Sam as the others form lines. I take my position in the back and shift cam views. This is much better than being a cop.

"Spread out," Sam yells.

She doesn't look like she's yelling, so I use eye movements to turn down the earpiece volume.

"Drop and give me 100 full one-handed pushups. Now."

When I drop, my head hits the padded helmet. I'll have to be careful of that. I ease into pushups. They're almost effortless with the suit's hydraulics. Sam has us do sit-ups, squats, jumping jacks, and a variety of moves to show what we can expect from the suits. Then she lines us up. "I want you to run across the gym and back. Learn to turn quickly."

I do, enjoying the exercise flexibility. I've almost forgotten my injuries.

"Now line up in pairs," Sam says. She points for me to stand across from Dara.

Not again.

"Now that you know how the suit works," Sam says, "let's see how you fight in one."

I flinch.

"Each pair stands on a square on the floor."

Dara and I are inside faint white lines, maybe ten by ten.

"Under no circumstances are you to leave that square," Sam says. "You do not win by pushing your opponent out. In fact, you both lose. I want to see movement, attack, and if you can stay within bounds, a clear winner. You have three minutes."

Oh, joy. I set my cams to monitor the square and my opponent. Dara hesitates, no doubt doing the same. I attack, kick her legs from under her, and send the amazon crashing onto concrete. Dara

91

jumps up, grabbing my waist, and we wrestle. It's not like before. I feel through haptic sensors where Dara touches my mech gear, but I don't feel pain. This raises the question: With the protection of the suit, how do you get a clear win?

It doesn't take long to find out. Dara flips me, clasps my arms with her legs and my legs with her arm. I can't move. Blood rushes to my head.

"Good job," Sam says. "Release your opponents. Run the ten-mile track out back and return your suits to their racks."

After Dara releases me, it takes a moment to orient so I can get to my feet. While I like the power of the suit, it will take time to master. And it won't give me any advantage over Dara.

* * *

Running in mech gear is clumsy until I get the hang of placing steps so I don't trip or fly through the air with no traction. It's like learning to walk on the moon. Yet by a half-mile, I get into a rhythm with most of the other recruits. Dara stays close. She won't let me beat her again, not with the suit.

When I pick up my pace, nearby trees and shrubs flash by. It's like being on the electric cycle. I lengthen my stride, pick up speed, and focus on forward motion to control the upward thrust that comes with each pace. By two miles, it becomes effortless.

My muscles don't ache, and in fact, I relish movement. What did Sam give me after I passed out? I've heard of miracle drugs, unapproved by FDA, that heal injuries and sprains. Does Sam experiment on her recruits? Is she using illegal substances like the memory enhancer? What about the contraceptive and tracking implants? Ordinary citizens aren't privy to any of this, since National Healthcare doesn't cover what the FDA doesn't approve.

I push into a full sprint, and still my muscles glide. Brandy and Margarite fall back, while Dara keeps up, huffing like a rhinoceros. I laugh, push myself to the max, and sprint into the gymnasium.

Unable to stop, I roll into a tumble and bang up against the wall. I jump to my feet. *This is amazing. I'm a cat with nine lives.* Falls don't hurt, and I land on my feet.

Dara crashes into me with a body-slam that should have knocked me out. I shove back, sending her soaring into the air. She lands in the middle of the gym. Other runners scatter. Dara gets to her feet and charges at me like a bull. Tapping my foot, I make like a bull ready to attack. I launch myself into the air. Dara jumps; we collide. I fly back, sprawling onto my back. Dara lands on top, grabs my right arm, and pulls it over my head. It reminds me of how she almost destroyed Janine.

"Stand down, Number One Grunt. Now!"

"Why?" Letting go, Dara gets to her feet and ambles toward Sam. She looks ready to use her mech strength to crush the commander. "I thought the point was to enhance our fighting ability."

"You think you've learned everything you can from me? Hang up your suit and meet me on the mats."

Dara hesitates, confused. Then she joins the others hanging up mech suits.

While I remove mine, I examine my body. Bruises should be spreading by now, but I'm amazed that they're gone. My muscles feel fine. I'm bouncing with energy. I hope the side effects of Sam's meds don't send me crashing later.

Surrounded by a dozen recruits removing gear, Dara mumbles, "This is a sick joke."

Brandy joins me and whispers, "I hear Sam's tough. This should be interesting."

I lead the way to the opposite side of the mat from Dara. I want to see the face of this amazon in battle when I'm not focused on survival. About half of the recruits cluster around Margarite as Dara steps onto the mat. Most of the rest stand along the sidelines, with me behind Sam. I imagine myself in her place.

It's hardly a fair fight. Sam's solid and stocky. Dara is tall, big all around, flexing muscle. She has a clear 50-pound advantage over the Commander. She bows to her audience and stretches. Sam stands frozen, as if she has second thoughts.

"Your move, Number One Grunt."

Dara beams as if Number One means anything more than that she showed up first on Sam's radar. She hunkers down, turns her face into a menacing scowl and charges across the mat. She thrusts her fist into Sam's jaw. Her punch fails to connect when Sam moves at the last moment. Dara flips onto her belly with a thud. Sam pulls the amazon's arms behind and cuffs her.

Kicking and hollering, Dara gets to her knees and then up to her feet with her hands cuffed behind. Her face transforms into the furies. She charges, goes for a head-butt into Sam's stomach. Sam dodges, drops the amazon, and gets Dara into a chokehold. "Relax before you hurt yourself."

Dara struggles for a couple of minutes before relaxing. Her face has her just-wait look. Sam releases Dara and stands back. I read humiliation across Dara's face.

Sam turns to address the recruits. "The first lesson of leadership is never put yourself in position to take advantage of a subordinate. I've made an exception with Dara for two reasons. First, she was itching to see if she could take me. Second, each of you needs to challenge and compensate for weaknesses. Dara's flaw is believing she's invincible because of size and strength. Those matter, but so do agility, experience, and intelligence. Now maybe she'll listen and do the real work of becoming a warrior."

Dara stands before Sam, ready to challenge again. Instead, she bows. "I'm ready to learn how you did that."

Sam scowls. "All in good time. I told you that mech warriors are the best and work together. You need to work out whatever hostility you have toward each other or toward me. The tournament is competition that produces a winner. In all else, including training, we work together because we can never be better than our weakest link."

Most of the recruits stand at attention. "We stand ready to deliver."

Not me. I stifle that thought and stand at attention. I hope Sam can't pick out which voices she hasn't heard.

THIRTEEN

After my second day of mech training, I'm wound up tighter than the springs in one of Mom's antique clocks. Mech gear is fascinating, but I don't like what it means. I scratch my head for any alternative, and come back to starting a restaurant.

I need to be alone to think, but that's not to be.

Little Brandy waits for me at the guardhouse. "It's a lot to take in," she says.

Nodding, I wave to a petite guard who stands at attention.

"Want to grab a sandwich or something?" Brandy asks.

"I have to get to work," I lie. I'm sure Voss won't miss me. Besides, I want Brooks to take Janine, which means I won't have a partner.

Brandy follows me out toward the cycles. "I don't mean to be a pest, but I hear there's a lot of teaming up. I want to team with you."

I knew it. I look at my cute little companion. She's hardly what I'd recruit for mech material. She's been quiet during training and struggles with the exercises yet keeps up with me when we run. Still, I could use an ally with Dara gathering her posse. "That's great, but right now I have to go to work."

"You need to eat."

"That's a great idea." Dara joins us and places her hand on my shoulder.

We're friends now, Dr. Jekyll?

"Let's go to the plantation and see what we can rustle up?"

LANCE ERLICK

I remove Dara's hand and move toward the rack of silver electric cycles, under the watchful eye of the petite guard. Maybe I shouldn't underestimate little Brandy.

While I want to be alone, I'm hungry. And it would be good to get to know Brandy, if I can get her away from the amazon.

"I have to work downtown," I say. "I'll grab something there."

With one arm around Brandy and the other around me, Dara pushes us toward the cycles. "Then downtown it is." She lowers her voice and adds: "Though our food's better."

I pull away. "Don't touch."

"Okay!" Dara holds up her hands, all defensive. "Just trying that teamwork thing Sam mentioned. Go have one of your cardboard burgers."

When I reach my cycle, Brandy joins me. She seems to want my protection from the amazon. Sorry to disappoint.

My taste-buds crave flavor, so I turn to Dara. "I don't suppose you know a place downtown with real food."

Dara grins and lowers her voice. "I might."

"What if we start our own restaurant with something between Tenn-tucky Bistro blah and your party food? A little variety and atmosphere. I'm certain we'd be popular."

"And draw the harmony police."

"I thought you were fearless."

Dara wags her finger at me. "You're on. I know where we can do some research." She gets on her cycle and heads toward town.

Margarite hurries to catch up. Brandy hesitates, but when I pull out, she joins me. When we reach downtown, we pass clusters of shops and restaurants near bus stops. Crowds of women mill about in Union-approved blah dresses, skorts, and pants intended to support the image of harmony.

For the first time, the restaurant idea becomes real. Dara knows girls who can spice up the food. She might have ways around the harmony police. It's my first bit of hope since I got arrested. I could get Janine out of security and make us a life close to Mom.

* * *

Dara pulls up in front of a storefront with traditional pre-war charm and a subdued red sign announcing Mario's. I like it already. After we park, Dara leads the way inside, always in charge.

The interior teems with curves and arches, subtle touches that make it distinct from Tenn-tucky Bistro. Tuscan pictures decorate

96

the walls. Bad news: only four customers, seated in the front. Dara takes a booth in the back, and with Margarite faces the entrance. Brandy and I face the back exit, a possible escape route.

"We don't know much about the business, so let's observe," Dara says. There she goes, giving orders.

"We need a cook," I say, "someone who can add zest to bring people in."

"I can cook," Brandy says, trying to be helpful. Her sweet auburn hair glimmers in subdued lighting. "But it won't be easy."

I nod. The Union bans salt, MSG, trans-fats, caffeine, sugar, and most spices.

"Mom says they used to put salt, pepper and sugar on each table," Brandy goes on. "Not anymore, and don't ask the waitress."

A waitress with wrinkled olive skin appears. She passes out laminated menus that look like they've been used for decades, with items we could get at Union Burgers & Subs. That's a letdown.

Dara hands back her menu. "I'll take a rare hamburger well-seasoned, fries, and a bustle-berry malt. Please." The last comes as an afterthought when the waitress stares.

Instead of arguing that Dara can't have what she ordered, the waitress turns to Margarite. She orders the same, as does Brandy. Curious, I make it unanimous.

After the waitress leaves, I whisper, "What was that all about? It's not on the menu."

"Mario's won't reject your order. Can't afford to, with Union Burgers across the street. This is what we have to prepare for."

While the décor has subtle architectural niceties, it doesn't have anything to offend Union harmony restrictions except perhaps pictures of the old country. I doubt the owner's been there, since travel has been restricted since before I was born. "We can do this. We'll need decorations that push the limits but don't cross harmony codes."

"The Italian theme works," Brandy says.

"Do any of us look Italian?" Dara asks.

I was going to suggest Dara did, but it's best not to stir that pot. "Don't be so negative. We have a cook and a theme."

"You're serious?" Dara asks.

"Why not?"

The droopy-eyed waitress brings four stoneware plates with chunky fries and pinkish-brown burgers on thick, buttery buns.

This definitely looks like the beef the Union bans.

Dara digs in. I stuff a rectangular fry into my mouth. The rich flavor delights with tastes I don't recognize. A tad salty and sweet, it doesn't taste greasy.

"Is this really a fry?" I ask.

"Tastes like one," Dara says.

"When have you had fries?"

"One of my foster moms liked to spice things up. Try the burger."

When I do, the buttery taste lingers. I can't decide whether I'm pleased by defying stupid Federal Union laws or tasting the food itself. The malt has a sweet berry flavor. I can't help smiling. "This is what I have in mind. Isn't it illegal?"

"Keep it down." Brandy sinks in her seat. "We don't need trouble."

Dara checks her wrist-com. "Maybe that is what we need. I got hold of Sam's miracle meds. I hear they're like steroids, only they don't put hair on your chest, thank God."

"What are you talking about?" I ask.

Dara places a thin brown bottle of pills on the table. "Special prescription for warriors. Try these. You'll be amazed how great you'll feel."

"Did you take these today?"

"This isn't basketball, dearie." Dara places her hand on mine: too friendly.

I pull away and put on my stony face. I don't want another fight.

"In mechs, we play for keeps." Dara pops a pill and downs it with malt. Then she offers pills to the others.

Thin-faced Margarite follows Dara's example. Brandy takes a pill and examines it as if she can tell anything by looking. I push the bottle of pills toward Dara. I'm not ingesting more unknown junk.

Dara pushes the small bottle toward me. "Take it. I have more. It enhances our performance, gives us an edge in the tournament, the arena, and as warriors."

I study the unlabeled bottle that holds some two dozen pills. If these work and Dara gets stronger, I won't stand a chance. I stuff the bottle into an inside pocket in my skorts and look to see if anyone noticed.

Two older cops I don't recognize barge in with two plain-clothed, pinched-faced women. The heavier cop rushes into the kitchen, along with the plain-clothes. They must be ISP, Illegal Substance Police.

"Did you call this in?" I whisper.

Dara grins. "Doing research on how quickly they respond and how they operate."

I put down my burger. "Let's go."

"Relax," Dara says.

One of the plain-clothes, an officious young prig with dyed-blonde hair, returns and grabs my plate. "We need this for evidence."

I glare at Dara. Brandy squeezes my hand like Janine does, but she isn't Janine. I pull away.

"All customers clear out," the priggish blonde says. "This establishment is closed for violating food laws."

When I start to get up, Dara grabs my arm. "Wait."

I drop back into my seat. After I hear the few other customers leave, the officious food enforcer returns to our table. "I said clear out."

"Not until you tell me what I've eaten," Dara says. "I trust the Union to make sure food is proper. Now you tell me it's not." Dara crosses her arms, tightening her dark eyes and pouty mouth.

The blonde looks flustered. She hasn't run into an obstacle like Dara before. "Very well. Stay seated while we inspect this."

When she heads back into the kitchen, the thin cop stands by the front door eyeing us. Dara takes another bite.

"You've got to be kidding," I say.

"Here, want some of mine?" She pushes her plate my way.

"I need to get to work."

Dara leans forward. "You're either serious about your restaurant or you're not."

"I am."

"Then let's see what they come back with. It took them five minutes to respond, not enough time to purge the place even if we have warning. They'll do preliminary tests on site. If it's obvious, they've got you. They'll do more thorough tests offsite."

To avoid her touching again, I lean back. "You've given this some thought?"

"Lots of girls have. Pulling it off is another matter. All it takes is one disgruntled customer."

Or a bitchy amazon trying to prove something.

The blonde returns, her eyes gray and face sagging. "The burger is turkey and soy. The potatoes are baked, not fried, though they were soaked in butter. We'll do more tests. The malt has too much sugar, but no caffeine or other illegal additives. You should be fine."

"But my friend never got her meal," Dara says.

"Which you won't pay for, since the restaurant is closing. Now go."

The blonde directs the cops to remove us. Dara looks ready to challenge them just because she can. Margarite takes her by the hand and leads her out.

Damn you, Dara. Mario's hasn't done anything wrong. They did what I want to do and you've shut them down. Maybe they'll reopen, but the Union doesn't like any hint of violating food laws. That smacks of rebellion. Once again, enforcement eliminates competition to official restaurant chains.

"Now we know what we're up against," Dara says. "You still want to do this?"

I nod and walk my cycle to the street so I can head for the police station six blocks away. The others tag along. I don't mind Brandy, but I'm not sure what Dara's up to. One moment she wants to fight. The next, she's my buddy, ready to help start my restaurant.

When I stop at the first light, a wisp of a boy darts into the shadows. *Are you from Michael's School?*

Dara parks her cycle.

"Leave him," I say. "I'm late for work."

Dara tugs me off my cycle. "Sweetie, you want to be a mech, you can't be afraid of guys."

I pull free. "I'm not. I'm—"

"Margarite, Brandy, close off his retreat. Let's show Sam some teamwork."

"Let's call it in," I say as Brandy and Margarite run to the other end of the alley. I'm torn. I'll have to betray either what I know to be right or my oath as a cop intern.

"Annabelle, I'm really trying here, "Dara says. "Sam wants us to work out our differences. I've humored your restaurant idea. Humor me on this." She pats my cheek.

When I hesitate, Dara grabs my wrist in an iron grip and pulls me down the alley toward where the boy disappeared. I pull free, but I follow. We meet up with the others by Dumpsters behind Mario's.

No more than 14, a slender boy with a dirt-smudged face and green student collar flees into the arms of Margarite and Brandy. His dirty hands clutch one of the tasty turkey burgers I tried before the blonde food-enforcer took it. He bites into it and cowers like a frightened mouse. He shrinks into his oversized jeans and jersey.

"What's your name, boy?" I ask. "Where do you belong?"

Dara grabs the boy by his green metallic collar and lifts him off the ground. "We don't need a name to tell this critter doesn't belong here."

The choking boy drops his sandwich. His thin arms and legs flail. He makes no attempt to fight.

With my sister recruits watching, I can't free the boy, and I fear what Dara will do to him. I alert my station from my wrist-com and turn to Dara. "Leave him. Patrols are on their way."

"Are you defending this boy?"

"No, but this isn't necessary." The boy's sad eyes tug at me.

Dara turns and slams the boy into the brick wall of Mario's. "That's for running and being where you're not supposed to be. If I had my remote, I'd give you a jolt to remember."

I pull Dara away from the wall. "Leave him for the cops. Don't do this."

Blood spills from the boy's crooked nose. Tears stream down his gritty cheeks. "Please."

Dara tosses the boy aside like garbage and grabs me. "I'm trying to work with you. Don't ever cross me again." Letting me go, she picks the boy up by the collar.

"Dara, don't. Mech cops are here."

Dara sets the boy on the ground and kicks him toward a black-shielded figure sprinting toward us. "He resisted arrest," Dara says, moving back.

The boy whimpers like Janine when she's afraid of the dark.

The mech cop picks him up like a twig. "I'll take him from here. Go about your business." The mech cop trots off toward city lockup.

I stare at the retreating boy, a scared mouse caught in a trap. You don't treat humans like this.

FOURTEEN

I reach the station, sneak in the back way to the small break room, and check the roster. Two interns wait for their partners while absorbed in their wrist-coms. My partner, Brooks, is out on patrol. Then I remember she's no longer my partner. She's with Janine, who signed on five days a week to get out of basketball practice.

I wander through the bullpen full of metal desks, and no cops. Is it another riot, a new breakout, or are they still after the Michael's boys? What can I do while I wait?

Voss' puppy, Lieutenant Scarlatti, intercepts me at Brooks' desk. "Keeping your own hours now?"

I hate how she checks up on me, as if I'm a child. "We caught a green-collar on the run. I called it in and had to wait until mech cops came."

"Likely excuse. We'll see. Lucky for you Captain Voss is out."

"I came to see if Brooks had anything for me."

"She had to respond to a call. Since you were late, she grabbed Janine." Now that Scarlatti has scored her points, she returns to her office.

What am I supposed to do without a partner? I can't go out on patrol. There's no other partner I want, certainly not Scarlatti. Besides, why break in an intern who's leaving? I scan in so I'll get credit toward my minimal intern pay.

I'm glad Scarlatti didn't assign me cleanup detail. I need to get out of sight before she remembers. Then it occurs to me: the captain's computer might have access to private records, and she's out. I might not get another chance to search for my birth mother.

I dig around the inner pocket of my skorts, past the illegal mech pills. My fingers rest on the chip with encrypted files on where my birth mother was during her first years in prison. It also has a copy of Lieutenant Scarlatti's access codes.

I head for the break room, detour to the small gym, and sneak up the back stairs to the small lobby controlled by Liz Cameron, special assistant to Voss the Boss. Liz drinks too much decaf coffee and has a weak bladder. Now that she's pregnant, she spends even more time in the bathroom. She's away from her desk again.

The captain's door is closed. I hurry over and find it unlocked. I slip inside, close the door, and shrink behind the big oak desk into Voss' cushy easy chair. I'm not proud of what I'm doing, but it's my way of staying connected to my birth mother.

I find Voss' security fob in her bottom desk drawer–sloppy security–and enter Scarlatti's access codes into the captain's security box. It isn't unusual for the lieutenant to use the captain's access, since hers is limited. Nor would it be unusual for her to research an intern outside normal channels while the captain was out. *So far, so good.*

Onto the virtual screen above the oak desk, I enter my birth mother's name: Dorothy Montgomery. I wait. Somewhere over the rainbow is a better place for her. But that's only a fairy tale. A file comes up, giving particulars of her arrest. She helped an unnamed man escape from prison and again from the mech arena. I know it's my dad, even though they erased his connection. They don't want me to know.

Dorothy received a trial. The prosecution presented evidence that she supplied guns to rebel Outlanders, helped several escape, withheld information that could have helped capture rebel leaders, and betrayed the Federal Union. The defense argued each point while presenting no evidence to refute the prosecution. I don't believe any of this except that my birth mother helped my dad escape and was torn from my arms when I was three. Bet the Union doesn't know I know.

Under "examination," which I interpret as torture, Dorothy admitted to the crimes and received a life sentence in lieu of execution as a traitor. *This is bullshit.* They sent her to Oak Ridge

Maximum Security Prison west of Knoxville.

Defense counsel petitioned to reverse her conviction. She attempted to escape. *Way to go, girl.*

They moved Dorothy to a prison in Michigan's Upper Peninsula. Another escape. They moved her to Florida. Another attempt. Then they sealed her records. Even the captain can't access these.

"I'll have to lock my office from now on." Red-faced, Voss the Boss fills the lower part of the doorway with her rotund figure.

Scrambling, I close my search and purge temp files. I hope I've concealed my purpose. "Files downstairs don't show much on the Outland and why boys are so eager to go," I say.

"Get the hell out of my seat before I put you behind bars. How dare you?"

I consider complimenting her comfy chair as I scoot around the oak desk, ditching my chip and pills in the dirt of the potted hibiscus plants. "Sorry, Captain. I was curious." I scoot for the door.

Voss blocks the way. "Empty your purse and pockets."

My blue vinyl purse is tiny, with a thin wallet, plain lipstick for chapped lips, tissues, and a stylus for my wrist-com. I empty those onto a corner of her polished oak desk and stand back while Voss examines each item. She looks through the wallet with my ID. It lists me as student with restricted travel privileges and cop intern with a few more. The chip can relay that to any of a million scanners around town, and at entry to public transport and cab services that enforce travel limitations. *Does my mech implant override those?*

While eyeing me, Voss fiddles her fat fingers on her wrist-com. Got to let my school and Sam know of my disharmony. "Now your pockets."

I show Voss my empty blouse pocket. I turn out two pockets of my skorts with a used tissue and some sugarless, tasteless gum for when my throat gets dry. I turn up my nose when she examines the tissue for vital national secrets among the germs.

The bloodhound, Voss the Boss, gives me her victory grin. "Now empty that inside pocket."

I release the skorts clasp and zipper. I show Voss that the inside pocket has only my access cards for the station, my home, and the mech base, all marked. I'm forming an apology in my head when I remember that Mom says it's best to be seen, not heard, when questioned. I wonder how she developed such instincts.

As Voss looks away and closes the door, I retrieve the pills and chip, tucking them into my inner pocket before I fasten up. Then I collect the contents of my purse and hang my head.

"Paperwork has you leaving for Hollander's Resocialization Facility in Nashville today," Voss says. "The state has other plans. I hope the mechs have better luck with you than I've had. You're a grave disappointment, an embarrassment to your family, your school, and your colleagues here on the force. What do you have to say for yourself?"

"I'm sorry, Captain. I won't let it happen again." There's nothing more I can learn here, anyway.

Voss scans her computer files. "Not good enough. The Outland is forbidden territory controlled by rebels. That's all you need to know. If you want, we can send you, like those who help runaways." Voss grins. "They get to be whores in Biltmoor." The Outland capital.

My stomach tightens. Is Voss capable of sending me for breaking into her office? I hang my head and maintain my stony silence.

"Has your renegade mother led you to believe burglary and theft are okay?"

Here comes the "spy on your family" bit. "No!" I catch myself before I say more. Defending the family makes it look like I have something to hide.

"Do you break into her office and read her files?"

"No!" Nothing confidential at least, just banned books and files I hoped would tell me about my parents. I've found nothing Mom held back and much evidence that she's tried to help.

"You haven't much to say for all your snooping. Has your mom taught you how to act when confronted by authority?"

I shake my head and pray I don't betray Mom with a wrong answer. "I live in a communal home. I've been taught harmony by living there." And rebelliousness at being told how to live.

"You seem defensive. Have you been interrogated often? Of course you have, by Harmony Director Surroc."

I hold my face so tightly blank, it's ready to fracture. I need the interrogation to end before I say something that hurts Mom. It's standard practice to get kids to betray family, which is why Mom keeps so many secrets even from Mama Helen and Mama Grace. Why she confides in me is a mystery. I figure it's because I won't leave the past alone. Burned into my soul is that single moment when my birth mother was torn away. Perhaps Mom thinks conspiring will keep me from doing something really stupid, like opening my mouth.

"I'm embarrassed and terribly sorry," I say. "Brooks was gone. I came to see what I could do for you. Liz was out. Your door was open. My curiosity took over."

There's a knock at the door. Voss probably wants to find a way to force the state to pull me from mechs and send me to Nashville. Instead, she opens the door. Mom stands there, her face filled with anger and distress. It's public humiliation time.

I hang my head lower. "I've shamed myself and my family. I'm so mortified, Mom."

Voss looks flustered. "Take this thing out of my sight before I throw her into jail."

Mom grabs my wrist and drags me out of Voss' office, down the stairs, and out into the parking lot without a word. I want to die, which is the point of this exercise. I've caused Voss to call Mom away from work to deal with her troublesome daughter again. I didn't even learn anything.

When we're in Mom's car, I buckle up, thankful I retained my chip. I don't want to lose all my research, what little it tells me. "I'm a terrible embarrassment. I didn't mean—"

"Cut the tripe, Belle. I'm angry with you for putting yourself in danger again. What was it this time? And why anger Captain Voss?"

"I tried to use the police database to find Dorothy Montgomery." I say her name so I won't forget her. "Voss was out. I thought she might have better access."

"And?" Mom pulls out of the parking lot and parks next to my cycle.

"Nothing you haven't told me except a pack of lies. Even the captain can't access recent files."

"That's what I've been telling you, Belle. Was it worth all this?"

"I hate that they keep her from me. I mean no disrespect, Mom.

I couldn't love you more if you were my birth mother. It's just—they took her and it's not right."

"No, it's not, but you know what they can do to you if you push this. Please don't."

Guilt worms its way into my gut. "Why aren't you mad at me for breaking in?"

"I know why you did it, Belle. I wish I could make this right. Promise me you'll drop it and let me keep digging."

"I'll try." I stifle a sob. I hate how I've hurt Mom and have nothing to show for it.

"That's all I ask. I want to find her, too. Dorothy was a dear friend, but even that can put us at risk. Few people know. The governor will do anything to make sure she doesn't resurface."

"And you, Mom?"

"I'll continue to do what I can. Please be more careful."

"What about Morgan?" I ask.

"I told you not to bring him up again."

"Mom, please."

"He's safe for now."

I nod. "I had to arrest another boy today. I would rather help you and—"

"We're done talking about this. Now go."

But I want to help.

* * *

I decide to spend the weekend at the mech base. It'll let me avoid the shame I've brought my family, and I won't have to listen to Therese gloating over how much better a daughter she is. I'd rather sleep outside in the bushes.

Sitting on my electric cycle, I watch Mom drive off. I don't know if I'm lucky that she understands or cursed that she isn't tougher on me. I'm ready to drive off and unwind along the quiet road to the base when Brooks drives up in her tiny gray two-seater. I have to laugh at how ridiculous she looks in that undersized squad car, while Scarlatti gets a four-seat sedan.

Janine crawls out of the passenger seat and joins me.

Brooks gets out and looks relaxed, her face less creased than when she works with me. "She's an easy student. Not that I don't miss the excitement of your company. She's done for the day. I'll clock her."

"Thanks." I smile, happy that things are working out for my sister.

Janine climbs on behind me and whispers, "Thanks for letting me partner with Brooks. She's great. I'm sorry. I should have asked. Can you give me a lift?"

Her arms tighten around my waist. I couldn't say no if I wanted to. I ease out behind a bus full of women at shift's end. "Brooks is a good mentor."

"I'm sorry I took her from you."

I don't have the heart to tell Janine that Voss wants to send me to Nashville. She still might if I fail mech training, which is another reason I'll spend the weekend on the base. I can't afford to fail.

"I'm not going home," I tell her.

"But Mom might be there. I've been so worried."

"Mom's okay. I spoke with her. When you get home you'll see for yourself. I'm going to the base. I have stuff to learn by Monday."

"Then I'm going with you."

"Not this time, Babe."

"I've never been. You could show me around."

"Not tonight."

I drop Janine off a block from our home so the family won't see me.

She hugs me like we'll meet again. "I'll miss you, Belle. Hurry home. I'll put cream on your wounds."

"I'm not fighting tonight," I say. "Now go, before I have to explain this to everyone else."

Janine pouts, but she goes. I wait down the street until I see her enter the townhouse.

FIFTEEN

With another spring thunderstorm threatening, I drive the speed limit until I reach the east end of town, then push to test the cycle's limits. I get it over 100. It feels like what I imagine a jet airplane would, though with wind in my face.

I push a red button to see what other cool things this cycle can do. Fins spread out before, beneath, and behind me. I'm airborne, a foot off the ground. The road curves. I spot lights off to the right. I can't get a ticket or I'll lose my cycle.

I brake. Nothing happens. I lean into the curve. The cycle doesn't turn and I have no control. A tree looms ahead. I punch the button. Fins retract. The cycle bounces on asphalt. I lean hard into the curve, and the cycle skids but responds. I make the turn and brake. Relieved, I take a deep breath. *I'd love to get this on a controlled track.*

With twilight settling in, rain pelts the asphalt. I pass a cop along the empty road. She doesn't pull me over, probably so she doesn't get soaked like me.

I reach the gate to the mech base. From the shelter of the guard shack, a petite guard lifts the gate. She waves me through before I can explain. That has me suspicious, but I'm on a mission not to wash out.

"Park in the courtyard," the guard says. "It'll stay dry over there." She points to an overhang alongside the building, and disappears inside the gatehouse.

It's getting dark and I feel pleasantly alone. A cool breeze brought in with the rain washes away the day's heat. I wouldn't mind staying out here, but I sense eyes watching me.

I reach the bullet-proof glass door into the building and hear a click. The door releases and opens a crack. Is my implant doing this? What other doors might this open?

Lights brighten in the lobby, removing shadows from the corridor. The base looks deserted, though I'm certain it operates 24/7. There's always something going on. My flats echo on the concrete floor as I move past the tiny room where we had instruction. My butt hurts recalling that stiff wooden seat.

I enter the dimly lit gym with weights along the side and find my locker. I change into my blue form-fitting uniform that carries none of the odor of sweat I'm sure I contributed today. Is it the fabric, or did Sam have these cleaned?

After changing, I break into a run. I need the adrenalin rush and runner's high. I push into a sprint, imagining I have mech gear so I could do a three-minute mile.

So far, I've learned little about my birth mother. I've met two boys too briefly to matter, and I have no idea how to find them or how to help them if I do. I would need transit routes and hiding places.

I finish ten laps and move to the free weights, pushing myself until I can barely lift my arms. Then I sneak into the bigger gym with the mech equipment. In dim light, the black suits loom along the wall like mechanical monsters that could come to life and attack me.

A dark figure glides through the shadows. I jump.

"If it isn't Number Two Grunt." Sam marches over in her blue dress uniform.

"Sorry, I thought I was alone. I want to work on my conditioning." I stop babbling.

"You're welcome any time."

"How did you know I was here?"

Sam grins. "Tracking implant. By the way, don't tempt that cop. She will nail you if you keep speeding."

My face burns. I try to divert attention. "I want to learn to fight like you do."

"You mean you want to hold your own against Dara."

"She's like a truck barreling down on me."

"Which is her weakness," Sam says. "Her standard tactic is to use bulk and strength to intimidate rivals into submission."

"It works."

"It hasn't worked on you. You seethe every time she takes charge. She wants to lead through intimidation. People only follow that so long. You have leadership potential, but you need to learn to focus your anger and energy. You fight distracted and scattered."

I nod. "Will you teach me to defend against her?"

Sam motions for me to follow her out of the gym. "You're not like the gung-ho recruits we usually get. They want to punish someone for whatever's wrong with their lives. I sense in you a need for creativity. You think we don't have it, that we're boot-licking robots."

That slices through me. Is she baiting me, pushing me as one of her tests?

"Under fire, robot-fighters die. Creativity saves lives. Let me show you something."

I follow Sam into a small room void of anything but an electronic panel on the wall and a large boxy contraption in the middle. The place smells of sweat that someone has tried to perfume away. I examine the box from all sides. There's just the seam for a door. "So?"

"It's a simulator. Climb in." Sam opens a panel, revealing a padded seat and cushioned enclosure. "We usually wait a week to introduce recruits so we don't overwhelm them. I think you're ready. Strap in tight. This will be a wild ride, similar to testing the mech suit."

I tuck myself into the unit. It foams around my legs and torso like a set of leotards without restricting movement. Sam inserts a mouthpiece between my lips and closes the door. The entire unit wraps snug like a straitjacket. It feels claustrophobic, but I'm not backing out. I breathe through the tube. With dry foam pressing against my face, I understand the need for the mouthpiece.

"Make sure it fits snug all around," Sam says. "It'll sense your moves and suggest others to stretch your range. I'll start it on level one. You can adjust this yourself either with eye or hand movements. Whatever you do, don't accelerate to level ten. You'll have time for that later."

Although I'm in an enclosed space, I can swing my arms and legs in all directions. I'm floating on cushions or in a pool, without the sluggish resistance. I can't feel any hard surfaces except beneath my feet when they touch down. When I walk, I lose the sensation of a confined space. Scenery changes: a walk by a lake. I run, swing my arms and jump. My legs move as if I'm on a treadmill.

"I have to step out," Sam says. "Keep it on level one until I return. I don't want you having problems without a spotter."

I hear and see Sam walk next to me by the lake. She waves, walks away, and vanishes into the scenery.

Now I'm alone in downtown Knoxville, where I inhale damp city air. I walk down the main street past stores selling Union-approved food and clothing. I pick up my pace and pass women shopping on their way home. I flex my arms and legs. Feel wind on my face. The imagery, sounds, even smells have me believing I'm there. I head for the cop station. When I enter, it's as chaotic as I remember. Is this the machine or a hallucination?

Scarlatti bolts out of her office, ready to make trouble for me. I sprint down the corridor and bump into Liz on the way to the break room for more decaf. I give her a hug. Will she remember this? With her downstairs, I rush upstairs to Voss' office. I open her door and step aside so she can't see me.

"Liz, that you?" Voss calls out. When she gets no reply, she scrapes her chair against the carpet and gets up.

I hear footsteps on the stairs. I'm trapped.

Calming my mind, I return to the simulator, and float. That was close and unnecessary. I can't learn any more from Voss. Do Sam's files have the answers? She must have better access than Voss. After all, Sam's charged with tracking enemies of the state and in fact imprisoned my birth mother.

When I imagine myself outside the simulator, the door is locked. I imagine myself in the corridor outside the simulator room. I head toward what I suspect is Sam's office, though I've never seen it or the building layout. The corridor elongates like Einstein's description of space-time warp. The closer I get to Sam's office, the slower I move and the farther away it appears. I'm in molasses. If I get any closer, I'll be in concrete.

I retreat to the simulator. I'm exhausted from the journey, despite being in the simulator the entire time.

So far, it's a cool game with fine sensory details. Since I'm here for training, I use eye movements to pull up a menu and change the setting to physical conditioning. I place myself beneath stationary weights and feel the strain on my arms. I push the 50-

pounder until I get it up. I do it again despite muscle strain until I get five lifts. I'm amazed my muscles respond in the same manner as when I did real weights. My arms tell me they've had enough.

I select simulated mech training. This time the suit envelopes me, unlike before when I had to assemble the legs, torso plates, neck plate, and helmet individually. With the suit and simulator, I run, jump, spin, and push myself to do impossible leaps. When I arch my back and tumble, gravity shifts from my feet to my back, over my head and back to my feet. I do these again until I'm convinced I could do this with just the suit.

What about a cat?

I transform into a feline and do leaps I imagine cats doing. I jump like a kangaroo, hold onto the gym beam like an orangutan, and drop like a cat. *I'll need more than nine lives if I keep this up.* With each change, the simulator gives me abilities of what I imagine, as if I'm a shape-shifter. *This is way more amazing than the mech suit. Maybe even addictive.* I'll have to watch that.

The simulator allows me any action that I can imagine being performed by a well-trained actor. I visualize myself as Superwoman and fly high over Knoxville. I could make it to the Outlands like this. Realizing this can't be true, I crash toward the ground. I imagine myself as a cat, but I'm too big. At this speed and height, even a cat could die. I imagine myself as a flying squirrel. They don't actually fly, but they glide. I land on the rooftop of my school, tumble and end up at the edge. I stare across the street at Michael's School for Boys, now less crowded.

I decide to face Dara on the mats without mech gear. She materializes across from me and hesitates. *This is false.* Yet, I'm scared out of my wits.

The simulation stops. The padding eases away. My exercise uniform is sweat-soaked from exertion. I chill as cool air rushes in.

Sam looks distracted. "Enough simulator for tonight. You don't want to overstress your vitals."

"Please don't send me home, Sam. I want to stay and learn." I've never found anything so liberating and empowering.

Sam considers this while I extract myself from the machine. I shiver from withdrawal. Except for the moment of facing Dara, the simulator felt cozy and wonderful. It lets me stretch and try new moves, even if it is all fantasy. My muscles tell me it was real and that I've had enough. The screen by the wall shows my elevated heart rate and blood pressure, which crashes down on me when I stand.

Sam steadies me. "Very well, I'll put you up for the night."

"Can I do some mech suit work first?"

"You're a glutton for punishment. Care to talk about it?"

I'm in over my head. I'm in the belly of my worst enemy. I can't share that with Sam. "The mechs are the best. I want to be my best." *Am I really giving her this bull?* I smile at my performance, though my legs tremble beneath me.

Sam escorts me to the big gymnasium. I suit up in mech gear; assemble piece by piece. I prefer the simulator approach, all at once. I hope the suit's hydraulics will compensate for my weary legs. Sam leaves, and the closing door echoes.

Blissfully alone, I wonder if Morgan is okay. Is he out under the stars? Hiding above some abandoned store?

Twinges of claustrophobia tickle the corners of my consciousness. I fasten the helmet and push through muscle fatigue to sprint the perimeter of the gym. I jump, executing quick side-step movements and moves I tried in the simulator. They don't work as well.

After a flip lands me on my back, winded, I stare up into the bleachers along one side of the gym. I see a figure that makes me think I'm back in the simulator. Realizing I'm not, I jump to my feet and sprint toward the bleachers before the figure disappears. I slow as I approach because Janine has become a frightened mouse, and yet she doesn't flee.

I remove my helmet. "What are you doing here? I told you not to get into trouble." I look for Sam. She's gone.

My sister smiles up at me now that she can see my face. "I knew you weren't coming home, so I came to you."

"Janine? What if cops pick you up out here?"

"I have your transit papers. The ones you left at home. When I told Sam I wanted to watch, she gave me a pass."

I go to the racks and remove my suit, starting with the neck plate. "Babe, I'm doing this for us, so you won't have to."

She follows me. "I know, Belle. You're so sweet, but I'm coming with you, so don't fuss."

"Does Mom know?"

Janine nods. "I told her we were doing sister bonding."

"You're a scoundrel, you know that?"

She grins so wide it reminds me of the Cheshire Cat.

When I get the suit off, I give Janine a hug and whisper, "I'll let you watch. You're not joining the mechs, though."

"You can't stop me watching since Sam gave permission, and I'll make up my own mind about the mechs."

I've seen this stubborn side of Janine before. There's no point pushing. *Later.*

Sam returns. "I see you have an audience. Are you ladies done for tonight?" She holds the door for us.

As much as I'm glad to see Janine, I want to yell at Sam for messing up my plans. "Can I spend the night so I can get an early start?"

Sam hustles down the khaki corridor toward the front lobby.

I catch up and stop her by the door. "I know it's a huge imposition, but I can't rest until I learn a few tricks to stand up to Dara."

Sam sighs. "You try an old lady's patience." She turns to Janine. "Are you up to sparring with your sister?"

You would have thought she'd offered Janine Christmas, birthday, the basketball championship and a dozen other reasons to celebrate.

Janine grabs my hands. "Can we? Can we?"

We've never fought, not physically at least. Not wanting to disappoint her, I nod.

Sam leads us back into the gym, where she produces a fight outfit for Janine. *Funny how she just happens to have one.* My sister and I change into form-fitted leotards that cover us from toe to gloves to neck. They show off Janine's slender waist, attractive legs, and pleasing upper body.

Sam directs us to enter a ringed mat to the side of the smaller gym. "These outfits have haptic sensors that measure pressure, deliver sensations of contact, and allow me to monitor, which helps us judge fights."

Touching my arm delivers a stronger response than I expect. *I don't like this.*

I stand across from Janine in the ring. She's so giddy she bounces. When she dances around behind me, I turn to face her. She scoots behind. I remind myself I'm teaching Janine and need to learn myself. I have to do something in order for Sam to give pointers.

Janine darts behind and jumps onto my back. I rotate, drop her, and land on top because she holds too tight. She gasps.

"Sorry." I barely stop myself from adding "Babe."

When I break free, Janine grabs my neck as if hanging onto a wild horse. Pulling away, I get behind her, drop onto the mat, and pin her. *Poor baby, you're really not a fighter.*

I get up, help Janine to her feet, and stand back. "I can't fight you, Janine. I can't muster the anger."

Sam gets into my face. "That was pathetic, Number Two Grunt. You've given me nothing to work with. You've taught Janine nothing."

I shrink back. When I look at Janine, the fight escapes me.

Sam moves closer until I feel her hot breath on my cheek. "Listen up, Number Two Grunt. If you fight out of anger, you lose. When you fight Dara, you're like a newborn, all movement and no focus. With focus you can defeat her. Waste any more of my time and I'll boot your ass out of the program."

Sam heads for the offices. "Lessons are over."

I catch up with Sam and struggle for breath. "I'm not quitting. But I won't hurt my sister."

"What about Brandy? Are you prepared to take her to the mat? Or is all your fight reserved for Dara?"

Janine cocks her head like she's trying to tell me something and I'm not listening.

"Give me tonight," I say. "I'll be ready for training in the morning."

"Very well. You can use the small suite in back of the gym. I've authorized your access. The door will respond to you and only you. Janine is welcome to stay, but she won't have access to locked doors. I'll be back at eight."

Sam marches away. I don't know if she's helping or not. She found my weakness: Janine.

My sister takes my hand and leads me back to the ringed mat. "I'm sorry I embarrassed you."

"Oh, Babe, you haven't. I don't belong here and neither do you."

"Then why are you here?"

I can't keep this from her. "Voss signed papers to send me to a re-socialization facility in Nashville. If I don't make it here, I'm gone."

Tears fill Janine's soft brown eyes. "Then we stay until we fix this." She pulls me into the ring.

I can't help admiring her determination. Yet I have no stomach to fight her. I stand as she prods, pokes and tries to stir me.

"Come on, Belle. You can do anything you set your mind to. I know you can. I won't stand by and let them take you away." I see fear in her eyes, the same fear of separation I experienced years ago.

Janine trips me. I go down hard.

Then she pins me, because I'm too careful.

We spar for another half-hour. She gives spirited fight with no style or experience, just gut and need and fear. I defend myself without hurting her. Her punches are more like slaps. I block, grab her and ease her onto the mat. In a real contest my opponent would nail me; Janine doesn't know what to do.

When I can't do this anymore, I climb out of the ring. She doesn't stop me.

I lead her to a little room with a double bed, tiny kitchenette, and small bathroom. After we change out of our sweaty fight outfits, I hold Janine while she cries herself to sleep.

I've let her down. For the first time in my life I don't know how to make this right.

SIXTEEN

Sam isn't in the gym at seven when Janine and I warm up. The commander doesn't show at eight when Janine and I stand in the ring ready to try again. I figure she watched our poor performance and gave up on me. Part of me wants to wash out. I brush those thoughts aside.

Janine takes my hand. "You want to dance?"

"Now?" I glare at her.

"Why not?"

"I can think of a dozen reasons, Babe." I take a deep breath because my anger isn't directed at her. "If I don't show Sam something, she'll kick me out."

That doesn't deter Janine in the slightest. Taking both my hands, she stands opposite me in the middle of the ring. "Fighting is nothing more than un-choreographed dance."

"What?"

"Let's choreograph a fight and see what we learn."

So we do.

In slow motion she punches. I block and hit. She moves. I drop her to the mat and show wrestling moves. Since I'm not hurting her, I exaggerate movements and use all that I've learned with mech gear and simulation, in slow motion. I'm proud of my clever sister coming up with this. She always was the smart one.

We get into a rhythm and speed things up. I throw her to the mat, ease her fall to maintain the slow motion effect and get behind her. I get her into a wrestling hold. She wiggles free and comes at me. The physical entanglement becomes a new level of bonding with her beyond dancing, and we're doing this without music.

We begin to move at two-thirds pace. I misjudge and hit her cheek. Guilt chokes my heart. "I'm sorry, Babe."

She shakes it off and returns with a huge grin. "Come on, Belle, you can do this. I can take it. I know you won't really hurt me."

We pick up the pace. I show her what I've learned in side-stepping, blocks and holds. I fight through fatigue, while her enthusiasm doesn't wane. Before I know it, we're fighting, not like Dara trying to injure, but hits, drops, and holds.

Janine gets me into a chokehold. I reverse and pin her. As I lie here holding her, my heart races. I'm so proud of Janine. She isn't the same feeble rabbit I fought last night.

Sam claps. "Well, Number Two Grunt. You are capable of learning. Tell me, what wisdom have you gained from mech gear, the simulator, and sparring with your sister?"

I let go and stand up. "That I'm capable of more than I thought."

"Maybe you won't be a complete waste of my time. Let's get you back into the simulator and into mech gear before you spar again." Sam narrows her eyes and turns to Janine. "If you're serious about learning, I have a simulator and mech suit for you."

Janine acts ready to kiss Sam's feet. "Really...I won't ...disappoint...oh my."

Sam pushes us all day Saturday, moving us from simulator to mech suits to sparring. By mid-afternoon I'm ready to collapse and Janine's dragging, but Sam doesn't let up.

She gives us pills like Dara had. "This will make you feel better."

Aching all over, I take mine. Janine follows my lead. Then Sam gives us a pea-green drink that smells as awful as it looks and tastes like sludge.

Within 10 minutes, I get my second wind. I'm ready to begin all over, though my muscles aren't so sure. Sam takes us through another grueling round of training. By six, I'm too tired to eat.

We retire to our tiny room. Janine collapses on the bed and falls asleep at once. I remove her top and examine her for bruises. I see faint, ghost-like images of where I'd hit her, much less than I expected, since she bruises easily. I sob to think I've hurt my baby sister, even though she kept urging me on.

She wakes, kisses me on the cheek and falls back on her pillow. "I'm okay, Belle, don't over-baby me."

I don't know how you over-baby. You either do or don't, but I get her meaning. She's okay with how things are going.

I'm not.

* * *

Monday morning, I feel like I've gone several rounds with Dara, and lost. I ask Janine to show me her bruises.

"I'm okay, Belle. Really."

"Show me."

While she changes into school clothes, I strain to see the effects of our punishing workout. They're gone. Must be Sam's meds. What about side effects?

In uniform, as always, Sam greets us outside the suite. "Let's go," she tells Janine. "We can't have you late for school." Sam escorts her past the classroom, infirmary, cafeteria, and conference room toward the lobby. I follow to satisfy myself my sister isn't limping or anything. She acts brave, like on her first day of school.

Sam puts Janine into a cab and sends her off. At times like this, I know Sam cares. But when the other recruits arrive in the gym, she yells at us to form up and corrals all 48 of us back into the tiny classroom. My sore butt isn't happy meeting the stiff wood seat again.

"Okay, grunts." Sam paces before us, holding that injector gun.

I cringe. Here we go again.

Sam's face tightens, which stretches that scar. "In two days you've covered what used to take a week. Now we begin your intensive daily training."

I should have rested over the weekend. Too late now.

"First, housekeeping. Then we'll get to more indoctrination, or as those who resist enlightenment call it, brainwashing, which we reserve for traitors."

That has my attention. I've heard rumors. Once I even got Mom to confirm that deep electronic brain probes were used to force prisoners to reveal their innermost thoughts. Sam's watching me, so I shut down that thought. I'm already spooked by the way she sees through me.

Sam begins up front by the door, injecting a slender brunette behind her left ear. "The auditory implant becomes important with the use of mech gear. It allows you to link up with sister warriors to

120

become a single fighting unit.

"While you wait, let's talk scenarios. As a warrior in gear, you'll have advantages over opponents, which we'll cover when we train with the suits. What about when you aren't wearing and encounter Outlanders kidnapping our citizens?"

I shudder, thinking of the risks Janine takes coming out here by herself.

"What would you do if confronted in a dark alley at night by an Outlander?" Sam asks.

Hannah, with dark chocolate hair and freckled face, raises her hand. "How would we know he's an Outlander? Do they wear signs?"

"Number Twelve Grunt, assume a man without a collar who accosts you in a dark place is an Outlander. You could assume he's lost. However, lapses in judgment will cost you your freedom and possibly your life. Anyone else?" Sam looks toward me.

I'm not about to demonstrate my ignorance.

Dara raises her hand. "I'd blind him, break his legs so he couldn't run and then cuff him. If he still gives me trouble—"

"That's enough, Number One Grunt. While you're taking out your anger on the suspect, his partner immobilizes you and carts you off to an uncertain future. You lose."

I'm glad I dodged that one.

"What you do is immobilize the suspect and determine if he's alone," Sam says. "Then you remove him as a threat, preferably with cuffs. I get to review your actions and will not tolerate unnecessary brutality. Is that clear?"

"Hoo-rah."

Sam reaches me with the injector gun. She holds my head in a firm grip, places the injector below my left ear, and fires. It feels like a bullet and burns like hell. When she moves on, I reach up and touch the spot, a negligible bump. I rub a drop of blood between my fingers, somewhat slippery before it dries. I reach up again, no more blood, and sigh. I don't want to let Janine go through this.

"Number Two Grunt! Have you left the room?" Sam stands over me, her eyes narrow, drawing her scars into a fearsome arc.

"I don't like shots, Commander. I was pushing past it."

Sam laughs, which pulls her scars taut. "That's a new one. The scenario: you're on patrol in the Outland in a team of three. One member is down, a good friend. The lone enemy who wounded her is getting away. You have shields and superior performance on your side. What do you do?"

"I run the bastard down and either capture or kill him, Commander."

"No, you don't. Next time, pay attention. Warriors operate in threes. If one is injured or killed, the other two set up a defensive perimeter. You wait for reinforcements or evacuate the downed warrior. Under no circumstances do you leave one of your team alone. That's unacceptable."

"Yes, Commander." I see the logic, but I also visualize my dad when three warriors he trained surrounded him and gave him no out. Did he choose death over brain-probes that might have betrayed my birth mother and me? Did their concern to protect me betray them? *How can I become a mech?* I bury that thought and hope I haven't missed anything else.

"This implant is your last for now." Sam looks at me, the weakling afraid of shots. "In addition to the auditory connection, it measures heart rate, blood pressure, oxygen in the blood and other life signs. It transmits them to our base via satellite. We'll know you're injured or dead before you do. It also allows us to monitor your health during tournament and arena tests."

I feel like a cog in this mech machine. These implants will tell Sam where I am at all times. So much for helping boys like Morgan.

"We have another tutorial and test before we return to conditioning. Stay alert. I'll be back in an hour."

No sooner does Sam close the door than the tutorial fires up. I catch a glimpse of Dara agitating to get out of her seat. I return my attention to the tutorial, realizing that anything less than 100 percent is unacceptable.

While the screen fills my head with virtual reality training and the mechanics and capabilities of mech gear, my thoughts flash to a different life. *I want my restaurant so I don't have to beat on my sister and friends to stay in the program. I want a way to bring my birth mother home and free Morgan and his friends.*

* * *

After an hour, it's like I've had a week's intern indoctrination. I'm thankful when Sam escorts us to the basement and gives us blue one-piece swim suits, the sleek full-body style I've seen in the Olympics.

While we change, no privacy, Dara sidles up next to me. "Where were you all weekend? We missed you at the plantation."

I grin, say nothing, and find a corner where I have at least a little privacy to pull on my swimsuit. I stuff my exercise uniform into a locker.

Still in her blue jacket and dress pants, Sam leads us out onto the deck of an Olympic-sized swimming pool. Six warriors from Friday's training line up across from us in blue one-piece swimsuits that show off their leg and arm muscles. It's like a half-dozen Daras, only smaller.

"Listen up, grunts. Part of conditioning involves holding your breath to swim the length of the pool underwater. You never can tell when that might save your life. I expect two minutes minimum from each of you. I'll test you now to see what you have. You can return after training and practice. Before you become a mech, you'll need to hold your breath three minutes and swim the length of the pool using various strokes in specified times posted on the board."

We line up along one side of the pool. Dara and Margarite stand on one side of me, and Brandy is on the other.

Sam addresses the warriors. "Show these grunts what to expect."

The six warriors line up at one end of the pool at attention. When Sam drops her arm, all six dive in a synchronized move. Gliding like fish, they scoot in unison the length of the pool underwater. I hold my breath from the moment they hit the water. My lungs burn by the time they're halfway, and I'm not exerting any effort. When they reach the end of the pool, they turn, out of synch, take a deep breath, and return. Again I hold my breath until they reach halfway.

After the warriors complete their lap, Sam steps aside. "Grunts, into the pool, now. Your implant will tell us if you're underwater and how long you hold your breath. The implant doesn't lie. For the first exercise, drop below the surface and hold your breath as long as you can. Once you come up, swim the width of the pool and back. Show me what you're capable of. Begin."

Eyes closed, I take a deep breath and jump in. I'm like a balloon ready to explode. I let out some air, open my eyes and see Dara,

Margarite, and Brandy bobbing nearby. Margarite dog-paddles, surfaces, and gasps for air. Dara hangs in the water, floating, with her victory grin. I adopt the limp approach. My lungs beg for air. I don't know how long I've been down. I forgot to count. I check my wrist-com and count off seconds.

Brandy stops treading water and floats with me. We're learning from each other. I guess that's the point. Two warriors float in the middle of the pool, this after doing two lengths. Margarite swims across as instructed. Brandy gives up and joins her. Dara eases toward me, her annoying grin wider. It's a staring contest while my lungs burn and she remains calm.

I'm ready to lose it when a warrior signals me to surface. I do. When I reach the surface, Dara and I are the last. I'm amazed. I guess I've got her to thank for that.

I gulp air and push my way across the pool. Dara sprints ahead. I'm too winded and exhausted to turn this into a contest. When I make it back, Dara places her mouth to my ear and whispers, "Told you to take those pills."

So she's making this about her and her meds.

"Out of the pool, grunts. Let's do some real work."

I hurry to avoid Dara, but she keeps up and so does Brandy, my other shadow. Along the way, we pass the electronic board showing that only six of us met the two-minute requirement. Brandy missed by five seconds. Nearby are posted best times in swim events. Sam's name is next to most. No wonder she's in amazing shape.

When we go to change out of our swimsuits, the warriors lead us into a huge communal shower with clusters of shower heads. *No way.* I don't think of myself as a prude or anything. Living with eight sisters, it's hard to find privacy, but at least I get private showers at school and at the cop station.

While I didn't pay attention to all the naked bodies when I put on my swimsuit, I can't avoid it now that nudes in all shapes and sizes surround me. Anyone who believes all women are created equal hasn't shared a communal shower. I can't help thinking my boobs are small, my hips a bit narrow and my waist too big.

Forty-seven other naked recruits and six warriors cluster around three-prong showers. Moving along the wall to the left, I pass three warriors chatting as if fully clothed. I move toward a shower head in a corner that offers some privacy away from Dara. She's attractive in the altogether for a big girl and intimidating even in the nude. When she heads my way, I cringe. How do I get her to leave me alone?

Brandy grabs my arm. I pull away but follow her toward a muscular brunette with high cheekbones, one of the six warriors. While we share a trio of shower heads, Brandy introduces me to her cousin. "Renee is the reason I joined the mechs. She told me all about the lifestyle and demands. I'd much rather do this than be a cop."

Renee looks me over.

Go ahead and say something about my tiny tits.

Her face is stern like Sam's, but with softness in her brown eyes. "Brandy has told me a lot about you, Annabelle. I've told her how important it is to find partners. I do hope you'll consider."

With Dara lingering nearby and looking left out, I nod. She gives me her angry eye while string-bean Margarite, who looks almost anorexic in the nude, holds her back.

I feel other eyes sizing me up, probably for something I don't want to do. I don't think of myself as ugly, just plain. And nudity should be private. My figure is trim from basketball and running, but I don't need the attention of Dara or anyone else.

"I'm overwhelmed," I admit.

"It's part of the training," Renee says. "Keeps you off balance and challenges assumptions about yourself, like communal showers. You get over it."

"I don't think so."

"We put our lives in each others' hands. We can't have secrets or hidden agendas that endanger sister warriors. We bare our bodies and souls. Our lifestyle brings emotional and sexual attachments. Yet even they can't be permitted to endanger sister warriors."

Thanks for the speech, Renee. Excuse me, but I don't want sex with you, or Dara, or Brandy, though she's cuter than I expected. I keep this to myself. I don't need enemies.

I smile and nod that I understand. At least I hope that's what it means.

SEVENTEEN

Back upstairs, Sam escorts twelve of us, including Dara, Margarite, Brandy, and Hannah. The six warriors from swimming join us when we reach the simulator Janine and I used over the weekend.

Sam goes through the basics with the group, what she already covered with me. She gives no indication she helped me over the weekend. *Thanks for that.*

"The purpose of the simulator is to stretch your mind and body," Sam says. "If you can visualize it, you can do it."

"I visualize becoming president of the Federal Union," Dara says, nodding to her posse.

Sam gets under her face. "Can you really?" She turns to Margarite. "Are you ready to vote your friend into the presidency? Do you think she has what it takes? Are you prepared to put your life in her hands on the battlefield?"

When other recruits back away, Dara glares at me like this is my doing.

"For this exercise, you'll work in pairs." Sam backs away.

I stand next to Brandy, hoping she'll be my partner.

Sam introduces Camilla, a ruddy-faced blonde, as a warrior-tech. Then she grabs me and points to Dara. "Room three."

Before I can protest, Camilla leads the way down the corridor and Sam introduces the next pair. She's determined to make me face my worst fears, daily.

Pairs of doors line the corridor. We enter a room with two boxy simulators like the one I used over the weekend. Dara picks the unit by the door. I open the other one. It still smells of sweat. After I climb onto the padded seat and adjust my breathing tube so I won't suffocate, the panel closes. Dry, gel-like foam fills the space around every part of my body in a snug but fluid fit.

After a brief demo, a refresher for me, I'm standing in the ring with Dara, who looks huge and intimidating as ever. I see behind and to the sides as if I were in a mech suit. We're alone except for Sam, who floats nearby. This must be how she monitors all six matchups.

Unused to the simulator, Dara hesitates. I rush forward and trip her. She drops like she would in the real world. Before I can take advantage, she gets to her feet and charges. When she hits, the haptic sensors inside my simulator deliver a punch, a lightning strike to the face that sends me reeling backward. If someone programmed this wrong, the machine could pulverize a body just like in a real fight. I might as well be in the ring with Dara. The pain radiating from my cheek is real.

She swings, alternating left and right as if she's hitting a punching bag. I deflect. She comes back with practiced blows. I use martial kicks and chops I've practiced and others I imagine from mech suit training. Dara adjusts quickly.

I want out of the simulator. This isn't fun. I find no switch or lever to turn it off. I punch, kick, and strike every which way. Dara hits my face and stomach, building into a rhythm. When I protect my face, she hits my stomach. I cover that and she punches my face. I repel a moment too late and kick. She deflects and hits me. I've got nothing left. My arms are inflamed. My muscles refuse to respond. When I throw a punch, my body doesn't follow through.

"Look into your opponent's eyes and anticipate what she'll do." The voice floating toward me sounds like Sam's. "Your life depends on it."

While I turn into a bloody pulp, Sam watches, monitors my vitals and does nothing. She could cut this off. My heart's racing. Can't she see that? I want to scream for her to stop. My voice doesn't cooperate.

Dara hits my eye. *Focus. Focus on what?* I begin to recognize a pattern to Dara's moves. She hits high, then low. I block a bit too late.

I shift my pattern. When she goes for my stomach, I tighten my inflamed muscles, and ram my fist into her throat. Dara chokes.

She doesn't hit back. I slug her in the stomach. She slumps over and swings for my gut. I double over in pain for a moment and finally rise up to hammer her throat. Gasping for air, Dara drops to her knees.

The simulator releases. I fall out onto the concrete floor, a mass of throbbing pain. Brandy takes my arm and helps me to my feet. "That was amazing," she whispers.

Renee takes my other arm, and together they practically carry me out of the simulator room. We pass through corridors to the nurse's station. From there, the infirmary radiates out to half a dozen small rooms. I have a feeling this will be my second home.

As Renee helps me to a bed, I glance at a mirror. Cuts and welts cover my face, and one eye is swollen. If I was plain before, what am I now?

Two warriors carry Dara on a stretcher to another room. There's an oxygen mask over her face. *I had to get her to stop.*

Nurse Kristina Wells shakes her head, which sends her auburn hair flopping about her leathery face. She hooks me up to another IV. I hate the thought of more meds, but whatever this is; I hope it fixes what I saw in the mirror.

Sam sends Nurse Wells away, closes the door, and lingers over me, a scowl on her scarred face. "Start fighting or you won't be much to look at."

"I tried," I say in a hoarse voice. "Why do I have to start with the toughest?"

"You still think she's the toughest?"

Brandy's cousin, Renee, moves between me and the commander. "Give me this grunt until Friday. I'll whip her into shape."

"You go easy on her and I'll have your ass, lieutenant."

"Understood, Commander."

I'm relieved I won't have to face Dara again until Friday. At least I hope that's what this means. Joining us, Brandy smiles and pats my hand. I don't pull away. Her cousin stood up for me on Brandy's behalf, and I need friends, lots of them, if I'm going to make it.

I turn toward Sam and croak, "I thought the simulator was a virtual experience."

Sam leans over me. "It was, Number Two Grunt. In a real fight you'd be dead. You have three choices. Become one of the best, worthy to stand with my warriors. Wash out. Or die. Don't waste your life. If you think training's too tough or that I'm too hard on you, then wash out. Right now."

I stare at the IV and shake my head.

"Then learn to fight."

When I'm alone with Brandy and Renee, I turn to Brandy with her sweet unmarred face. "How was your simulation?"

Renee pats her cousin's shoulder. "I gave her a few pointers, which I'll give you if you don't embarrass me."

"I'll do my best."

"Hannah's a tough talker and strong, but she has limited range. I told Brandy to think outside her comfort zone and hit Hannah where she wouldn't expect it. She got in some tough blows, though nothing like Dara. Sam wanted you to teach Dara a lesson today and you did. You just need a few pointers."

"Isn't that cheating?" I ask.

Renee laughs, which accentuates her high cheekbones. "Annabelle, as mechs there's nothing we won't do for each other. There's a bond I can't describe, stronger than family. Wait until you try the mech com-link. You'll know what it means to be one with another warrior. As trainees, we break down your inhibitions so you're ready for this. You fight afraid."

"Dara is huge and muscular."

"So is a horse, but humans ride horses, not the other way. Think of her like a horse."

"You mean a bronco that has to be broken." I watch welts fade on my arms. This must be the effect of Sam's meds.

"Exactly. Challenge your ways of looking at her. Force yourself to adapt. Expand your breadth of actions. Above all, recognize what your opponent is doing and what her weaknesses are."

"Was that Sam's voice I heard in the simulator?"

"Mine," Renee says. "Auditory distortion makes it difficult to tell."

"Thanks for saving my life."

"Come on, I want to show you something."

Renee removes my IV and leads us back to the simulator area, into another room where four recruits wait. Six boxy machines, chunkier than the simulator, squat in the middle of this room.

I'm surprised rail-thin Margarite isn't with Dara. She looks more relaxed than before. Of the others, Vivian is a sturdy blonde built like Sam, though without her toughness. Tara is a compact brunette with a crooked nose she could have gotten in a fight. Then there's freckle-faced Hannah with her dark chocolate hair. She looks like the toughest of the bunch, except that Brandy beat her. She scowls and grumbles under her breath.

Renee brushes back her brown hair and faces Hannah. "Now that you know what the simulator can do, don't make me use it against you."

Hannah and her freckles shrink into a corner.

"This is the VR room, where we review fights," Renee says. Along one wall are a control panel and six screens. She assigns each of us to a VR unit and hands us blue uniforms with tight cloth hoods. Thanks to the tutorial, I recognize the nano-fabric.

I look for a place to change, but Sam isn't big on privacy. When Brandy strips down, I turn toward the corner and pull on the stretchy suit and hood.

"These haptic outfits connect you to the VR unit and give you the sensation of being in the fight. It's like the simulator, but less intense."

I climb inside my VR machine and sit down. The tight uniform is less intense than the full body pressure of the simulator's foam. No controls are visible. I see the other five machines and Renee, who stands by a monitor where she can view all six of us.

"We'll revisit your fight from your opponent's perspective and then your own. Think about how to attack yourselves when in your opponent's view. Look for weaknesses to exploit, because your opponent will. Learn what you have to change."

With Renee controlling the images, I see her and the other five recruits in the gym by ringed mats. Sweet Brandy looks unnerved at Hannah getting the benefit of fight insight. She'll have to work harder next time. Renee can't afford to go easy on her cousin. I pray the haptic sensors won't pulverize me. I still have welts from the simulator.

I enter the ring as Dara and tower over a frightened mouse; this other Annabelle begs to be ground into dust. While I see and feel what Dara did, I can't act on the fight as I did in the simulator. As Dara I move in on myself. It's disorienting, as if fighting my twin. I throw punches at my own face and stomach and get into a rhythm. I sense the music of my pattern and the results as this other

Annabelle Scott, me, gets her brains bashed in. I swear I'll never let Janine go through this.

Concentrating on the fight, I experience elation at my mastery of the ring as I beat this other Annabelle. Then revulsion grips me that I'm hurting someone, and that someone is me.

Focus! That other Annabelle's responses are slow. She leaves herself open and fails to protect her face and stomach. *How pathetic.* Is this what Dara felt or is it a chemical enhancement from the drugs and the IV, activated by the VR equipment?

"Focus on your opponent's eyes," Renee says over the com. "Feel the energy inside her, what's driving her. What's her next move? Psych her out. Get her to believe you own her and can do as you will."

That's where Dara has me. When I look into this Annabelle's eyes, I spot weaknesses I can exploit. I see submission, defeat.

Then I see something new. The thrust to the throat comes out of nowhere. It's a tap that doesn't choke me, not as Dara felt it, but it breaks my concentration. When I look again on my Annabelle opponent, all bloodied before me, she has me. She slams my stomach and my throat. I look into those eyes and spot the transition from defeat into–not victory, exactly, but resolve and determination. This Annabelle's eyes are focused. They bear into me. I'm no longer dominating. This makes me hesitate. Then the fight is over.

"You see the change in focus," Renee says.

I nod. "Yes."

"That's what Sam wants from you, what you need to deliver in order for me to put my life in your hands. The early Annabelle I don't want. She'll get me killed. The later Annabelle can stand shoulder to shoulder with the best after more training. Harness that."

I expect Renee to release me from the virtual reality playback. Instead she runs it again from several angles, from both Dara's view and mine, which is disorienting. When this Annabelle fights back, I notice dynamic intensity in her and doubt in Dara. Dara's angry but no longer confident of victory.

When Renee releases me, I pull off the VR cloth helmet and see myself reflected in the steel enclosure. Eye swelling is down, cuts have stopped bleeding, and I don't see bruises. Yet they're still visible. Sam didn't bandage me. Like her scars, she let my wounds show, a badge that I'm a warrior, *don't mess with me.*

When the six of us assemble, Renee opens the door. "Now that you've reviewed your fights, I need you back in the simulators to learn martial arts."

I'm ready to collapse. Mention of the simulator has blood rushing in my ears. Brandy joins me. I imagine escaping down the khaki corridors toward freedom. Looking up at me, Brandy reminds me of Janine and why I'm here. Brandy's afraid. That's all I need to stop wallowing in my own grief.

I follow Renee into a smaller room with two simulators. I climb into a unit across from Brandy and insert my mouthpiece. Warm gel-like foam envelopes me, reminding me that I have to fight or get beaten.

Visuals light up. Brandy stands across from me in a ring, frightened. She doesn't want this either.

Renee steps forward. "The simulator supports your body to ease movements and muscle fatigue while building muscle memory of moves we'll show you. Pay attention like you did with your tutorial, but remember, this is physical conditioning. Don't think; just do moves as close to what you see as possible. There's no body contact in this, although it appears that you have an opponent."

That thought releases so much tension I float. My feet no longer touch whatever substitutes for a floor.

"We'll push you to an extreme your body can't handle without the simulator. If you give this your full attention and effort, you can pick up two weeks of training in a day. We'll begin with karate and move to kick-boxing, wrestling, and a wide range of other martial arts."

Suddenly my body tumbles out of control. I'm back in the pool, underwater, holding my breath, and sinking. I can't breathe. I don't know which way is up.

"Annabelle, are you okay?" It's Renee.

"I'm sinking."

"You're not in a pool. Use the tube and steady your breathing. Relax your body. Let it float. There, is that better?"

My feet hit something solid. I stand, determined to tough my way through this. When Renee starts the karate demonstration, the simulator takes over, moving my limbs to duplicate the moves. I've become a puppet.

"Repetition provides muscle memory," Renee says.

My mind fills with images and movements. I can't keep track of what I'm learning, if I'm learning. My body resists continual battering, but the machine demands more.

EIGHTEEN

By the time Renee lets me out of the simulator, I've zoned out like I do in basketball practice when I know the moves and don't have to think. With every muscle burning, I collapse into a chair by the monitoring equipment.

Sam barges in. "On your feet, grunts. You're not on holiday. Double-time to the gym."

Sister recruits slump onto the floor. We all reek of sweat. It's 2 p.m., and we've been in the simulator two hours. It seems like 20, and I'm famished.

Renee hustles me and the rest of her recruits out toward the gym.

"When do we break for lunch?" I rub my stomach.

When we reach the gym, Renee gathers us around. "Listen up. This is intensive training. We don't have time to waste. While your stomachs won't agree, we injected you with nutritional supplements after your fights to last you until dinner. You need to push your limits. Now give me 30 pushups and 30 sit-ups, and meet me by the weights."

This is crazy. But I can't disappoint my team: little Brandy, wiry Margarite, freckle-faced Hannah, tough-blonde Vivian, or Tara, with her crooked nose. It's amazing how I feel part of this unit after only a few hours. Is it because we've all been through shocking fights and grueling training?

I finish first and linger with Brandy, who struggles to get the last of her sit-ups. If we're a team, then we stick together and help each other. Yet in the tournament I'll have to fight these girls, and I don't want to.

On the weights I'm too weary to press 50 pounds before Renee sends us out for a 10-mile run. I don't have it in me to sprint, even though Renee runs alongside, prodding us. At least I don't have Dara to contend with. Tough-looking Vivian is the weakest runner. I run next to her, give her encouragement and with it, urge myself on. It gives me an excuse not to burn myself out.

By the time I stumble back toward the gym, my stomach's in knots. I'm ready to eat anything in sight. With my muscles in full rebellion, I collapse by the door. Brandy helps me to my feet before my muscles cramp and freeze up. We look like survivors of the Bataan Death March helping each other back inside. It's only four. When is dinner?

"Let's see some hustle." Renee sounds like Sam. "Get into mech gear and show me what you learned in simulation."

I'm in a daze floating into the big gym, as if I'm in the simulator watching a whole other Annabelle. I can barely lift the pieces of the mech suit off the rack. I step into the leg units and need Brandy's help to heft the front and back plates up and snap them into place. I hope hydraulics will offset this weariness. I'd hate to pass out in all this gear.

When I get the helmet on and take my first steps, I feel spastic. My muscles move to their own sagging will. Across from me Brandy tries chops and kicks that are intimidating with the force and speed enhancements of the suit. Renee pairs us at one end of the big gym.

When she gives the signal, Brandy attacks. My body responds with block and thrust moves from the simulator that I didn't know before today. Adrenaline brushes my exhaustion aside. Knowing the suit protects Brandy, I let my thrusts connect with her mech-shielded body. We explode into jabs and chops.

I'm getting the hang of this when Renee stops us. "Take off the suits and face each other in the ring."

It takes all my effort to remove the gear. My muscles scream for relief. I follow Brandy into one of the rings. We bow and approach to engage. I can't raise my arms to defend myself. I try to focus and see Brandy barely able to stand.

135

"That's enough for today," Sam announces. "Get cleaned up. Chow's in the cafeteria. Then you're free to go."

For a nano-second I'm disappointed that I worked myself up to fight and had it called off. Then Brandy collapses into my arms and hangs there.

I keep from falling and steady her. "You okay?"

"Legs gave out. You?"

"Same." I put my arm under hers and help her toward the showers in the back of the gym.

It's only the six of us. I'm too exhausted to feel self-conscious, not only about communal showers, but helping each other out of sweaty clothes, and looking our best afterwards.

When we drag ourselves into the cafeteria, Dara sits in the middle, bragging to her posse about how tough and awesome she is. I lead Renee's grunts to the back corner. We slump around a table with steaming bowls of stew. I expect something security bland and am delighted by a pinch of salt and spice and big chunks of chicken.

Renee joins us, her face softened. "You grunts did well today. It's a long journey. It'll be rough throughout, so if you're having second thoughts…"

We all shake our heads, though I'm certain we all want to quit.

* * *

After what seems a month of conditioning and training and filling my mind and body with who knows what, all I want to do is crawl into a corner and die. But if I don't go see Janine, she'll come to me, taking far too many risks, and exposing herself to more of the mech world.

I'm on my way out of the building when Sam grabs me. "A word, please."

I follow her, expecting we'll head to her office. Instead, she pulls me past the empty nurse's station into the small infirmary I used earlier.

"Remove your clothes and hop up." Sam points to the bed. "You're in no condition to be tooling about town. I don't fancy losing recruits to stupidity."

"I–"

"Relax, Number Two Grunt. This won't take long. Then you can be on your way."

I relax into the thin mattress and imagine sleeping for weeks.

"I'm fine."

"Your medical implant says otherwise. Your blood pressure's up. You lack electrolytes. If you don't get relief, you face systemic failure."

I don't know whether to feel impressed that she knows, grateful that she cares, or abused that I'm just an asset she has to protect.

Sam has me lie face down and starts an IV. While she fills my body with more chemicals, she applies warm, soothing cream to my back.

"What are all these chemicals doing to me? I mean, IVs, pills and—"

"I could tell you I don't know, but that won't be satisfying." Sam applies cream across my back and down my legs and arms.

I'm on fire like hot chocolate on a chilly night. While the cream and the IV warm me, I relax. Layers of tension peel away as if I'm bundled for an Antarctic expedition that turned into a desert stroll.

"I could tell you it's top secret and if I told you…well, you get the idea."

Relaxing more, I stop caring what she's giving me, because it's what I need.

"The cream is a muscle relaxer and toner. Nano-particles penetrate deep into muscle tissue to nourish and rejuvenate. The IV will replenish fluids, electrolytes and other elements you're lacking. It helps your body expel excess lactic acid and other toxins. We're almost done."

"Thanks. Sometimes I think you hate me, and then you act nice."

"Don't make too much of this." Sam stops with the cream. "You had a tough fight today. If you return, I'm confident you'll make it to the end. That choice is yours. As for tending your medical needs, I do that for any warrior or recruit who needs it. I can't afford to play favorites. You're the only one who needed medical attention tonight."

Sam removes the IV. "Get dressed and get some sleep. I'll expect you here at eight if you wish to continue."

* * *

By the time I reach the cop station, my muscles no longer burn. I long to see Janine, download my misery from today and frighten her away from the mechs.

Brooks is not at her cluttered desk. I check the roster in the break room. She's out.

"They left ten minutes ago," Scarlatti says. "Got a lead on some boys."

I freeze. What if one of the boys gets angry enough to grab Janine? I hope Morgan wouldn't, but what about the others? "Where did they go? I can offer backup."

"You don't have a partner." Which means I'm no longer needed. Scarlatti carries her victory back to her office.

I trot upstairs to Liz's desk and get her to tell me where Voss and Brooks went. Then I zip out on my cycle. Reaching the sprawling University of Tennessee campus, I pull up beside six squad sedans and Brooks' two-seater. Voss is giving the cops instructions in full view of an abandoned dorm that's boarded up on the first floor. I spot Janine snug inside the little bug. *Such an obedient girl.*

I pop the door open and almost get jolted when Janine aims her stun-gun at me. She drops the gun and scrambles out to give me a hug. "You survived. Do you need me to—" She stops and straightens up when Brooks walks over.

Brooks pats my sore shoulder. "To what do we owe a mech trainee gracing our humble lives?"

"I thought you could use more backup," I say.

"So you don't think I can handle myself." Janine gives me her pouty face.

"You don't know how many boys are out here, do you?"

"We don't," Brooks admits. "Let's go. We get the back."

She hands me a stun-gun and leads the way around the tall brick building that awaits a tear-down or remodel, probably into apartments.

When we reach the back stairs, I take Janine's hand. She pulls away. I've hurt her feelings, but this is her first raid and we don't know what to expect.

"You go ahead," I say. "I'll hang back in case you need anything."

Brooks nods and leads Janine up concrete stairs. When they disappear into the former dorm building, I slip behind one of six green Dumpsters. This is the first time I've been without a partner. All I have is this one-shot zapper and the collar remote. And that works only if the boys haven't masked their collars. I hold one in each hand.

Not only am I exhausted from the mech workout, I feel vulnerable and stupid. I should have gone in with Brooks and Janine. Instead, I've caved to my sister's pouting and put myself in danger. I'm in no condition to defend myself.

Glancing out from behind Dumpsters that stink of rotten food, I wonder where the rest of Voss' cops are. Anyone hiding in this abandoned dorm would look for the back way out. I don't see any other cops. Voss has the entire force out front with only Brooks and my baby sister covering the back. *Plus stupid me.*

The crash of metal startles me. I fall away from the Dumpster and come face-to-face with a boy climbing down. Big and menacing, he towers over me. I recognize the handsome face beneath the tuft of red hair. *Morgan?* My knees are too weak to stand; my mouth too dry to talk. My hands tremble with the collar remote and stun-gun. Even if I trigger the remote, his collar is masked.

He stares down, a flash of recognition.

Gazing up, I struggle for breath. I study his sweet, boyish face: a masculine face, no longer muddy. I'm awash with feelings I don't have around girls, and didn't have around Brad. My heart races. I need to capture him. It's my job. I want to run off with him and talk and explore. I'm paralyzed, though not by fear. What shall I do?

"Are you going to use that on me?" he asks in a gentle bass voice. "If not, then I need to go." He smiles and backs away. "Thank your mom again for me, and thank you for helping." He turns and sprints down the alley.

"Wait." *Where are you from? What do you like? Where will you go? When can I see you again?* I take a deep breath and aim the stun-gun at his back. *Don't go.* My hand shakes. I can't trigger the stupid thing. He wants what I want: freedom. *Godspeed.*

Getting to my feet, I hear footsteps. *More boys?* The stun-gun triggers, firing electrodes and a pulse toward the street, into thin air. Morgan disappears around a corner. *How stupid. Now I have no weapons. All I have are my bare hands, and whatever I've learned today.*

I jump from beside the Dumpster and launch an attack, some combination of simulated martial arts. I halt inches from Janine's face. She stands, petrified. I drop my spent stun-gun and hold her. "I'm sorry. I had company."

Janine's eyes glaze over.

"Babe, talk to me. Tell me you're okay."

Her face seems to explode while her hands thrust to my throat. I almost have a heart attack.

"Got you back." She lowers her hands. "So you did learn something today."

"If you two are finished…" Brooks says. "What happened?"

I take a deep breath, lean against the Dumpster, and steal a glance down the alley to make sure Morgan is gone. I miss him already. "I hid behind the Dumpster. A boy jumped me. There may have been two or three. He hit me and ran. I didn't see much."

"Which way?"

I hope Brooks doesn't notice the moment of indecision. I point toward the street, where I discharged my stun-gun. "I fired but missed. I had no other weapons, so I hid and looked for other boys. When I looked back, he was gone."

"We caught three," Brooks says, walking away.

"You met an honest to goodness boy," Janine whispers. She looks more excited than scared.

"His collar was masked, so the remote didn't work," I add.

I lead the way around the former dorm to the cars and my cycle. Janine holds my arm and looks furtively in all directions as if she expects the boy to jump her.

I've never really met Morgan, yet I can't help replaying two missed opportunities. It's like I've known him for months. We've been watching each other from across the street. Then, when I come face-to-face, I blow it.

I'm not a good cop, either. I let him go.

Will I ever see you again?

* * *

Since the shift is over, Brooks returns to the station to clock Janine out. When I give my sister a lift home, she holds onto me from behind tighter than usual. I really frightened her, but she had to put up a good front for Brooks. After all, if she can't be a mech or a cop, they'll ship her off to transit patrol or worse.

Mom's car isn't in the garage when we get there, which isn't unusual. I wonder whether she's helping my redhead. If so, I pray Voss didn't capture her.

Janine takes my hand and leads me past Mama Helen, who's reading some medical report on her e-pad, and Mama Grace, talking to Sarah. Therese must be upstairs with the other girls, supervising homework. She's always been a better role model than me.

When we reach our bedroom, Janine shuts the door and locks it. Then she comes at me and throws me onto the bed. "I want to do mech training with you, Belle. You terrified me tonight. I don't like being terrified of you." She breaks down sobbing in my arms.

I hold her and stroke her soft brown hair until she stops crying.

Her face brightens. She gets up and tugs me to my feet. "Come on. Show me."

I grab her arms and steady her. She lost her anchor today, and I'm to blame. "I don't want to fight, Babe. I don't even like the mechs. I just want you safe. I'm so sorry about scaring you."

Janine pushes and tries to throw me. When I can't stop her, I wrestle her to the hardwood floor and pin her arms and legs. Only then does she relax, purring like she does at night.

"You will stay tonight, won't you?" she asks. A mixture of playfulness and worry lines crosses her soft face.

I nod and let go. "But I have to be there early. Now if you don't mind, I'm exhausted. We'll talk mechs over the weekend."

I toss her the last so she won't think I've abandoned her. Then I take her downstairs and fix her a bland turkey sandwich. She won't leave my side. In fact, when I go to bed early, Janine follows like my shadow.

NINETEEN

Each day for the rest of the week begins with simulator fights, virtual reality reviews, and simulator martial arts training with Renee and her recruits. We see other teams during general instruction in the morning, as we move from activity to activity, and at meals, where we cluster in our own groups with our warrior trainers.

Dara leads her group and seems to dominate her trainer, which could be dangerous. She eyes me like she can't wait for a rematch. I avoid her when I can and watch her work out when we pass her group in gym. I'm convinced that no amount of martial arts training will enable me to stand up to her in the tournament.

While my mind and muscles stretch to include various shades of Chinese, Korean, and Japanese martial arts, along with boxing and kick-boxing, I replay how I scared Janine. Instead of sending her away from mechs, now she wants to share this with me. I can't let that happen.

At dinner on Tuesday, Margarite grabs the seat next to me. She seems upset at how Dara has moved on, gathering new friends, and excluding her.

I decide to be friendly. Between bites of chicken stew, I tell her, "Your fight technique has improved a lot."

Margarite beams. Her little face brightens, quite pretty. I hadn't noticed before, when all I saw was Dara's poodle.

"Someone needs to kick her down a notch," Margarite whispers.

I'm surprised to hear her say anything against Dara. I know she's afraid, even though she says Dara hasn't hurt her.

"I can't imagine who," I reply, because while I'm improving, so is the amazon.

Margarite lifts a spoonful of stew. Her hand shakes, so she puts it down. "Her arrogance will be her undoing."

I let that go. "She's a powerful fighter," I tell Margarite. "I don't see anyone capable of taking her. She's a shoe-in to win the tournament."

"I think you can. Deep inside, she's afraid of you."

I don't believe that for a moment. Yet the seed plants itself. I look over at Dara and she glares back without interrupting whatever tale she's entertaining her group with.

When dinner's over, I hang back until Dara and her crew leave. I don't want to get sucked into another of her parties. At the door, I hear voices in the corridor, recognize several warrior-trainers, and hold my breath.

"What's the pool up to?" I hear Dara's trainer ask.

"Five thousand," a second warrior says.

"Who you got in the final?" Renee asks.

"Dara and Rox," Dara's trainer says and adds, "with Dara winning, of course."

Rox is a loner like me. She has caramel-colored skin and short, coal-black hair. She hangs in the middle of the pack in all activities, trying not to draw attention. I'm surprised to hear her picked.

"What about Annabelle?" Renee asks.

"She'll wash out before round two," the second warrior says. "She's brittle outside and squishy inside. You saw how she let Dara tear her apart."

No one tells me I can't.

Two more recruits washed out between Friday and Monday and three more today, which brings us down to 43. Only 32 make it to the tournament. Eleven more have to leave. *Not me!*

* * *

Wednesday afternoon, we return to mech gear training with a difference. Renee breaks us into two teams: string-bean Margarite and thin Tara join slender Hannah, while short Brandy and stocky Vivian join me. I look at my belly. Am I getting chubby? I'll have to watch what I eat. Or is this one of the side effects of the meds?

After we suit up and put on our shiny black helmets, Renee has us sit with our teams while she activates our com-link. "You'll find the multi-tasking aspects of com-link disorienting. That's natural. You'll get used to it."

The first thing I notice is breathing: mine, Brandy's and Vivian's. I see three forward views, one for each of us, in addition to my rear view and peripherals. It's like the tutorial and martial arts simulations; too much information bombards me at once. I'm not sure where to direct my attention.

"Team leaders: Number Two Grunt and Number Twelve Grunt. Stand and move forward so your teammates can sense a single member's movement."

I'm not sure how I got picked as team leader. I hope this rotates, though I don't see anyone I want to follow. Margarite is thin to the point of frailty, and a definite follower.

Brandy is short and easily frightened. She's done well in training, but she leeches onto me like Margarite did with Dara.

Blonde Vivian is a tough girl, built like Sam, yet struggles in training. She's not what Renee would want next to her in battle.

Tara is a compact, slender brunette with a crooked nose that makes her look like she lost a fight. She drags herself through training, barely keeping up. I expect her to wash out before the tournament.

With her striking chocolate brown hair, Hannah appears to be the strongest in our group and most likely to do well in the tournament. Brandy beat her in the initial fight, but she had coaching. Number Twelve Hannah's the one I need to watch.

Getting to my feet is disorienting. Only one forward view changes. I take a step and see the gym before me and my profile from the perspective of my team. It gives new meaning to the phrase "watch your back." I see the polished black shields of my exoskeleton and helmet as I move. Then I trip because I'm not watching where I'm going.

"Okay, two and twelve," Renee says. "Face off. Get used to seeing a wider perspective of the battlefield before you engage. Then commence mild fighting. The purpose isn't the fight but to test linkage with your team."

I stand across from Hannah. Her black-encased profile fills my view. I see us from Brandy's perspective, but Vivian watches Hannah's teammates. *Good girl.* I approach Hannah and throw a punch, see it in two views as she deflects, clashing shield on shield.

Hannah attacks, throwing several punches to show off and take control. I crouch down and thrust my shielded fist into her gut. That sends her up toward the rafters. Tara jumps to her feet and races to her teammate's aid. Seeing this from Vivian's perspective, I turn, punch, and knock Tara sideways.

Vivian gets to her feet, followed by Brandy and Margarite. Pretty soon all six of us are brawling. It's hard to know who is who since we all look alike in our black mech gear. Coordinating my three views, I decide who is friend and foe. "Brandy, step back."

When she does, I get a clear shot at one of our opponents and take it, knocking the recruit back. Two opponents pounce on me. I drop to my knees and punch the leg of one attacker. She goes down. My teammates pull the other attacker away. When the first opponent gets to her feet, I pull my team back into a line and face them.

"Very good," Renee says. "First, don't use names on the com-link, in case we get hacked. Use first initials. If you have name confusion use two initials, never names. Second, as you've seen, it can be confusing in battle to know friend from foe. Quickly orient yourselves using com and cams to deal with any threat. Now, pick up the fighting. Stretch yourselves and see what you can do."

My body is exhausted from our morning workout, yet I can't let my team down. "Can the other team hear our com?"

"No, but in battle, you can't be certain. Be brief and cryptic."

While Hannah's team moves in to attack, I start to give orders and realize I could garble B and V. "Bravo, move left. Victor, cover my back."

Someone hits me in the gut. I don't feel the punch, just the thrust back. I should be airborne, but Vivian braces me. I swing around and hit the opponent to my left at the same time Brandy does, knocking our opponent back against the wall. Vivian takes the brunt of the attack behind me. When I turn, Brandy hits the middle attacker and I bring her down. Vivian is down. Now it's Brandy and me against a lone attacker. I'm guessing Hannah.

While her teammates recover, Brandy and I hammer Hannah from two sides. "Victor, are you okay?" I ask.

"Watch your left," Vivian says.

I turn in time to watch Brandy get hammered. Hannah knocks Vivian down and then it's three on me. They pounce. I jump. Someone grabs my leg and throws me back against the concrete floor. The suit shields most of the impact, but I'm gasping for air. When I catch my breath, Hannah has us stacked side-by-side like logs. *This is why everyone has me washing out.*

Seeing Hannah and her team with chains, ready to bind us, I have to act. "Backward somersaults on three, two, one."

I spin back and get dizzy with all views revolving. We land on our feet, sort of.

"Charge and punch low," I say and lead my team forward. In the middle, Hannah acts disoriented. Her teammates swing the chains. Brandy and Vivian duck. I get clobbered. The suit jerks in all directions, sends me in spasms to the ground. I can't get my suit to respond. Coming to my aid, my teammates are encircled and incapacitated.

Hannah stands over me with a foot on my chest. How humiliating. I waltzed into a trap.

*　*　*

Thursday afternoon, after simulated martial arts, each of us passes the pool tests. Then we return to mech training.

I'm getting the hang of mech speed and mobility, what it can and can't do. One thing's for sure: it can't protect me from my own rash acts.

I prefer mech training over simulators because it's real movement with an addictive sense of power and freedom. I imagine fleeing into the Outland to look for George. I'd find Morgan and help Mom take boys over the border. I'm certain that's what she's doing. After all, both Morgan and Brad thanked me for her. But neither made it to the Outland, and now she's disappeared.

After we do mobility exercises and fight as teams in the large mech gym, Renee, in gear, takes us outside. Behind the compound is the shooting range, a wide expanse of scrub brush and dirt leading to a set of targets in the distance.

"We've mounted weapons in your suits," Renee says. "When you're in position, I'll activate. This is live ammunition. While we designed mech shields to resist this ammo, they're not invincible. Only aim at the targets. Line up with your teams."

I take my team to the left side where we lie on the ground and face square targets with concentric circles. I imagine crawling through brush like this at the border to escape.

Targets look too far at 50 meters. I don't trust my high scores during cop intern video training as anything more than encouragement to keep playing.

"Each team has sets of three targets. One at a time, have your team take six shots each. Number Two Grunt, go first."

"Victor." I stick to false names.

Vivian shoots three .45-caliber rounds into bushes. In her view I watch her line up her arm-mounted weapon. "Victor, try a little to the left."

She misses the final three shots. Tara goes next and hits her target for the other team. That's discouraging.

"Bravo, it's your turn," I say.

Brandy hits the edge of two targets and then strikes bushes. Mech hydraulic drives accentuate her shaking hands.

Margarite nails a bulls-eye and a couple of side shots.

When it's my turn, I take a deep breath and hold it like I do during intern video shooting. I aim at the target Brandy missed and ease off a shot. I can't see where it went; I must have flinched. I shoot five more rounds. All I see are untouched targets with circles surrounding dark centers. *Oh, well.*

Robots place targets at 75 and 100 meters. We take turns shooting at each distance. I strain to make out the targets. By the time the targets are at 150 meters, I'm so agitated that I fire twice toward each. I can't tell if I hit anything. *Does this darned suit have a scope?* I can't find it.

"Line up," Renee yells over the com-link.

We stand before the scrub-brush range with no targets. *I can do this.*

"In time you'll train with and without mech gear. We expect you to hit targets every time. Remember, in combat your life depends on it. Now I'll have you test machine pellets so you'll know how this feels. They're automatic. Don't waste ammo. Watch what it does to a target."

A scarecrow dummy in the shape of an arena brute appears 15 meters away, hovering above scrub-brush. Hannah approaches the line and faces the target. She aims and shoots. It sounds like a drill as a spray of pellets tears the center out of the dummy.

Excited, Hannah yells loud enough for me to hear. She disintegrates the head and works her way down the body until only a stump remains.

I can't see what joy she gets from destroying things, although if

I imagine the dummy as the mechs who killed my dad, I could get close.

Are those warriors still here? Sam is. It was 13 years ago. Mechs sign on for six-year tours, but some may have stuck around.

Mom said Sam was upset about my dad. The commander wasn't involved; the warriors who train us aren't old enough. I make a mental note to check mech files, which means breaking into Sam's office. If I get caught this time I'll share a cell, though nowhere near my birth mother.

I let other recruits go before me. Each shreds the dummy. When it's my turn, I imagine Morgan's face on the dummy, and I can't shoot. As a mech, will I have to obey or die? Did those who killed Dad have a choice? If not, then Sam is responsible.

I imagine her face on the dummy and fire a short blast into the neck, severing the head. I stop. While I hate mechs, I have no reason to hate Sam, yet.

"Bravo," Renee says. "If this were a battle, you have the most remaining ammo to face other threats. Remember, dominate, but don't leave yourself without weapons."

TWENTY

By Friday afternoon, I'm ready for the weekend and rest. Mom has been absent all week. According to messages she left with Mama Grace, she has too much legislative work. *No way.* I know better. Those boys are still on the loose, at least some of them. I pray that coincidence doesn't occur to the rest of the family or to Sam, Voss or Governor Battani.

Expecting another afternoon in mech gear, I follow Renee out to the gym. Instead, I see other groups gathered around four raised fighting rings. Dara is in one with Rox, who favors a swollen eye and bloody nose. Dara has a few welts, but that doesn't slow her down. She attacks Rox with relentless punches, chops, and kicks. It's a brutal barrage, yet warriors have money on Rox. *I don't get it. At least no one will lose money on me, unless they bet on me washing out before the tournament.*

While I change into my blue fight outfit with haptic sensors and thin padded gloves, I study Dara's relentless attack. *There's no way she's afraid of me.*

As if she hears my thoughts, Margarite grabs my arm. "Don't let her intimidate you."

I've lost before I get into the ring, but I refuse to let those gambling warriors get the better of me.

When Rox goes down and doesn't get up, Sam calls the fight. Dara raises her own hands in victory. She looks proud, as if Rox was her main competitor. The warriors certainly think so.

Two warriors move Rox to a stretcher and carry her out. I feel bad for her and hope she won't wash out over this. I approach the ring with Dara. *Let's get this over.*

Sam motions for Dara to step down, and then takes the platform as a stage. While she ought to be sweltering in that dress uniform, she doesn't show it.

"Okay, grunts. Let's see what a week of training by top warriors has done for you. We're down to 42 recruits. Each of you has passed many hurdles. You wouldn't be here if I didn't think you had a chance. However, no one gets favorite treatment. In battle that makes you weak.

"You each have strengths you can use against opponents if you anticipate moves and concentrate your energy. I ask you to dig deeper than you have ever dug before; deeper than you have in simulation. Deeper than you have in mech suit training."

Sam scans the faces of recruits before she continues. "Rule Thirteen, my good luck rule, is this: When deprived of all weapons, of all means of protecting yourself, find new ones. This means if your opponent gets the upper hand, change the game to your advantage. That won't be easy, because a good opponent will do the same to you. Never assume victory is yours to take. Never assume your opponent has you beat. There's always one more move you can make. Reach for it."

"Hoo-rah."

The rah-rah pumps me up. Then I realize: *this is suicide.* If neither side backs down, the fight can't end until one, or both, are dead.

I'm staring at the exit when Renee taps my arm and leads me to a ring.

"Stay focused," Renee says. "Capra is tough, but she's not Dara."

Dara climbs into another ring and nods to Capra, a sandy-blonde member of Dara's group. Though smaller than Dara, she's big and boisterous: "I'll bury you."

Her warrior-trainer restrains her, while pushing her into the ring.

"It's Dara's style," Renee whispers. "It only works if you let it."

I feel no animosity toward Capra, though she wants to show everyone she can pound me.

I enter the ring, stretch, and adopt a stance like Sam did with Dara. Capra glares at me until Sam signals to begin. Capra charges across the ring. Before she can hit me, I drop down and thrust my right fist up into her ribcage. I hear an "oof." She hits the ropes and bounces back swinging.

She hits my right arm with a paralyzing jab. She swings at my face. I explode at her like I did at Janine. I deliver a coordinated triple thrust: a chop to the neck, a fist to the face, and my right foot to her knee. She blocks both hands. I hit her knee hard. She goes down howling.

I feel bad until she gets back on her feet, or rather foot, and hobbles toward me. When deprived of weapons, find more. *Thanks, Sam.* What should have been my victory has Capra coming back for more.

She launches a barrage of boxing punches I've seen Dara use. I fall back. *Think. What else can I use?*

Hobbling toward me, Capra attacks again. Not wanting to injure her, I favor her bad leg. I block a blow to my jaw. She hits me hard on my left shoulder. *I can't take much more.* When she comes at me again, I fall back into the corner. With nowhere to go, I jump, grab the padded steel post and kick both legs into Capra's gut. This launches her across the platform onto her butt.

She gets up on one foot and hobbles toward me. *She's a surrogate for a Dara. If I can't handle her, then Dara has me.* Capra charges. I block her punches. She launches her injured foot toward my knee. I grab her foot, rotate and drop. Screaming, Capra pounds my back as we crash to the platform. When I get up, she doesn't.

Sam calls the fight. *I'm so sorry.*

When I stand back for the stretcher to take Capra, I glance at Dara. She pauses her fight to scowl. The once cute brunette across from her is a mess. When she refuses to go down, Dara delivers punishing blows until the brunette drops her arms in defeat. Sam stops their fight.

There's evil in Dara, a thug who enjoys beating on girls. I see it in her grin.

When I climb out of the ring, Brandy, Margarite and Vivian surround me.

Margarite pats my arm. "Good job."

Rubbing my sore shoulder, I watch Hannah in the ring with a tall, slender Hispanic girl who is getting the worst of the match. Tara prepares for her own fight. At least we didn't lose anyone to Dara. *Yet.*

When the fights end, I've held my own against one of Dara's posse. Brandy and Margarite didn't fare so well and had to be carried out on stretchers. We gather in the infirmary, where Sam provides us those troubling IVs. I don't see the nurse. Then we hobble to the lobby and freedom.

It's Friday. I don't want to see the mech base until Monday.

Looking less boisterous, Capra greets me in the courtyard and offers her hand. "No hard feelings, I hope. You did better than I expected. Two more washed out today."

"How's the knee?"

"Sam says it'll mend by Monday. I'd be proud to serve with you."

Where did that come from? I wonder what Dara and others are saying about me.

Butting in, Dara places her arm around my shoulder. "You deserve a party to beat all."

I remove her arm. "I am beat."

"I've got my money on you," Dara whispers.

She kisses my cheek, which twists my anger in several directions.

"Come on," she says. "Everyone's partying tonight. If you don't show, you'll be missed."

I doubt that. "I want to check some restaurant locations," I lie.

"Then we'll do that and meet the others later. I've got some thoughts."

Even though I'll probably regret it, I agree. There's no way to pull off the restaurant idea without help.

* * *

While the others head to the party, Dara, Margarite, Brandy and I take our cycles downtown. I can't tell if the others are just humoring me, particularly Dara, whose Dr. Jekyll and Ms. Hyde behavior has me on guard.

I drive through the Kingston/Northshore area to find vacant stores. When I pull up to a stop, Dara pulls up next to me.

Shaking her head, she asks, "What are you thinking?"

"We need to rent a vacant building near bus stops for traffic."

Brandy joins us, pointing. "There's one up the street."

"This won't work," Dara says. "Look at Union Burgers over there. They're empty, even though they're next to the bus stop. People should be eating out now that it's evening, but they're not."

"What do you suggest?" I ask.

Dara grins. *Another little victory.* "Something downtown near the university. We'll get lunch traffic, some breakfast, and plenty of dinner traffic."

While Brandy and Margarite start off toward downtown, Dara grabs my arm. Ugh, too much touching. "You wouldn't happen to know what happened to that boy we caught, would you?"

I pull my arm away. "What boy?"

"Last Friday we caught two boys. One escaped around the time you left."

My eyes narrow, and then I recall Brad. "What would I do with a boy?"

"Just answer the question."

Brandy and Margarite stop and turn around.

"I have no idea what you're talking about," I say. "I've never been with a boy."

Dara studies me. I'm not sure she's buying this.

"Someone helped those boys escape," she says. "I was interrogating one. He couldn't tell me much. When we went back for the other one, he was gone."

I try to mask my fear. Dara's trying to find Mom. "What did you learn?"

"Only that some traitorous bitch was involved."

"And where are the boys?"

"I told you. One escaped. The other—well, he's not talking."

I'm glad I helped Brad. Did he get away?

When Margarite returns, Dara grins and burns rubber, heading downtown. She leads the way to the Cumberland/Henley area. I spot an empty sub shop on the corner with windows soaped so we can't see in. There's a Tenn-tucky Bistro across the street, the campus is down a ways, and there's a bus stop nearby.

"This is what I'm talking about," Dara says.

I nod, and snap a picture with my wrist-com, including the number listed in the window. "Okay, we have the place. Brandy, did you create a menu?"

She hands me crinkled pages. Most of what she wrote I'd find at the bistro across the street. I shake my head. "We can't draw customers this way."

Brandy brushes auburn hair from her face. "We could use chili peppers. That's not on the banned list. I checked."

"I thought we wanted Italian."

"What does that mean when we can't use garlic, salt, or sauce additives?"

"We can use olive oils," I say. "There has to be something other than chili."

"There's been talk of banning that as well."

I look at Dara. "What do you think?"

The amazon brightens up and takes charge. "We use small quantities of garlic and other spices. Just enough so customers sense something delightful and come back, without being able to identify what. We could use dopamine stimulators."

"You mean get our customers addicted?" I say.

"It could work."

"And land us in prison."

Dara throws up her hands. "I'm just saying."

"I want to do this," I say.

Brandy sidles next to me. "I'm in."

Margarite looks skeptical. Dara shakes my hand. "Let's do it."

"We have to contact the landlord and arrange a meeting with the food and zoning commission."

"I'm one step ahead of you," Dara says. "We have a meeting with the commission at three next Friday. We need to provide them location, menu, and ambiance."

"Really." This is the best news I've had all week. "I'll be ready." I could bring Janine into the business and keep her out of mechs. Then I could imagine helping Mom on the side with escaped boys, maybe even find Morgan.

"Let's celebrate." Dara starts to pull away. "Come on, the party won't wait all night."

It would for you. I don't want to spend the evening with Dara, but if I want my restaurant, I have to humor her. Besides, I need to know if she's on Mom's trail. "OK," I tell her.

When we reach Farragut, Dara stops and opens a canvas bag strapped to her cycle.

I pull up next to her and spot dark clouds moving in from the west, another thunderstorm. "What now?"

Margarite hangs back. She's along for whatever ride Dara has in mind. Brandy pulls up close.

Dara hands me and Brandy pink flat squares. "Put these patches over the implant behind your ear. It'll shield the GPS so Sam can't track us." She applies a pink patch behind her ear.

I do likewise. "What about the other implant?"

"That's a contraceptive. Don't worry about it. Let's go."

When we reach the plantation house with its ornate pillars, mech-provided electric cycles litter the front drive. I count 35. Inside the palatial hall a strong, energetic beat plays in the background. I don't see any of Dara's basketball crowd, only mech recruits. *She has moved on.* While I'm sure Sam wouldn't like this, I can't imagine her tossing us all out. Then she couldn't have her precious televised semi-annual tournaments and mech finals.

While Dara goes to greet sister recruits and make a little speech to show she's in charge, sweet little Brandy pulls me aside. "I'm not into drinking, so whenever you want to leave, grab me."

I smile. A girl after my own heart. "Let's mingle. Then we'll go. Say in forty-five."

I figure she'll mingle, but she stays close. I refuse the drinks several recruits pass around and join freckle-faced Hannah with her dark chocolate hair. She beams with confidence over today's fight. I imagine Dara bloodying her.

"What happened to those boys Dara caught last week?" I ask.

Hannah shakes her head. "Lucky one got away. I didn't see the one she took into the cellar, but I heard enough screams to keep me up that night and the next. Something's seriously wrong with that girl. She takes too much pleasure in hurting people. I'm thinking of dropping out."

"Don't be too hasty," I say. "Some of us would miss you."

"Thanks." Hannah downs a caramel liquid and heads for the bar.

Across the way, Capra limps toward the bar. Her knee will take time to heal even with Sam's meds. Meanwhile, other recruits will attack her injury in a fight. How do we bond as sister warriors when we're expected to exploit each others' weaknesses? It makes no sense.

I get a glass of water from the bar and hand one to Brandy, who smiles in appreciation.

Nearby, stocky Vivian swigs clear alcohol and turns to me. "Pity the final isn't shooting."

"Why?" I ask over the beat of thumping music.

"You're kidding me? You hit the bulls-eye each time."

I drop my water glass and stare at her. "What are you talking about? I missed the targets."

"They're electronically scored. You hit the black center each time."

No way. I have no training except cop video games. "Are you pulling my leg?"

"You really don't know?"

I shake my head. Good to know I have something to offer, though with weapons like machine pellets, accuracy isn't required. "You don't have to worry about me in the finals."

"Don't count yourself out," Vivian says. "I hear Renee has money on you."

"First, she shouldn't play favorites. Second, Hannah's the toughest in our group."

Hannah butts in. "We'll find out soon enough." She grabs a drink and leaves.

And competition is supposed to make us bond.

"Don't mind her," Vivian says. "She's still riding high from today. You did well."

I excuse myself to talk to Capra. She limps to a dusty sofa and slumps down.

"I'm sorry about the knee," I say.

"I'll heal."

"It stinks that we're expected to beat up on each other."

Capra looks at me with sad, dark eyes. "Dara wanted me to destroy you today. I'm sorry. She likes you, but she doesn't want to face you in the tournament."

"Why not? I have no skills she can't overwhelm."

"Something's driving you," Capra says. "When you fought Dara, you should have gone down. She had you. Yet you rose up like Sam says. You found something more to throw at her. You're a natural."

I don't know what to say. I'm anything but a natural. I don't belong here. I'm a pussycat, not a fighter, despite feeling rebellious most of the time. "I want to make it into mechs, and I know we have to be tough, but why can't Sam train us without making us destroy each other?"

Capra frowns. "That kind of fighting is sport. She wants us to realize this is for real. Lives depend on our performance."

"Have Sam look at that knee and give you a support brace. Every girl here will use it against you."

"I know. You've caused me to doubt. I suppose even that's good. I was convinced I could take you."

I smile and notice Rox hovering over Brandy, who looks miserable. I join them. "You put up a good fight."

"What would you know?" Rox slurs her words and takes another drink of clear liquid.

"I've lost to Dara several times."

"Losing counts for shit." She wraps her arm around Brandy, who winces.

I take Brandy's hand. "Let's dance."

She practically chases me to the middle of the room where several other girls dance to a lively tune. "Thanks," she whispers. "I want to be left alone. Not by you, of course."

"Ready to leave?"

She nods.

I dance and lead her toward the exit.

Dara intercepts us. "Leaving so soon?"

"I promised Janine and Mom I'd take them out tonight." It's a lie I'd welcome doing.

"And you?" Dara glares at Brandy.

"I'm sick to my stomach and would prefer not to drive back alone."

Dara looks skeptical.

TWENTY-ONE

With Brandy beside me, I ride away from the plantation, wondering if I'll bump into Brad or Morgan. I hope they've gotten far away from Dara. I ride with Brandy as far as Farragut, then text Janine to find out if she's at work. Unable to reach her, I call Brooks.

"She left an hour ago," Brooks tells me. "Everything okay?"

"I wanted to give her a lift."

When I pull into our garage, Mom's car is gone. This emptiness tugs at me. Now I am worried. Is she looking for Janine, or helping boys escape? While I'm proud of what she does, I worry they'll take her, or Dara will grab her.

I enter the great room, hoping to find Janine at least. Mama Grace drops a tray in the kitchen to grab me. She pulls me into Mom's office, a first. I smile and wave to Mama Helen on the way. Therese ignores me and gathers three sisters to head upstairs, where Sara must be. I hope I'll find Janine in our room.

Mama Grace closes the door, her plump face pulled taut. "Cora hasn't come home all week and now Janine's late."

"She had to work." Has Mama Grace guessed what Mom's doing? Mom said never to mention these things, even to the other moms.

Mama Grace fidgets with the back of a worn vinyl chair. "You're probably right, but it's not like Janine to stay out late and not call. She's always been good. Now she's quit basketball. She goes to parties. I mean, it's okay when you're with her."

You wouldn't think so if you knew how Janine spent last weekend.

"I thought Janine was with you, Belle. I expected Cora when you came in."

I hug Mama Grace to calm her worries. I'm amazed at how much love she has, as if it could grow a thousand-fold with a larger family. I wouldn't wish that responsibility on her, though. It makes me doubt I'll ever have kids and put them through what I've seen.

"Don't worry, Mama Grace, I'm sure we got our signals crossed. I didn't get to the station until after she left. We were going to meet for dinner." I'm surprised at how the lies roll off my tongue. "I'll find her and let you know our plans."

"You're not spending another weekend at that wretched base, are you?"

"I have much to learn, and Janine likes to watch." And participate.

On my way out, I wave to Mama Helen. Therese eyes me like my social disease will spread while guarding the stairs lest I decide to go up.

Back on my cycle, I race toward the base, praying Janine is there, since she doesn't answer text or call. I slow during the last mile up the base road and see that cop waiting. I smile and keep going. *Not tonight.*

The petite guard waves me through the gate to the base. I park my cycle and hurry through the dark lobby and down dimly lit corridors. Most of the base personnel have left. The infirmary is dark. Most of the girls, even injured ones like Rox and Capra, are at the party.

When I enter the gym and turn on lights, I hear weeping. The sobs sound like Janine's. I scour the gym. The weights are in the far corner, near the entrance to the mech-suit gym. Four fight rings line one wall, bleachers the other. I don't see her.

I stop, listen, and follow the sound to the bleachers. I still don't see her until I climb behind, and find her cowering like a mouse in the corner.

"What in the world are you doing in there?"

Brown hair covers her eyes. "Something's wrong with Mom, and no one will tell me."

So that's what got Mama Grace so upset. I don't know what to say that won't make things worse.

I get as close as I can without climbing under the cramped bleachers. "I'm here, Babe. Why didn't you answer texts or calls?"

Janine brushes her hair aside. Tears glisten in her eyes. "I'm losing my family, Belle. Mom stopped coming home and you're joining mechs."

"Please come out. I need to get you home. Mama Grace is worried sick."

"I know. Call her and tell her I'm with you. Then teach me what you've learned this week."

"Janine?" Of all the things she's worried about, why this? "I can't. I banged you up last weekend. I don't want to fight you."

"Don't you want me to learn to protect myself?"

"I'll teach you to defend yourself, but not mech training. It's too brutal."

"If you won't teach me, I'll find that party I'm not supposed to know about. Dara will train me."

"Don't you dare."

"Then it's settled. I'm spending the weekend with you." She crawls out from under the bleachers and gives me a hug.

I hold her tight. I can't stand to see her afraid. She's my "Babe," my baby sister.

* * *

I take Janine toward the small suite off the gym to get her cleaned up. The door behind me slams.

"I thought I heard you." Sam marches up to us with a sly grin. "I almost called when Janine showed up, but I figured you were having too much fun at that illegal party." Sam reaches behind my ear and rips the patch off, along with a clump of hair.

I wince, shrink back, and stare at the concrete floor.

"Don't imagine I haven't thought of all the tricks." Sam winks at Janine, who looks worried for me. "At least you didn't speed. That cop almost pulled over the cab Janine took."

I look up. "I'm sorry, Commander. You said recruits should bond." *Do you have any life outside the mechs and keeping tabs on us?*

"Then you've learned something. While you and your sister are welcome to spend the weekend, why don't you go home and spend it with your family?"

I straighten up. "I can't afford to wash out, Commander." I lower my voice. "I'm struggling." And worried about Mom. I don't

160

want to be the cause of her getting caught like my birth mother. Besides, I've been thinking of what prison information Sam might have access to, if I can figure out how to get to her files.

Sam turns to Janine. "Since you're back, I presume you agree to undergo rigorous training."

"I do, Commander." Janine squeezes my hand: don't fuss.

"Training begins at eight." Sam turns to me. "Janine will train with you only while there are no other recruits."

No! Vulture. Did you overhear me tell Janine I'd train her?

Sam leaves. I take Janine into the suite. Lying next to her in the double bed, I consider all the reasons for taking her home.

"I don't want you signing the release, Babe. This place is brutal."

"I'm sorry, Belle. I've made up my mind. I know you won't really hurt me."

"But that's part of the training. Sam encourages us not to give up no matter what. I watched Dara beat up a tough girl who wouldn't yield. Sam finally stopped the fight when this girl couldn't lift her arms to defend herself. I busted a girl's leg because she got the better of me. I didn't know what else to do."

Janine smiles like when she used to beg me to take her down to the river. "I'm sure Sam has a purpose."

"I'm not sure that's a good thing. She creates trained killers. I don't want that."

"Then quit, and I won't bring it up again."

Now I've gone and done it. I've let Janine know my reservations. Next she'll want to know why. "Get some sleep, Babe. Training is exhausting."

* * *

In the morning, over my objections, Janine signs the release. I don't think it's legal to have a 15-year-old sign, but when I call Mom, she's not available.

"Don't do this, Janine. Mom will be angry."

"Did you sign?" she asks, her pretty face all pinched.

Janine is radiant when Sam leads us into the virtual reality lab. It's as if this is the greatest toy imaginable. And except for getting banged up, I guess it is.

"Can I review Annabelle's fights?" Janine asks Sam.

"Janine, don't," I say.

"Stop babying me."

161

Knowing she can't get hurt in VR, I relent. After all, if she sees how bloodied I was, it might put her off joining.

While Sam lets Janine experience my fights, I review those of my competitors. It's time I become familiar with what I'm up against so I don't get surprised like I did with Capra. After reviewing the members of Dara's training group, I view other members of her posse, and other recruits. I notice moves I haven't tried and file those away for simulator training.

On a good day I could handle maybe nine of the girls, yet I recall what Capra said about believing she could take me. *Don't get cocky.* There are a dozen like Dara and Rox who can take me every time. Reviewing Capra's fights, I realize how lucky I was. Her overconfidence cost her. No surprise, Dara is the strongest fighter.

I pull up haptic memory of her fight with Rox. The black girl had great form at first and got in solid punches and kicks that would have sliced me up. Then Dara exploded in a dozen swift, powerful moves. Rox fell back, unable to get her blocks up in time. Dara kept attacking. Tiring, Rox no longer did. Yet instead of surrendering, she stood and let Dara use her like a punching bag until she collapsed.

When the three of us break for lunch in a small cafeteria, I have mixed feelings about Sam. She's the vulture plucking Janine, yet she also spent her morning training us. "What's the value in injuring each other when we should be coming together? And now our partners are injured."

Sam sets turkey sandwiches on the table, sighs, and turns to Janine. "What do you think?"

Janine picks up her sandwich and puts it back down. "I agree with Annabelle. In basketball practice, I would never injure someone I rely on."

Sam sits across from us. "I'd prefer none of you get injured. However, my mission is to save lives." Sam looks at me. "Tell me what you've learned this week. It'll be good for Janine to hear."

"Reach deep and never give up. But if neither side gives up, someone gets injured or dies."

"True, but in combat you'll face tough opponents who won't give up."

"So you weed out the weak and injured." *Like me.*

"It's unfortunate." Sam manages to take bites between talking. "Ask yourself: in combat, wouldn't you like to know the best are

162

next to you, prepared to face whatever comes at you?"

"I guess."

"No guesswork. You know this. Capra congratulated you today because now she respects you. She didn't before. Her knee will heal. I now have two stronger recruits, you because you stood up to her, and her because she knows she can't do this alone. Dara still thinks she can. She might not be there for sister warriors."

I'm amazed at how candid Sam is, given how tight-lipped Voss has been. "I'll do my best in the tournament, Commander, knowing that if I lose I'm not disqualified."

"Is that a question?"

"I know you accept more than one recruit every six months."

Sam laughs. "You want to ask about the arena tests."

"Why does the final have to be to the death?"

"Combat imperative. When faced with a brutal enemy, you either kill or get killed. I don't relish losing a single warrior."

"But—"

"Number Two Grunt, every girl in the program is concerned about the arena, petrified even, with the exception of Dara. It's part of the test for you to come to grips with your fears. I won't have warriors who relish killing. That goes against our values. On the other hand, I can't have warriors who hesitate when duty calls."

"I know. That costs lives," I say.

"We monitor you well. You may suffer serious injuries, for which I'm sorry. But during training, few are life-threatening."

"I understand, Commander. I wish there was another way."

Janine devours her sandwich, her eyes following the conversation.

Sam nods. "I've wrestled with this for 17 years. I didn't settle on this program without much teeth-gnashing. What you suffer from is failure of imagination. You'll never be better than you imagine for yourself. If you think small, you'll stay small. Imagine bigger. If mechs isn't right for you, that's okay. Either way, don't limit your thinking."

You mean like the Union does, telling me I'm stuck with security?

"Let me show you something." Not waiting for a response, Sam leads us out of the cafeteria.

I bring my sandwich and a glass of water, and eat while I walk, trying to keep up with Janine. Sam leads us past a locked door off the lobby, and down a long khaki corridor identical to the others. Using retinal scans, voice recognition, and fingerprint, Sam unlocks a steel door into a large room lined with electronics. "This is the command center."

The middle of the room is filled with 100 uncomfortable wood seats like those used for the tutorial. Janine's attention flows to dozens of screens along two walls showing Knoxville and rural scenes.

Sam continues, "This is one of several control facilities that can be self-contained if we come under attack. What you see displayed are roving images of the border, no-man's-land, and certain locations on this and the other side of the border."

While I eat and watch, Sam moves to a large screen. "This tracks recruits. As you see, thirty are still partying southwest of Knoxville."

I'm fixated on the screen. Is there anything Sam can't track? Suddenly I'm glad I didn't go looking for Mom. I might have gotten her killed or imprisoned.

Janine scans other screens. "What about the boys from Michael's School? Since they wear collars, can't you track them?"

"I don't want to give away all our secrets, but someone provided effective shields. Twenty-eight boys disappeared off the grid. That's how we know they had help. We'll find them. There are few places boys can hide. If they make for the border, we'll grab them."

Sam points to another screen. "Here we track the boys at Michael's School and those who escaped and didn't mask their tracking chips. We've caught all but three of them."

Sam uses a laser pointer to show where those boys are. The signal fades on one, another, then the third. Sam drops into a seat before a console, a virtual screen where she moves icons to recover the signals. *Way to go, Mom. Best get moving. Is Morgan with you?*

While Sam tries to find the missing boys, I finish my turkey sandwich, moist and flavorful. Must be real turkey. I put the plate down by a coffee machine. "Is this real?"

When Sam doesn't answer, I move to monitors of the Outland. The only images I've seen of the forbidden lands were Union-approved boogie-man stories to scare me into obeying the law. Some showed kidnapped girls dragged away. Others had Outlanders attacking innocent civilians before they retreated into the Outland. Newsreels end with mech troops saving the day.

Janine looks over my shoulder and absorbs all this like she does at school. "It's desolate out there."

And peaceful. I nod.

A half-mile-wide clearing created with the help of mechs surrounds the Outland so we can monitor border crossings. I don't see a soul. Before the war, the Great Smoky Mountains were a national park, a beauty we no longer can visit, except as mechs.

"This is a lot of equipment." Janine admires a dozen work stations along one wall crammed with electronics.

"It's a big responsibility watching the border," I say. *And millions of males still in the Union.* I pray Mom gets away. I need to distract Sam before she gets too clever.

I approach Sam. "Can you take us to the simulator so we can train?"

Sam moves icons onscreen. All I can tell is that she's trying to zero in on Mom and Morgan.

Sam doesn't look up. "Give me a minute. I'm checking surveillance around where the boys disappeared."

"I thought we didn't use surveillance on citizens, only on collared people."

"Usually we don't."

I watch Sam scan street by street. "But you've got street and building cams all over?"

"Un-huh."

"Do you have surveillance inside buildings? I mean, what happens if they go into a bank?"

"We cover public buildings, bus and train stations, and banks because of robbery risks."

I can't get Sam to look up or slow her scan of street views. "Do you have cams inside where Dara has her party?"

"No, but maybe I should. Look, I need to concentrate."

"I'm curious. When I become a mech, will I be using this equipment to help you find people?" I'm powerless again to keep them from taking my mom.

"Annabelle, give me a few minutes?" It's the first time Sam has used my first name since I entered the program.

Think, Annabelle. "Uh, Janine and I could help." I clutch my glass of water. "We have eyes if you tell us what to look for."

That brings Janine over like an overeager puppy. "Can we? That would be maxi-grand. I've always wanted to catch the bad guys. It would be just like on the videos. It would mean so much to me."

Sam looks up. "I appreciate your enthusiasm, but I have business to conduct. I don't think this is a malfunction."

Mom's image flashes onscreen. I drop my drinking glass. Water splashes across the electronic tabletop. The glass tumbles to the concrete floor without shattering. It's probably some polymer.

"I'm so sorry, Commander. I'm a klutz." I pick up the glass and grab Janine's wrist. *Think fast.* "Sam's right. Let's wander over to simulation and get some practice."

Blood thunders in my ears. I ignore Janine's pouty face and push her toward the door.

Sam joins us. "I can't have you wandering through this section. Come on." She sighs. "I'll take you over."

Janine looks up at me, puzzled. *Time to distract her.* "So this is where your office is, Commander," I say, fishing.

"Too noisy. I'm down the next corridor."

Good to know. We pass it on the way to the simulators. *Now how do I get back here and past security when Sam monitors everything?*

I pray Mom's image is too fuzzy for Sam to recognize. I don't think Janine saw, but who else is watching? *Oh, Mom, don't let them take you.*

TWENTY-TWO

By the time we reach the simulator room, my stomach threatens to bring up that turkey sandwich. *What have you done, Mom? I can't lose you, too.* I shield my face from Sam as she turns us over to Camilla, the ruddy-faced warrior-tech who is recalibrating the simulators.

After Sam leaves, Janine whispers, "You look like you've seen a ghost."

I give her my can't-talk look, which leaves worry-lines spreading across her forehead. Not as worried as I am. Mom says I need to think of the consequences before I act. *I get it, Mom.*

I climb into a simulator and take comfort in the foam that engulfs me. "Put us both into martial arts training, Janine on level one, me on five."

"Are you sure?" the technician asks.

"Janine isn't ready for level two," I say.

"I mean you."

"Level five, Camilla, please." I tremble so hard I'm glad I'm enclosed in the simulator so she can't see.

"Your pulse and blood pressure are off the chart. I should—"

"Camilla, put me into level five."

The program fires up. The machine pushes my body to kick, thrust, and dodge every which way. Fighting to keep lunch down, I dig into rigorous exercise to overwhelm my feelings of helplessness and loss, of my world turned upside down. Toxins build in my bloodstream as muscles reach exhaustion and act spastic.

The session ends. The panel opens. Camilla stands there, her ruddy face taut. "Blood pressure's down, but your pulse is racing. And we have to get you hydrated."

That means another IV and more of Sam's meds. I don't protest when Camilla and Janine help me to the infirmary. After Camilla sets up the IV, she leaves.

Janine holds my free hand tight. "Talk to me."

Looking away, I shake my head. All I see are consequences. I helped Morgan and brought him home. I got Mom involved. Now Sam's hunting them.

Janine moves the IV, and sits on my lap. "Belle, you're scaring me."

"Just cramps."

"Don't give me that. Did you see that boy from Michael's?"

I have to give her something. "This feels like a prison camp. Sam watches everything we do. How did we get like this?"

"We give up some freedoms to protect what we need." The Federal Union party line.

"I'm okay, sis. I just found it overwhelming. Then I overdid it."

"I'll say. The tech said you were on the verge of a heart attack. Belle, don't you dare do that to me."

I hold Janine and get an idea. When Camilla returns, I ask, "Can we explore the mech suit com-link without the suit?"

"Sure." Camilla checks my vitals and removes the IV. Then she leads us out of the infirmary and down the hall.

I struggle to keep up. "Can we get a private channel for Janine and me?"

"You mean unmonitored?" Camilla asks.

"And not recorded?"

"Sure, why?"

"She's my sister, and I want a private moment with her."

"Ah." The husky tech smiles and leads us into a small room with two sound enclosures. "First we need to give Janine the auditory implant. Is that okay?"

Janine nods, with excitement that disturbs me.

Camilla gives Janine the injection behind her ear and attaches the com-link helmet, similar to mech suits, but lighter. I attach my own and enter my sound room.

After the tech leaves, Janine whispers. It's like in our room at night, except I can't feel her breath on my ear. "Now will you tell me what's troubling you?"

It's strange to have her thoughts bypass my eardrum and penetrate my skull like telepathy. I don't so much hear her words as think them myself. It makes me wonder if Sam can root around in my brain. I have to believe she's monitoring this conversation.

"Watching the surveillance got me thinking of every time I cut school or went down by the river or off to the woods. It's creepy to think someone watches everything I do." I vocalize these thoughts and hope this will satisfy Janine.

"Then I have good reason to worry when you do."

I savor Janine's thoughts inside me. It's a deeper connection with her.

"I like this as well," Janine says.

But I didn't say anything. I try to block my thoughts. Have I accidentally shared thoughts with my mech team? I'll have to watch that. I project an idea: If you hear me, say 17.

"Seventeen. Of course I hear you. We're linked."

She's far too casual about this. Her facility with technology amazes me. *Janine, I didn't vocalize 17. This link allows us to share thoughts. I think we can block some and project others, not sure how.*

"Fascinating," Janine projects. "Thanks for sharing, but I need you to tell me what's wrong."

I sense the difference when I receive her thoughts as opposed to her spoken words. I try to decide how to calm her without revealing too much.

"I feel crushing pain, Belle. How can I help?" Internal thoughts.

Just by being here. I sense her blood pressure drop and calmness return to her thoughts. This intimacy reminds me of twins I once knew. Reading Janine's thoughts, I feel for the first time that I'm not alone; feel it deep within my chest.

"I feel the same," Janine thinks. "I wish we could do this all the time."

So do I, but I'm convinced Sam is monitoring us. We continue in this vein for a long time, savoring the bond as much as the thoughts. When I sever the link, the tech returns, which confirms that we weren't alone. Now what can I do for Mom?

"Sam will meet you for dinner," Camilla says, showing us out.

* * *

I sit across from Sam and hold my trembling hands beneath the table. I'm starved, but it doesn't look like I'll be eating. "Did you catch those boys?" I smile, widening my eyes.

Sam scowls. "We're after something more cunning than boys."

"What?" Janine scoops up a spoonful of thick chicken stew.

"The Underground Railroad, modeled after the one during the first Civil War. They traffic in moving males over the border. They've been dormant for a year. Now they're using sophisticated techniques to circumvent our surveillance."

"You won't let them get away, will you?" Janine looks worried, for all the wrong reasons.

"Not if I can help it." This doesn't sound like the same confident Sam who faced off against Dara. It gives me hope.

"If I were a mech—"

I stomp on Janine's foot, expecting her to yell. She doesn't.

Instead, she turns to me. "But I haven't even been admitted to the training program."

"Eat up." Sam gazes at me. "Trust me; it tastes better than what you'll get in town."

I keep my hands from trembling long enough to get a bite. It's quite tasty, salt and something that tingles my taste buds. This wasn't available during the week. Only the best for mech warriors who put their lives on the line. Is this another fringe benefit? Ah, goodies for the privileged few. My hands shake.

"You okay?" Sam asks.

I nod. I'm so self-conscious, I can't eat. "I overdid it in the simulator."

"So I hear."

"Did you learn anything from our com-link session?"

Sam's eyes narrow. "You asked for a private session. Those aren't monitored or recorded. We use them when we have two recruits or warriors with difficulty communicating."

I'm still not convinced.

"Did it work for you?" Sam asks.

"It was terrific," Janine says.

I bump her leg: *say no more.* Wish we had thought-sharing now. I'm playing a cat and mouse game with Sam. I'm the mouse, and Janine's what? I'm afraid to think—the bait?

After dinner, I take Janine to the VR room and have Camilla set us up to review fights. I let Janine experience the same arena fights I do with sensory detail, in a vain hope it will discourage her. I'm shocked by the intensity. Unlike broadcast and promo videos, VR puts us into the fight. These warriors-to-be are so well trained, I'm not sure even Dara could defeat them.

They face huge muscle-men on steroids trained to kill, and whose only salvation is to win, at least for the day. Even though I'm not in the arena, I feel the terror. I hope this gives Janine second thoughts. It's so intense I'm surprised most of the girls win.

When a brute charges toward me like a bull, I break the connection. I've had enough. I crawl out of the VR booth to find Janine going strong. She grunts as she imagines herself in the fight. Camilla stands by a screen and monitors the session. "Blood pressure is strong. Pulse is racing as expected."

I watch the brute grab the recruit, Janine, and throw her onto her back. She refuses to cave as the brute crushes her throat. Feeling ill, I terminate Janine's session. Not all the girls win. Trust Janine to get one who doesn't. That should change her mind.

Janine's pretty face is ashen when I pull her from the VR booth. She falls into my arms, whimpering, trembling, and looks up at me with flooded eyes. "You don't have to do this."

I do, unless I get my restaurant.

* * *

Janine and I train on Sunday, and then we both go home. I have to get away from the base before another tough week, and she needs to get her head back into school. I park my cycle in the garage next to Mom's car and sigh in relief. Janine dismounts and rushes into the great room. By the time I enter, Janine is in hysterics, with Mama Grace and Mama Helen holding her. *Mom?*

Mama Grace takes me in her chubby arms before I can reach Mom's office. "She's okay. She's resting. Don't disturb her."

I don't see any sisters downstairs, not even Sarah, who often reads in the corner with Helen.

"The girls are in their rooms," Mama Helen says. "We've had a scare, what with all those boys loose. Best you two go to your room for the night."

Though I need a week's worth of rest, I have to see Mom. Not with Janine. I lead my sister upstairs, trying to act calm. "I'm sure she's fine. You can talk to her in the morning."

When we reach our bedroom, Sarah is sitting on her bed, reading her touch-screen. "Why do we have to stay in our rooms?"

I give Sarah a hug. "We're home now, kiddo. You're safe."

"I want to see Robin and Kelly. It's not fair."

Sarah hasn't thought to sneak down the hall to visit her sisters. She's not rebellious like me. "I'm sure tomorrow will be fine."

Sarah buries her head in her pillow and pretends to have a fit now that she has an audience. Janine jumps into the suite bathroom before I can. I take the opportunity to slip out of the room and down the pastel-flowered hall to Mom's room.

I ease the door open, no squeak, and enter the bedroom, guided only by a nightlight. I climb into bed next to Mom. Once my eyes adjust, I study her weathered face. I don't see any wounds, but then it's too dark to see bruising. I've imagined Mom in a fight, or tortured. I can't hold back my tears.

Mom opens her dark eyes. "Belle?"

I feel her warm breath on my cheek and the sour odor of fear.

"I know, Mom. I was in Sam's control room when your image came up."

"Oh, dear. Did Janine see?"

"Mom! That's the least of your worries. I can't lose you. I can't. And neither can she. I know your work is important, but you must stop. Promise me."

"I'm sorry, Belle. It's getting harder."

"I shouldn't have brought Morgan home. I didn't know what else to do."

Mom strokes my face. "You did fine, Belle. Morgan's a good boy, smart, with lots of heart. Reminds me a bit of George."

"Me, too, Mom."

"Before you brought him, I was trying to connect with him. He'd put out feelers that he had a way to get boys out of that school."

"You're kidding, Mom. Seriously?"

Mom smiles. "Of all the boys you could have brought, of all the places you could have brought him, you brought him here. I was upset because I never wanted you involved."

"Involved, Mom. If I lose you I'll declare war on the Federal Union. I swear."

"Promise me you won't. Janine and Sarah need you."

"Then stop," I say. "You've done enough."

"I can't, Belle. When I see injustice I have to act. No one else will."

"I know. I'm so proud of you, but I've already lost one mom.

They have your image. Even though it's fuzzy, if they post, someone will recognize you."

"There's nothing more I can do right now. The boys are safe for the moment."

"Where's Morgan?" I ask.

"Best you don't know. He told me again to thank you."

I sigh. What would it be like to hold him? Then I tell Mom about Brad. "He was with Morgan and mentioned a woman. I assume it was you. I pray they can't identify you."

Mom nods. "We caught up with him, but his friend didn't make it."

"I know." I take a deep breath. "Being in mechs, they expect me to help catch boys, not to free them."

"Go to Janine before she suspects."

TWENTY-THREE

This week's training is more intense. Even after the weekend practice of VR and the simulator, I struggle. Then comes Friday, two fights each. In my first, Sam matches me against Tara from my training group. When I stand across from her in the ring, all I see is her crooked nose. She refuses to talk about how she got it. *Did a bully like Dara abuse you?* The slender brunette dances toward me. *I don't want to break that nose again.*

Tara attacks, using a barrage of chops, pokes, kicks and punches. I block, get a few blows into her stomach, and block some more. I avoid her nose.

Sam watches our fight. "Focus on the eyes. Use them to help you anticipate moves. Then channel your opponent's energy against her." Great advice if you weren't also telling Tara.

My slender opponent comes at me with a barrage of punches and kicks. I think of Capra—*don't break her knee*—and Tara's nose. I like Tara. I don't want to injure her. She lands a combination to my stomach, doubles me over. *This has to end.*

My muscles explode. I hammer her nose from right and left. She blocks, hits back. Horrified, I watch the nose straighten and bend, straighten and bend as if someone else is doing this. She drops to the ground and holds her face. What have I done? I was so fixated on her nose that when she pushed me, that's what I hit.

I drop to the bloodstained mat to help her. "I'm so sorry."

"Leave me alone. I'm quitting. Okay. You win."

Two warriors escort Tara away, her hands soaked in blood.

I glare at Sam. *Why are you pushing us like this? Is this necessary?*

Before I can recover, Sam gives me fresh gloves and pushes me into the ring across from Rox, caramel complexion, short black hair and scarred face. Rox has something to prove. At the signal, she attacks with confidence and force. I stare into her eyes, anticipate moves, block, retreat, and look for weaknesses.

I know from VR training that she's a tough fighter, compact, and more versatile than Dara. Rox has muscles and upper body strength I lack. She has endurance to outlast me. Whatever I'm going to do, I have to act before she wears me down. Rox comes at me again, boxing moves, powerful blows that splatter pain over my blocking arms. She can knock me out if she gets a clean punch. I can only retreat so long.

Rox dances toward me, quick on her feet. She throws a one-two-three set of punches. I deflect despite sharp pain up and down my arms. She charges with another combination, the third a power blow. I don't deflect the second hit, take it on the chin with more of a jolt than I expect.

I ram my fist with all the thrust I can muster up beneath her jaw. I connect when she does. My head snaps back, pain splashes my face. I miss her jaw and hit her neck. I feel the crunch of cartilage. My blow throws her back. Rox hits the ropes and crumbles to the mat, holding her neck. Terror and anger fill her eyes as she struggles to her feet and comes at me. It's no longer a one-two-three. She lashes at me in a rhythm like a punching bag. I block, protect my head. Rox slams my stomach. I go down.

When I come to, I'm lying on a bed in the infirmary staring up at bright LED lights, white ceiling, and a worried expression on Sam's face.

"You lost focus, Number Two Grunt."

I groan and will my stomach to stop ripping me apart. I see the reliable IV. Both of my arms are bright red.

"Instead of obsessing on how not to hurt your opponents and playing defense, you need to go on offense. I would have thought you'd have learned that in basketball. You have the skill and drive to do much better. Unless, that is, you're ready to wash out."

I shake my head. *Not until I know Mom is safe.*

"I take that to mean you're not washing out. If that's true, stop lounging about and get your sorry ass out to the gym." Sam removes the IV.

On the way out of the infirmary, I nod to nurse Wells and glance at the digital clock. I've been out for an hour. My stomach is cramping so badly I can hardly walk.

"Stand tall, grunt. Show the others what you're made of."

Mush? As I enter the gym, other recruits wrap up their fights. The welts on my arms begin to fade. I'd love to know what psychotropic drugs Sam's giving me to put up with this. Mechs use what works. Yeah.

After fighters crawl out of the rings, Sam climbs onto a platform and gathers us around. I expect another round of fights, since Sam likes to surprise us. With my luck I'll get Dara so I can end this. Why keep torturing myself? I'm buying time. I check my wrist-com and start to raise my arm, but it hasn't the strength.

"All right, grunts," Sam says. "You've survived another tough week. You think you're ready to be mechs?"

"Hoo-rah."

"You have three more weeks of tough training before the tournament. While the purpose of training is to turn you into effective fighters to protect our society, the tournament and arena are hurdles you face to prove you're ready. Today I want to share that we're creating a new mech unit along the TexSoCal frontier."

No! I signed up so I could stay in Knoxville. I slide behind Dara to keep a low profile.

"Our initial group will consist of five senior veterans, 10 seasoned warriors and 15 new recruits. We'll bestow on you the honor of forming the core of a new unit. I need volunteers. If I don't get them…well, let's just say there be 15 volunteers."

* * *

After Sam lets the others leave, she pulls me into the infirmary.

I sit on a bed with my top off while she inserts another IV. I'm covered in welts and the beginnings of bruises. "This medicine is dangerous, isn't it?"

She nods and examines my wounds. "No more than internal injuries."

"Nano-tech?"

"I can't discuss the particulars. You should be fine by the time you go to bed. Depending on how late you party." She winks.

Now that I know Sam tracks us even with Dara's patches, I should tell my sister recruits. When I reach my cycle, Dara, Margarite, and Brandy are waiting.

Dara mounts her cycle. "Hope you didn't forget our meeting with the zoning board. We ready to do this?"

I get on my cycle. "How did you get Sam to let us out early?"

Pleased that I know it was her, Dara grins. "I told her it would be a good gesture after such a tough week."

I suspect Sam knows about the restaurant, since she knows everything else. After all, she'll track us to the zoning commission.

We ride. I smile, thinking we have location, menus, and friends to support the restaurant. I've even prepared a presentation. Still, the closer we get to downtown, the more anxious I become at meeting the Knoxville Food and Zoning Commission.

The offices are in a dingy brick building across from the state capital. We could walk from here to dinner if we had our restaurant.

Brandy and Margarite sit on a wooden bench in a dark gray hallway outside the zoning office so we don't crowd the official. Dara and I go in and sit across from Zoning Officer Kelly Wong with her thirtyish smiley face. She has posters of President Tatiana Zell and Governor Georgiana Battani on the wall behind her, standing guard over a small window that overlooks the square. Another true believer.

An ancient, shriveled-up gray woman enters the room and sits across from me.

"Excuse me," I say to Kelly Wong. "I thought we were only meeting with you today."

"Henrietta Sharpe is Harmony Administrator over food and entertainment."

I try to shrug it off. This is my chance. Those posters stare back at me. Taking a deep breath, I put up a 3D holographic layout of our reconfigured sub shop that will allow more mingling with comports and videogames. "It will let college students and teens meet and–"

"Drink and do drugs and stir up trouble," the Harmony Administrator says. "I had to shut down three of these last month."

"Being able to mingle and let off steam will be good for harmony." I smile, proud of my quick response.

"Show me your drink list," the Harmony Administrator says.

I display the usual Union-approved bland beverages, and two I want to add. One has a hint of caffeine, though not enough to

177

stimulate the blood; the other has a taste of cherry sweetener.

"I can't approve these. You're underage for alcohol."

"We won't offer alcohol." I look to Dara for support. She just sits.

The Harmony Administrator ignores me and keys into her wrist-com with trembling fingers. "What about food?"

Air drains from my lungs. I display Brandy's food choices. The Harmony Administrator removes everything we added to the Union Burgers & Subs menu.

"There's nothing about those that are disharmonious or injurious to our health," I say.

"Who made you our public welfare expert?" The Harmony Administrator squints at me and taps at her com. "What about music? No retro groups. Nothing that spurs disharmony. No loud music that disturbs neighbors."

I display our choices in a hologram over the table: energetic, spiced-up versions of approved music, no disharmony in the lyrics. I plan more if I get the shop open. "Something to burn off teen energy," I volunteer, "so we can become more harmonic."

"Unacceptable. Elevated music leads to hearing loss and aberrant behavior, raising medical costs and disharmony. I can't allow this."

"What can we offer other than what's at Union Burgers & Subs?"

"I'm not the one who thinks we need a new restaurant." She gives me a smug grin and taps at her com.

Dara remains passive. *What gives?* But it's futile. It's like staring into Dara's eyes in the ring and knowing it's over. Sam would say to dig deep to find something else to fight with. I could say girls go to illegal parties because they have no outlets, but the Harmony Administrator would take me into custody until I told her where they were.

"I want to offer girls variety." I keep my voice level.

The gray Harmony Administrator stands. "Variety leads to inequality. Inequality leads to disharmony." More Union sound-bites.

"Please work with me," I say, fishing for any way to keep this alive. "I'm new at this. I could use your guidance." I smile up at her. "Could you help us develop the right food, drink, and music?"

The old woman shuffles toward the door. "Young lady, my job

isn't to design restaurants. If you want to know what we've approved, go to Union Burgers & Subs or Tenn-tucky Bistro. We monitor them and find them acceptable."

"But girls hunger to try new things."

The ancient woman's eyes narrow into slits. "The Union has need of your services in the mechs. Don't waste our time with girlish nonsense." She slams the door, letting me know this answer is final.

I feel like I do after fights, but without Sam's magic IV.

In the gray hallway, Dara marches ahead with Margarite in tow. Brandy joins me, mirroring the resignation in my face. "I'm sorry. It would have been fun."

I hurry to catch up with Dara while considering what else I could have said or done. In the lobby, I catch a puff of well-coiffed brown hair: Emily Battani. Why is she here? Beside her, the governor looks through me like I'm a speck not worth flicking off her navy blue blazer.

The governor disappears before I can muster the courage to say anything. Good thing. I'd only make it worse for Mom.

When we reach the cycles, I'm fuming.

Dara turns to me. "That was a waste of time."

"Where were you in there?"

"Would it have mattered? Face it. They don't want a legitimate restaurant."

"Meaning?"

"We create an illegal one, but don't expect it to pay. We'll need regular jobs to avoid suspicion."

I don't like Dara's idea, despite its rebellious nature. I want something for Janine that won't get her into trouble. I don't see how to make this work.

Now I'm stuck with mechs on the TexSoCal frontier, or Hollander's Resocialization Facility in Nashville.

* * *

After Dara rides off with Margarite, I turn to Brandy. "I don't want to party tonight."

"Neither do I. You want to grab a tasty Union burger?"

I shake my head. I need to be alone, which is impossible in a crowded communal house. I don't want to wander to my usual spots and give those up to Sam. "Maybe another time."

Brandy smiles. "I can be good company." Her interest is more than friendly, though she's not pushy. "We can go sit somewhere. I can be quiet if you'd like. Let's just get away."

"Not tonight." I don't want to tell her how much pent-up frustration I have when I can't even tell my sister.

We ride until we reach the cop station. Then I wave her on and close my eyes. I'm not ready to see Janine. I need to let go of things I can't tell her first. I'm tempted to take the cycle east and find a way to cross the border into the Outland to look for George.

I wouldn't make it to the border with Sam tracking my movements. First I'd have to dig out the implants, or find someone to do it. Dara might if I tell her Sam uses them to track her. If I did, I could make a run for it, to the Outland or out west.

I'd look for my birth mother at that prison in Oregon. I'd magically break her out. I don't know where we'd go, but somewhere I could be with her and Mom and Janine and Sarah. We'd find George, of course. But the Union is a broad landscape. I wouldn't know where to begin.

Even if I can't find them, I could flee. I wouldn't have to take another day of Voss or Dara. I wouldn't have to turn myself into an animal so I can compete in the tournament and face brutes in the arena. Once I become a mech, they'll expect me to capture my redheaded Morgan.

Opening my eyes, I peel out into the street and head west toward freedom. I get halfway down the block before I realize Janine's arms are tight around my tender stomach. When did she show up? All my fight vanishes. I can't leave her to face Voss and mechs on her own.

When I pull the cycle into the garage and park next to Mom's car, *thank God,* Janine whispers, "They didn't accept your restaurant plan, did they?"

I shake my head, dismount and face her. "How did you know? I wanted it to be a surprise."

Janine hugs me and tucks her chin on my shoulder. "I'm so sorry. You do so much for me. I wasn't going to say anything, but Emily bragged about how her mom would squash it. Then you almost threw me off the back of your cycle."

"I'm sorry, Babe. I'm—"

"Hey. Thanks. You know I hate buses."

So the governor did interfere. Why am I not surprised? "I

thought the restaurant would be a chance for us to work together and not have to fight."

"Come on," Janine says. "Mom's home."

As much as I want to be alone, I'm excited to see Mom. And worried.

Janine goes in first, gets a big hug from Mama Grace, and greets Mama Helen and each of our sisters. She's much better at relationship small-talk than I am. She even softens Therese's smug look. This allows me to make quick greetings and hunt down Mom in her office.

I close the door, turn on harmony music, and wait. Mom looks exhausted and worried, yet thankfully not injured. I've seen enough of that in the past few weeks for a lifetime.

She gives me a hug. "I know you had your heart set on opening a restaurant."

"Does everyone know?"

"I wish you'd said something, Belle. I could have run interference. Instead, the governor killed it before I could intervene. Then she gloated about how we need to root out infections."

I pull away. "It was a stupid idea. I wanted something for Janine and me not to have to do security." I bite back tears.

I realize I'm thinking of becoming a fighter to avoid becoming one. It makes no sense and perfect sense. I have to become a mech for Janine, George, Mom, Morgan, and my birth mother.

Mom dries my cheeks. I've soaked her shoulder.

"Let it out, Belle," she says. "You need to let it all out."

I dry my eyes and look at her. "I know now that I have to commit to mechs. After I become one, I want to help you."

"Promise you won't. Don't push the feds. They can take everything from you, even make you disappear."

"I'm going to help the boys, Mom. Just tell me how."

TWENTY-FOUR

With no acceptable alternative to the mechs and only 11 days until the tournament, I eliminate all distractions and move into the tiny suite off the gym at the mech base. I skip Dara's parties.

Before leaving, I tell Mom, "I won't be home unless victorious or in a casket." She doesn't appreciate my weak attempt at humor.

I spend the weekend training with Janine from seven in the morning until late at night. We use VR to review prior tournament and arena events as well as fights by sister recruits. In simulation, I experiment with every conceivable martial art, pushing my body in ways it wasn't designed to move until I can barely stand.

Several times, Camilla cuts off sessions so Sam can give me an IV and meds. I no longer ask what's in them.

While Janine does martial arts, I use the simulator to fight virtual opponents, composites of warriors who trained the equipment. Level eight becomes so realistic I can no longer tell the difference from real fights, right down to cuts and welts, though Camilla says this level is set at only 90 percent of full impact.

I push my body too hard, but if I wash out, it's Nashville. Another idea percolates within me: I could use my position with mechs to help boys, if I survive that long.

Knowing I'll have to face Dara, I run through each of her recorded fights in the simulator and in the ring. I find a virtual opponent as big as Dara and face her. Each time she bloodies me until the tech stops my session.

After Sam patches me up, I return for more. The virtual fighter isn't Dara, but despite running through every conceivable martial art, I can't come close to defeating her, not even once.

Sunday afternoon, after Sam patches me again, she pulls Janine and me into the gym, which smells of stale sweat despite the cleaning crew doing their best. "There's only so much you can learn through simulation," Sam says.

"I refuse to fight my sister," I say.

Janine shoves me. "You promised to teach me to defend myself."

"Haven't I done that?"

"You've helped, but I'll never know until I face a real opponent." She gives me her satisfied smile that says she has me.

"Not this time, Janine."

Sam frowns. "I didn't bring you here to squabble." She turns to me. "In the ring, Number Two Grunt. Show me what you've learned."

My jaw drops. "I can't, Sam."

The commander climbs between the ropes. "Number Two. On the double."

Janine squeezes my hand for reassurance. I climb in and face the compact commander. My knees shake. *She's the best. She's my boss.* Her eyes tell me she's in control.

Sam stands in the middle of the ring. "You're problem is you try to defend against every opponent."

"Isn't that natural?" I look around, thankful for no more audience than my sister.

"You can't win on defense. Given enough time, good opponents will take you down. You're blessed with enough skill that when an opponent hurts you enough, you fight back. It's time to take offense. I want you to attack me relentlessly."

I look from Janine to Sam. "You mean like Dara?"

"No. She attacks with brute force. She has a few surprises in store for her. While the betting pool has her winning, it goes back and forth as to who has the best shot of facing her. That's where the fun begins. Many bet on Rox until you took her down. That fluke won you a fight, and a following."

"People think I can win?"

"You're not a bully like Dara," Sam says. "Or a natural fighter like Rox or Capra. You don't want to be here. I can accept that."

Curse you for seeing through me.

183

"In my book, you're a better potential leader than the gung-ho types. They'll have to respect you in order to follow, but you won't waste resources on futile or meaningless missions, will you?"

I shake my head.

"You've come close to quitting. Your choice. You wonder why I waste time on you. I see potential if you're willing to work. The others will either make it and become good fighters, or not and end up elsewhere. You have the potential to lead troops into battle. Now attack. Show me everything you've learned."

Fixing my gaze on Sam, I approach with tentative steps. She stares into my eyes. I stare back and thrust my fist toward her chin. Sam blocks, moves aside and waits for my next move. When I attack again, I realize she intimidates by reputation and calm.

I chop and thrust. She blocks. I kick. She deflects. I go for pressure points that vanish at moment of impact. *She's good.* I box, kick, body block, everything I've learned in simulation. When she stops me, I withdraw to get my breath and bearings. Janine studies me like her schoolwork.

"Is that all you've got?" Sam asks.

"You could have annihilated me a dozen times."

"I'm not here to destroy you," Sam says. "I want you to really attack this time."

"I don't want to hurt you."

"And so you telegraph every move so I can block you. Have my eyes betrayed me?"

I shake my head.

I prepare to throw a punch and chop instead. I catch Sam's leg and throw her. She counters, tossing me back against the ropes.

"Better," Sam says. "Confuse the eyes. Come in for the kill. Imagine I'm Dara in the tournament. I have to win. It's a huge embarrassment if I don't. I've bloodied you and won't let up."

I go for a kick, punch and chop in quick succession. In a real fight she'd hammer me. I ignore that, get a few strikes, and fall back to prepare another attack.

"You've just shown me what you have and then given up your advantage," Sam says. "You've given me time to regroup. This is Dara you're fighting. She never backs off. If you get in, exploit it. No time to think."

I launch another attack. This time Sam blocks everything I

throw at her. When I can't find any weaknesses to exploit, I pull away.

"See. You had me, but when you return, you have nothing. Again."

Janine holds rapt attention on the fight, no doubt glamorizing me standing up to the great Samantha Hernandez. Her eyes betray that she's ready to sign up.

I throw everything I have at Sam, quick jabs, a faked body-block I turn into a kick and punch. I get inside and connect with her jaw. Feel horrible. Sam drops me to the floor, flips me over like a fish and pins me. I can't breathe.

"What did I say about betraying yourself?" Sam says. "If this were combat you'd be dead. Empathy is admirable, but not in a fight. Don't worry about your opponent. When she's had enough, she can yield. The only time that'll be an automatic wash-out will be in the arena. Get up and show me the fight you started with."

I do, yet no matter what I throw at Sam, she blocks and deflects. I can never be as good as her. If that means I fail, then what?

Janine watches with more wide-eyed enthusiasm than I can tolerate.

* * *

While Janine goes to school and the cop intern program, I train with Renee and her recruits. In addition to VR, simulator, and mech work, I spar with each of my team. I miss Tara. Without her, we have an odd number for matchups.

Hannah is our strongest. She comes at me in the ring with speed, as if she has an extra set of arms and legs.

I don't want to fight Margarite. She puts her heart into it, but loses to each of us. Brandy and Vivian match up well. Since we don't fight to the death like in the Friday bouts, I hold my own with both of them.

The infirmary becomes my second home. I get Sam's IVs several times a day without the nurse's assistance. I worry about becoming addicted to whatever Sam gives me. Yet it does heal welts, bruises and sprains so I can return to training.

"Where is Nurse Wells?" I ask Sam.

"She's preparing brutes for the arena."

"Does that include boys from Michael's School?"

Sam's eyes narrow. She doesn't answer, but I detect a yes.

At lunch on Thursday, Dara takes the seat across from me. "You still sore over the restaurant?"

The others stare at me, except Brandy and Margarite. "I'm not happy about it," I say.

"You didn't show up afterwards." She glares at Brandy. "Neither did you. You two hooking up?"

"None of your business," I tell her.

"I'm making it my business."

"No," Brandy says. "I went home and slept off my disappointment."

Thank you, Brandy.

"I'll expect you both tomorrow night," Dara says. "We're bringing entertainment."

I decide not to warn her about Sam's surveillance.

At night in my bed in the back of the gym, I'm alone. I'd craved this before. Now it haunts me. Janine's absence leaves a gaping hole. I pray she's okay, that Mom's home, and Sam hasn't caught her. I pray for Morgan and my birth mother, wherever she is.

That thought lifts me from bed and the little suite. I wander to the simulation room, now dark. I turn on lights and scan the control panel in the corner where Camilla works. I activate the virtual keyboard, which is not password protected, and find nothing but simulations, VR, and fights.

I leave the simulator and move down the hall to the infirmary. It's locked. I don't imagine it has anything except medical files. Further on, muffled voices come from the corridor to the command center. One voice is Sam's.

Easing my feet along gray concrete, I head for the corridor to Sam's office. She has to have access to prison files. After all, she monitors collar activity. My birth mother would be wearing one like a dog. I shudder at the image.

When I reach the door to the corridor, red lights flash. *Access denied.* I try the handle anyhow. It's locked. I turn, face Sam, and hang my head. "Couldn't sleep."

"So you decided to snoop."

"You know so much I wondered what you have on me, Janine, and my family." I force a smile.

Sam's eyes narrow. "You don't want to get on my wrong side."

"No, Commander, I don't. I'm sorry. I miss my family."

"You're free to leave."

"I don't want to go," I say. "I need more training." *Lots more.*

"Then don't abuse my hospitality. You wouldn't be the first who tried to break into my office."

"I'm sorry, Commander." *Just don't kick me out.*

"Come on, grunt. Have a cup of coffee with me. You can watch surveillance."

Stunned, I follow Sam into the command room.

The coffee she gives me is bitter and sweet with a powerful aroma I've never experienced before. It gives my brain a buzz. "Is this the real thing?"

"It helps when I have a late night. We're tracking another breakout, a boys' school on the north side. We caught all but seven who vanished. Someone is providing knowledge and tools to beat the system."

"Wasn't me," I say.

Sam's smile stretches her scar. "I suspect not, since Dara didn't change party locations." She points to recruits clustered at the plantation. "Last week she brought two escaped boys they found. One got away and disappeared. You don't want to know what she did with the other one. When we found him—well, you don't want to know."

Brad's friend?

"Capturing boys is part of what mechs do. Let me show you something else." Sam pulls up video of three bearded men without collars moving at night. It's the border area with the half-mile wide clearing in the background.

"Why don't we put up a wall?"

"Don't need it," Sam says. "Surveillance picks up all movement, and we respond quickly."

Three mechs surround the men. The men fire. The mechs cut down two with machine pellets. The last man surrenders. A mech cuffs him and carries him like a sack of flour away from the border.

"An important part of our job is preventing intrusions," Sam says.

I turn my attention to a different set of cams, inside and around the large concrete structure that houses the arena and the brutes that fight there. Outside is a well-lit parking lot for guests who come to see tournament and arena fights twice a year. Inside are plush seats around a dirt floor arena. "What's the purpose of fight training when we'll have mech gear?"

"The suit provides tools. It doesn't build character or warrior mentality. I don't want my warriors using the gear as a crutch. It makes you soft. This isn't a game. We don't fight eight-to-five, and yet warriors go home every day to their families. I have a tough balance to maintain. We've lost fewer warriors per 100 missions than any other unit. I want to keep it that way."

I can't take my eyes off the arena cams, and the dreaded grounds upon which my future rests.

TWENTY-FIVE

The final weekend before the tournament, I hide in my suite off the gym while other recruits leave. I don't want to deal with Dara and her parties. I don't want to deal with Brandy. I have to figure out how to survive the tournament and the arena when I don't want to hurt anyone.

When Janine pounds on my door, I'm nursing wounds from three rounds of fights: a win, a loss, and a draw at the buzzer.

She closes the door behind her and studies me. "You look terrible."

"We can't have this happen to you," I answer, "so you won't be signing up, will you?"

She gives me her I-won't-say-but-you-can't-stop-me look and gives me a hug. I welcome the closeness and realize how much I've missed her.

Janine's insatiable curiosity pushes me back to VR, simulator, and mech work until I want to scream for her to stop. Then she looks up at me with big brown eyes and says, "Belle, if you want to quit, fine, but I won't have them killing you out there."

I don't have the heart to tell her how much the governor wants to destroy our family, beginning with sending me away. It makes me wonder: Does the governor know my birth mother? Where was she when they sent Dorothy away?

Come Sunday afternoon, unable to take any more physical abuse, I hook up with Janine on the com-link. I have to be careful what I think, because I crave this insane connection with her. It defies physics. I feel her all around and inside as well. It's as if we're two aspects of the same person.

"I know what you mean." Janine plants her thoughts with mine. "When the other girls heard how Emily ruined your restaurant plans, they were so mean. I felt sorry for her...for a nano-second. I mean some girls look down on us as security-trackers, but they hate Emily. We'll always have each other."

It's that bond that keeps me from telling her I'm adopted. I like things as they are. *I'm proud of you, Babe. So proud.*

"That's why I need to join mechs, so we can be together always."

"Don't spoil things, Babe. It would kill me for you to get hurt."

"I know, Belle. All the girls have the opportunity to learn the same stuff, which gives an advantage to the bigger, stronger ones. Yet what happens if a tough fighter like Rox washes out? What if she gets angry and spiteful, and uses her fight training around town? I'm scared of so many trained, angry girls out there."

I wish I could see Janine's face. She sounds terrified. I want to say something comforting. I think of all those trained girls, angry at a society that put them here. What if I could harness them somehow?

"Belle, you've gone dark on me. It's lonely when you do that."

"I'm sorry, Babe. Just thinking about what you said. I wish things were different."

"Like what?"

I take a deep breath. "Like where you and I had other paths than security. You know they'll tell Sarah this year."

"No! She's—she needs protecting."

That's how I feel about Janine. "The Union has needs and decided our family should contribute." Janine and Sarah don't deserve to be in this position. I let that twinge of anger subside.

When Janine pulls me out of the com-booth, her face screws up in disappointment. I've let her down. I couldn't give her this connection. "I'm sorry, Babe. The tournament has me messed up inside."

"Come on." Janine takes my hand and drags me past Camilla.

"I don't have the energy," I say when she leads me into the mech gym. "I'm beginning to crash."

"I know. Suit up." Janine pulls out my mech gear and helps me put it on, legs first.

When I resist, she gives me her determined pouty face. Out of exhaustion, I cave.

Despite claustrophobic closeness, I like the feel of the mech suit. It's empowering and safe with all the shielded protection around me, the crutch Sam refers to. Janine suits up with too much eagerness.

The com-link kicks in. I relax, amazed that I could feel any closer to Janine. "I don't want to fight."

"Then let's do gymnastics like when we were little."

"Leap, pitch, roll," I say, and together we do our old programs.

There's comfort in performing routines we could do in our sleep. The mech gear accentuates and accelerates our movements, turning small moves into grand ones that have us filling the huge mech gym with jumps, dives and spins.

Through the com-link, Janine shares memories of school gymnastics, the playground at the center of our development, even sneaking down to the river, where we would get muddy just to feel free. The combination of com-link and exercise washes away the tournament, the arena, losing my restaurant, Dara, the governor, even my anger over what they've done to my birth mother. All I want is to savor this safe connection with Janine.

When I collapse in the middle of the gym, unable to move, I realize we've spent an hour here. I'm drenched in sweat, yet I feel better than I have since the arrest.

Janine drops next to me. "Wish we'd had these suits growing up."

"So do I, Babe. Now I need to rest. Tomorrow is prep. Tuesday is round one."

* * *

Monday is a blur of instruction and warm-up in preparation for the tournament. Arena preparation will come on Friday before the first test on Saturday.

"Why can't we complete the tournament before the arena so we can focus?" I ask Sam on Tuesday before we begin.

"Because, grunts, you won't get that opportunity in combat. You might as well get used to it."

Never get comfortable, she likes to say. My butt recalls that from tutorial.

"Only the last arena test and the final two tournament rounds are televised," Sam says, "to avoid embarrassment to the recruits."

And to the program, I'm sure.

The first round is critical. Sixteen girls will lose. Whether we continue and have a chance at becoming a mech depends on how well we perform. Fold too quickly and you wash out.

We change into fight outfits, which cover our entire bodies, including our hair and the top of our heads. Sam assembles us in the mech gym. Then she and a dozen uniformed warriors lead us down a gray underground tunnel. It's in sharp contrast to the usual khaki of the mech base itself. At the end of the tunnel, we reach gray steel doors. Behind them is the large concrete arena structure on the north side of the base that has its own parking lot, which I've seen from the command center.

Chattering among themselves, the warriors head off down a side corridor to take up seats in the stands. Sam opens the steel doors. We emerge into a sheltered concrete dugout beneath the arena seats with another steel door before us that leads into the arena. Along the side walls are large screens with views of the arena's dirt floor and the empty theater seats that surround the arena. Warriors begin to fill seats around the rim, above 10-foot walls.

Judges sit above, in enclosed box seats, though most of the contests are scored electronically using sensors in our fight uniforms.

In the middle of the wide dirt-floor arena, Sam has set up four raised ringed platforms. There will be 32 fighters in 16 fights, four at a time, which means there are four fight times. Sam hasn't told us who we'll fight or in which group. We don't get to prepare because we won't get that luxury in combat.

More warriors take first-row seats overlooking the railing and arena. Renee comes up and wishes each of her group luck. I'll need more than that. I need a miracle, especially if I get Dara. I pray I don't embarrass myself and wash out in round one. I'm sure all the girls feel this way, except Dara.

She stands tall and flexes her thick muscles. I'm certain she's on enhancement pills. I pity whoever gets her. Problem is, if you refuse to yield like Sam demands, you'll get injured or killed. If you give up, you're out.

"She's so full of herself," Brandy whispers in my ear.

I laugh, which lets out tension. Dara eyes me. I fix my gaze on her. *Give her nothing*, I remind myself. *Thanks, Sam.*

Sam calls the first round of fighters. Dara gets a girl my size and build. Sam also calls Margarite and Vivian, though not to face each other. Led by Dara, eight recruits step into the dirt-floor arena and approach their respective rings. Dara's is closest. I hear conversations above us as warriors place bets. Each was here and succeeded where I fear to fail.

Fighters enter their rings, face each other, and fall back into their corners.

Sam stands in the middle of the four rings, dwarfed by the platforms, yet her bass voice commands, "Rules are simple. You're here to win, not to destroy your opponent. Losing this round will not wash you out of the program. Poor performance will. That means I'd better see a warrior's focus and determination. Dig deep into your bag of tricks. Victory in the tournament gives advantages in the arena. We've never had a final four wash out. That should motivate you. Now make us proud."

Sam walks among the platforms where she can watch fights up close. I'm certain she'll review video and VR afterward.

When I look around, other recruits are riveted on the screens showing fight platforms. My attention is on Dara when the buzzer sounds. She thrusts herself out of her corner and approaches my stand-in like a bulldozer.

Dara swings; the girl sidesteps and hammers Dara's shoulder. Dara looks stunned, then spins around. Her opponent rams her fist into Dara's jaw. Dara winces and smacks her left fist into the girl's face. She follows with a powerful right. The girl flies backward, hits the ropes and bounces. She tries to get her balance. Dara punches her hard in the stomach, drops her to the ground and pins her. Fight over.

Stunned by the swiftness, I can't concentrate on the other fights. After Sam calls the match, Dara climbs out of the ring. She isn't even winded. Grinning for the cams, she approaches the dugout. Sam directs her toward the stands. "No contact with those who haven't fought."

I'm staring at Dara onscreen when Brandy shakes me. "Our turn."

The door opens and she nudges me into the arena. My legs tremble as Brandy guides me to Dara's fight-platform. I can hold my own with Brandy, but I don't want to hurt her. I've watched fights by all the recruits marching into the arena. The one who worries me most is Amy, who's my size with coal black hair. When she smiles, she has a sweet face, but her scowl reminds me of Dara in a bad mood. Whoever I get, I don't want to embarrass myself before warriors, Sam, and the other recruits.

"You okay?" Brandy asks.

I start to apologize in advance for the fight. Then I notice Amy at the edge of my platform, scowling like Dara. I read in her face that she has tuned out all distractions. She's focused on defeating me. I've heard warriors have money riding on her.

When Sam nods, I climb up into the ring and face Amy with her tight, determined eyes. She reminds me of Sam in the way she moves. She's learned a lot from the Commander, a lot she'll use against me.

A buzzer blares. *Don't embarrass yourself.* I look at Amy. Behind her I see Janine in the back of the stands. She's not supposed to be here. It's a closed tournament.

A fist connects with my jaw. Pain explodes like electric shock. The high ribbed ceiling of the arena appears before me. Amy drops on top of me.

I can't wash out.

Rotating, I thrust my fist below Amy's ribs. She lands beside me, winded. I follow through, grab her arms behind her, and pin her legs. Hunkering down, I splay her legs. She bucks me up and down like a bronco. I push her arms higher until she screams. Sam calls the fight.

I made it. But I've embarrassed myself. After I crawl out of the ring, I head for the stands. Janine's gone.

Sam grabs my arm. "Have I taught you nothing?"

"I'm sorry, Commander. I didn't expect—"

"Always expect the unexpected."

"You invited her?"

"You opened yourself to defeat. Next time you won't be so lucky. Go sit with Dara and the others."

So Janine isn't here to comfort, but to distract, to display my weakness. I hate Sam for this, and I'm disappointed in Janine for going along with the scheme. Did she know?

When I reach the stands, Brandy joins me. Her face is cut and bruised, but she smiles. "Live to fight another day."

Yeah, if fighting's what you love to do. "I made a stupid mistake and got lucky."

"Don't discount luck. I suspect it was more than that." Brandy leads me to where Dara sits near a group of uniformed warriors.

I look across the hall and don't see Janine. Sam's not playing fair to bring her to a closed round. I could have washed out. I want to be mad at my sister, and I would be if I'd lost.

Dara wraps her arm around my shoulder. "Glad you made it. I like Amy, but her skills aren't deep enough."

I remove her arm. "Your opponent gave you some trouble."

"Not really. Sam said she wanted performance, not just a win, so I gave her something to remember me by."

And for other recruits to think about.

We all expect Dara to win. Thus anyone who keeps winning will face her at some point. It jinxes our fights. Fall to a lesser opponent; it won't hurt as much.

TWENTY-SIX

With tournament round one over, Sam brings us together in the stuffy tutorial room with stiff-back chairs to review the fights in 3D.

Two recruits wash out: the one Dara fought, and another. I'm surprised Amy survives the cut. She's a better fighter than how she performed. I was lucky. None of my group washes out, though I'm surprised Margarite survived. On video she turns out to be scrappier than I imagined. Her opponent underestimates her and fails to press her advantage. Just before the buzzer, Margarite blasts into an attack that takes her opponent down. Judges give Margarite the win. I'll have to watch her.

When Sam dismisses us, I call and text Janine. No response. I'm anxious to find her to understand what's going on.

Sam grabs me. "Not so fast, Number Two Grunt."

Dara's waiting in the lobby, no doubt to psych me out for Thursday's fight or to drag me to her stupid party. Either way, I'm not disappointed when Sam pulls me down the corridor.

We enter the infirmary. "What is it, Commander?"

Instead of hooking me up to an IV, she injects me with some of her nano-meds. "You're bruising around the face. You won't want your mom and sister to see you this way."

"I was pathetic today, Commander. I'm capable of more."

"You lost focus. You also showed me you're capable of reaching deep when you need to. I don't think you realize how hard you hit Amy. I'm surprised you didn't kill her."

196

I'm petrified at that thought.

"We didn't wash her out, because she'll recover for Saturday's arena. We've seen enough to believe she'll perform well. We don't wash girls out to punish them. We wash them out to avoid losing them in the final test or in combat."

"And you're afraid I'll ruin your record?"

Sam laughs. "I'm proud of our record because I'm proud of my girls. Forget the record. Are you sure you want to continue? In the arena final, you'll have a large audience, including family. You distract too easily."

"I'm sorry, Commander."

"Cut the bullshit. Do you want to become a mech?"

No! "I stand ready to deliver, Commander."

Sam shakes her head and tosses the needle into the hazmat bin. "You're incorrigible. Come on, you have work to do."

Sam keeps me afterward; detention for disappointing her and myself. She takes me to the gym where we put on haptic fight suits. I follow her into the ring, imagining a night where she turns me into a bloody pulp and puts me back together with her meds so I can do it again.

Still in dress uniform, Sam stands across from me, looking a lot like Amy. Is that why Sam matched us up?

"Okay, as exhausted as you are," she says, "you're going to stand and defend against my attacks while I quiz you on the strengths and weaknesses of your opponents."

Sam assumes a boxer's pose. "Dara." She jabs.

I block and sidestep. "She's big, powerful, intimidating, charges relentlessly."

Sam kicks, hits my side. I tumble against the ropes.

"Focus," Sam says.

But focus and multi-tasking seem at odds. I block a thrust at my throat. "Her biggest weakness is relying on intimidation and strength at the expense of creativity." I attack.

Sam grabs my wrist and drops me to the mat. "I said defend, not attack."

"You said I need to attack more."

Sam helps me to my feet. "Right now I want you to concentrate on me while scanning your memory about competitors. You don't have time to prepare for each fight, although it gets easier as the tournament progresses. Then in the final you'll know. But that won't help you in the arena or in combat. Now focus."

She gives me name after name, then attacks, using tactics of that recruit. I force myself to stare into her dark eyes to anticipate her moves. My mind turns to a mush of names and faces of my 15 remaining competitors along with what they do well and poorly. I struggle to keep my arms up to defend as I drag myself around the ring. My stomach tells me I've missed at least one meal. If we had windows, I'd expect the morning sun. Still Sam grills me.

She attacks with new moves. "What about Annabelle Scott?"

"She lacks focus," I say. "She isn't as strong as other recruits, in particular Dara. She gets distracted because she doesn't want to hurt sister recruits."

Sam jabs. "What about strengths?"

I fall back and without false modesty say, "I don't know what she has to help her win."

"Then you fail." Sam lunges at me.

Sidestepping, I thrust out my right arm and plant my foot. Sam goes down with a thud.

"I'm sick and tired of your questions." I jump her and go for a pin. She pulls away.

Sam stands and helps me up. "Good. Now what are Annabelle's strengths?"

I catch my breath. "When you arouse my anger, I dig deep."

"Exactly. You need to channel that anger so you can dig deep and focus earlier in the fight, before your opponent has a chance to defeat you or cause you serious injury."

"Why are you taking so much time with a misfit like me, Commander?"

She climbs out of the ring. "Come on, let's get you some grub."

I change into my blouse and skorts, and follow her to the cafeteria. I feel sorry for Sam. She seems lonely, isolated, spending evenings and weekends on base by herself.

She heats up another batch of chicken stew and sits across from me. "You remind me of a young woman I once knew. She was full of ideals and fight, though not in a physical way. We trained together. She became an effective marine."

Staring at the steaming stew, I think of my birth mother. "What happened to her?"

Sam shakes her head and sighs. "She died during the war. Got ambushed. If I place too much expectation on you, I apologize.

She was a dear friend who wanted kids after the war."

"I'm sorry." I don't know what else to say.

"Not your doing. Anyway, if you want out of the program, I won't try to change your mind, but if you want in, you have serious work and not much time."

* * *

On Wednesday, Sam has the 30 remaining recruits train hard on simulator, physical conditioning, and sparring. No more mech suits or VR. I spar with each of Renee's group and then against another group.

Wednesday night I hide in the infirmary while the others leave. Then I return to VR to relive the fight habits of my 15 competitors. I'm dying to talk to Janine, but after the scare in round one, I concentrate on training.

On Thursday, after a morning of warm-ups and preparation with my team, I call and text Janine not to come. I don't need her distracting me again. I hear nothing.

Standing in the arena dugout with fifteen other recruits, I see onscreen more warriors gathered in the stands, making bets, along with 14 recruits who lost in round one. No visitors, no Janine. Was she a mirage I wanted to see? It's not like her to ignore me.

For the first group of four fights, Sam matches Vivian against Dara. Vivian puts up a good fight for a minute and a half. Then Dara clobbers her. Vivian goes down and remains still. When Dara drops on top to pin her, Sam calls the match. I don't think Dara injured her enough to wash out. I hope she performed well enough to stay if she wants to.

Freckle-faced Hannah fights Dara's big friend Capra, takes a beating, and goes down. I'm sad to see two of my teammates lose. Brandy, Margarite, and I fight in the second group of four. At least I don't get Dara.

Sam matches me against Zoe, a mousy girl with scraggly brown hair. She's been quiet, hiding in the shadows of other recruits, yet I've seen her explode during fights.

Inside the ring, we bow. The buzzer sounds. There in the stands is Janine. My eyes water. *Not again.* I blink to make the mirage disappear. It doesn't.

Zoe attacks. I punch. She deflects and drops me to the mat. I bounce to my feet and pounce on her. She throws me back and charges. I attack; she chops. Everything I throw at her, she deflects and hurls back at me. She's as scrappy a fighter as I've seen in VR.

I replay my ordeal with Sam. Repeat Zoe's strengths and weaknesses. Defend against her repeated attacks. She mastered every martial art thrown at us by the simulator. Focused and disciplined, she attacks in bursts. Otherwise she keeps her body compact and protected. She's quick on her feet, with a strong right jab and a quick kick off a spin. She's versatile, changing moves as she comes at me.

I dodge another attack. I've seen her in VR. I guess she's seen me. Her eyes betray her an instant before each move despite attempts to conceal. I spot Janine in the stands. *Focus, Annabelle, focus.*

Zoe launches a patterned attack. I grab her leg, throw her to the mat, and drop on top of her. She pushes me off. We wrestle. I hope I'm giving a better performance than on Tuesday. Don't want to do anything stupid. It would be easy to let Zoe have this. Then I won't have to fight Dara. I'd be free to concentrate on the arena.

Zoe drops me to the ground and goes to pin me. My face mashes against the canvas floor. *This could be it.* I see Janine in the stands. *She'll know.* I thrust up and throw Zoe back, catching her off guard. I tangle her arm in the ropes and twist her around until she can't move.

The referee calls the match. My heart thunders like I'm having a heart attack. *Fool, you had an out.* I look up into the stands and can't find Janine. *What are you doing to me?*

Crawling out of the ring, I realize there are only eight of us left. Brandy's out. Margarite remains, the weakest member of our team.

Brandy shakes my hand and pats my shoulder. "Congrats."

"Sorry you're out," I tell her.

"I'm not." Brandy looks over at Dara.

Did she chicken out? Did Zoe let me win so she wouldn't have to face Dara? The amazon has become an even more dominant fighter. She's mastered simulator moves with more power behind them.

* * *

Before I can duck into the infirmary or bathroom, Dara grabs me and nudges me toward the exit. "You did well today. A lot of people had their money on Zoe and me in the final."

"I don't think anyone's betting against you."

Dara laughs. "Don't wimp out on me tonight. We have a lot to celebrate. And don't forget to wear a patch."

I nod. "I'll try, but I have to do something first." I need to see Janine and find out why she's avoiding me.

To escape Sam holding me another night, I leave the base with Dara.

Janine's appearances leave me disturbed, particularly when I don't hear from her. Did I see Janine, or is my mind playing tricks on me? That's something I need to find out face-to-face.

I text, call, and leave voicemail, asking if she'd like a ride home. I don't hear. I break off from the pack when we reach downtown and head for the cop station. When I enter the usually noisy central hall, there's a hush quieter than church. I look around and don't see Brooks or Janine. All other eyes fall on me.

Scarlatti bounces toward me with her smell-me look. "Well, if it isn't little-miss-know-it-all. Come to gloat?"

"I came to see if you had work for me. If not, I'll wait for Janine."

"She's out with Brooks. Don't pretend you didn't know the office pool had you washing out today."

That blow practically doubles me over. I know Voss hates me. I assume it's because Mom opposes the governor who appointed Voss. I expect the same from Voss' puppy. But the others? "I'll wait outside."

"Captain wants to see you."

I wander up the dark stairs to find Liz emptying another mug of watered down, caffeine-free coffee. *Yuck.* Now that Sam has given me the real thing, this isn't even mud.

Liz doesn't look up as I go in. Voss sits at her desk and acts busy while eyeing me. How much did she lose betting against me? I hope she doesn't punish Janine for this. The thought slams me. Did Voss put Janine up to distracting me?

"Sit down," she says. When I do, Voss stands over me. "You think you're better than the rest of us."

Where does that come from? I'm rebellious, yes. I want to see my birth mother and George and Morgan. But I'm far from thinking I'm better. If I did, I'd have Dara to put me in my place, as well as Sam.

"No comeback today."

I eye the hibiscus plant where I hid my valuables earlier. "Captain, I don't know what I've done to you."

"Don't you?" Voss retreats behind her desk but doesn't sit down. She fidgets with controls to her keyboard. "You don't have what it takes to be a mech. You don't have what it takes to be a cop, either. I see you on the other side of the law. In which case, you've made some powerful enemies."

I hang my head. "I'm ashamed and sorry for breaking into your office, Captain. I've never done anything like that before and never will again. I didn't ask to be tracked to security, but I want to do well at it." *Are you using Janine?* I can't think how to ask that won't come back to hurt my sister.

Voss glares at me and fidgets. "I'm sure you think so. Either straighten out or you'll end up in Nashville, or worse."

"I understand, Captain. Do you have anything for me tonight?"

"Not until you finish your mech fantasy. Now go."

I scurry from her office and down the stairs.

I reach my cycle and wait for Janine. When Brooks pulls up in her ridiculous bug-car, I get off my cycle to greet them. I don't know what to say to Janine. Something has come between us that could tear at the fabric of our bond.

Brooks gives me a thumbs-up. "I knew you had it in you."

"You're in the office pool?"

She grins. "I'm cleaning up, thanks to you."

"Don't bet too much. I don't see anyone beating Dara."

"Don't sell yourself short.

When Janine joins us, Brooks says, "I'll check your sister out and let you two catch up." She hurries into the station.

Janine grabs my hands and looks up at me with her doe-eyes. "Don't hate me. Sam invited me to the tournament."

"Sam? Why?"

"She said you needed something only I could provide. I feel terrible about distracting you." Tears fill her big brown eyes.

Her confession dissolves my anger. This innocence is why she doesn't belong in mechs. I hold her. "Don't cry, Babe. Sam's teaching me to focus despite distractions. You're the biggest distraction I have."

"Then I won't come."

"I'm doing this for you, Babe, for us. Sam's right." I surprise myself with this revelation about the vulture. "I've been weak. I'm losing because I can't focus on defeating my opponents. I'm not very good, but she thinks I have a chance."

Janine looks away. "I wanted to tell you. That's why Sam took my wrist-com and gave me this one. It only has Mom's number. I don't remember yours and I didn't want to tell Mom and–" Janine looks up with sweet moist eyes. "I'm so proud of you."

I hold her tight. "It's okay, Babe. I couldn't understand why you didn't respond to my messages or why you showed up for the fights and disappeared."

"Sam doesn't want the others to see me or they'll think she's playing favorites."

When I reach my cycle, I turn to Janine. "Babe, I'm scared. The next rounds will get worse. If I survive, I'll have to face Dara."

"You wanted to give up today, didn't you?"

"Let's go."

"Take me with you." Janine's mouth forms a sweet little pout.

I should take her home, but I miss her, and I don't want to go home.

TWENTY-SEVEN

When we reach the plantation house, I hide the cycle in the woods away from the road and the mansion. Then I give Janine the fob. "Hold on to this. If anything bad happens, promise me you'll get yourself home."

"Belle? What's going on?"

"I don't know. I have a bad feeling."

Janine swats a mosquito and gives me her pouty face. "I'm staying with you."

"Then I'm taking you home."

Janine's shoulders sag.

I count 29 cycles out front, all the remaining recruits. Then I lead her inside to the drowning beat of sassy music. It's a warm, muggy evening. Thankfully, Dara has the air conditioning on inside the great hall. Recruits huddle in small groups, some outfitted in flashy dresses that fail the harmony test, along with makeup like a Halloween ball. No one washed out today, which surprises me.

Bruised from her fight with Dara, Vivian doesn't look so tough as she bounds over to me. "Glad that's over. I thought she was going to kill me."

I nod. That's something to look forward to.

Dara brings drinks in chipped crystal for Janine and me. "I've watered yours down. I know you don't like alcohol. None for the sibling."

The way she looks at Janine, I wonder if she saw my sister at the match. While Dara wanders off distributing drinks, the music grows louder, certainly not harmonious. What would Sam think? She's monitoring us. She knows we're here, the victors and the vanquished, all except for two who washed out in the first round.

Several girls move to the middle of the hall to dance. Two recruits proposition Janine, who clings to me and looks up for protection. I smile and pull her close. Hanging together is all we need tonight.

Dara joins us. "How about a dance?" She grabs my hand.

When Janine moves away, I use her as my excuse. "My sister's not feeling well. We're going to walk it off."

Dara glares like she wants to push, then returns to the bar. I take Janine by the hand and whisper, "Sorry about that."

"Thanks for not leaving me. I feel like a gazelle surrounded by lions."

A fast gazelle, I hope. "I should take you home." I head for the exit and step outside into twilight to crickets, mosquitoes and something else.

"I want to stay with you, Belle."

"Remember what I said. Get on the cycle and go home."

"Belle?"

"Just do it." I lead her to the edge of the woods. We slosh through soggy weeds; there must have had a flash thunderstorm while we were inside. When she won't leave me, I lead Janine toward the cycle.

Choppers buzz overhead. Armored vehicles in green camouflage thunder up the road. When we reach the cycle, I crouch down and pull Janine into the bushes. Mech trucks spill up the muddy road.

"What's happening, Belle?"

"Sam's rounding us up. I have to go back. She won't leave until she has all the recruits. After she does, take the cycle and go home."

"You won't have transport."

"I'll call you now that we've synchronized phones. Do this for me."

With twilight fading into dark, Janine crouches down. I run to the front of the mansion where choppers are landing. I approach the lead truck to distract them.

Four warriors in combat gear with blackened faces emerge from an armored vehicle, along with a warrior in mech gear. Several other vehicles unload. Six mech warriors take positions around the mansion and shine lights on the huge ancient structure. Renee and others move into the house. One of the warriors grabs me.

"What's going on?" I have a good idea.

"Shut your trap and get into the wagon." The warrior shoves me into an empty armored truck with bench seats and bars on the single window in back. I sit on one side. It's going to be a very long night.

Warriors shout. In the dark I count nine bodies thrown in with me, two quite drunk. One chucks it onto the floor. Putrid odor fills the cramped, steamy space, making me want to empty my stomach. I'm glad I didn't drink.

Dara argues, then goes silent.

"Tranquilize anyone else who resists," a warrior says.

I pray Janine gets away. Mom has enough heartache with me to have to worry about my sister. Through the tiny back window, I watch warriors load cycles onto a truck and drive off.

"How the hell did they find us?" Capra asks.

"Shut up or I'll tranquilize the lot of you."

Why did Sam wait until now to raid? Sweat streams down my neck. The humidity inside the truck is so high I expect it to rain in here. The door slams shut. There's a scrape of metal as bolts latch. Then we bounce down the road, heading deeper into the woods. The smell of vomit overwhelms, along with mosquitoes feasting on our damp skin.

After some 20 minutes, our truck stops. Two others stop alongside, in addition to several armored vehicles.

Sam's bass voice carries. "While many of you are done with the tournament, you all face the arena on Saturday. Do you imagine you have time to party? Do you believe being a grunt exempts you from harmony laws? We'll have the food, drink, and music examined. Infractions may cause recruits to wash out, face disciplinary action, or worse.

"If no one comes forward to take responsibility, I'll hold each of you accountable. Think carefully before you test me on this. Any recruit not on base and in assembly at eight tomorrow morning will wash out. Goodnight, ladies."

A moment later the armored vehicles and choppers take off. We're surrounded in this stinking pressure cooker by thick darkness, the buzz of mosquitoes, a racket of crickets, and groans.

I try to stand; the roof isn't high enough. "We have to get out of here and back to base by eight. You heard the Commander."

The girl who sat next to me slumps onto the bench where I sat. Her friend, the one who vacated her stomach, falls on top of her. In the dark, I can't see much.

"What's the point?" Margarite says from the back. "Sam's going to kick us out anyhow."

"We all know Dara's responsible for the food, drink, and music," Capra says. "I'm not taking the fall for her."

"I say we turn her in," Hannah says.

"Go ahead," Vivian says.

"Brandy," I say.

"Yes."

"Capra, is your entire team here?"

"I think so."

"Then listen to me." I wish I could see faces. "This is another of Sam's tests. She's invested too much to wash us all out."

"Don't be so sure," Capra says.

"We're here by team. We can rat out other teams to save ourselves and lose by fighting among ourselves, or we can work together and find a way back to base."

"I'm in," Capra says.

"Let's get the door open for starters."

I move to the front of our compartment and try the door. It doesn't budge. There's no access to the cab. The only other opening is the little barred window; when I grab the bars, they don't budge. "Dara, you out there?"

"Yeah." She sounds groggy, tranquilized maybe. "What do you have in mind?"

"What if we put our backs into it and kick the doors out?"

"Already tried. Must be bolted on the outside."

I return to the window and grab the bars again. "Any way to pry loose one of the window bars?"

"Trying," Dara says. "They're solid. We need a hammer."

"What about one of the benches?"

Banging and grunts come from the trucks to my left and right as we try to pry the wooden bench off the floor. "Ours won't budge," I say.

"Same here," Dara says.

"No luck," says Kara, a muscular, pasty-faced blonde who has risen in the rankings with two tournament wins.

"Does anyone have something hard we could use against either the benches or the window bars?" I ask.

Groans and grumbling.

"I'm not giving up," I say. "Remember what Sam says, reach deeper. Come on, grunts. Let's show her we deserve to be mechs."

"Who put you in charge?" Dara asked.

"Then you take charge. I don't care. I'm not letting my mech career die here. Sam says when you lose all defenses and weapons, dig deep and find something else."

"Why don't you bash that hard skull of yours against the bars and see if that helps," Kara says.

"Hannah," I say. "Back to back against the door. What do you say?"

"I'm game."

I move to the door with my back to Hannah. With her pushing me, I kick. The door won't give. I kick again and again, letting my frustration and anger rise. I imagine Janine's face in the tournament encouraging me to stay in the fight. I kick again and the door swings open. Hannah pushes so hard I tumble out into mud at the feet of–*Janine?*

She helps me up.

"I sent you home." I stare into her sweet face lit by moonlight. Our trucks are clustered in a muddy ravine.

"You're welcome."

"What's going on?" Dara asks.

"We're out." In dim moonlight I look at the bolt on the door; there's no lock. I motion for Janine to open the truck to my left while I go to Dara's truck.

"How's that possible?" Dara groans.

"Stand back," I say, releasing the bolt.

The door flies open. Dara tumbles out into the mud. "Thanks. I guess I owe you."

Janine returns to my side.

"You?" Dara says. "Are you part of this?"

"I don't think so."

"I told her to skedaddle when I heard trucks coming," I say.

"And you returned?" Dara asked.

I nod. "Didn't want to miss out on whatever Sam has planned."

"Okay, girls," Dara says. "Let's get these trucks out of the ditch and back on the road." Dara turns to Janine. "Thanks, little sister."

Janine clutches my hand, while I shield her from Dara.

It takes two hours to get all three trucks out of the ravine and facing the plantation. It takes another hour in the dark to make our way to the mansion. Since it's past midnight and we have to be on base at eight, we drive the three trucks straight to the mech center.

Sam's waiting when we reach the gate. She expects us, because she can track our movements. Sam escorts the muddy lot of us to the gym, where she has spread out 30 thin mattresses. "This will be your home for now. Anyone leaving base will wash out. If you can't handle this, leave now."

Sam waits a moment. We each move to pick out a mattress, all except for Janine, who stands by the door. Before I can go to her and thank her for saving our asses, Sam escorts her away.

Sam never mentions the party, the illegal food, drink or music. What has me pissed is that she's using Janine.

* * *

Saturday morning, Sam escorts us back to the arena with our mech gear. The arena looks much bigger without the four raised tournament platforms. The 10-foot wall prevents escape. There's a padded platform in the middle where recruits can go to catch their breath or wash out. There's nowhere to hide, no place to escape brutes who will enter the arena to challenge us. I smell sweat and fear more than I did during the tournament, more than any disinfectant can remove. This isn't how I want to meet boys.

At least the first arena test is in full mech body armor. We face three brutes at once, musclemen from nearby prisons and escapees pumped up on steroids to make the contest more challenging. At any time we can signal to wash out and escape injury or death. But by now, none of us want to quit, for reasons we don't share. We can't show weakness.

The advantage of winning the first two rounds of the tournament is that I get to see other trainees in the arena before my turn. Those who lost round one go first. Those who lost round two follow. The eight still in the tournament go last. Unlike the tournament, there's one match at a time, and 30 of us. This will take our entire Saturday. I can't miss seeing live action to prepare myself. At least there's no audience, except other trainees, and warriors here to cover their bets.

I sit in the lowest level of the stands with Dara, Margarite and Brandy. I feel numb watching match after match. Too much violence.

Next up is Vivian, the tough blonde from my group who fell to Dara in round two. I suspect she quit rather than let Dara injure her so she could compete today. She has something to prove.

In full black body armor, Vivian stands beside the padded centerpiece facing the three doors the brutes use. The idea is to get over our fear of fighting big opponents in stages. In the first arena test, you win if you get all three brutes down and cuffed. You lose if they remove your helmet. It's not a fight to the death, but I don't relish facing three fighters at once. Even with my mech suit advantages, they look intimidating.

Vivian stretches and flexes her mech joints, showing fluid movements she'll need to stand victorious. I hold my breath, feeling the tension and adrenalin rush, unfocused at this point. I don't want to burn out before my contest.

All three steel doors open. Men in bulging haptic suits saunter onto the field for this single-elimination round, the first of several tests. They spot each other and their target. Though Sam says they've had no contact beforehand, they would know to work together to defeat the armored warrior. Remove her helmet and win the round. They'll receive rewards Sam doesn't mention, while the recruit washes out.

With a nod, the men rush toward Vivian. I watch and consider: should I wait for them to reach me, or rush them?

Vivian turns. She runs full force at the one on her left and thrusts her clenched mech glove into the man's gut, sending him backward. She chases his retreating body, putting distance between herself and his companions.

He tumbles onto the dirt, winces, then scrambles to his feet. She hits him again. He grabs her shielded arm and reaches for her helmet clasp. She slams him full force into the padded wall, knocking the wind out of him. Then she throws him over the 10-foot wall into the stands.

When the remaining two brutes close in, she jumps over them. While a mech warrior removes the brute from the stands, Vivian runs toward the centerpiece to catch her breath. The two men run toward her, side-by-side so she can't separate them. She waits until they get close and jumps, grabbing one from behind. The other brute climbs onto her shoulders, reaches up and removes one helmet clasp. Three more and she's out.

She dives into a somersault and drops her mech weight on the man as he pops the second clasp. It looks easier than it must be to use the suit to advantage. The third man climbs onto her back, pulls the third clasp. Vivian cuffs the second man, then drops back and scrapes the last man off her shoulders.

She turns to face her last opponent. He steps back. She charges, sidestepping at the last moment. He lunges for the clasp. She slams her mech arm across his neck, sending him sprawling, and cuffs him.

Vivian stands victorious. I tell myself: be aware of your helmet clasps, but don't obsess or you're done. It reminds me of losing focus during the tournament.

Yawning, Dara grabs Margarite and leaves.

Brandy and I sit through the next contest. I like Hannah, a good runner and strong competitor, the strongest in Renee's group. She should do well, but she hesitates when the men charge at her. Instead of singling one out, she jumps when they converge. One of the brutes catches her foot.

At first I don't recognize the guy, so bulked up on steroids. It's the boy from Michael's school, my redhead, Morgan. *Damn it all.* All those risks, all that effort, and he didn't get away. My stomach knots. How can Sam force him into this life like my dad? And the final contest is to the death? I force myself to watch.

Hannah kicks to free herself. Morgan slams her down and bangs her helmet onto the ground. That has to hurt, despite the padding. The men converge, ripping open her helmet clasps. By the time Hannah stirs, they've released three. She scrambles to her feet and scurries away with all three in pursuit. She runs around the arena, tiring herself out. She'll want to reattach the clasps. That's an automatic wash-out.

Morgan directs the other two to corner her. It's more a suggestion than a command. I can't take my eyes off him.

Each time the men attack, Hannah jumps and runs, with the suit giving her speed and agility. She can't win this way, though; time will run out. Pulling out a set of cuffs, she waits until the men charge. She darts sideways around the one on the right and cuffs one of his hands, then struggles to get the other hand and finally cuffs it.

Two men jump her and fight over the last clasp. She throws Morgan. *Don't hurt him.* He flies through the air, clutching her helmet.

The third man attacks. Terror fills Hannah's freckled face. The judge triggers the man's collar, sending him into convulsions. Two mechs jump into the arena and escort Hannah away. She's out of the program. Too bad. I liked working with her. Is this what happened to Voss and Scarlatti?

Morgan backs up toward his door, which opens for him. He disappears into darkness to wait for the next fight.

Brandy is up next. I can't watch my sweet, stocky teammate who acts sweet like Janine. Instead, I scan the stands for my sister. I don't need to be surprised again, not when a split second can end my chances and I've already been distracted once, by Morgan. I don't see Janine. When I look back into the arena, Brandy has two men cuffed, and she's still standing. She takes the last one down and looks my way. I should have watched.

I get suited up. When I return, Dara's in the arena. She painted a red sword on the front of her helmet, against regulations.

When the doors open, Dara charges the man in the middle, sprinting with the full power of her oversized mech suit. The man enters the arena and stops mid-stride. His partners stare, no doubt confused. They eye their target: the helmet and latches.

When Dara reaches the man in the middle, he grabs for her helmet. Dara thrusts the full force of her mech fist into his nose. She mashes him back against the closed steel door. His head looks like a crushed melon. He collapses onto the dirt.

Dara rushes the man to her left before the two can team up. She slams her mech fist into his stomach, then grabs his jaw, yanks, and snaps his neck. Pushing aside the body, she faces the third man. He looks much less intimidating before this large mech. She grabs his neck and throws him to the ground. He reaches up, releases one of her helmet latches, and slumps into a puff of dirt. The judge sounds the alarm and calls the match.

It happens so fast the judge must be as stunned as I am...and as the men were.

"This is not a fight to the death," the judge reminds us. "You will receive penalties."

Two of the men are dead. The other doesn't move.

If, a big if, I keep winning, I'll face Dara in the tournament. She's a killer. But if I quit, I can't help Morgan, a need that swells up inside, distracting me from my own contest.

TWENTY-EIGHT

Viewing the other matches makes me dread my own. I wait in the dugout, watching onscreen as mech warriors carry out the three men. Brandy joins me. I should have watched her fight.

"You have to eliminate one brute any way you can," Brandy says, stripping off her mech gear. Aside from sweat stains on her clothing, she doesn't look like she's been in a fight.

"Not like Dara."

"You know what I mean. You don't have to kill them, but you can't be afraid of hurting them."

"Why would you say that?"

Brandy lowers her voice. "I didn't want to hurt them either. I saw you look at that boy. This is just a trial to see if you qualify. Don't get booted out like Hannah."

"I don't intend to." While this is the easiest of the arena trials, my stomach tightens. Brandy escorts me to the door, then leaves. The wait takes forever. My throat tightens until I feel like I'm choking.

When my door opens, I march out to the middle of the arena and wait before the three doors the men will use. Nothing so far has prepared me for the terror of standing here, surrounded by 10-foot walls, on my own. My suit fills with sweat and fear. I taste bile. Splotches of reddish brown cover the dirt before me, the blood they'll clean up at the end of the day.

I look through the entire audience of warriors and recruits without spotting Janine. Then I check the rear projection, and her sweet baby-face peeks above the barrier. *Oh, no! Not today.*

The doors open. I hesitate. A flash of fear screams for me to seek shelter behind the padded centerpiece. Up close, these boys are huge musclemen, the kind who could tear you apart.

I can't hate them…no time for sentimentality…*focus.*

The brutes run toward me. I run at the middle guy, a scruffy black-haired ruffian, and pull a set of cuffs from my utility belt. At the last moment, I jump to the left, grab one man's wrist and slap on the cuff. He reaches for my helmet. I grab his other wrist, cuff it, and land on top of him with a thud. I tumble away as the other two converge.

I twist, thrilling at the mech power, and thrust my gloved fist into Black-hair's gut, harder than I'd planned. He flies, landing spread-eagled onto the dirt.

As the third man jumps me, I get a cuff onto his wrist. He unfastens a clasp of my helmet. I cuff his other wrist, in front, and trip him.

Black-hair recovers and grabs for my helmet. If he gets the last clasp and removes my helmet, he could bash my brains in before the judge can shock him into submission. *Focus.*

I cuff his forward wrist, twist, and grab his other wrist. The third man jumps me, removes the second clasp, and goes for the third, as I cuff Black-hair's second wrist behind him.

My helmet sits lopsided, held by a single clasp. I jump into a somersault and pray the helmet doesn't come off and decapitate me. With another set of cuffs, I clasp the third man's wrist. I land on top of him and hear a ghastly groan. He reaches for my last clasp.

I'm losing it.

I yank away, pull his leg up, and clasp his right arm to his left leg behind him. The man lies face down in the dirt, trying to scoot around and reach my last clasp.

When no buzzer signals victory, I check the other two men. They're down. I must not have this one right. I release his left hand and wrestle to get both his hands together behind him. He rolls free and unlatches my last clasp. I drop my mech-weight onto him, pull both hands behind, and cuff him. The buzzer sounds.

My heart races so hard I can barely breathe. I'm covered in sweat. Trembling, I look up into the stands for Janine. She gives me a nod and disappears.

215

Mechs run into the arena to cart the men back to their dungeons. I stare across the arena into the blackness beyond those three doors. They must lead to underground tunnels. The dungeons might lie beneath the arena like at the Bastille or the Coliseum in Rome.

I have to save Morgan, save these boys. Who could help me? I can't involve Mom or Janine. Brandy is too sweet like Janine. Dara hates boys. What about Kristina Wells, the nurse? She's nice and has access, but she works for Sam.

"Number Two, clear the arena," Sam yells into my com-link.

* * *

On Monday, Sam pulls the eight of us into the arena for tournament round three. I move like a zombie, praying I don't get Dara. I shouldn't have spent Sunday wearing myself out in VR and simulation. I try to figure how to take a fall in the match without looking obvious.

I want to talk to Sam about her using Janine, and I'd love to get back into the command center to check for weaknesses in Sam's arena surveillance. But I couldn't find Sam after Saturday's arena fights, and now I can't get her away from the six warriors who escort us to the arena. When we reach the dugout, four platforms stand in the middle of the arena. We'll all fight at once.

Dara puts her arm around me and Margarite, and pulls tight. "After today, we're down to a final four. Then we're televised. I'd love to get Sam into the ring again."

I pull away. I'm certain Sam could still take her, but Dara makes it clear she'll dominate today. Capra, the big sandy blonde, shakes her head. Kara, a solidly muscular, pasty-faced girl, has moved up in the betting. When I look into the stands, I glimpse Janine.

Capra pushes me into the arena. I realize I've zoned out again. I look into the stands, and this time I don't see Janine. Dara takes Margarite aside and whispers.

Capra matches up with a tough little brunette. Margarite heads off with Sally, a girl in cornrows who I'm sure will tear her apart. Dara gets into the ring with a big-boned Hispanic girl who looks horrified to have drawn the amazon.

Kara bumps fists with me before we climb into the fourth ring. I like this pasty-face blonde, who carries sadness like mine and refuses to talk about it. Facing her in the ring, I see fire in her eyes to survive another round. I feel kinship with Kara and don't want

216

to hurt her; this could be my chance to bow out to a friend. But as if she can read my thoughts, which she can, Janine pops up behind Kara in the stands.

When my sister's face disappears, a fist swings toward my jaw. I rotate away and kick Kara's leg. She sidesteps and jumps me. I have an inside shot at her nose. I don't take it. I'm on defense now.

Kara drops me onto the padded floor and goes for an easy pin. I could end this now, but no matter which way I look I see Janine inside my head like our private com-link.

I struggle to break free. Kara pulls my arm back to finish me. I thrust out my limbs, get her off-balance and reverse on her. She won't give up. Instead of punching or chopping as we've trained, she keeps the fight in close, where we can't do much damage.

While I scoot out from under Kara's trap, I spot Sam glaring at me. Is it so obvious I'm not giving this my all? I want out gracefully. This isn't graceful.

Kara tackles me. I reverse on her, throw her onto her stomach and pin her. It's a solid move Sam can respect. Kara doesn't struggle. I have my victory, yet I don't feel victorious.

Sam has a disgusted look on her face. She wants us to tear each other apart, which doesn't make sense. Why not have the arena tests before the tournament?

We wait for the bell to announce that I've won. Kara whispers, "Thanks."

She's a good person, and I'm glad I haven't hurt her. I hope this doesn't wash her out. Of course the televised fights won't be so tame. We'll have millions of eyes on us to notice if we don't give our all.

After my buzzer sounds, I check Dara's match and see her deliver the final blow. The announcer declares her victory as well as Capra's.

All eyes fall on Margarite and Sally. I bet if Sally's cornrows went straight, her hair would be longer than mine. It's another reason to like her, even though she's fighting my teammate.

Sally attacks while Margarite cowers. My teammate should be down by now, but she parries every move. Sally looks frustrated. She reaches deep, comes in with a combination punch, kick, and chop. Margarite drops her, pinning her against the corner post. Sally taps out.

I'm stunned. Dara's relieved. Margarite gets to her feet as if she has no idea what happened. We're the final four. After Dara hugs Capra and Margarite, she moves in on me. I pull away.

I have a one-third chance of facing Dara in the semi-final. If I don't draw her for the semi and manage to win, I'll face her in the final. There's a nightmarish inevitability to this. On the other hand, as a mech, I can't imagine anyone I'd rather have at my side. I'd welcome Capra, but Margarite is less of a fighter than I am.

I look for Janine. As usual, she disappears after the fights. I duck into the infirmary. No doubt, now that Sam isn't holding us overnight, Dara will want us all to party at the plantation. I don't want to listen to her gloat about how good she is because she has big bones and good genes, good fighter genes.

* * *

Even though my body wants to crawl into a hole and hibernate, I long to find Mom and see if she can help with Morgan again.

Sam grabs me as I leave the infirmary and pulls me into her small cafeteria. "That was the most pathetic fighting I've ever wasted my time on," she says. She closes the door and heats a container of chicken stew.

"Kara's a powerful fighter."

"I didn't see that today. You think I don't know what's going on?" Her eyes narrow.

"I'm surrounded by better fighters, except maybe for Margarite."

"Then you've learned nothing." Sam places a bowl of stew in front of me. "You think Dara's this great fighter because she's big."

"I—"

"Eat up. You need your strength. If I see this pitiful performance on the televised matches, I'll wash all four of you out."

"Commander…" I start, then hesitate. I'm on defense again.

"Do I need an auger to dig the words out?"

I'm flustered, afraid I'll betray myself. "I don't like how you're using Janine and trying to recruit her."

"Does that piss you off?"

"Yes."

"Does it get you to fight harder?" Sam sits across from me.

"That's not the point, Commander. She's innocent, underage, and—"

"If you were in a life and death situation with her as a hostage, what would you do?"

Tears begin to blur my vision, I take a deep breath. "I'd do whatever it takes to protect her."

"Then use that to give you an edge in the tournament and the arena."

I glare at her. "Your setup isn't fair. Why not have all the arena tests before the tournament?"

"You admit you're slacking."

I stare into the bowl of chicken stew, hungry, but too shaky to eat. "We're handicapped by any injuries we take into the arena."

"I have one purpose in the training program: to save lives."

Sam digs into her stew and lets me sit with her words. I've heard them before, and I expect she'll lecture me to overcome whatever uncertainty I encounter in the fog of war.

"Eat up," Sam says. "I'm warming up to browbeat you grunts tomorrow. Every recruit wants to lose without injury so she doesn't have to face Dara. You all want to preserve yourselves for the arena. That won't save you. If you don't give this your all, you will lose in the arena. If by luck you make it through the arena without learning these lessons, you'll get killed or get your mech team killed as well. Do you want out?"

"No, Commander."

"You don't sound convinced."

"I stand ready to deliver," I bark.

"Then see that you do, which means staying on the base tonight." Sam gets up and places a third bowl of stew on the table.

There goes my chance to ask if I can see the command center again. Sam opens the pantry door. Janine enters and sits next to me.

"I'll leave you two to talk." Sam leaves with her bowl.

Janine grips my hand. "I'm sorry I distracted you again, but Sam says I have to in order to get you ready." Her big brown eyes water.

I take a deep breath. "I know, Babe. How's Mom?"

"Gone again. She has us all worried. I feel like our family is spinning out of control." She stops and tightens her soft face to keep from crying, putting on her brave face for me.

I can't help smiling. "I'm glad you came, but I wish you hadn't seen my pathetic performance."

"You saved yourself for tomorrow."

I close my eyes. I can't fool Janine. I haven't fooled Sam. From here on, there's no hiding that I'm not a fighter. But then what?

"How long can you stay?" I ask.

"As long as you need me. I told Mama Grace I might spend the night."

Janine doesn't give me a chance to relax. She pushes me in VR and simulation. I go over all the footage for Dara, Capra, and Margarite. I only have these three to learn for Wednesday's tournament semi-final. Dara and Capra are stronger than me, and Margarite keeps surprising. Besides, I have arena round two first.

At the same time, I go over the thinnest of plans in my head: weaknesses in Sam's arena surveillance, and what little I know about layouts of the arena and holding cells.

TWENTY-NINE

Tuesday morning we're back in the arena, with a padded centerpiece instead of tournament platforms. The stands are empty except for wagering warriors and recruits awaiting their turn. I don't see Janine. Unlike the tournament, which is down to four fighters, here all 28 recruits have to fight. Tournament rankings have scheduled me among the last four.

For this ordeal, we fight one man, without our helmets. If he taps your head, sensors in his glove record the contact; he wins, you wash out. To win, you must cuff your opponent.

"As a warrior, you need to take control of any combat situation," Sam says. "Mistakes cost lives. I won't wish you luck, because this is all about focus. Recognize opportunities and grab them." Sam directs the first recruit into the arena, a slender girl who has lost too many fights yet isn't willing to give up.

The rest of us move to the stands or the dugout based on fight times. One by one, men—or rather boys beefed up for this test— enter the arena. I don't see Morgan. Aside from those who faced Dara, how many are incapable of fighting?

Dara pulls the four finalists together, as if we're a team despite fighting alone. It will be different come the tournament. For now, I don't fight it.

The recruits fight with greater concentration than in the tournament. After all, the tournament is for victory. The arena can kill your mech prospects. When Vivian enters the arena and dodges an attack by diving into a somersault, I worry for her. After all, the suit gives speed and agility, but without the helmet, landing on your head can be terminal. She spins away, attacks, and cuffs the guy.

"Don't let size intimidate you," Sam says as encouragement. I swear she's staring at me. I glance at Dara. *Easier said than done.*

I cheer for Vivian and Brandy and take pleasure that they don't wash out. We've only lost Hannah and Tara from my team. *More pressure not to embarrass myself.*

I'm first of the final four, and grateful to get this over. In the dugout with me, Dara pats my mech-shielded shoulder. Margarite smiles like a wretched mouse.

Capra gives me a nod. "Knock 'em dead."

I'd rather not.

By the time I enter the arena, surrounded by 10-foot concrete walls, I'm drenched in sweat. I turn the mech gear air conditioning full blast. It doesn't help. *No helmet,* I remind myself. *Focus. Don't try anything that involves landing on my head.*

I locate Janine in the bleachers. She gives me a knowing look. *Focus. Is that why you're distracting me?*

I have a better idea. While I wait for my steroid-enhanced opponent to enter the arena, I run the perimeter and keep a watchful eye on all three doors. I have cuffs ready in my left hand. *Take no chances. Take no prisoners. Keep moving; loosen up; overcome fear. Focus.* Sweat.

A huge man with scraggly brown beard and hair stumbles into the dirt-floor arena, most likely because he was pushed. He glances around, sees me, and charges my way. I brace myself.

When the muscle-bound man nears, I jump. He leaps and reaches for my head. I block his tap with my left arm and cuff his wrist. I stare into his dark bearded face and bloodshot eyes, and smell whatever spicy food he ate. I want to puke. He growls like a ravenous beast and tries to head-butt me, a victory for him. I raise my head. He hits my mech collar instead. He kicks, connecting with my mech armor.

While we tumble, I twist his right arm behind his back. His muscle is no match for mech hydraulics. I hear the click of the cuffs as we land in the dirt, me on top with my arms pinned beneath. I can't move my arms. No buzzer.

He tries to head-butt me again. Using my legs, I thrust aside, miss his hit and get my right arm free. I flip him onto his belly so the judges can see I've properly cuffed him. The buzzer sounds.

It's over. I survived. Janine is beaming. Yet I don't feel victorious or proud, only numb.

I sit in my sweaty mech gear, watching the final three contests. My breath catches when Morgan enters the arena to challenge Capra. I don't know who to root for. I don't want my redhead hurt, but I like Capra.

Taking a cue from me, she trots around the arena and charges at the redhead. She gets him off balance with her aggressiveness, and cuffs him before he can tap her. I don't think she hurt him.

I take a deep breath. A black-shielded mech warrior escorts Morgan back through his door into the maze of corridors and rooms I imagine beneath the arena. There are 28 of us, which means at least that many men, probably more, in case they're injured in earlier arena rounds. I'd guess 40, maybe 50.

Something tells me that can't be right. I think it over. The first arena test involved three men each. Okay, then 90 men, maybe.

I try to imagine the space needed to house, feed, and train that many men and keep them separated and secured. I sketch it out in my mind: the entire floor-space of the arena and then some, two floors with a dungeon. There have to be passages to the outside for supplies and transporting the men. Sam probably has those tunnels face away from the base so that we recruits wouldn't see them. Most likely they face the Outland.

Scrawny Margarite enters the arena. I suspect Dara has been held until last so everyone will stick around.

Margarite starts like I did, but when she approaches the burly, black-bearded man, she chickens out. I can't say the man chases her around the arena. The suit lets her run three times faster, like a gazelle. Just when I expect Sam to wash her out, Margarite jumps over the padded centerpiece and lands on top of the man. She gets her cuffs on him and stands up.

The string-bean brunette bows to the audience. All I hear are groans.

Dara grins.

Now it's her turn. With her bare head dwarfed by the oversized mech suit, Dara charges into the arena and stands next to the middle door. It dawns on me that the men never use the same door twice, which means she has a fifty-fifty chance. That door opens, and a husky guy emerges.

Dara slams the boy against the 10-foot wall and cuffs him even before he begins to fight. After watching the other contests, this quick ending is a disappointment. Warriors boo. Dara scowls back at them as the buzzer acknowledges her win.

I run to the mech gym and change out of my gear. Though covered in sweat, I don't shower. I'll do that later, alone. Instead, I make my way to the suite off the gym, strip down, and dab myself with a cold washcloth.

Two arena tests down, two to go, only worse.

I judge when the other recruits have settled down for the evening. Then I make my way to the simulator and VR. I should have lost to Kara. I can't afford to let that happen tomorrow.

* * *

For the fourth tournament round, there are only four of us: the amazon Dara, wiry Margarite, big sandy-blonde Capra, and me. Two fights, televised, one at a time before an audience. Warriors escort us through the gray underground tunnel toward the arena.

I don't know yet who I'll have to fight. Dara terrifies me. Margarite's slight form reminds me of Janine. I don't want to hurt Capra, and she's capable of destroying me so I can't face the arena.

Dara holds me back as Margarite and Capra reach the steel door to enter the dugout. "I'd wish you luck, but the arena is what counts."

I nod. *I already got that.*

Dara draws her arm around me in a chokehold. "I suggest you take a fall. Let Margarite have her victory. I need to put on a good show in the final round."

I pull away. "How can you be so sure you won't get me today?"

She grins.

"Don't be so sure Capra can't take you," I tell her.

"Focus on the arena. Let Margarite win or I'll seek out your little sister." Dara hurries toward the doorway.

I lunge.

Dara slams me against the concrete wall. "Save it for the arena. Just don't forget."

The steel door opens. Light bathes the gray concrete chamber.

I hold myself back. I can't show anger in front of the crowd. Dara timed this to make me lose focus.

She marches through the dugout into the arena to cheers. Margarite follows in her shadow. Capra shuffles behind with a sullen look. Did Dara talk to her?

The thunderous roar of the cheering crowd resonates off the arched ceiling. We're gladiators on spectacle for the masses, a distraction from their bland lives. Every seat is filled. Sam will televise this for all to see.

Two warriors in fight uniforms march away from the raised platform. They were a warm-up to our event.

I scan faces in the crowd without spotting Janine. *Need to focus.* Head high, I stride across the dirt arena toward the single ring in the middle, a confined space with no escape. I feel like mushy oatmeal. All these people, all these bets, and Dara rigged the odds. Or did she? Everyone knows she'll win. She's the biggest and best fighter, a natural.

I'm shocked when the announcer calls Dara for the first contest. I would have thought they'd keep the best until last. The crowd cheers.

The announcer shouts, "Capra." Like Dara said. How did she know? Has she rigged everything in her favor? My legs wobble.

I can't get excited about this fight when the outcome is known. Capra puts up a good fight, more like a show. She's no match for the amazon.

I scan the audience, face by face, for Janine. My eyes water.

The buzzer sounds. I return my attention to the ring to see Capra on the ground covered in blood. She fought harder than Dara wanted and was punished for it.

While Dara takes her bow, two warriors in crisp blue uniforms climb into the ring and put Capra on a stretcher. *And this is entertainment?*

Dara turns to me and scowls: *Let Margarite win.* Why? What does it matter? Yet she's right. It would spare me having to fight the amazon.

"For fight two, we have Annabelle Scott," the announcer says.

The crowd is subdued except for excited clapping in the back, Janine standing next to Mom and Mama Helen. *How did I miss them before?*

I don't get cheers like Dara. I'm not expected to win. *Well, to hell with you.*

"Facing Margarite Olivetti," the announcer adds.

The crowd cheers, but not as much as for Dara.

Smelling sweat and a heavy odor of fear, I climb into the ring. I bow toward the crowd and then toward Margarite. She bows, her face gripped in a catatonic stare, as if she's on drugs. I wonder whether Dara gave her Sam's meds.

I think of all the reasons to let Margarite win. She's on my team. I like her. She's vulnerable like Janine. It would spare me fighting an angered Dara. Does she have money on this?

It occurs to me that Dara might throw the final fight to Margarite to thumb her nose at Sam and the tournament. This slap at the mech program appeals to me. On the other hand, Sam knows I went easy on Kara. If I throw this, she could kick me out and send me to Nashville. I have to put on a good show.

The buzzer announces the fight. A jumble of shouts crash down on me from the audience. I break out of my daze to see Janine's face, tight with worry. *Focus.*

Margarite taps my jaw. I lose my balance and crash onto the padded platform. She drops next to me. She starts to get me into a chokehold, and I haven't begun to fight. I push up, kick out and nail her right leg. This sends her howling into her corner. Embarrassed, I get to my feet. The crowd jeers.

While I gather my wits, Margarite gets to her feet and stands there, confused. Her prior fights have been against aggressive recruits chasing her around the ring. At this rate, Sam will throw us both out.

When I lunge, she kicks. I grab her foot and send her flying against the ropes. She bounces back, catching me unprepared. She hammers my stomach. When I fall back, she jumps me. We wrestle. She tries to get behind. She's much scrappier than I'd imagined. I have to concentrate to keep her from getting behind me.

Dara must have told her to win at all costs. *Is the amazon afraid of little ole me?* Did she arrange to fight Capra so she wouldn't have to fight her in the final? Did she threaten me, hoping I'd buckle? I don't want a rematch. All I have to do is quit struggling and this is over.

Needing to put on a good show, I squirm away and get to my feet. Margarite scrambles behind me. She's scrappy. *No time to be impressed. Yet, this could be it. Let her have this. It's one less fight.*

Janine's face appears as if five feet away. She's disappointed.

I ram my elbow into Margarite's ribs. When she twists away, I fake a kick to her head. She winces. I jump her, pin her arms, and get her into a chokehold. She tries to kick her way out. I pin her legs with mine. She wiggles, squirms and tries to break free, but I hold tight. *I will not let Dara order me around.*

When the buzzer announces the end of the fight, I let go. Margarite falls limp into my arms, her neck bright red. She's barely breathing. I hope she'll be okay.

I stand. The crowd cheers. *Three more fights.*

Margarite shakes my hand and smiles. "I'd be honored to serve with you."

"And I you. You're a much better fighter than I thought."

She smiles, but she needs help getting out of the ring.

When I climb out, Sam grabs my arm and pulls me and Dara away from the ring. She bows to the audience and holds our hands high. "Here are the two finalists. Friday we will name a new champion."

Sam looks pleased with the fights, or is that her public face?

When Sam leaves, Dara pulls me into an embrace and whispers, "I warned you to let Margarite win. I'll enjoy tearing you apart. Then I'll have at your sister."

I shove Dara away. "Don't you—"

Janine pushes between us. "Good fight. Both of you." She shakes Dara's hand and smiles up at her.

When Dara strokes Janine's brown hair, my sister pulls me away.

Leaving, Dara gives me her evil eye. On Friday she'll turn me into a bloody pulp, unable to complete the arena final on Saturday.

Oh, Lord, what have I done?

THIRTY

While well-dressed reporters hover around Dara, Janine takes me through the dugout and the holding chamber that leads underground back to the mech base. I'm thankful not to have to talk to reporters. I'm not sure what I'd say about Dara or the program.

As we pass through the stuffy gray tunnel, Dara's threat sinks in. She's manipulating me so I'll lose concentration, and it's working. I glance at Janine, who looks up, not sure whether to talk or let me have quiet time. My eyes tear up at how well she reads me, how close we are. If only I could tell her I'm adopted, like that would fix anything. *It won't.*

I stop before we reach the gym. "I wish you wouldn't pop up at critical times during my fights and then disappear."

She smiles. "Until today, I wasn't supposed to be here, remember. It's just ... you zone out like you do in basketball. You need to keep focus no matter what."

"Who's the big sister here?"

"You are, Belle. I'll always look up to you, but during fights you need to focus." She cups her hand to my ear and whispers, "I know you want to run, but you can't unless you take me."

Guilt. "Janine? Think about—"

She places her finger to my lips and leads me through the gray tunnel to the mech gym. I'm not sure what to make of this. I ache from the fight. I want to hurt Dara for threatening us, for using Janine against me.

228

When we reach the suite off the gym, the door releases, and Janine pulls me inside. I collapse onto the bed. She removes my sweat-soaked fight uniform and applies cream to my bruised and aching muscles. "I told Sam that Dara threatened to kill you."

I sit up. "You what?"

Janine pushes me down and continues, "I stretched things a little, but seeing how she looked at you today and what she said, not by much."

I hate that she witnessed that. I sit up and pull the sheet around me. "Janine, I never should have—"

"Stop feeling sorry for yourself. And don't you dare let Dara tear us apart. Lie down and let me finish." She pushes me down, removes the sheet, and applies cream. "Belle, you're the only part of my life I could always count on. Mom is gone so much. Even when she's around, she's distracted."

"She loves you very much."

"I know, Belle. Please don't push me away. I couldn't bear it. It's been hard enough since you joined the mech program."

"Maybe it's time to grow up and stop following me before you get hurt."

Janine gets up and paces the tiled floor. "Here I've been selfish. With all you have going on, I've been thinking about my needs." She takes my hands. "What I really need from you more than anything is to concentrate so you won't get hurt. Don't let Dara hurt you. Can you do that for me?"

I nod. "I'll be okay. Dara wanted me to throw the fight today. I couldn't. I wanted to, but I saw disappointment in your face. I couldn't fake it."

"That wasn't my face, Belle. I'm okay if you lose. Promise you won't die. You don't get to do that. I don't know what I'd do if I lost you. My heart aches enough watching you fight. Wash out of the program. Just come home in one piece."

Oh, Janine, how I've wronged you by putting too much on your tender shoulders. You're the mother ripped from my arms and the daughter I must shield from such pain. You're the sister I can't have and the best friend I keep deep secrets from. You're what keeps me going in the face of adversity. I've asked too much of you.

But now I must ask one more thing.

Unable to leave the base, I take Janine to see Camilla. The tech hooks us up with unmonitored com-link, though I suspect even that isn't private.

When we connect, I feel questions in Janine's mind and worry in her heart. As we savor the connection, I feel calmer than I have in days, and more determined.

"Janine?" I use thought transference rather than verbal.

"I'm here, Belle."

"I wanted a private moment, and everything on base is monitored, maybe even this."

"Please don't use this to push me away." Janine sounds frantic.

"I'm not, Babe. I miss Mom. I hate that I can't leave base to see her."

"She's exhausted, but fine. She stayed home all day and rested so she could see you fight."

I close my eyes. If there was any other way to help Morgan, I'd stop now. My heart aches for this boy I don't even know. "Babe, tell her the family should be safe. Sam has captured the escapees from Michael's School."

"Really? All of them?"

"Listen to me, Babe. Tell her what I tell you."

"Okay. You don't have to yell in my head."

"Tell her my wounds will heal when she and I gather by the Wells."

I have no idea if Mom will understand my cryptic message or be able to help, but I have to try. I can't do this alone.

* * *

After shuffling Janine off to school, I prepare myself for the third arena test. For this contest, we fight in teams of three without mech armor against one man, nine teams in all. I'm not ready. At least the meds Janine gave me were stronger than usual, probably Sam's. I don't like how Sam draws her in. I'm angry that Janine talked to the commander about Dara, but my sister's scared. I can't hate her for that.

Sam lines us up in the gray underground tunnel outside the dugout in our haptic fight uniforms and light arena boots.

Dara grabs me from behind. "Looking forward to tomorrow? I am. I'll be thinking about it all day. You won't be able to give up, because all eyes will be on us."

I take a deep, slow breath. *Focus on today.* I smile and stand back a row, where I can keep Dara in view.

"Listen up," Sam says. "Team leaders for today's test will be as follows."

She reads off the names of the final eight from the tournament plus Zoe, my second opponent. I think of who I want on my team. Sam chooses. I get Brandy and Vivian from my group. They gather around me. I'm sweating in my fight uniform. I risk my teammates today if I zone out.

Sam paces before us. "No audience today. The purpose of this test is to face a strong opponent without body armor. Even with your three-on-one advantage, don't be fooled into overconfidence. Your objective is to work together to cuff the man. His objective is to tap your head and you're out. This is not fight-to-the death. If it were, the tap could signify a fatal blow. Sense your team and your opponent at all times. Failure costs your entire team the program. Stay focused, channel your energy, and recognize opportunities."

Steel doors open. Sam leads all but Zoe's team to the lower level of the stands by team so we can watch. Zoe enters the arena and arranges her team. As leader, I should have wisdom for my team. I don't. The men Sam brings are strong, on steroids, and motivated to take us out. I have no idea what she promised them. Maybe those who win don't have to face the final fight to the death.

"Let's watch the fights and see what we can learn," I say, since that's what I plan to do.

Brandy turns her attention from me to the arena.

Vivian looks unconvinced. "These guys are huge. All they have to do is come out swinging and–"

"Stop it right there," I say. "I don't plan on washing out today."

Brandy squeezes my hand. "Vivian's right. We should jump the guy as soon as he comes out."

"Agreed, but we have to figure how to work together."

"How about if Vivian and I each grab an arm," Brandy says, "and you cuff him."

"He'll swat us away," Vivian says, her eyes narrow.

"We each need to prepare to cuff him and be flexible," I say.

The first man out is my steroid-enhanced redhead, looking bigger than before. I tell myself it's because we're close enough to be in the arena. Dara scowls at me from across the way.

Zoe's team runs toward Morgan, and he toward them. At the last minute, he veers right and thrusts his hand at the head of Zoe's left flank. Zoe throws herself at his arm, slaps on one side of the cuffs. Morgan brings his left arm around to tap Zoe. Her right flank slaps on a separate cuff and pulls down to prevent the tap. But two separate cuffs don't count. He swings his arms to throw the recruits off. They hold tight to the cuffs while Zoe's left flank barrels into his legs, toppling him onto his back. I'm rooting for Morgan.

It's like pictures in Mom's library of Gulliver's Travels, when the little people tie Gulliver down. Morgan thrashes about, trying to get up. Zoe holds on and so does her right flank. They can't turn him over. Zoe calls her team away to regroup. Morgan gets up and fastens the open ends of the cuffs, so the girls can't use them. *Clever. Go, Red.*

Swinging the cuffs, he charges. The girls scatter. Without mech gear, they aren't fast enough to outrun him. He picks the right flanker. I force myself to look. When he closes in on his target, the other two recruits converge.

The right flanker drops and tackles him. Zoe and the other girl grab his arms and pull them back. When the right flanker joins them, they get the cuffs on his wrists and step back. I'm glad for Zoe and her team yet sad for my redhead.

I watch the next four fights without learning anything that gives me confidence. The only advantages we have against the man/boy are three-on-one and martial arts training. He has training as well as size and strength, yet we don't lose any recruits in the first five fights.

Margarite goes next. Her team acts tentative, yet I've seen her turn defeat into victory.

This gets me thinking. What happens if I lose? Dara wins the tournament by default. They send me to Nashville. Janine would be at the mercy of Dara and others taking advantage of her kind and trusting nature. And Morgan would be stuck here, or dead.

I brush those thoughts away as the man in the arena taps out Chloe. Margarite's right flanker is a muscular girl who can't get out of his way after she gets one cuff on.

"Chloe, clear the arena," the judge announces.

A mech warrior enters the arena to escort Chloe out. She's fuming that she washed out because of Margarite's hesitation.

When the man tries to close the cuff, Margarite's left flanker body-blocks, sending him onto his stomach. She pulls back the cuffed arm. He taps her head with his free hand. Margarite grabs the open cuff and whips it onto his other wrist before he can tap her. He rolls on top.

She gasps for air, but she has him cuffed. Her hesitation forced two good recruits out of the program. *Curse you, Margarite. And damn you, Dara, for pulling her along.*

Capra's team wins, as does Dara's. I'm baffled that I'm last. And pissed when warriors leave the stands. *Am I invisible? Is this because I don't go to Dara's parties and promote myself among the warriors?* Dara exits to the underground tunnel with her team.

I turn to my team. "If we can trip the guy and get him on his belly, then two of us can hold onto his arms while the third cuffs him."

"Which two?" Vivian asks.

"One of us has to tackle him without getting tapped out. The other two go for the arms. Then the tackler brings the cuffs."

Brandy smiles. "Let's do this."

Bless your enthusiasm. I nod and lead my team into the arena. This is my first time onto the dirt floor in the light boots Sam provided. In the nearly empty stands, I spot Janine's face. I nod. She nods back. *Focus.*

I've paid attention to the use of doors: never the same one twice. It's probably so they don't come in contact while waiting to enter the arena. The last was the middle door. While the order appears random, the middle and left doors have been used three times. I position my team by the right door, praying for the element of surprise. I stand to one side of the steel door with my teammates on the other. Bloodstains mar the gray wall where Dara attacked a man.

When the door creaks open, a husky, light-bearded man emerges, big as a tree. *It's only your imagination, Belle. Focus.*

He spots me to his right before noticing the others. When he looks away, I thrust my body into his legs. Vivian hesitates. Brandy jumps on him and turns her head so he can't tap her out. The man flips over me and lands on his right side. When he tries to get up, Vivian cuffs his left wrist and holds on for dear life.

I crawl out from under him and grab his right arm. I slap on a cuff. He pushes me away and tries to get up. Brandy jumps onto his back. He grunts and rolls flat on his belly. Brandy pulls the two cuffs together and acts confused.

He pulls his arms free and starts to get up. With bile in my throat, I see fear in Vivian's eyes. Brandy falls away. We've lost our advantage. *Focus. I'm not going home today.*

Grabbing his right wrist, I roll over, back-to-back with the man. I strain to hold his arm twisted behind him and grab the cuff attached to his left wrist with my right hand. With Brandy's help I yank it back. Vivian jumps up and fastens the cuffs. *Huge mistake.* I'm chained to the man's back, pinned. I can't wiggle free.

Behind me, the massive man tries to tap out at least one of us. When he can't, he tightens up and strains his muscles, crushes the air from my lungs. I pull up on the cuffed wrists to get air as the buzzer sounds. A mech warrior sprints into the arena.

How stupid. I focused so hard on cuffing the man I didn't think beyond that, to the consequences. In real combat, I'm dead. The black-shielded mech removes the cuffs and pulls me free.

Face flushed with relief, Vivian helps me to my feet. "We did it."

Brandy pats my shoulder. "Thanks."

Sam greets me and drags me toward the tunnel. "You have a death wish?"

Pulling free, I keep up with her. "I refuse to wash out of the program."

"I have no use for warriors with suicidal thoughts."

I grab her arm. "I don't—"

Sam slams me against the gray concrete wall and presses her arm against my throat. I start to pass out.

"Don't presume I'm one of your sister grunts. Do you believe you're ready to face Dara?" She lets go.

I slump to the gray concrete floor. I've lost any doubts over whether Sam could handle Dara. I stand uneasily. "I'm sorry, Commander. I don't have a death wish or delusions about fighting Dara. I'm certain she'll tear me apart, but I will not back down."

"Even if she injures you so you can't complete the final arena test?"

I touch my tender neck. "I hope you can put me back together so I can."

Sam laughs, a deep laugh I haven't heard before. "Come on, I'll see to your neck. I won't apologize. You know grabbing me is inappropriate."

234

Maybe so, but an apology would have helped. I hang my head.

There's no nurse in the infirmary, so Sam gives me an injection of something, and three rainbow pills.

That's when I realize the corridors are unusually quiet. "Where are the other recruits?"

"I gave them the night off. They're probably at the plantation."

My eyes light up. "Then I can go? Home, I mean?"

"Are you that confident about facing Dara?"

My mind spins–Morgan–Dara–what to do? If I don't survive Dara, I can't help Morgan. "Will you train me to face Dara?"

"I have a busy night. With only one opponent, you should be able to focus."

Think fast, Belle. "I want to go home and talk to Janine. Then I'll return to train."

* * *

I race my cycle home, careful to avoid speed traps. I know this entire jumbled scheme of breaking those boys out of a mech command center is nuts. If Sam catches me, she'll go through my emails and calls. If I take off hunting for Mom, it would alert Sam. *Damn this tracking device.* Janine has one, too. I'm certain of it. I should walk away. Do my fights. Become a mech and protect my family. *I can't.*

When I pull into the garage, I'm stunned to see Mom's car. I enter the great room to a hug from Mama Grace, a wave from Mama Helen, and a scowl from Therese. Some things never change.

"Janine's upstairs with Sarah," Mama Grace says.

"And Mom?" Seeing her office door closed, I don't wait for a reply. I knock and enter.

Mom looks up from behind her desk. Dark gray eyes carry more than their usual sadness. "I got your cryptic message."

I close the door, lock it, and turn on her harmony music.

Mom puts her finger to her lips and pulls me behind her desk into her spacious closet lit only by a nightlight. She triggers something, and a guttural hum surrounds us. "I thought we were in the clear. Mechs came out of nowhere. They rounded up the boys. I was lucky to get away."

"I can't let them kill Morgan, Mom. I have to do something."

"I figured that's what you had in mind. This is an elite military base, Belle, under tight surveillance, and with mechs on patrol."

"I've learned a few things about bypassing security," I say. "I've mapped out where Sam holds the men."

"You've been there?"

"When I was in Sam's command center, I was thinking how I'd escape. It's in my blood, Mom."

Her eyes narrow. "You've seen the control room? It's one bit of information we've never had before."

"Sam gave us a tour." I turn on a flash beam. "The arena has gaps in security. There's a tunnel on the northeast side, leading toward the Outlands." Quickly I draw a sketch on a piece of paper. "That's where she transports the men to keep them away from recruits, the base, and off-screen for anyone in the command center."

"Interesting."

"The cams point outward to pick up anyone approaching the base from the side. If you come from the direction of the border, you miss the cams."

"It's too dangerous, Belle."

"I know you're part of the Underground, Mom. You oppose the governor. You got George to safety. You helped my birth mother. You helped Morgan. I saw you on Sam's surveillance."

Mom holds up her hands. "Okay, but we need time to plan."

"There's a nurse, Kristina Wells. She might be sympathetic."

"I pray Sam doesn't think so. She used to work with Helen at the hospital before Sam recruited her. I was afraid that was the other part of your message."

"Would she help?" I ask.

"Hard to say. Think—"

"I know. Think of the consequences. But if we do nothing, Morgan and the other men will die. I can't sit by. If Battani and others want the men gone, then let them go. The arena is barbaric. I can't kill, Mom. I don't know what I'll do come Saturday."

Mom squeezes my hand. "Then quit and come home."

"I won't be coming home if I quit. Mom, I've never felt like this before. I need to do this."

Mom sighs. "I can't promise anything on such short notice. I won't be able to approach Nurse Wells until tomorrow."

"Will you do it?"

"Sam will have the men heavily guarded before the televised

236

fights with the entire place on lockdown. Even if we get them out, we need time and logistics to get them to the border. If they put the televised arena broadcast on hold for lack of men, you can bet all resources will be on hunting them down. Unless we divert Sam's attention, we're doomed."

"That's not good enough."

"I'm sorry. There is no way to get the men out before the fight."

Dig deeper, Sam would say. "If we can't save them before, what about after?"

"You mean those who survive?"

Focus, Annabelle. "Even though Sam says it's a fight to the death, some of the men are only injured or unconscious. That's how I can avoid killing."

"But most of the men won't survive."

"There has to be over 100 men, because there were three for each recruit for the first arena test. Only 25 will fight in the final. Wells can bring the rest to that tunnel, and your friends can escort them to the border."

"After the fight, some will need medical attention."

"I'm counting on it. All we need is a distraction. Mom, we can do this. How can you let me know if Wells will help?"

Mom shakes her head. "You're incorrigible, Belle. Okay, if she shows up after your fight to tend to your unconscious opponent, then she's on board."

"Thanks, Mom. You're the best." I hug her. "I have to get back to the base."

"Don't get your hopes up, Belle. This is a long shot."

THIRTY-ONE

After I say hello and goodbye to Janine, I return to the base. I wander to the VR room and rotate through all the footage of Dara fighting. Then I do the same in the simulator. I'm not ready to fight Dara and can't imagine I'll ever be. She's a one-woman army.

Needing a break, I bypass the cafeteria, enter the gym, and head toward the suite. I feel so alone. I wish Sam had medicine for that gaping wound.

Tomorrow I face Dara, who wants to kill me and hurt my baby sister. Saturday, Sam expects me to kill a boy to become a mech. If I fail, they'll send me to an uncertain future, away from those I love. If I win, I get to destroy families, round up boys, and bring them here so Sam can pump them up on steroids to train more warriors.

I want to find the lost boys and escort them over the border where they'll have a chance. Will Mom come through? Have I put my family in needless danger? I'd help Morgan directly if I could turn off how Sam tracks me. But I can't be sure Sam hasn't anticipated every move I could make. After all, she seems to always be a step ahead of me.

What I need is a diversion to distract Sam. All eyes will be on the contest, on me either killing or dying. I have one of the last two fights. Maybe Wells and Mom could take the other men while I fight, but then I might as well kill my opponent. Otherwise Sam will torture him for what he doesn't know. At least Sam won't need to guard the men so closely while I fight, since my opponent and

Dara's will be the last two to appear. Mom can't miss my fight without being obvious, though. Being one of the last fighters has to factor into this.

The steroid-enhanced men are bigger and stronger than me. They can hurt me in well-advertised ways despite my martial arts training. And this time I get no mech gear.

Sounds crazy, but I'm convinced my brain has a mind of its own. When my thoughts clear, I'm standing in the dusty dark arena before one of those doors. It's locked from the inside, no handle, no access from the arena. *Wouldn't want these lost boys to escape.*

Leaning against the middle steel door in shadows from dim emergency lights, I sense testosterone on the other side. It stirs my blood in frightening ways. My heart races.

I want to see Morgan, to tell him—tell him what? I can't make sense of images and urges. It's not love. That requires interaction. This is more basic, something the Federal Union attacks like an evil disease.

I pull myself away from the arena, suddenly afraid. Have I put everything at risk by coming here? Another need resurfaces: to find my birth mother, and with it, a plan.

I hurry through the dark corridors toward Sam's office. If anyone has access to prison files, she does. And if Sam kicks me out of the program tomorrow, this might be my last chance.

The steel door to Sam's wing of the compound is open. The corridor is dimly lit, filled with shadows. I ease along the wall, looking for micro-cams. I avoid jerky motion that might draw attention.

I reach Sam's office. The door is closed. When I touch the handle, the door releases. I freeze. Did my implant do this?

It takes a minute to silently ease the door open. Long shadows bathe the room, lit by moonlight streaming through a high window. Nothing resembles the commander's stocky frame. *Good. She's not in.*

Easing in, I close the door and tiptoe across the tiled floor to Sam's plain metal desk. Streaks of moonlight provide enough brightness to keep me from bumping into things. I sit behind her desk in a stiff chair and feel around to activate her virtual keyboard and screen. I'm so close to finding my birth mother that my hands tremble. My heart thumps in my throat.

The screen activates with views of the arena underground and tunnel not seen in the command center. So Sam *does* watch the back door from her office. That's not good.

Blinding lights burst my concentration. A powerful arm hauls me backward toward the door. My backside meets the hard surface of a wooden chair.

Sam stands over me with that menacing scar. "You don't want to make an enemy of me."

A moment later and you'd know what I'm looking for. I have that, at least.

I stare at the gray tiled floor. "I'm sorry, Commander." I swallow hard. *Sorry, Mom. Sorry, Morgan.* I guess I'm off to Nashville.

"Save it. You went to the arena, and I don't think it was to prepare for tomorrow. Are you that overconfident?"

"I want to know more about the boys." A half-truth.

"They're criminals. That's all you need to know."

"What are their crimes that they deserve to die here?"

Sam leans closer. "That's not your concern. As for fighting to the death, it's critical that warriors face death and be willing to take a life. Otherwise, they put themselves and sister warriors in danger, like Margarite did today."

I tremble, trying to hold my blank face. *What's my punishment?*

She glares at me; says nothing.

"I faced death today, Commander. It was stupid, but I didn't back down. Killing a boy won't make me a better warrior."

Sam sits on the corner of her desk and stares down at me. "Maybe not, but it's required, unless you choose to wash out."

"I won't."

"We'll see."

"Why do you treat me different from the others?" I ask.

Sam rises and hovers over me. "Do I?"

"You haven't said you're throwing me out because of tonight."

That brings a smile to Sam's face. "Do you really believe I treat you differently in the tournament or in the arena?"

"No."

"Do I offer any favoritism when you're in the group?"

"No," I say. "But you let me use the facilities at night and on weekends."

"I offer that to every recruit."

And here I was beginning to think of Sam as a mentor instead of a vulture. "Why do you keep using Janine?"

"Ah. Your burden in life."

"She's not a burden."

"Have you considered that she no longer needs your protection?"

You don't know her like I do. "She's too trusting."

"Of you?"

"No!" *Maybe.*

Sam sits behind her desk and turns off the screen. "You don't want her to be a mech."

"She's too sweet to become a warrior. Please don't turn her into a killer."

"That's not your decision."

I bristle and take a deep breath. "I'll do whatever you ask. Don't drag her into this."

"Get some rest. You'll need your energy and focus tomorrow on Dara, not Janine."

But I can't separate my need to protect Janine from my need to face Dara.

THIRTY-TWO

Friday evening. I can't eat before the fight; my stomach's in knots. Wearing my black haptic fight-suit, I loosen up in the dugout beneath the arena. Out there, warriors display fight maneuvers to entertain and warm up the crowd. Three warriors stand guard to separate me from Dara, who growls in the opposite corner of the dugout. Brandy and Vivian give me words of encouragement that barely register above the din of the crowd.

"After taking down that brute yesterday, you can do this," Brandy whispers.

However, no one except Sam has come close to holding their own with Dara.

When the steel door opens, Dara rushes into the arena. The crowd explodes in applause. I float over the threshold toward the single ringed platform in the middle of the dirt floor, and smell the sweat of a thousand fights. Voices thunder in my ears. I see Mom in the stands. Her blank expression doesn't tell me whether she reached Nurse Wells. Janine nods when she has my attention. *Focus. I get it, Babe.*

While gliding toward the ring, I spot Captain Voss seated next to the governor in one of the box seats. Emily points my way. Warriors have cheap seats in the back where they place final bets. Odds have reached 300 to one. *I wouldn't place a buck on me.* Dara strides up to the ringed platform as if she has already won.

She bows to the audience and receives cheers and applause. I give a slight bow and hear catcalls. *Let's get this over.*

Sam, in dress blues, joins us in the center. Her bass voice resonates over the speakers. "Ladies, we present to you the final match of the Spring Knoxville Warrior Tournament. These recruits proved themselves worthy to stand before you as they prepare to step up to the challenge of defending our precious Union. Each has defeated four challengers to qualify for this match. I present to you Dara Tobias and Annabelle Scott."

The crowd cheers as I imagine they did in Roman times for the gladiatorial spectacle. They chant "Dara the Terror." With odds at 300 to one, I wonder who took the other side of that bet besides Brooks. I hope she didn't wager too much.

Sam motions for us to climb into the ring and raises her hand for quiet. "Victory today comes when one contestant pins or knocks the other down for the count."

Sam climbs into the ring, which she hasn't done before. She turns off the mike. "Keep this clean. I want a good performance for the audience. Make me proud." She shakes both our hands and climbs out.

Is this because Janine spoke to her about Dara? I look into the stands and match the intensity I see in Janine's face.

Across from me stands Dara in her gray fight-suit. "Are you ready to be destroyed? Are you prepared to die?"

Intimidation doesn't begin to describe the steely gaze Dara holds on me. *Submit.* She's the biggest, strongest, meanest mother in the valley. I break the spell with a glance up into the stands. Mom's face betrays the same fear I feel. Next to her, Janine sits in a trance, as if telling me on the mech com-link that I can do this.

Dara lunges forward with confidence, throwing her powerful physical presence at this pathetic excuse of a grunt—me. Where did I get the arrogance to believe I could hold my own against her? I don't have her killer instincts.

"When I finish with you, I'll seduce your sister and turn her into primordial mush." Dara hits me in the stomach, sending me crashing to the matted floor.

Pain. Radiated heat. My stomach rebels.

I bounce away from my tormentor. *You've crossed the line. You may be an amazon, but amazons are myths. It's time to bust this one wide open.*

Dara lunges and grabs. I leap aside, take her by the neck, and thrust her to the ground. Scrambling behind, I get her into a chokehold. She wrenches my arm loose. I can't hold on.

Rolling, she gets on top. "You want to play rough? You don't belong in the mechs, and I'll prove it."

Don't tell me I can't. I thrust Dara off and kick her thigh. She winces. I take no pleasure in it.

"You should have let Margarite win." Dara moves toward me, slower, more cautious.

I attack, two punches to the head. She blocks, then kicks my legs from under me. I slam into the mat. She drops. I roll away, spin and slam my arm onto the back of her neck. It feels like I'm fighting a man in the arena. Dara's muscles are thick from pumping meds and iron.

She gets to her feet and comes at me as if she could do this all day. "You think you're clever, spending extra time training. It won't help you."

She kicks my legs. I jump to avoid her. She throws a right hook like a knife jab. I deflect, fall against the ropes, and drop to the mat. It's as if a bus hit me. I should stay down, but then she'll go after Janine.

When Dara approaches, I scramble away and get behind her. She turns. I rise up and clobber her jaw with my left. I follow through with a right that she blocks. The red imprint of my fist mars her face. It doesn't slow her down. Dara lunges. I punch her stomach and chop her arm. She wallops my left arm and sends me crashing down.

I'm exhausted, tired of time on the mat. I don't see anything I can use against her. She's too well padded, with muscle. I get up.

Dara charges. "This will end badly for you."

She kicks. I sidestep. Her punch glances off my jaw. She follows with a punch to the stomach. I block. It doesn't matter; I careen backward.

I stay on my feet, bracing for another attack. She swings what could be a knockout blow to the jaw. I block and go down, missing the brunt of the thrust. I hit her hard in the gut.

She winces, falls back and comes at me again. "Let the punishment begin. When I'm done with you, you won't be able to fight in the arena."

I get behind her. She turns and pushes me into a corner. I want to take the fall. She won't let me. I block; she pounds my arms. I want to scream: *This is the end.* Dara has me surrounded. I can't get momentum to attack. She hits, hits, hits, spreading welts over my arms, legs and shoulders. I kick her thigh and fall against the ropes. When I bounce back, she hits me.

This has to stop. I fall. She lifts me with uppercuts to my stomach and jaw.

I focus on Dara's eyes, trying to anticipate her moves, which come too fast. I envision her energy as my own. I'm fading. *Fight the pain.* I thrust out both arms and kick. I drop and scurry to the middle of the ring. When she turns, I punch. She blocks.

I retreat and deliver a kick to the stomach. We both go down. As I get up, I see Janine's worried face. *Focus. Take the fall. Make up your mind.*

I've become a cross between a frightened mouse and a cornered rattler, without venom. Dara ambles toward me. I lunge at her midsection to throw her. She laughs, grabs me, and tosses me onto the padded platform. Dropping hard, I scramble away.

"Now I'm going to finish you off," Dara announces as she gets to her feet.

Take the fall. Stay down. But she won't let me.

On any of a thousand other nights, I'd lose without mercy to a true amazon warrior who deserves the title. *Not tonight.*

You will not touch Janine.

Anger bubbles up inside—all-consuming fury full of destruction. Some evil thing grabs hold. All that venom turns on Dara. In some perverse way, she's the mech who destroyed my family.

Before she charges again, I lunge and grab her left wrist as she did Janine's in the game. I twist to throw my weight in a leveraged move against her elbow.

"No! I yield," Dara cries out.

I let go and kick her feet from under her. She goes down hard on her belly. I get her into a chokehold. This time, despite fury in her face, Dara doesn't resist. "I yield."

The buzzer sounds. I get up. Defeat spreads over her face like a dark cloud. I hold out my hand to help Dara up.

She refuses, gets to her feet, and scowls. "I underestimated you." She reaches out and clasps my hand. "You didn't fold under pressure."

I grin. "I have you to thank for that."

* * *

I take my bows before a boisterous crowd and shake hands with reporters until mine is raw. Then I flee down the gray underground corridor to the little suite off the gym, where I drop onto the bed. I need to be alone.

Through the door to the gym, I hear recruits and warriors congratulate me, shouting about how I upset Dara the Terror. I want to hide from the shame of what I did. It might not be illegal. Sam says there are no illegal moves. But it violates something inside me to attempt serious injury for Sam's stupid tournament. Worse than that, I'm now the symbol of the hated mechs. Each day I grow closer to what I despise.

No miracles will bring back my birth mother. None can save my dad. None will spare me tomorrow, having to kill a boy or wash out and be sent away. If I'd taken the fall, I wouldn't be a symbol of anything.

Stop feeling sorry for yourself, Belle.

I stand. At least now, Dara might think twice before hurting Janine.

After the voices outside fade and I'm certain the others are off partying with Dara, I'm ready to venture out. I need medical attention before facing the arena tomorrow.

When the door swings open, Janine falls inward, almost banging her head on the tiled floor. I catch her. "What are you doing here?"

Janine looks up, all innocence. "I'm glad to see you, too. You survived. You had me worried."

She hugs me, the best medicine I know. It takes all my waning strength to keep from breaking down. I want to tell her everything. After all, she never wavered being here for me. "Is Mom with you?"

"She went home. I explained how hard it is when you win and can't share because the victory is yours alone."

"You're full of it."

Janine grins. "She bought it. Let's get you to the infirmary."

"I'm okay."

"Stop acting so brave around me."

She takes my hand and pulls me across the gym and down the dimly lit corridor to the infirmary. When we get there, the nurse is gone. *Did Mom talk to her?*

Sam sits in the corner, studying a medical screen. "You found her."

"You read medical charts?" I ask.

"Before the war I was a doctor as well as a marine. Now let me look at you."

I remove my blue sweat-soaked fight uniform. *Too many red splotches and the beginnings of bruises.* I have to stay strong when I see Janine's eyes moisten. She turns away.

"I'll say this for you," Sam says. "You're not a quitter."

She jabs an IV into my arm. I wince. Everything hurts. Janine grips my other hand too tightly.

"Probably your best outcome," Sam says. "Dara wanted to make an example out of you. Now she'll respect you. So will the others."

I don't care. Instead, I savor electric warmth. Maybe it's Janine revitalizing me, though I suspect it's Sam's miracle drugs. They'll probably shorten my life by 20 years, as well as leave me infertile.

"I suggest no training tonight. Just rest," Sam says. "You'll need all your wits tomorrow. Training won't help. I saw more focus today than I've seen from you before. That's what you'll need tomorrow."

Sam leaves, brings us both some stew, and leaves us alone.

With the IV in my arm, I sit up and try to feed myself, but I can't lift my arms.

Janine feeds me as I've done for her when she's been sick. "You've never asked why I was so afraid of the dark, Belle."

Between bites of savory chunky chicken, I manage: "It's nothing to be ashamed of."

"I'm not." She grips my right hand as she feeds me. "It's because Mom was always working. I felt a terrible separation. I couldn't have verbalized that then, but I know it now."

I nod. I know that separation well.

"You were always there for me. You held me, and I needed that. Sounds crazy, but despite only being a year older, you've been like my surrogate mom as well as my best friend and sister. Now save your strength and get better. You have another fight coming up."

THIRTY-THREE

Winning the tournament lets me go last in the arena on Saturday. The good news: I get to see how other recruits face the final test. The worst part is the wait, seeing myself in each fight, 24 before me. I still haven't found a reliable distraction to keep Sam from looking for injured boys trying to escape.

The crowded concrete dugout reeks of sweat, fear, and dust from the arena. The stands roar with chants and jeers for individual favorites. Within the dugout, we watch the fights on large wall-screens.

Standing tall, Dara bumps fists with me and the others. "Knock them dead today. All of you. And I do mean dead. We've earned the right to be here. Let's show our audience what we're made of."

"Hoo-rah," most recruits chant in response.

I weep for the boys who won't make it. I pray we can save Morgan and the others. Sam introduces a scrappy brunette and lets in a single male for a no-holds-barred fight to the death. Recruits can tap out, with armored mechs on hand should the boy fail to back off. The guys have no such option. For them it's kill, force the recruit to yield, or die. Sam says it's as close to combat as we'll get in training. But it's still wrong.

The door opens to let in another recruit, and I look up into the stands to see Mom, Janine, and Sarah. Mom's face gives no indication as to whether we're on. Next to them are Mama Helen, and Mama Grace's eldest, June, another adoptee. No Therese, so much for sisterly support.

In box seats over one end of the arena, I spot the Governor, Emily, Captain Voss, and Lieutenant Scarlatti. *What a cozy crew.* How do Voss and Scarlatti feel watching what they failed? I'm certain they've bet against me.

"They want a gladiatorial spectacle; let's give them one," Dara says when the door closes.

"Hoo-rah."

I mouth the chant with no enthusiasm. I can't kill for the pleasure of spectators, particularly the bloated Governor Battani and her backstabbing daughter. I want to see Captain Voss and Lieutenant Scarlatti in the arena pleading for mercy. I stop my internal rant when mousy Zoe enters the arena.

With scraggly brown hair over a plain pale face, Zoe strikes me as the straight-A student who struggles to put what she knows into practice. Yet she survived this far.

The bald man who enters by the left door looks huge, with rippling muscles and a thick neck. Zoe charges. *Good. Get him before he can use his size to advantage.* Baldy braces himself, ready to pounce. At the last moment, Zoe jumps and kicks. He leaps and rams his fist into her face. Disoriented, she tumbles onto the dirt and scrambles away.

She runs for the padded centerpiece. He closes in. Zoe scrambles over a padded rock and up to the top to catch her breath. She hasn't much time as she sizes him up. Zoe looks tiny in comparison. *Where did Sam find this guy? Is he what I have to look forward to?*

The bald man makes his way around the centerpiece. Zoe jumps him. She kicks his shoulder and tries to get away. He grabs her ankle, pulls her down, and slams her against the rock. Padding or not, that has to hurt. Phantom pain shoots up my spine.

He kicks her knee, snapping it like a twig. Zoe slumps to the ground. He grabs her right arm and rams the elbow. Before he does more damage, someone triggers his collar. The man collapses while a black-shielded mech warrior sprints into the arena.

Panting, Zoe lies against the rock. Her body twitching, she yells, "I could have taken him."

The brutality and suddenness of her defeat stun me. While medics can repair her knee and elbow, she's out of the program. I wipe sweat trickling down my neck. How much more of this can I take? And what's the point? As mechs, we'll fight in threes with mech suits. When will we ever face this type of situation?

I'm surprised Zoe, as the fourteenth fighter, is the first recruit to fail. Some won with kicks to the groin and gruesome acts like clawing a boy's eyes out. Others like Amy made up in speed and agility what they lacked in body mass. She went for the throat.

Next recruit is Jane, a tough girl who fell in the second tournament round. Stronger in training than in the tournament–probably took a fall to avoid Dara–she fights hard in the opening minutes, then loses focus like I do. A blow to the head stuns her. Before she recovers, her opponent crushes her neck against the wall. The way she slumps to the ground tells me she's gone.

I can't breathe. The dugout closes in around me. I'm ready to lose it even before I get into the arena. Dara glares at me. I turn away.

The next few fights are tough, as Sam matches stronger opponents with the better recruits. One girl yields, while most survive. The male body count rises. Why couldn't I save them? Is this part of Battani's plan to eradicate boys? She sits in her box seat, cheering on fighters. We lost Jane. Other recruits suffered serious injuries. *For what?*

I'm numb by the time Vivian steps into the arena. She looks shell-shocked. I hope she yields before her opponent does irreparable harm. She hides behind the padded centerpiece. Bad move. A muscle-bound boy with goatee appears, looking around for his target. Not seeing her, he runs the perimeter of the arena. Vivian scoots around the centerpiece to avoid him.

The boy looks up at the crowd, raising his hands. The crowd yells. I can't make out anything coherent as Vivian sprints toward him. Realizing what the crowd is yelling, he turns. She jumps and plants both feet into his belly. The boy crashes against the wall and hits his head. He doesn't get up.

Vivian scrambles behind, grabs his neck and gets him into a chokehold. I suspect he's already dead. Another boy I can't help.

Vivian bows to the cheering crowd. I eye the door behind me, imagining gray underground tunnels leading back to the base. Craving escape, I don't know where I'd go. If I'm captured, it's off to Nashville or worse. I need to stay and find some way to distract Sam.

I worry when Brandy enters the dirt arena. I like her as a friend. She's a good fighter, but she doesn't have the killer instinct.

She opens with Vivian's move, hiding behind the centerpiece. The crowd hisses at her. The light-bearded man who enters from the right door takes a jog around the arena and attacks the centerpiece, climbing to the top.

Towering over Brandy, the man jumps. Brandy leaps up and launches the full thrust of her fist to his throat. He lands on top of her. She crawls out from under, gets behind, and goes for a chokehold. He tries to loosen her arm, digging his fingers into her, until finally he relaxes and goes limp. She holds until the judge calls the fight.

So far, what I've seen, aside from brutality, are lucky moves.

Dara's fight is the last one before mine. She swaggers into the arena and bows to the crowd. Cheers fill the chamber. Despite losing to me, she still has star power. She's the one they came to see.

The left door opens, and a man enters. He is not the biggest I've seen, but still big. I suspect he's also more agile than the others. Certainly, he's the best Sam could find for Dara the Terror. I don't want to think what Sam has for me.

Dara approaches the man. They exchange punches and kicks. The man attacks, Dara blocks. Anger fills her face when she attacks him. He's bigger, but she makes up for that with viciousness. He hammers her; she hammers him. He tries to wrestle her to the ground. Dara kicks and punches him hard enough that he backs off.

So far, she's been in the arena longer than anyone else. He attacks, trying to dominate with his size. Dara won't have any of that. While they slug it out, he cuts her face and she bloodies his nose. He spits out a tooth and then another. Dara has met her match. She can't dominate this opponent, and she doesn't seem to know what to do.

I'm exhausted watching them. I root for her not out of friendship but because I see myself in there when she's done.

They kick and bite and chop and slug their way around the arena, tearing each other apart. When the guy looks ready to knock home the winning blow, Dara digs deeper and hits him with a barrage that stuns him. Yet she can't get the upper hand.

He's waiting her out, letting her tire. Once she's spent, shown all her tactics, he'll move in for the kill. And this will be a kill. I see it in both their eyes. I pull away, ashamed by my involvement in this brutality. I can't watch. I don't want to see either get killed.

Turning my back to the screen, I lean against the concrete wall. The arena boots weigh heavily on my feet. I need to find a diversion. I'm alone now. All the other recruits have gone into the arena. If I run and make my break for freedom, that could create a diversion, but it would lead to lockdown and doom my family and the men.

The crowd cheers like thunder above me. I return my gaze to the screen. With blood-splattered face, Dara stands over the man, her foot on his chest.

She's made for the arena. I'm not.

* * *

The announcer calls my name. I can't breathe. The door to the arena opens. The reek of death clogs my sinuses, along with the stench of sweat and fear from dozens of earlier fights.

I push myself into the arena and hide behind the centerpiece. Time is not my ally. I break into a jog and feel a jolt of adrenalin. The middle door opens, revealing the outline of a large man. I stop behind the padded rocks.

None of my prior training, tournament, or arena contests prepared me to stand alone across the dirt arena from this muscle-man on steroids. He's twice my size, built like a side of beef—*hell, the entire bull.* I have no weapons. My instinct is to yield, to climb the wall and escape.

Hiding behind the centerpiece, I clear my mind. *Focus.* I recognize the tuft of red hair, the man—boy really. It's Morgan with rippling muscles. Though not much older than me, he carries the scars of steroid enhanced fights. His eyes betray that he doesn't want to be here, doesn't want to fight to the death. He doesn't deserve to die.

How do I spare his life without giving up mine or having to ship off to Nashville? Where do I find a diversion so that he can escape with the others?

Jane died here today. Zoe almost did. It's fight to the death. Whether I die or wash out, it's terminal.

The boy is motivated. I see that in his eyes as he searches for me. He can die here. He has to make me yield, or kill me. Then he gets a reprieve to train warriors as my dad did. I won't survive long in this struggle.

Morgan hesitates when I step out from behind the centerpiece.

Does he recognize me? Does he remember how terrified I was when he jumped from the Dumpster behind that abandoned dorm? How I made no effort to stop him?

From across the dirt arena, he sizes me up. I see fear in his eyes. *Me, too.* "Hi," I say, rather shyly.

"No talking," a judge yells over the loudspeaker.

I glance up into stands packed with warriors, trainees, families, and Knoxville dignitaries. The Governor catches my attention, sitting next to Captain Voss in a box seat. Mom sits in the far back with an intense look on her face I interpret as worry. Next to her, Janine looks like she does when I lose focus in a game.

The boy glares at me. I stare back. It's a staring contest. *I can handle that. Stay focused; see his energy as part of my own.*

He makes no attempt to lunge at me. *Do you expect me to make the first move? Are you psyching me?*

"Commence fighting or we will disqualify you."

Thanks for the pressure, Sam. If the purpose is to get past my fear of facing bigger opponents, well, I'm standing my ground. The sheer mass of the boy reminds me that he can snap my limbs, like what happened to Zoe. Or he could squeeze the breath from my lungs until I pass out. Then there isn't much I can do to avoid washing out, except die.

Jeering and chants float down from the stands. They help me focus. I won't give up without a fight. *Spare Morgan; create a distraction.*

I move toward him, dance to the side. He moves with surprising agility given his bulk. I've watched him in earlier contests. He's a tough competitor. As winner of the tournament, I'd expect nothing less. I can't think of him as a brute, though. I fake a move to the left. He grabs for me. I scoot aside, slamming a kick to his solar plexus. *Sorry.*

He winces, rotates and grabs me. I pull away and kick his legs from under him. He doesn't go down. Up close, I see scars on his face that weren't there earlier. My eyes tear up. *I don't want to hurt you. Have they traumatized you, like a bull with no way out?*

I can't afford sentimentality. Looking up in the stands, I see Janine's worried face. *I know, Babe, focus.* I need to put on a good show for the crowd first.

I spin around behind him and jump. When he moves to counter, I ram my fist into his neck. *Sorry again.* He coughs, flexes his biceps, and struggles for breath. He moves with me. I can't take advantage, can't get behind him.

I'm sweating; he isn't. *Not good.* He looks like he can keep this up for hours. I'm not sure how to end this in my favor. I can spare him if I yield, but then what? Nashville re-socialization.

He kicks my legs from under me, grabs my waist and throws me down. I scramble away and get to my feet. *Focus.*

He lunges. I spin free, jump, and ram my arm into the back of his neck. He remains standing. I kick him hard in the gut. He grabs my foot, twists me off balance, and thrusts me onto the dirt. He jumps on top of me, grabs me from behind in a chokehold, and pins my legs.

Morgan is firm yet gentle. I could almost feel safe in his arms, except he's choking me. I'm a turtle on its back. His aroma filters into my nostrils.

I can't give up. This isn't enough diversion. I can't free Morgan this way or save myself. My mind scratches for options. I pray Sam doesn't call the fight due to my racing heartbeat.

Engulfed in Morgan's masculine odor of sweat and fear, I wrench at his arm clasped around my neck. Bulging biceps tighten, choking off my oxygen. I dig stubby fingernails into his flesh. Though he winces, he doesn't loosen his grip. I look up and see Janine's horrified expression: *don't do it, don't die proving a point.*

I can't yield. That's its own death sentence. I jerk my limbs in all directions but I can't get leverage to free myself. I poke his face. He grabs my arms. I'm trapped. Beginning to fade.

Morgan whispers in my ear. "Finish me or wash out. Otherwise I have to finish you."

THIRTY-FOUR

Up in the stands, another horror unfolds. A dark-haired cop intern leaps out of her seat. She raises a pistol and lunges toward Mom.

Mom! I struggle for oxygen. *Think, Annabelle. Focus. Dig deep. Make your opponent's energy your own.* But I have two opponents, and I'm losing consciousness.

I thrust arms and legs in opposing directions and butt my head back. Can't get leverage.

Janine leaps from her seat and grabs the gun. She wrestles the assassin. The gun drops. I cling to consciousness as Janine thrusts the cop intern back against the railing with such fight as I've never seen in her before.

When Morgan turns toward the commotion, I wrench my arms, ram elbows into his ribs, and squirm free. The cop intern jumps the railing and lands in the arena. Then she turns toward me.

I face Morgan. "In a moment, you'll have two to fight. I'll stand back if you remove the intruder."

The dimpled intern gets to her feet and charges toward us. Morgan runs to intercept. He grabs the intern and throws her against the wall. The intern pulls a knife from her belt, and slits her own throat. He drops her. A black-shielded warrior jumps into the arena.

Morgan backs away and returns to me. He nods, and assumes attack position. Behind him, the mech warrior picks up the assassin and carries her through one of the doors used by the men.

I glance up into the stands and see in Janine's face a fighter's determination. It fills me with such pride and grit to do what I must. *Mom, is this your diversion? Are we on?* I can't tell from her somber expression.

"Sorry, I have no choice," Morgan says.

Ah, but you do. And so do I.

He lunges at me. I move an instant quicker than before, with a thrust to his gut. *Focus. Feel his energy as my own.*

I get behind and kick his right knee to drop him onto the dirt. He leaps to his feet and grabs me. I find pressure points in his hand. He reaches for my neck. I hit him again and again. He doesn't slow.

Simulations return to me. I know where to hit to kill him. I see his boyish face and hesitate. Two opportunities flash by. I'm telegraphing my moves. I can't bring myself to kill Morgan. *Oh Mother, Dad, am I about to become a dreaded mech?*

He grabs me from behind in a chokehold. Before he can lock my feet, I throw him, landing on top of him on my back. *Bad move.* He cuts off my windpipe. I'm a balloon ready to pop.

He grasps my right wrist. I tap him behind the ear, on the side of the head and various other points, yet I can't apply enough pressure. His grip tightens, cutting off oxygen. I start to pass out. *All I have to do is tap my hand and it's over, the terror, the fight, and a career with the mechs I don't want.* In the stands, I see Mom willing me to do so. Janine begs me to yield before I die.

Not going to happen. My brain craves oxygen. I only have seconds before it no longer matters. *Think, Annabelle, think. It's him or me.*

I jab my free hand toward his face. When he grabs for my wrist, I ram the heel of my boot up into his groin and yank at his arm around my neck. *Sorry.* Arching my body like in the simulator, I pull free, sucking in air. I thrust my fist into his neck and ram his windpipe. When he falls away struggling for breath, I grab him from behind in a chokehold.

"Yield and I'll let you live," I whisper.

I feel his throbbing pulse against my arm and ease up. *Will you let me have this?* While I hold tight, I inhale his masculine musky scent, filled with fear and virility. I try to be as gentle as he was with me.

"I've injured you enough that you'll need to see the nurse," I whisper in his ear. "Accept her help."

His body falls limp. I ease up and wait a minute, two. *Will he rise up and attack me?* When he doesn't, I let go and stand. I don't feel victorious, but I did beat him without killing him.

Bowing to the cheering crowd, I see relief in Mom's face. Janine looks like she's won the most important championship ever.

I keep a wary eye on Morgan, hoping he's okay and Mom can get him out. If not, have I done him a favor? Maybe not, but at least I didn't kill him.

* * *

While I wait for the judge's verdict, I stand over the boy, who plays dead, I hope. What would it have been like to sit with him, take walks in the forbidden mountains, and have him hold me without choking? I feel no animosity. I want to take his hand, lift him up beside me and announce–what? That he's in the same straitjacket I am, a life with few choices, only a separate room.

The crowd's cheering transforms into a cacophony of a thousand conversations. Janine jumps the railing and runs over. I hug her, savoring the embrace. "I'm so proud of you," I say. "I see you no longer need protecting."

Janine looks down, wounded. "I've always wanted to be like you, Belle."

"Why? You're the smart, lovable basketball star."

"Only so you'll be proud of me. I let you protect me because you seem to need that."

I'm stunned, but I can't be angry with her.

Smiling, Janine clutches my hand as if we might never see each other again. "Then you won't mind my following you into the mechs?"

"No! I couldn't bear this for you."

"Then it's settled. Sisters stick together. Besides, someone has to watch your back like I did at the basketball game."

Looking deep into Janine's sweet brown eyes, I realize the truth. While I worried about Margarite hurting her, Janine must have stepped in to keep the fight from escalating. *Good girl.* "Promise you'll talk to me before you sign up."

"Judge's decision is final," a shrill voice screeches over the loudspeaker. "Annabelle failed the final test." The crowd howls derisively.

What? No! All that work...

I throw my suit's sensor-filled hoodie to the ground. Janine grabs my upper arm and pulls me back before I do something more rebellious. "How can they say that, Belle? What happens now?"

My throat is so tight I can barely get the words out. "I'm out of the mech program." *I almost died. For what? For this? You can't do this to me.*

Black-shielded mech warriors move my redhead onto a stretcher. I struggle for breath.

"It'll be okay, Belle. You'll see."

I scan the three doors out of the arena without seeing any sign of Nurse Wells. Wiping my brow, I stand tall, holding my head high. I won't give the crowd the satisfaction of bowing to their contempt.

This is the first time the tournament winner failed. I'll never live this down. Dara stands in the opening to the dugout, a gloating look on her big face. She's still the champion, the amazon afraid of no one, willing to do whatever it takes to win.

My victory is: *I defied you all.* Maybe Morgan won't have much of a life, but it won't be because of me. I might even find a way to free him.

I don't see Mom in the stands. Still no sign of Nurse Wells.

Janine whispers in my ear, "None of this matters. You did basketball, cop internship, mech training, and a thousand other things for me. I'm so grateful, but it's time for you to stop doing for me and figure out what you want. I'll be fine as long as you don't push me away."

"One day you'll have to stop following me," I say.

"Maybe, but today isn't that day."

Sam approaches. In other contests, she congratulated the victor and welcomed the recruit as a mech warrior. This time, her scarred face gives no clue to what she's thinking.

Behind her, mech warriors carry Morgan out of the arena through the middle door. There to receive him is Nurse Kristina Wells. She looks at me and disappears. I keep my face blank. *Now I have to distract Sam.*

She's flanked by two warriors I haven't seen before. Sam stops five feet from me. "Former recruit, report to my office now to surrender your gear." Sam turns and walks toward the tunnel to the base.

I have to stop her. "Sam? Please give me another chance." I try to follow.

The two warriors block me at the dugout while Sam walks on. Something hits me on the head: a rotten apple. The crowd hollers angry insults. I'm ready to pick up the spoiled fruit and hunt for targets.

Janine grabs me and whispers, "I'm still proud of you."

The middle door of the arena closes.

Mom joins us and gives me a hug. "It's done, Belle. Time to move onto other things."

"Mom?"

She nods. "You gave me such a scare. I thought I'd lost you." She winks.

"And I you."

"I guess some people don't like me making waves. I'll have to be more careful in future." Mom squeezes Janine's hand and mine. "I'm so lucky to have amazing daughters."

Janine's the amazing one. I guess I'm not the only one with secrets. I think of all her training, how much she absorbed, always the good student. "I'm proud of you…" I start to say "Babe" and catch myself.

Janine looks up with a knowing smile. I glance at the middle door. *Holy hell. I've got to stop Sam from going to the command center.*

* * *

I enter Sam's austere office, bathed in LED light, and stand on a worn area rug by her plain metal desk. She turns off her holographic screen.

Focus. Use your opponent's energy against her. You taught me well, Sam. Reap what you sowed. "I'm so sorry and ashamed I've disappointed you, Commander. You've invested so much time and energy in me, and I've let you down. I believe I can show myself to be worthy. I'm prepared to do whatever it takes to become a mech if I can stay in Knoxville. You know that."

"Relax, private."

Keep her attention. The longer she focuses on me, the better chance Morgan and the others have. If there were a problem, Sam wouldn't be so calm.

I continue. "I know you expected me to kill him, Commander. I showed you that I could. I stood up to a stronger opponent, faced my fears and defeated him. But I won't kill for some contest. You know I won't let you down in combat." *Forgive me for saying this.*

"Private, sit down. I'm neither angry nor disappointed in your performance. You demonstrated remarkable leadership instincts today and throughout the program."

I collapse into a stiff wooden chair. "Did…did…did you say 'private'?"

"That's correct, soldier. You've passed every hurdle I've thrown at you with style and fortitude."

I struggle for air. *Got to stall.* "I don't understand."

"I'm sorry for what I've put you through. I needed to be certain you could handle a very special assignment."

"What do you mean?"

"It required me to disavow you publicly. I want you to report back to Captain Voss. Keep your eyes open. Tell me anything that stinks in that operation."

I take a deep breath. *I'm not heading to Nashville?* "She washed out of your program, didn't she?"

Sam leans forward, her face serious. "I can't give you details at this time."

"What about the captain's threat to send me to that Nashville re-socialization facility?"

"Your high-profile finish put that off the table. However, don't you dare get caught again crossing the line. If you've learned anything in training, I hope it's to focus and channel your opponent's energy."

Focus, right. I watch the clock behind her tick off the minutes.

"You failed to do that with Voss. You wasted precious capital on your juvenile escapade of breaking into her office."

I swallow hard. "You know about that?" *Is there anything you don't know? What about my birth mother? What about Mom and the boys?*

Sam laughs. "Voss isn't discreet. Not one of my better students. She'd relish having you back so she can say 'I told you so.' You'll need to bite back your anger and focus on the goal."

"Which is…?"

"Find out what she does with money siphoned off departmental funds. What's she doing with Lieutenant Scarlatti and her special team? Something tells me you'll enjoy taking them down."

"Why would they trust me?" I ask.

"They won't, but they'll be so focused on rubbing your nose in your public humiliation they won't see the bigger picture, unless you slip up. This will be incredibly dangerous. You'll be on your own. I believe you're the perfect warrior to pull this off. When you do, you'll receive full mech warrior honors. You have more training to complete, which we'll have to do on the side. You are a warrior if you choose to be. I hope you will."

It's a lot of pressure and responsibility for being 16, but I feel much older, and Voss won't expect this. Precious minutes tick away. *Good.* "I don't know what to say."

"Think about it, but don't take too long."

"I don't have to, Commander. I'll accept." I can't believe how the words fly out of my mouth.

"Very well, then." Sam stands and shakes my hand. "Welcome to the mechs. Be forewarned. You cannot tell a soul, not your sister, not your mom, no one."

"I understand, Commander." I'm not ready to leave. "What about the boys who survived today?"

Sam steps back and seems to consider. "We'll give them medical attention. I don't suspect Morgan will need much after your little love fest."

I try to hide my embarrassment. I pray I'm not blushing.

"I have business to tend to," Sam says with a wave of her hand. "I'll contact you next week to arrange to meet."

It's still too soon. "Can I see the boy when he recovers?" *Nice touch.*

"That wouldn't be appropriate."

"What will become of him?"

"We'll use him to train, just not in the final arena test. After today, I can't rely on him fighting to the death. He might choose to sacrifice himself, which would defeat the purpose of the exercise."

Better than that, right now, I hope, he's on his way to the Outland. If Sam catches him, it won't go well. "How did you know I wouldn't kill him?"

Sam settles into her wooden seat and drums her fingers on the desk. "All through your training, you've hesitated to attack unless you had to. You've challenged me over this requirement several times. I figured matching you with the boy you spared during the university raid would push you."

"Is there anything you don't see?" *Like Nurse Wells and the boys fleeing?*

Sam grins. "Very little."

Every minute I stall is precious. "Since you knew about Dara's parties, why did you let them continue?"

Sam's face brightens. "As a leader, you'll learn to do what you must to build a team. Dara has natural charisma because of her physical presence. She tried to take charge. You showed a different leadership that enticed me to take you on. I told you I'd give you the tools to stand up to her, and you did."

"I'm not proud of how I won."

"You gave her a taste of what she tried to do to Janine. That earned her respect and that of the other warriors. You also taught Dara she doesn't have all the answers."

We still need more time. "You took the other side of the tournament bets against me, didn't you?"

Sam's face softens more than I've seen. "Putting a thousand at risk won us 300 grand, enough to fund your assignment without drawing unwanted attention."

"Is there anything you haven't planned?"

She shrugs. "Janine isn't the helpless little girl you take her for."

"So I saw."

"I've watched her train. She's bright, strong, and a quick learner. When your Mom warned me of a potential threat, I gave Janine an earpiece."

"You used my sister again?"

"I figured she would be the closest to intercept," Sam says. "I know you don't want her to join the mechs, but we can make her a good home here."

"Please don't pressure her or use your planning magic to get her to join."

"I won't," Sam says. "As for you, if you ever pull another stunt like letting your opponent get you into a terminal chokehold, I'll kill you myself."

I get to my feet. "I stand ready to deliver." *And to find my birth mother and adopted brother George.*

The clock behind Sam keeps ticking away. Nurse Wells and the boys have a 40-minute head start.

I'll be seeing you, Morgan.

ACKNOWLEDGMENTS

I want to thank my wife, Sue, for putting up with my devotion to writing. I am grateful to Laurie Scheer from the University of Wisconsin for being a burr in my side when I needed it. I am also grateful to my writing groups for their input over the years: The Troubadours, The Barrington Writers Workshop, and the Algonquin Area Writers Group. I especially wish to thank my editor, Leah Carson, for her patience and diligence in making up for my editorial shortcomings and keeping me on the right track.

ABOUT THE AUTHOR

Lance Erlick has lived and traveled throughout the United States and Europe, as well as visiting Asia. Inspired by his father's aerospace engineering work on such cutting-edge projects as Apollo and the original GPS, and his love of stories, including the works of Asimov and Heinlein, Lance has been writing since he was eleven.

He took numerous detours along the way, solving business problems for companies ranging from automobiles, to electronics, kitchen cabinets and boats, which he supplemented after hours by reading and writing science fiction.

He has two grown sons and lives with his wife in the Chicago area, where he's working on his next novel, as well as a sequel to *The Rebel Within*. The best definition he can come up with for his writing is science fiction for those who don't normally read science fiction.

Find out more about the author and his work at LanceErlick.com.